the WILD BOY

Warren Rochelle

GOLDEN GRYPHON PRESS • 2001

This is a work of fiction. All the characters and events portrayed in this novel are either fictitious or are used fictitiously.

Copyright © 2001 by Warren Rochelle

LIBRARY OF CONGRESS CATALOGING-IN-PUBLICATION DATA
Rochelle, Warren
  The Wild Boy/Warren Rochelle — 1st ed.
    p.   cm
  ISBN 1-930846-04-5 (hardcover : alk. paper)
  1. Human-alien encounters—Fiction. 2. Fathers and sons—Fiction. I. Title.

PS3618.O34W5   2001
813'.6—dc21   2001018969

for
Ellen McQueen

Your first pain, you carry it with you like a lodestone in your breast because all tenderness will come from there. You must carry it through your whole life but you must not circle around it.
— Jane Bowles

We love because it's the only true adventure.
— Nikki Giovanni

Acknowledgments

Thanks to my family and my friends; especially my fellow students in the UNC Greensboro MFA Creative Writing Program in 1989–91; the members of my MFA thesis committee (the thesis was this novel's original incarnation) at UNC Greensboro, Fred Chappell, Bob Langenfeld, and Lee Zacharias—especially Fred, committee chair and my coach and mentor; Jim Clark, the program's director; my teachers over the years who believed in me, especially Dorothy McNeill, Eric Baylin, Rachel Simon, Weldon Thornton, Marianne Gingher, and Doris Betts; the librarians in the Chapel Hill-Carrboro City Schools and at the Chapel Hill Public Library; my colleagues at Limestone College and Mary Washington College; Maria C. Riegger for making sure the Spanish is perfecto; and my editor, Gary Turner, at Golden Gryphon Press, who made this process great fun.

Warren Rochelle
Fredericksburg, Virginia
October, 2000

The Wild Boy

Prologue: Emium

Search Fleet Departure, T minus 1 year
11 Snowmoon 11214, in the 43rd Year of
the Left Emperor Orfassian

CORVIAX LANDED HIS PERSONAL FLYER, AS THE AGREE-
ment stated, one ten-stride from the Double Fountains, in the
center of the Old Gardens. The snow was heavy on the omerian
trees from last night's storm, the lowest branches scraping the
terrace. The snow was about a tenth-stride deep in the gardens,
but the heat stones marked a clear path out. He was fifteen tenstrides from the South River Gate. Just one ten-stride from the
Gate was a small plain brown door, just tall enough to admit an
Iani. It was through this door Corviax was to enter the imperial
palace, the Palace of Mazes.

His toeclaws clicking on the smooth heat stones, Corviax
walked slowly down the steps from the fountain. At the bottom,
he stopped and sniffed the cold air. The agreement had been
explicit: no one else at all was to be anywhere near—not in the
gardens, or on the river, or even in the palace. The great triangular
palace—each of its pinkstone wings a leg of one of three nested
triangles, all enclosing the inner triangle, the heart—was to be
totally empty, except for Corviax and the Emperor. (There was
snow on the palace roof; had his father forgotten to order the
activation of the heat stones there?)

Corviax knew his father would be waiting for him in the inner

3

triangle, in the little waiting room behind the Left Throne. Favvy would be waiting for Corviax just as he had done when Corviax was little and they were playing the maze game in the palace. After Corviax's tutors had dismissed him, he had to take a different route through the palace to get to his father in the little waiting room. He could repeat no route twice and the time to get there never varied. Sometimes Corviax would get there just as the alarm rang. He would be panting, his tongue out, all his claws extended. Other times, Corviax would be already rubbing his head into his father's broad palm, Corviax's rumbling only a little softer than his father's. Other times, the alarm would ring long before Corviax was anywhere near the throne room. His father had to come and find him then. Corviax had to stand very still, exactly where the alarm had caught him, listening for the sound of his father's toeclaws on the polished floor.

Corviax could smell no other Lindauzi anywhere near the palace. He turned around slowly, wondering if his father had truly evacuated every Lindauzi—male and female, adult and youngling, royal, menial, merchanter, military, priestly castes—from the neighborhoods surrounding the palace. Or had his father just ordered people off the streets. Not that there were many left anyway. Many of the tall red, pink, and orange houses were already completely empty— and had been half-empty since the Extinction. The father and mother would begin the ritual by killing all the younglings: one quick laser bolt while they slept. Then, the menials, who would kneel, one by one, in the mealroom. (Corviax had heard that sometimes the laser pistol would need a recharge and there would be a mad, silent scramble, running and jumping over bodies, the air stinking of singed fur.) The parents would be last, by the house's double fountains, or in the house gardens, flanked on one side by the Iani wing and on the other by the Lindauzi wing. Kwava juice, freshly squeezed. Wrist-slashing, slow bleeding. Two laser bolts. It didn't matter.

There was the dome of the Great Temple, just visible behind the nearest house. A thin ribbon of smoke curled up and out of the gaping hole in the top of the dome. The insides must still be burning, Corviax thought, even though the last battle before the truce had been three days ago. Corviax had personally fired the laser cannon at the dome: *This will make him listen, stop the fighting, the suicides, I don't care if it is the Great Temple and packed with priests.*

Smashing the dome had worked.

The suicides stopped and a truce was announced. Too many of the white-furred pink-eyed priests had died when the huge iridescent dome had shattered in fire, raining flaming shards down into the sanctuary. A priest had to answer the two questions before any suicide could begin. And if the Dissenters would attack the Temple. . . .

Ah, there *was* someone nearby. Corviax inhaled deeply: there, to his left, the orange-and-pink-and-yellow house with the rounded doors. Not native-born, returning colonials. There they were, two of them, two shadows in a third story window. Were they from Aven? Volis? Ilgobar? Zachanassia, the farthest out? How far had the two shadows traveled, leaving their homes, their lives, to return and die? And to have to live in a house emptied by ritual suicides—*murders*, Corviax corrected himself, murders —and to live in that bloodied house, knowing they were going to die there as well. Or revert, intelligence scattering like leaves in a storm.

No.

Corviax shook himself. He willed his crest to subside, his fangs to retract.

There was nothing to fear.

Corviax raked his fur with his claws, searching out any snarls he had missed the three times before. He didn't want his father to raise his lower lip in that slow way he had that said his son, the Crown Prince, Heir to the Left Throne, was not presentable.

Let's get this over with. And it's snowing again.

He looked back at the house of the two shadows. They were gone or had opaqued the window. And the wind had shifted: now the smoke from the smoldering temple was drifting over the city, no longer a thread but a thinning cloud. The smoke mixed with snow, big, feathery flakes, falling thick and fast.

The South River Gate was open, as was the small plain brown door into the palace. Corviax hesitated before going inside. He knew his father wouldn't trick him, but not everyone was as honorable as his father. The Council of Elders had wanted Corviax's head on a stake at the old city gates. And there was the Iani story of the warring brothers, princes, rivals for the same crown, twins, born five minutes apart. One brother was fair, the other was dark. But no one remembered, in the confusion of the birth, who was the older. The civil war had raged for years, laying waste to one of the fairest provinces on South Continent. Finally a truce had been negotiated and the two brothers had agreed to meet in

the old country house where they had been born. The dark
brother arrived first, to an empty house, and went inside to wait.
An hour later, the fair brother arrived, only to be burned down as
he stepped out of his flyer. Not by the dark brother, but by a
fanatical lieutenant who was convinced the dark brother was
making a terrible mistake and that his fair brother would betray
him. The dark brother shot the lieutenant himself, but his fair
brother was no less dead.

One of Corviax's lieutenants had told him this story just before
he had left for this meeting. This lieutenant probably had a reper-
toire of such stories, suitable for telling before sailing a boat or
taking a shuttle to the orbital stations or the lunar colonies.

Once inside the palace, Corviax felt his body relax, his heart
slow down, his crest subside. No more ghosts or stories haunted
him for the rest of the walk through the palace to the little room
behind the throne room. Corviax trailed his claws on the walls the
way he had as a youngling, leaving fading pink trails as he walked.

The door to the throne room was open. Corviax's toeclaws
clicking on the smooth, smooth floor sounded impossibly loud.
But then the last time he had been in this room, it had been
packed with Lindauzi. Their rumblings had filled the room as they
brushed against each other, pressing, touching. Tufts of black,
brown, grey, red, and even white fur littered the thick carpet. Why
had his father taken the carpet out for this meeting? Surely not
to hear Corviax's toeclaws on the floor.

The party had been to honor Corviax's oldest sister's upright
day, thirty years erect. His father had announced the evacuation
of the colonies at the party, just after the serving of platters of
sweetened whitefish. Corviax had speared five chunks with his
claws and was eating them one by one when his father began talking, his words dropping into the noise like stones, silence rippling
out in wider and wider circles. All the colonies were to be evacuated. All the colonials were to come home. The silence had
reached Corviax as he sucked off the third fish chunk, a cold,
noiseless wave muting him where he stood.

The Debates were over and the decision had been made:
acquiescence, resignation, defeat.

The suicide rate had doubled the next day.

Corviax had left the palace the day after and civil war had
broken out within the month.

That had been a year ago and today was the first time Corviax
had returned to Emium and the palace.

Corviax crossed the throne room—three ten-strides from the entrance to the door of the little room. He laid his open palm on the lock and waited, as the lock pressed back, first his finger pads and claw tips, then, his palm, finally his entire hand. Satisfied that he was indeed Corviax luOrfassian laSardath luCorviax Alerian, Crown Prince, the palm lock glowed white and the door slid open.

"Hello, Father," Corviax said softly, trying to repress his rumbling, the movement of his ears.

His father, Left and only Emperor of Lindauzian, sat in his favorite arm chair, reading from an old, thick, cloth-bound volume in his lap. Corviax winced, recognizing the fat tome, *The Book of The Forest*—not his father's copy, but the Right Emperor's copy. The book had been passed down, parent to oldest child, since the beginning of the Empire. That book had sat on a low table by the Right Throne since the Extinction. No one had moved it, touched it, dusted it.

Corviax could smell the book, its soft old pages, from where he stood: dust, years, time, the bath oils of the old Right Emperor, his father's hands, his mother's, even his own. Sweat, tears, spilled morning juice, death. Corviax hated the book and he hated what he knew his father was reading, the story of the First Meeting. Lord Madaan and Lady Aurelian had called the Iani out of the trees and the Lindauzi out of the caves and dark, hiding places, and called them each to come to the heart of the Forest, where the hand of one was given the hand of the other.

Lies, lies, old priest's tales, nursery stories, half-remembered dreams, imagined history. Lies, lies, lies.

"Where will you go, Corvy? Where will you take them?" his father asked softly, still not looking up from the book.

"Out. Farther than Zachanassia—archaeologists found evidence on the Zachanassian moons of the Iani's alien origins—star charts marking their travels—marking their colonies. We are going to finally use the stardrive to follow these charts to the only near Iani world, to another large primate civilization. You know that. And we are going to find them, recreate the bond, heart to heart, mind to mind, soul to—"

"Don't, not here, in this room where you sat in my lap, your head on my chest, your rumbling echoing my own. Don't blaspheme here, not anymore," his father growled, his ears flat, the tips of his fangs showing. "Those words will never be said on any Lindauzi world, by any Lindauzi, ever again. Not in this life, only in the Great Forest—"

"They will, Father. I've promised. We will find others like the Iani with whom we can bond—"

"There is no other species like the Iani, no other." His father slammed shut the heavy book and stood, his fangs and claws fully extended, his crest erect. He took one step toward Corviax and stopped, his crest suddenly slumping. "I'm sorry. There is no point in shouting."

You were roaring.

"I'm sorry, Corvy," his father repeated. "I wanted one last time to try and persuade you to stop, to acquiesce and accept, before it is too late, before you went." The Emperor re-opened *The Book of The Forest* and held it out to Corviax. "Here, son; it's all in here."

Corviax stepped back and shook his head.

"Father, this is *your* last chance to be persuaded. Come with me, support me, believe in me. Believe in science, in archaeology, in linguistics, in lindology. Believe in the truth. *The Book of The Forest* is a collection of old stories written by some Iani to give religious validation to what their science had already done. They found us in the caves, in the burrows and tamed us: we were their pets. And after who knows how many generations of eugenic breeding and gene surgery, we stood upright and took their hands with our modified paws and finally talked back with our modified mouths. The Lord Madaan and the Lady Aurelian were Iani gene surgeons. The stories are all metaphoric. Large primates made their pets sapient. The emotional bond was already there—they just bred for it, enhanced it. The Iani made us, Father. They *made* us. I'm not against religion, against God—the Reformed Madaanic preach the Iani as being the hands of God—"

Corviax stopped talking and stepped back. His father's ears were flat against his head and his crest was erect from his forehead to the base of his spine. His fangs and claws were fully extended; his chest fully expanded; the fur on his back stood up like bristles on a brush. His father's growling came from deep in his throat. His father's eyes had grown dark and clouded.

"I know you are furious, beyond furious," Corviax said quickly, taking yet another step back, "but, listen, please, just listen. And answer me. Why do you ignore the evidence and go on interplanetary news and tell every Lindauzu and every Lindauza to ignore it? There are those skeletons, different-sized skeletons in the Aderf Valley, in the Conger Basin. And the ruins in the Galerian Islands, those laboratories. Computer loops with eugenic breeding charts, thousands of years old—"

"Bones are bones. Different-sized skeletons are children and adults. Those loops can't be verified." His father was roaring.

"But they have been verified, Father. Let me finish. I know you will never believe me. It all happened so long ago that no one will ever know why the Iani—and maybe the Lindauzi collaborated, or maybe they were never told, who knows—wrote *The Book of The Forest*. No one will ever know why they lied and taught those lies as truth, as religion. But it happened, Father. We were bred to be the perfect partners—emotional symbionts—of large primates. There is so little mammalian life on this planet; maybe they were just lonely."

"I've read the Planned Evolution journal articles, Corvy. I have heard the news reports and the Dissenter speeches and the Debates. You are very eloquent . . ."

He hasn't called me Corvy since we played the maze game here, in the Palace of Mazes. Didn't he ever wonder, after the Debates began, why that is a universal Lindauzi children's game?

". . . but all the piles of bones and all the ruins and cryptic charts left behind for us to puzzle over did not change what happened and will not change what is happening. The Lord Madaan and the Lady Aurelian have called us back to the Great Forest. They called the Iani first, and now they are calling us. Even if I believed in your science, that still wouldn't change."

"But there is hope, Father. Hope. Science gives us one tiny bit of hope: the Iani probably came from another world. They found us here; this is where we came from, not them. Or maybe they brought us with them; there are even hints of that, as you know. We are going to find that other world, find more large primates who can save us. No more ritual suicides, no more atavistic reversions."

"*Probably* came. You fought a civil war, killed thousands for *probably*."

"*Came*. I fought a war for *came* and for life. You are choosing death. There is DNA and RNA evidence, differences between the Iani and the rest of this planet's biosphere, archaeological evidence. Historical evidence. This gives new meaning to all those stories of the first meeting, the first village. And those charts the Zachanassian archaeologists found: they have meaning. They mean it can be done again. We are going to follow those star charts. There are small primates, ruminants, reptiles on all the colony worlds, parallels, analogues to life here. Life isn't some special purview of Lindauzian. The Iani raised us to sapience, to the bond, and we can recreate that bond, we can find their star-cousins and save ourselves."

His father shook his head.

"Disease killed the Iani. There was no way to prevent it, no way to stop it, or even slow it down. In one generation all the Lindauzi were alone. I remember my father's, Yorx, the last Right Emperor, and your grandmother's, Vian; I watched them both die. Acquiesce and accept. I'm asking you for the last time. You are the Crown Prince, heir to the Left Throne. Lead our people to an honorable end, a just and righteous death."

"I will lead them to a just and righteous life."

His father growled deep in his throat, his chest, and then he threw back his head and sucked air, once, twice, thrice. Then he looked at Corviax one last time and when Corviax returned his father's gaze without speaking, his father turned completely around and presented Corviax his back, his crest and fur erect.

The ultimate sign of displeasure and dismissal: Corviax no longer existed; he had no name; the Emperor had no son.

"Good-bye, Father," Corviax said. He had never wanted more in his life to run back to his father, to press his head into his father's open palm, to feel his father's claws rake his fur. He wanted to roll over, as he had done in the nursery and show his father his belly and let his father scratch and rub his expanded chest.

"Father, when I find them, the star Iani, and when we have bonded with them, heart to heart, mind to mind, soul to soul, I will bring them back here to Lindauzian, to Emium, the City of Mazes. I will lead them through all the twists and turns to you here, in the Palace of Mazes. Wait for me, Father. Don't follow Mother into the Great Forest."

Corviax did not walk straight out of the Palace of Mazes. Instead, he took a lift to the third floor, to the family apartments. He stepped out into a wide, open room, its floor soft with a thick, blood-red carpet, smaller pink, red, orange, and yellow rugs scattered here and there. Great lumpy pillows, in shades of brown, green, blue, and grey, overflowed out of huge woven baskets. Beside each basket of pillows were thick, rough scratching posts. It was in this room he had sat with his mother and father and sisters after morning temple and before the noon meal. A family portrait hung on the far wall. The nearest wall, the window-wall, was transparent and Corviax saw the snow was heavy now. The sky was grey and white. Below, obscured by the snow, were the family gardens, the very heart of the palace, laid out in its own tiny maze of trees, bushes, and stone paths, still visible thanks to the heat stones. There was a small, double fountain in the very center, which his father had turned off years ago.

There was, of course, another family room, a double, next to the one Corviax stood in. But its door had always been locked.

Corviax went down a long hallway, lined with grazing pots, and then in and out of the kitchen, the sand baths, the sleeping rooms, until he got to the one he had slept in as a youngling. It was small, and now it seemed crowded with its jumble of pillows and cave-boxes. He raked his claws on the rough wall, streaked with years of claw marks. His childhood books were there, on low, inset shelves and he took them with him when he left.

He took the next lift to the ground floor, and left the way he came, out through the small door, into the heavy snow, through the South River Gate, and through the Old Gardens, on the path lined with omerian trees, their broad leaves making dark pools of shadows on the white snow. He stored his books in the back of his flyer, climbed in, whispered *go*, and flew away.

A year and a month later, on 7 Icemoon 11215, Corviax was the last of a million Dissenters to board the hodge-podge interstellar fleet assembled beyond the orbit of the last world in the home system. Over twenty times that number had wanted to leave and follow him in the Search for the other Iani home, for the Iani star-cousins, to see where the star charts would take them — for whatever truth they had wanted to believe.

Corviax had let the imperial computer net choose which Lindauzi were to accompany him on the Search. Technicians had fed information from the personal databanks, data collected at key points during every Lindauzi's life: birth, upright day, sexual puberty, sexual and emotional bonding. Lindauzi had been finding their sex-mates and bond-mates through computer matching for generations. More ignored proof, Corviax thought, as he had watched the technicians make the data transfer into a program designed to determine the highest empathic quotient. Why didn't anyone ever wonder why we have never stopped breeding ourselves? Why, if we weren't artificially bred to sapience, and to bond, didn't we choose our partners through love, affection? Maybe no one noticed because it was always there; a fish would be the last to discover water. Had even the Iani forgotten? There

were so many records, so much data, lost during the Extinction—
there would be no final answers.

The million selected for berths in the Search fleet weren't all
Dissenters or Reformed Madaanics. There were imperial nobles,
peasants and servants, warriors, priests of every sect on the planet,
returned colonials, professors—Lindauzi of every caste. The one
thing they all had in common was high empathic quotients. Corviax wondered if this million were simply the most desperate? The
most in need of emotional symbiosis? Had those with true high
EQs already died or reverted or committed suicide? Millions *had*
chosen suicide during the Disorders following the Extinction.
There were many who had never bonded—were incapable of
bonding. But, they tended to die young, forever outside the true
communion, denied reproduction privileges, university admission
and employment. Not that the bonding privileges meant anything
now.

There were riots when the names of the Million began scrolling across screens. The suicide rate went up another percentage
point when the invitations were zapped to each online household,
to each public terminal, displayed on all the newsnets. Corviax
demanded and received imperial troops to protect those who did
accept as they began to leave for Emium Station and the shuttles
from there to the fleet. Priests organized demonstrations at every
train terminal, every boat dock, every spaceport. The worst demonstrations were in Emium itself. Thirty reversions occurred in
the middle of the screaming priest-led mob. The troops fired into
the mobs as those accepting made their way to the spaceport. The
air stank with the smell of burned fur. Departure, and the riots
and demonstrations, the suicides and reversions, lasted for seven
days.

When the last, except for the support staff on Emium Station,
were being settled in the fleet, undergoing preparation for coldsleep, Corviax called his father one last time. For too long he
stared at the imperial seal on the screen as the recorded voice of
the palace operator asked him over and over again if he wanted
to leave a message with the Chief of Staff of the Imperial Household. If so, please say accept. For further choices, please say
options. Otherwise, say end to sever the comlink.

Corviax leaned his head against the screen, his crest drooping.
He sighed heavily and stood and looked around. He was in the
comcenter for Emium Station. All around him were computer
consoles, vidscreens, instrumentation pads, and the murmur of

voices from the newsnets and television networks being received from the planet. On one screen, a commentator, a red-furred Lindauza with a too-pink snout, was reporting the most recent reversions, in a city in the Greater Archipelago. The reversions, she insisted, were a reaction to the imminent departure of the Search fleet. Racial betrayal and heresy was the theme on another screen, the broadcast from the Mother Temple. The High Priest, an old, old Lindauzu, peered out with tired, watery, pink eyes. Blasphemy, blasphemy, hell, damnation, soul-murder . . .

Corviax pressed the central mute and all the voices stopped. He listened to the recorded voice of the palace operator for one more time.

"End. Good-bye, Father," Corviax said, and left the room to board the shuttle for the fleet.

Chapter I

Caleb, 15 October 2155, Early Morning

"CALEB. CALEB! KAAY-LUBB! COME BACK HERE THIS minute. Do you hear me? Get yourself back here . . ."

I hate Aunt Sara. I hateherIhateherIhateher.

Caleb was running with Aunt Sara yelling behind him, her words falling like hot hail around him. He didn't look back, he ran. Past the Jackson's picture (no stopping to kneel, no time, and besides, Papa never had), out the door and through the white columns, down the steps, and out onto the hard clay walk (careful, jump over the broken bits of old brick, chunks of asphalt and concrete, great way to sprain an ankle, and then she *would* catch him), and into the gardens. Max ran behind Caleb, his high quick bark a counterpoint to Aunt Sara's yelling.

"KKKaaaaayyyy-lllubbbbb! You are going to be sorry, you'll wish you had never been born, you little good-for-nothing brat."

She stopped. Caleb darted behind a tree and risked a quick look behind him. Aunt Sara had gone back inside Jackson, no doubt with smoke pouring out of her nostrils. God, he hated her. No point in going back in until she had cooled off. Davy was asleep; he'd be all right. Now, where was Max?

Caleb stood ankle-deep in the last of the predawn fog, a damp white-greyness which drifted across and around tree trunks, softening and obscuring the edges of the chunks of sidewalk and street, the brick walls still standing, and what was left of the tribal garden. The two night-watchers stood at opposite ends of the garden. One covered a yawn, swallowed air, glanced disinterestedly at Caleb, nodded, and turned away. The other didn't even bother to cover his mouth. Caleb felt his face grow warm; the two men had seen everything, heard everything. And would tell everybody. Well, it wasn't the first time he had come tearing out of Jackson with Aunt Sara yelling behind him. At least this time she hadn't thrown rocks and rotten vegetables at him, Caleb thought as he touched the fresh scar on his leg from that episode.

They shouldn't be watching me, anyway. They are supposed to be watching for Lindauzi. The monsters and their hounds could sneak up on these two sleepyheads and it'd all be over in a minute. Max?

"Max? Max, here, here boy."

The sky was still grey-blue, and sprinkled with stars, a fading moon. The garden was mostly weeds now, with only a few cornstalks still standing, brown and brittle, dead vines, empty beanpoles. Only the pumpkins were left, scattered about like the plastic balls Caleb had once found in the Mall with Papa. It was as if some giant child out of the fairy tales had been playing and forgotten to pick up his toys. The trees were just beginning to change color: the maple leaves were both green and red-gold, as if there was a hidden fire inside, slowly burning.

Ah, there was Max. Caleb could see the dog's tail in the middle of the garden, wagging in what was left of the squash and cucumber vines, a dark brown wiry antenna. "Stay, boy, I'm coming." Caleb made his way through the weeds, dead cornstalks, beanpoles and more weeds until he found Max snuffling around what looked like the remains of a very large and quite dead rat. The dog looked up and barked at Caleb: *neatstuffhuhcanweplaywithithuh-huh?*

"No, we can't. C'mon, boy," Caleb said and scooped the dog up. He made his way through the rest of the garden and then down another clay path, bordered on both sides by asphalt and cement chunks. The farther away from Aunt Sara the better. He went past the old kiln, the silver maples, and then down into the street. Caleb walked carefully there, as the tribe hadn't bothered to clear out what was left of the old pavement. Grass and weeds had split the pavement into irregular chunks of different sizes and shapes. The tangle of weeds made it hard to see where to walk on

the uneven surfaces. Caleb stepped gingerly, with Max whimpering in his arms.

*She called me a dirty little halver. A foul-mouthed brat. Just
because I yelled at her in Lindauzi. So what? She'd be even angrier
if she knew what I said in Lindauzi. Call me a halver. I wish I was
fourteen — she couldn't bother me then, I'd be an adult. I'd take Davy
and tell her to go to hell. I hate herIhateherIhateher.*

But he was only eleven and Davy was four. Where would they
go? And the tribal elders claimed they needed Lindauzi-speakers.
No one else in Jackson's Tribe knew any Lindauzi. Even if they
did, they would never speak it aloud. It was the speech of nightmares, of the furred monster aliens, the human-killers.

Caleb stopped at the street corner. He looked back over his
shoulder. No one. It was too early for anybody but the watchmen
to be out, anyway. He took a deep breath and exhaled in a noisy
whoosh. There, he felt a little better. Imagining Aunt Sara walking
back inside and tripping down the stairs and whacking her head
on the wall made him feel a lot better. Max whimpered again and
Caleb let Max down and the dog pressed close to his feet, tugging
at Caleb's boots with his feet.

"It's OK, buddy, go on and run. She never follows us, she just
likes to yell," Caleb said in a low voice. He knelt down to stroke
the dog's rough mottled skin and scratch behind the floppy ears.

"Let's just walk. We'll go back in a while. Let's go this way,"
Caleb said and pointed to his left, down Tate Street. He stood,
sighing. He knew Tate Street like the back of his hand. He looked
back up McIver: more completely familiar territory. The old green
and white street signs were gone, carefully stored down in the
lower levels of Jackson as prized relics of the years before the
Sickness and the Arrival. Caleb knew, like every other Jacksoner,
every street name by heart. He could name all the buildings on
Tate Street as well; Papa had taught him that, even though
neither Papa nor anybody else knew what had been a particular
building's purpose. To Caleb's left, so the litany went, were The
Corner, Hallmark Cards, The Clothesline, The Exchange, Coffeehouse, Hong Kong, Sisters, Spoon's Bar, Addam's Bookstore.
Across the street were Valencia's, New York Pizza, Copy-One,
and so on.

Caleb could remember all the names, all the way to where
Tate ended at Lee Street. But then he had a perfect memory: he
forgot nothing. He could remember Papa's exact words when he
had explained why to Caleb: *The Lindauzi bred humans, Caleb, for*

different traits. Perfect memory, intelligence, longevity, stamina, endurance, strength, empathy. I know you don't know what all those words mean yet; I'll explain them to you in a while. They wanted us to be a certain way for their Grand Project—but, never mind that. As for what Hong Kong and Pizza are, I don't know, son. I do know New York was one of the biggest of the human cities before the Lindauzi Arrival. Umium, their capital, is there now. Remember, I told you they took me there with Phlarx to go to school and I got very sick. . . .

Caleb remembered, just like he remembered everything. Some things he wished he could forget, like all the mean things Aunt Sara had said to him since Papa had left. He shook his head. He couldn't forget, yes, but then he could think of something else, like following Max down Tate Street.

Caleb kicked up the leaves as he walked. Tate Street was deep in leaves and broken branches. Trees grew between what was left of the pavement, tall pines and oak and maple and sweetgum saplings. Vines crawled in and out of the empty windows, twining around the shards and spears of leftover glass. Max was a few feet away, snuffling and sniffing. Probably another dead rat, Caleb thought. There couldn't possibly be anything left to find on Tate Street. The tribe had scavenged Tate Street so many times over the years that there was little, if anything, worth finding. All the old stores, from The Corner on, were empty, except for rats' and mice nests, snakes, and thick spider webs. Oh, there were little things, bits and pieces of glass, metal, plastic, but not much else.

It was dawn; he could just see the sky beginning to change color, with streaks of yellow and orange staining the grey-blue. Caleb's stomach growled. Maybe if he concentrated on looking for something, anything, he wouldn't feel hungry. He wasn't hoping to find anything really special. Maybe one of the metal pop-top rings tribal women made into necklaces or some of the plastic loops which were woven together to make tunics. Or one of those tiny multi-colored glass balls Papa called marbles, even though he also called some of the big slabs of smooth white stone marble, too. Another puzzle from the past. The marbles Caleb liked the best were one color, and when he held them in his hand, they cast a shadow of that color, a tiny little blue or green or red shadow.

Mama had worn one of the pop-top necklaces in long graceful loops. The necklace jingled as she walked. Caleb remembered playing with her necklace, pulling it slowly through his fingers and then swinging it back and forth, back and forth.

There was nothing new in the leaves this morning. Caleb wondered what Aunt Sara was doing. He hoped she had gotten so mad that her face had turned bright red and exploded, just the way puffballs did when he kicked them. If Papa were still here, she wouldn't have even dared to be so mean, Caleb thought. Aunt Sara had hated Papa, but she had been afraid of him, too. Papa had shielded Caleb and his little brother from the hard stares and the sharp words. Such things never seemed to bother Papa as much as they did Caleb. Maybe it was because he was a grown-up.

Papa didn't think so. "Things could be a whole lot worse, son. You waste too much time worrying over things you can't change —just like your mother did."

Papa worried over nothing. Caleb, on the other hand, worried about everything. He lay awake at night, replaying whatever had happened, imagining what he wished he could have said or done. It didn't help that he could replay every conversation verbatim. Papa called Caleb an old man pretending to be a little boy.

Max waited for Caleb at Addam's Bookstore, the last named building before the beginning of the tangle of vines and trees marking where the old houses had once stood. Max looked up at Caleb: *Tooslowletsgoletsgo.* Caleb knew where each house had once been. The trees that grew out of the old cellars and foundations weren't as tall as those around them. The other trees were towering, growing up and over the middle of the old street to create a green-turning-red-and-gold-and-yellow canopy. Thick vines and briar brambles covered the old rotting boards and broken bricks. Caleb was sure he might find a few small things in the undergrowth, but not much. Jacksoners had scavenged here as well.

"I'm coming, I'm coming." Caleb had told no one he could hear Max's doggy thoughts. Or that he was beginning to sense how others felt, see their feelings shining around them, like a corona of light. Aunt Sara had been surrounded by a red fire this morning. It had only been in the past month or so that Caleb had been able to see these personal coronas. He would be watching someone and there it would be, like flames flickering around them. And as the light shimmered, Caleb felt how the other felt; he could almost reach out and touch the anger or fear or worry or love. Papa could have explained and had even hinted there would be changes the older Caleb got. Puberty he called it. Caleb didn't know and he didn't dare ask or tell anyone. It would be only one more thing for them to hate him for. Besides, he could only see the coronas some times and then just for a little while. On the other hand, it was getting easier and easier to understand Max. Feeling how much Max loved him was almost embarrassing. But, then, he frustrated Max, not being able to smell or hear well enough *smellthisyoucan'tuhyournoseistoolittlejustsniff.* . . .

When Caleb came to the next corner, he stopped to pick up Max. Holding the little dog against his chest, Caleb shuffled his way across Tate Street and sat down on a low stone wall. He held Max tighter and pressed his face into the dog. Usually Max hated to be held and would squirm to get away. Today he seemed content to stay in Caleb's arms *IloveyouMasterIloveyouCableblove.* . . .

By now the sun was well above the trees. The blue sky had been scoured of clouds. Caleb looked up and down the street. Nobody but him and Max. He wasn't surprised; he knew where everybody was. The night-watchers had gone inside; the day-watchers were at their posts, gnawing on dried strips of deer meat and maybe an apple or two. The always-burning fire beneath the huge black iron cauldron would have been resurrected from its banked night coals and would be licking around the cauldron's fat bottom. Inside the cauldron the stew would be beginning to bubble, its aroma fingering its way throughout Jackson, awakening anyone who might still be asleep.

I'm so hungry.

Caleb's stomach growled at the thought of the hot stew ladled out into the rough wooden bowls. One or two of the elders would have one of the precious plastic bowls. No one dared used one of the even more precious porcelain bowls. A third elder would be standing in front of the cauldron to recite the food blessing, calling on Father Art in heaven to make the food wholesome and good and that it would fill the empty stomachs.

Caleb hoped Aunt Sara would still be so mad she wouldn't be able to swallow her food. Maybe she would even choke on it. She would be standing there, talking to anybody who would listen, waving her free arm and going on and on about what a worthless no-good boy Caleb was and whatever was she going to do with him and if he wasn't her own sister's son she would have had the elders expel him long before this why . . . Then she would gag and choke and have to spit all her food out, her face red and wrinkled, the anybody whaling on her back. *Father Art, since you're so angry, be angry at her.*

Davy was probably awake now. Caleb winced. He wasn't there and Davy, who was just four, would have to deal with Aunt Sara all by himself. She hated Davy only a little less than she hated Caleb.

"Take care of Davy for me, Caleb," Papa had said just before he left. "Take care of your little brother."

"I will, Papa. I promise."

At least Caleb looked like most Jacksoners. Only his dark blue eyes marked him as different from the other short, dusky-skinned and dark curly-haired tribe folk. Davy looked more like Papa and Papa was fair, golden hair, blue eyes that seemed to have a white light behind them, and fair skin, fairer than even the fairest of the Footwashers and the Covenant-keepers.

Caleb's stomach growled. He knew he should go back up to Jackson. Aunt Sara was probably already slapping Davy around, making him wait to eat after her two boys did. And besides, he was really hungry; he should go home. *I don't want to go home, though. Not to stay. I want to go get Davy and go. . . . Where? Where could we go and live? Where could two boys and a dog go around here?*

But who said they had to stay around Jackson? Papa had said more than once the world was a huge place, they had no idea how huge. He had seen it from space, from the Lindauzi space station when he was a boy. *The world is a great ball, Caleb, a great turning ball. You can't even see people from up there, just the clouds and the ocean and the land, green and brown and red and yellow. . . .* Davy and Caleb could go anywhere. They could go to the summer country, where they would not only be free of Aunt Sara and her anger, but of the Lindauzi as well. The summer country, or so the stories went, was a warm, gentle place, by a green-blue sea, with white, white sand. Fruit with strange and wonderful names — oranges, grapefruits, bananas, lemons, tangerines — grew on trees with branches close to the ground. You could just reach out your hand and pick something to eat.

Papa hadn't known where the summer country was or how to get there, except to go south, then southeast. "It's just an old story, Caleb," he had said, shaking his head. Mama had believed it was real. "Walk with the sunset on your right and the sunrise on your left. When you come to the end of this land, this earth, take sail over the sea and when you see the white sand a line against the sky, you will know you are almost there. That's how to get there," she had said.

Caleb saw something glinting in the sunlight and, still clutching Max, he leaned down and picked up a pop-top. *I wish I could give it to Mama for her necklace.* Aunt Sara had that necklace now, along with everything else her younger sister had that had been worth saving. After Papa had disappeared, she had taken everything, telling Caleb boys didn't need women's things. "Remember her in your dreams," Aunt Sara had snapped.

It had been a dream about Papa that had caused this morning's fight. Caleb had woken up calling for Papa. Now the dream seemed distant and faint. Caleb wondered if he had even dreamed it at all. In the dream, Papa had been somewhere in the east, toward the sunrise, toward the nearest Lindauzi plantations. In the dream Caleb could see Papa but he couldn't get to him. And Papa didn't seem to be able to hear, no matter how loud and long Caleb said his name.

Caleb looked up. Something was in the eastern sky, and it was moving fast. A cloud, a dark storm cloud? Could a cloud move that fast? Now he could make it out — that shape . . . three shapes. The trees started shaking and waving as if there had been a sudden wind just as before a storm. There was a low hum in the air. This wasn't a surprise storm cloud. These dark shapes in the sky that were getting closer and closer were Lindauzi airships. All the stories were explicit about their size, shape, sound, and speed. Caleb had never seen one, but he knew. He watched as the three moved apart, one staying in the rear, one moving to Caleb's right, and the third straight toward him. This airship was flying low, just above the trees, its vibrations knocking them about, showering the street with even more leaves. The ship cast a long wide shadow. By now Max was hysterical and Caleb let him go. The little dog ran in circles, barking at the ship then running back, turning, barking, running back again *badbadbadrunhidebad.*

"Come back here, Max," Caleb shouted. The Lindauzi hated dogs; they killed them when and wherever they saw them. Another story told at night around the fire, Caleb thought. Was it true? The airship stories were true, there one was, a half-block away, now moving very slowly, as if it had all the time in the world. And the other two — one was gone, but Caleb could see the other hovering at a distance — over what? The Footwashers? The oldest of the Lindauzi stories, of the moment of the Arrival, over one hundred and fifty years ago, told of men and women in the biggest and greatest of the old cities, New York, ill and tired, afraid, the Sickness everywhere. They came out of where they had been hiding, rubbing their eyes, blinking, to watch a sky filled with dark shadows, dark descending shadows.

Papa had told Caleb exactly what the Lindauzi looked like. They were taller than any human, even the tall hounds and the long-legged racers they had bred. The Lindauzi were completely covered with fur. Their hands and feet were clawed. They had muzzles, snouts, instead of noses, like the tribal dogs, but shorter and blunter. Their fangs were shorter than any dog's, and they could retract and extend them, like their claws. Lindauzi eyes were yellow or golden-brown. According to the stories, the Lindauzi looked like a cross between bears and panthers, and Papa had agreed. Mama said the Lindauzi were supposed to smell when they got wet, like dogs, a thick sour smell. Papa had shrugged when Caleb asked him about the smell. "It never bothered me. They just smelled when they were wet. And besides, they said we had a smell, too." (Max had agreed: *allyouhaveyourownsmell ilike-yours. . . .*)

Once before Papa had left, the Jacksoner hunters had brought home a massive black bear. Its skin covered an entire wall.

"The Lindauzi are just about as tall," Papa had said as Caleb stroked the pelt, "but their fur is softer. Much, much softer." Papa had reached up then with one hand and brushed across the fur with his open fingers. Caleb had wanted to ask Papa what he was seeing and what he was remembering. Papa's eyes had gone far away.

Caleb turned himself into a ball, his hands over his head, his feet tucked under his buttocks, and waited until the shadow was gone and he could feel the sun again. Maybe he was too small for the Lindauzi to notice and they would go away and he would be safe. Max kept barking frantically and pulling at Caleb's tunic sleeve with his teeth *dangerdangerbaddangerbadbad. . . .*

"Shut up, Max. Please. Shut up," Caleb begged. If the Lindauzi were listening through their airship, they would both be dead. He looked up to see the airship down the street, slowly turning toward Jackson. The trees were still. The last of the sudden leaf shower drifted to the ground. Where was it going now? Caleb stood. There it was, hovering above Jackson's white columns and the broken tooth of the old tower. Flying around the airship, like angry wasps, were the small flyers of the hounds. Instead of stingers, they were shooting out thin needles of light.

"Lasers," Caleb whispered. The fiery weapon of the hounds, which meant their hunterbeasts were with them as well. They were hunting — not for rabbits or deer or possums, or even for foxes or bears. From time to time, as everybody in the tribe knew, the hounds and their beasts hunted humans. The hounds and their beasts didn't just chase humans. They hunted them down and killed them, cutting off their heads as trophies. Everyone. Men, women, boys, girls, babies.

Davy.

"Davy. Not Davy."

Caleb took off running. He didn't look back or call for Max; he knew the little dog was right behind him *hurryrunrunbadobad-Calebrunrun.* Up the street, right, then past the kiln. Up a little hill. Through still dewy grass, stumbling, jumping over broken cement, asphalt, bricks. Shoving back low branches and saplings. One snapped back and slapped Caleb in the mouth. He fell hard on the ground. He tasted blood, salty and warm in his mouth.

Screams. Screams louder than any he had ever heard, different screamers. Barking that became shrieking. Then one screamer, another, stopped. Hunterbeasts snarling, growling. Caleb pushed himself up, wiped the blood off his mouth, started running again. There were the dogs, the beasts, the dogs biting at the beasts' legs. The hunterbeasts were more than three times the size of the biggest dogs. They had scaly reptilian skin and a crest of sharp spikes that ran from their heads to their barbed tails. Giant lizards whose whiplike forked tongues and talons drew blood and shrieks from the terrified dogs who were all running now, their attack-lust swallowed by their fear.

"Their tongues are poisonous," Papa had said. "It takes a little while, but one or two flicks makes you dizzy, slows you down. Three or four and you are out."

"Max, come back, Max, come back, come baaaaccckkkk!"

ImcomingImcomingCaleb—

It was too late. One of the four beasts' tails snagged Max on his head and he fell, whimpering *hurtCalebhurtstop* and before Caleb could move, the return stroke ripped the dog open. Then another beast, with one quick taloned slash, finished the job. Caleb felt a doggy tongue on his face, quick and light, and, just as quickly, it was gone. A few dogs escaped, howling. The beasts made short work of the rest. Then the monsters galloped off toward Jackson.

MaxohMax. Davy.

Caleb spit out blood and bark and started running. He had to get there, he had to get there, now, now, now. He stopped at the gardens, gasping, wiping more blood. The gardens were in flames and all the trees Caleb could see were great torches. The heat pushed him back as if it were a giant hand. Through the smoke and the fire, Caleb could see the motionless airship and the flyers, dropping to the ground, one by one by one.

"Davvveeeee!"

"Go back, boy, go back, run, they're killing us, run, boy, run . . ."

Caleb jerked around. It was Ezra, the tanner, pushing his way out of the smoke.

"Run, get away. . . ."

Ezra staggered and fell, twitched, and was still. Caleb saw a hole in his back, where the leather had been burned away; he smelled the burnt flesh. Ezra's tunic was soaked in blood. The flesh on one side of his face and up and down his legs had been torn and ripped. Beast tongue marks made angry red stripes all over the man. For a brief, brief moment, Ezra's corona glowed bright yellow, then an intense hot white, and, then, like Max's ghost tongue, was gone.

Caleb reached out his hand toward the man and froze again as another scream came from Jackson. "I'm sorry, Ezra, I'm sorry, but I have to go find Davy," he whispered and turned to run again but met another man, Micah, the fisherman, swaying out of the smoke. Blood covered Micah's hands and face, as if he were wearing red gloves and a red mask. Micah fell beside Ezra, making a dull thud that Caleb almost couldn't hear over the sounds of the fire and beasts.

He had to find Davy, but how? There was no way Caleb could get into Jackson. If he got past the smoke and the fire, there were the hounds and the hunterbeasts outside the columns, and being dead wouldn't help his little brother. The airship still remained over the broken stub of the old tower, motionless, appearing and reappearing as the winds shifted the smoke. A few of the flyers hovered around the ship, like great bumblebees, bobbing up and down in the air. And the hounds and beasts Caleb couldn't see, and Davy, were all down inside Jackson.

"The tunnel, the one under the garden, or the one that comes out by the big magnolia, I could go in one of those tunnels and find—" No. Neither way would work. And there was something else, something Papa had said, something Papa had made Caleb and Davy learn—if Caleb could just think, oh, it was so hard to make himself think.

A beast snarled and growled—where was it? Caleb couldn't see it, the smoke was getting thicker as the fire consumed the garden, so he ran. Was the beast behind him, were those beast-feet hitting the ground? Or his heart, hammering? Caleb ran. He ran past the old brick wall that had separated the garden from the old street, College Av, and then across the street, jumping from asphalt chunk to asphalt chunk, and then, sure the beast was upon him, he jumped and rolled down a thick grassy bank. Finally he crawled into the green and black shadows beneath the magnolia that guarded the tunnel mouth. He lay still against the ground, the big dry leaves crunching beneath his body.

I have to think. Something Papa said. A place to go if I couldn't go home. A place to wait, a sanctuary.

"But why couldn't I go home, Papa?" Caleb had asked.

"A flood, a fire, it doesn't matter. You just go there and wait in the field by the little lake, there's a tunnel mouth there. You just go there and wait."

The hounds were going to kill everyone in Jackson. Caleb knew this. He had heard it said more times than he could remember. And after everybody was dead, the heads would be collected and what the beasts had left of the bodies would lie where they had fallen for the birds and rats. Hounds didn't bother to bury humans. They would, though, collect any hunterbeast killed by Jacksoner arrows, spears, and knives. There wouldn't be many beast bodies to collect.

Caleb rolled over and sat up. His mouth hurt. He was hungry. And it felt safe here at the bottom of the hill, beneath the magnolia, safe in its thicket of branches, its piles of leaves. He couldn't hear any more screams, or feel the fire. There was just a little smoke. Behind Caleb was the huge thick tree trunk and behind it was the tunnel entrance, a dark hole in the hillside, completely hidden by the tree. The tunnel led straight into the heart of Jackson, but just before it reached the living quarters, there was a side tunnel which was the way to the field and the little lake where Papa had told Caleb to wait if he couldn't go home.

Caleb had to crouch to enter the tunnel. Once inside he smelled smoke again and cool earth and dust and mildew from the shelves on both sides of him, which were filled with books, books, books, and more books. There were books everywhere. The shelves were stuffed. Books lay on top of each other, on the tunnel floor (made out of asphalt chunks), in high stacks, and loose, as if they were light enough to be scattered by any wind finding its way through the thick magnolia branches into the tunnel. It would have to be a hurakin, Caleb thought, and the air would be filled with magnolia leaves and books flapping their pages. Thick, fat books (maybe they wouldn't fly too well), skinny books. Red, blue, black, white, grey, and brown books. Books with torn and ripped bindings, pages spilling out, more leaves to take flight. Books that looked almost new, their plastic covers still shiny.

There had been little warning years ago, before Caleb was born, so the story went, when a tired, red-eyed messenger had come to tell the Jacksoners that the Lindauzi were burning human books. They were blowing up the old libraries, he said, between gulps of water, tearing down their walls so that no brick lay on top of another. He had run the last part of the way. Everyone knew Jacksoners kept the old books. The messenger ate just enough to get his energy back and went on. Farther up the road there were more book keepers.

Mama had told Caleb the story, the fevered, desperate, day-and-night job of moving as many of the books as possible, hour after hour, books passing from hand to hand to hand in a long human chain.

"People still say it was stupid," Mama said once when she and Caleb were alone in the very tunnel in which Caleb now stood. Farther in, he thought, past the turn for the side tunnel, in the old part, built before the Arrival. They had been bent over a book which she had been making Caleb read aloud. "There are books here that even Readers can't read. I tried looking in the dictionaries and still some of the words don't make any sense. People said we should just let the Lindauzi burn them. Books and the things inside them didn't do humans any good when the Lindauzi came.

"But, Caleb, there was a time when people could read these books," she said, gesturing with an open hand toward the shelves. "Before the Arrival, people read and understood all these books." They were sitting beneath one of the gratings open to the sky. The sunlight falling through made white bars on the yellow pages.

Mama had taught Caleb (and he had been teaching Davy) every square inch of the tunnels, each turn, each twist, and each exit and entrance. Caleb set off, letting the tips of his fingers touch the spines of the books.

"These books are proof we were once more than we are, son. And a promise we can be that again." Still, Caleb knew, the books were not the tribe's greatest treasures. The books were the tribe's trust, a promise made in the past out of which the tribe had grown, and were guarded, cherished, and protected. But the greater reverence was given to the relics kept in the glass cases in the upstairs of Jackson, next to the picture of Jackson himself. Inside the glass cases were precious, whole cups of the white plastic styrofoam. Plastic forks with no tines missing, uncracked spoons, knives still sharp, with tiny, tiny teeth, aluminum cans carefully polished. Mama had taught Caleb how to read the words on each can: Coca-Cola, Schlitz, Miller Lite. One of the tribe's greatest heirlooms was six unopened golden-colored aluminum cans labeled Coors, all connected by rings of plastic.

Each family had its own cherished set of styrofoam cups. Caleb kept the four left by Mama and Papa wrapped in a soft piece of leather in one corner of the space he and Davy shared. He would let Davy use the cups only once a week. Caleb would first wash his hands and then slowly pour water from the gourd-cup into the styrofoam. They would drink slowly, savoring the special flavor the cups gave the water.

Davy and the family cups, Caleb knew, weren't far from where the tunnel split, one fork leading into Jackson itself, the other leading outward. Smoke was rolling out of the Jackson fork like hot fog. Caleb could feel the heat against his skin. Three bodies blocked the way into Jackson. Behind them, inside the smoke and the fire, Caleb could hear the Lindauzi shouts of the hounds. He almost turned left: *I can do it. Davy's just over there, waiting for me, holding on to our cups.*

The hounds were closer. And Davy knew the special place. Papa had made sure he knew, Caleb remembered. He wouldn't stay; he'd go there.

Caleb saw a hound, a blurred shape in the smoke, moving toward him. Behind the hound was a beast, another blurred shape.

He took off, running, into the right fork.

The special place was beyond the end of this tunnel and down another street, past more buildings, trees, and out into an open field and a small shallow lake, cupped by low hills. Tall grasses grew on the hills. Caleb and Davy and Papa had run and played and rolled there many times.

"Your mother loved this place, boys," Papa said once, "and I want you boys to love it, too. She came to pray here, she said, because all the churches were either destroyed or scavenged or just empty, with broken windows, mice, and rotting wood. Myself, I am never sure who to pray to. There's Father Art in Jackson, Jehovah for the Footwashers, and Yahweh for the Covenant-keepers. Phlarx took me with him to Lord Madaan and Lady Aurelian's Temple at Kinsella. Maybe they are all the same; I just don't know."

Phlarx was the Lindauzi with whom Papa had grown up. When Papa talked about Phlarx, usually at night when Caleb and Davy were in bed, his eyes would grow dark and his voice would become thick and heavy. At times in his sleep, Papa called for Phlarx; other times for Mama. Sometimes he said their names together in the same breath.

Caleb shook his head. He wanted to think only of the safe place as he made his way through the tunnel's darkness. More books on both sides, and on the tunnel floor more asphalt chunks. The little lake, the grassy hills. His little brother rolling and laughing. Papa catching him and tossing him in the air as Davy laughed still harder. *Mama swaying in the grass, humming. Davy will remember, he will go there. He's gonna be sitting in the grass by the lake, waiting for me. Keep him safe, Father Art, Jehovah, Yahweh, Lord Madaan.*

He stepped out of the tunnel into the basement of a building, Strong, he remembered. The lake and the hills were on the other side of Strong, through another thicket of trees. The basement was filled with a jumble of iron rectangular frames, rods, and poles. A narrow path had been cleared through the iron jumble to stairs and the outside. Caleb found himself on a low cement platform. Behind him and above Strong's roof, Caleb could see smoke billowing up and darkening the sky. He stood by a tree that grew up against the platform, one hand touching the bark, the other hand unconsciously drawing a line down his nose, his lips, and his chin. He felt the cut from the branch that had slapped his face. It felt sore and tender and wet.

The hounds' flyers were up in the air, darker shapes in the smoke. Caleb couldn't see the Lindauzi airship. As Caleb watched, the flyers started to rise, all at the same time. Hanging below them was a shimmering, translucent net, a net Papa had told him was the same stuff that made the shimmering domes of light over every Lindauzi city and plantation. The golden net sagged from its weight, causing the flyers to rise very slowly. At the net's bottom its golden color was streaked with red from the heads it carried.

Caleb turned and climbed down from the platform and made his way into the thicket between him and the lake. It was another jumble, this time of thick, knotted roots, vines, and spider webs.

He found the path and walking bent made his way to the other side, into the safe place, to stand on a low hill. Caleb could see the sunlight reflected from the smooth clear surface of the lake. A slight breeze brushed across the grasses.

There was no one there. Caleb looked back quickly: what looked like the entire sky was filled with black smoke. In front of him were the sun and the lake and the hills. It was as if the world had been divided in half, one half burning and turning black, the other untouched and empty.

"Davy? Davveeee?"

Caleb shouted his brother's name over and over, but his voice was the only sound he heard.

"Maybe he's waiting for me in that short tunnel," Caleb said, thinking of the tunnel running between the wing of Strong he had just come out of, and its other wing, which he could just see through the thicket. Back through the thicket's narrow path, then down into the basement, up into the building, through a long hall, and down again, into another basement. This basement was another jumble of iron and pipes. The tunnel's entrance was a door on the far side. Caleb peered in and called for Davy again. His voice echoed and bounced, but there was no answer. *He can't be back in Jackson. Davy was supposed to come here. But he's only four years old.*

Take care of your brother, Caleb.

Caleb sat down in the doorway, his back to the frame, half in and half out. He was really hungry and tired. Davy wasn't where he was supposed to be. And this Strong basement—he hadn't noticed the other so much—was cool and still. *I'll wait. He'll come. And Papa will come, too, just like in my dream this morning.* He wondered what time it was—noon, maybe. There wasn't enough light coming through the narrow windows at the top of the basement walls, and he didn't feel like getting up and going back outside. Noon sounded good enough.

Caleb yawned and then lay down inside the doorway, feeling safer in the shadows of the tunnel entrance. He pressed his stomach against the floor, hoping that might make his hunger go away. He closed his eyes, thinking how it would be if it were night and he was at home in Jackson. All around him he would have been able to hear the sounds of others sleeping: the gentle rhythmic breathing, the wordless calls, legs and arms rearranging, bodies shifting. Davy always slept right beside Caleb. His little brother was a restless sleeper, turning and throwing out his arms, murmuring words and making little sounds. Now in the tunnel, sleepy and tired and hungry, Caleb found everything too quiet, too still.

Before, when he couldn't sleep, either Mama, or Papa, after she died, would have come in and found Caleb awake and told him a story. Aunt Sara never did after Papa left, so Caleb told himself the stories Mama and Papa had, over and over again, until they became one long story. He remembered the stories exactly as his parents had told them, down to nuances of inflection and tone, the gestures they repeated each time they told a tale.

Once upon a time there was a tribe of people who called themselves Jacksoners. They took their name from the place where they had lived since the Lindauzi Arrival, and the place took its name from the painting of Jackson that hung inside the door, just past the white columns, and surrounded by the glass cases with the tribal treasures. Nobody knew anymore who Jackson was or why his painting was on the wall or what he had done to have the place named for him. They just knew the building was called Jackson in his honor and before his image, each Jacksoner bent the knee.

They were sure Jackson wasn't Father Art, God. Jackson's face was seen every day. Everybody knew Father Art and His Son had turned Their backs on humans, or why else would the Lindauzi be here and have done what they had done? It was as it had been for Job, but Father Art had given the Lindauzi even more power than Satan.

Every day one of the eldest prayed Father Art would turn around, show His face, and deliver them from evil. Over the years the prayers had grown shorter and sadder. Fewer and fewer of the old hymns were sung; the words "Joyful, joyful, we adore thee" left a bitter taste.

The tribe lived below the ground in a warren of interlocking tunnels, passages, and rooms. Some were there when the tribe began to live in Jackson; some had been dug out over the years as the tribe grew and more room was needed.

While no Jacksoner was sure who Jackson was, they all knew what the building itself had been used for before the aliens had come. Jackson had been a library, and it had been surrounded by a school of many buildings. Cached in the tunnels, crammed into overcrowded shelves, the old books, or what was left of them after one hundred and fifty years, remained, cared for with great devotion. The books were dusted and wiped clean, stacked and restacked. This was done slowly and carefully: each action, each gesture a prayer.

The books were rarely, if ever, opened, for the simple reason that most Jacksoners could not read them.

Each Jacksoner wore a necklace made of stone and wooden beads and one smooth flat stone or a metal circle on which was scratched his or her given name and family name. Each year a stone or wooden bead was added, one for each year of life. For all but a few Jacksoners, the names on their life-necklaces were all they could read.

There was one family who could read the old books: the Hulberts. It was this family who preserved the old arts of reading and writing. Only Hulberts scratched the name of each new Jacksoner on his or her name-stone or name-plate. Only a Hulbert taught the children a few years later how to write their names. Only a Hulbert kept track of the tribal calendar, moving the stone each morning from one day-brick to the next. Others told stories around the night-fires; Hulberts read them from the old books. There was always a Hulbert among the tribal elders, or there had been until the time of this story.

There were just two Hulberts then, Mary and her older sister, Sara. Their father had died from an infected leg; their mother in childbirth, the baby dying with her. Of the two sisters, Mary, or so everybody said, was by far the prettier: great brown eyes, and long shining dark hair falling to her waist in a curly mane. Many of the young men were in love with Mary and wanted to marry her: Ezra, the tanner, Jesse the hunter, Micah, the fisherman, and his brother, Jonah. But she would have none of them. Jesse, in despair, married Sara, though neither loved the other.

When Mary finally did marry, she chose a man from outside Jackson. Not a man from the nearest tribe, the Footwashers. Not a man from the tribe beyond the Footwashers, the Covenant-keepers. No, Mary shocked the tribe: her man came from the Lindauzi. He was a Lindauzi pet, born and bred for life in the Lindauzi cities and plantations. A man different from any Jacksoner: taller, bigger, stronger, and of questionable humanity.

Mary found her Lindauzi-bred man in the snow. Ilox was the name which he had when she found him and the name she always called him. She found Ilox on one of the coldest days in the year with snow heavy on the ground. More fell by the hour and the wind moaned as it sculpted the snow into graceful curves and twists.

She had awakened early in the morning, bundled up in furs, and went outside to walk in the snow. Even so, the wind brought the cold against her skin, rubbing her face raw. Still, Mary liked walking alone in the snow. If nothing else, she couldn't hear her sister's nagging: Choose a man! You're a Hulbert, a Reader; you have a responsibility to marry and have children for Jackson. Choose a man! And that was just one thing Sara harped on, as the list of Mary's short-comings seemed endless. With only the wind talking with the trees and the white and the grey sky, Mary felt as if she had the world to herself.

Then she saw him.

At first Mary thought it was a big dog or a bear who had died in the snow. But when she knelt down and brushed the snow away, she found a man. A tall, fair-skinned, blond, blue-eyed man, naked, and barely alive. It took a long time for the man to open his eyes. Mary pounded and massaged his chest for what seemed like forever until, at last, the man's eyes blinked and opened. He stared up at her and then slowly raised one hand to touch her face.

Later, Mary said it was at the moment of the man's touch that she fell in love. She helped him to his feet, giving him her furs to cover his body. The walk back to Jackson seemed to take even longer than it had taken the man to wake up. Most of what the man said Mary could not understand, but by the time she had him wrapped up in furs and near the fire, she knew his name, Ilox. He had said it over and over, pointing to himself: Ilox, Ilox, Eeeellloxxxxx, with the wind carrying away the final sound to knock snow off the trees.

No one in Jackson believed Mary when she said she wanted to marry Ilox. Sara told her she was crazy. The elders said no Jacksoner could marry a man who they couldn't be sure was human. Then Mary told them she was forgetting how to read, and the tribe had never had just one reader before.

Ilox and Mary's first child was born dead. Many Jacksoners nodded their heads knowingly and muttered amongst themselves: you see, Lindauzi humans are changed. They aren't like us; they are different. Bad blood kills babies. The birth of their second child, a big healthy boy named Caleb, only made the talkers whisper a little more softly.

Mary lived to have one more child, Davy, who was born when Caleb was seven. By then the tribe had grudgingly accepted Ilox, and some even let him write their babies' names on the name-stones at birth. That Ilox had learned how to read, write, and speak American so quickly had been considered nothing short of miraculous. But Mary's death in childbirth set the tall blond man and his two sons apart.

People no longer bothered to lower their voices. They made the sign of protection against evil, crosses drawn openly in the air. They would turn back or go out of their way so their paths wouldn't cross.

Only Ilox's gift of reading and writing saved him and his sons from expulsion.

Ilox seemed not to care so few Jacksoners trusted him or believed he was as human as they. He raised his two sons, read for the tribe, and argued with Sara. He was a good, kind, and gentle man who told Caleb and Davy many, many stories about the Lindauzi and being raised in a Lindauzi house. He secretly taught them to speak the aliens' speech, telling them that someday it would help them to know the snarling, growling language.

In the summer of Caleb's eleventh year, Papa came to Caleb and Davy to tell them he was going on a short trip. Neither boy wanted Papa to go.

"Stay, Papa," Davy said, pulling at Papa's sleeve.

"For once the tribe has admitted it really needs me, boys," Papa had told them. "They know I know Lindauzi speech and they know I can sense the Lindauzi. A Footwasher hunter told Ezra he saw an airship nearby and we have to know if they're coming. Don't you see? This is the first time anyone has seen an airship anywhere near Jackson for years and years. It could mean the Lindauzi are going to send their hounds out after us. I have to go."

Caleb didn't see, but he woke up early to tell Papa good-bye on the day he left. Papa had already gone. He was supposed to be back in two days. Two days passed, then three, a week, then two. At the end of a month, the elders declared Ilox, the husband of the Reader, Mary Hulbert, to be dead. Their two sons were to be raised by their Aunt Sara.

Aunt Sara had not loved her sister. She had hated her sister's husband more than anybody else in Jackson. She hated their children: Caleb, because he reminded her of Mary; Davy, because he reminded her of Ilox. It was a hatred born of jealousy. Mary and Ilox had loved each other; Sara and Jesse did not, could not. And one morning, just after Mary's death, Jesse had disappeared. (No one in Jackson was surprised.) It wasn't fair. Mary had been more beautiful than her sister, and she had found a man to love her. And people liked Mary. Sara was respected because she was a Reader; she was not liked. Sara hated her, him, and the children.

Caleb became her scapegoat. It was Caleb who was forced to empty out the night-waste buckets every morning. It was Caleb who was forced to serve Aunt Sara and her two sons. He fetched, he carried, he cleaned, he raised Davy, and he hated his aunt in return. Then one morning in October, Caleb had a dream that Papa was near and that Papa needed him.

"It's just a dream; go back to sleep," Aunt Sara had said. "Or I will find something for you to do. Now, go on."

Caleb and Aunt Sara had yelled and shouted, and Caleb and his dog had run away.

And then the Lindauzi and their hounds came.

Caleb fell asleep, still waiting.

Interchapter 1

Surveillance

From the Journal of Corviax luOrfassian laSardath luCorviax Alerian, Crown Prince of Lindauzian, Heir to the Left Throne, Supreme Commander of The Search Fleet, 26 Thawmoon 11372, the 135th year of the Search, the 60th year of Surveillance

I wish I could send a message to Favvy.

The techs tell me it would be pointless: he wouldn't receive the message before he died, and that he might already be dead, from old age, from reversion, from suicide. We have yet to re-establish contact with Lindauzian, not that it would matter. Any transmission we would receive would be at least 135 years old — from the year we left. We would still know nothing of what the homeworld is like now.

Would Favvy kill himself? Would he take his own life at the first signs of reversion? Would I? I don't know. The father I loved wouldn't have turned his back to me, and watched me leave without a word, a sign, a gesture. That father is a stranger and he might kill himself, if he thought it the will of Madaan. The father I would send a message is the father in my dreams, the father who played maze with me and found me in the corridors, whose hand was so big I could press my entire head into it, the father who knew just where to scratch behind my ears.

Favvy, I found them, the large primates, the star-cousins of the Iani. They are related, the DNA scans have been done again and again. The Search is over, now the Grand Project must begin. We have found the star-cousins of the Iani.

I am sure.

We have been in shielded cometary orbit for sixty of their years, with the crew awake in cycles programmed into the sleep viruses. We have been sending scout ships to their world for almost as long. We have been monitoring, recording, and analyzing their television and radio broadcasts. We have collected, studied, and tested their books, newspapers, magazines, music recordings. Toys, household appliances, transportation vehicles, serving utensils, clothing, food, and drink.

The specimens are afraid, of course. But memory viruses should make their returns bearable, and their recollections of us only fleeting dreams. The memory viruses will, of course, always be resident, albeit dormant, waiting for a trigger of recognition for an endorphin release. The specimens — and there are many now — will like us, want to be with us.

It is their empathy, latent and manifest, that has convinced me more than anything else that we have found the Iani's original world, or another colony like Lindauzian. These large primates have legends of being visited by powerful beings all throughout their history. They have legends of planetary disasters as well — Atlantis, Lemuria, Mu — which would explain why they are so technologically primitive.

The physical similarities are startling; there has been only minor genetic drift, some mutation —

But I was writing about their empathic abilities. Crude, unrefined, rough, untrained. But it is so, so strong in potential. These large primates love and love intensely and with great passion. They love their children, their mates, their parents, their friends, and their pets. These star-Iani form powerful and emotional bonds with their companion animals. It is this bonding ability and need that made us and now it will save us.

I wish we could save them all. But the weak and sick must be culled, the survivors bred and modified for the bond. The viral suborbital torpedoes are ready. There will be two launches, now, with first stage plague viruses, and then, in twenty years, the second stage. Fleet sociologists have timed the second stage release for a major calendar event for these Iani — what do they call it — I should know, I have studied the data and analyses enough. Millennium — in twenty or so years, their calendar will register the passing of a thousand years, a time marked by omens and portents. The second stage viruses will, with the subsequent planetary collapse, prime them to welcome us, to love us, as saviors.

I know: millions upon millions will die. But our entire species may die if the Grand Project fails. And the survivors—they will have the bond, heart to heart, mind to mind, soul to soul.

It will be worth all the deaths, the pain, the suffering.

It will.

Chapter II

Ilox, 2125-2136

I LOX TOSSED THE RED BALL AGAINST THE KENNEL door: bounce off the metal, bounce again, then back into his hands. He leaned down for the next toss, and stopped. There was a familiar heat in his joints, a prickling at the back of his neck, and his arm hair stood up. Lindauzi — somewhere near, getting closer. He glanced quickly around the choosing pen and then outside: no Lindauzi in sight. That just meant, though, that they were on the other side of the nursery. None of the other boy-pups in the pen, of course, felt anything. Two were trying to climb the shield-wall, and kept slipping to land in a heap at the bottom. Two more were playing catch with another ball. One more, Arxes, Ilox's litter mate, was asleep, curled up on a soft foam pad in the corner.

He brushed the sand off his buttocks and stomach and rolled the ball at Arxes's pad. He shrugged and twisted his head, trying to shake off the heat on his neck. But no amount of twisting or shrugging or even shaking would do any good. Ilox used to wonder why the others never felt the Lindauzi, and for a long time, he thought everybody did. He had sensed them since forever, even, or so the dams told him, when he was a baby-pup and still sucking from a nurse-dam. When the kennel vet came, so her story went, to examine and inoculate the new infant pups, Ilox would start crying even before the Lindauza came into the pen. When she picked him up to set him on the examining table, he squirmed and twisted and cried even louder, as if her touch hurt.

"But my claws are retracted," the vet protested to the nurse-dam after giving Ilox his shots. "Why is this one crying and acting out like this? Has he been sick?"

The dam shook her head, shrugged and took Ilox back into the nursery. He didn't stop crying until the vet left the kennel. It wasn't long before the entire kennel knew when any Lindauzi was near: Ilox's cries were an alarm that set them all scurrying and running. For those in the choosing pens it was a chance to straighten hair, brush off dirt, wipe away leftover food. By the time he learned to walk, Ilox had also learned to hide his sensitivity from the Lindauzi. Instead of crying when he felt the prickling and heat, Ilox would pull away from the others and become very still and watchful.

Now that Ilox was seven, he was beginning to tell one Lindauzi from another. There were three coming to the kennel this morning. One was Oldoch the kennelmaster, and Ilox felt his worry, and just beneath it, a tinge of fear. It was Morix, the plantation lord, that Oldoch feared, and Ilox also felt the older Lindauzu's dark presence, his steady, sure strength. The third Lindauzu was unfamiliar, and what Ilox felt was equally unfamiliar: a peculiar heat in his chest, a tightening in his throat, tears in his eyes.

Ilox shook himself, forcing all three responses to recede. He ran his fingers through his hair and waited in the center of the pen. There, they were almost—*now,* Ilox thought—and the door into the kennel slid open and there they were. Oldoch was talking excitedly and waving his arms. Beside him was a taller, blond-furred Lindauzu, Morix, who was listening intently to Oldoch, his ears up and alert. A youngling walked just behind Morix.

"I told you he would be waiting for us. This cross is the most successful yet. The vet told me about him and I've been keeping an eye on Ilox ever since. This one, my Lord Morix, is the pick of his litter and is manifesting most of the gene complexes we are breeding his line for. You know, it would be so much easier if we could just do with them what we do with the hunterbeasts, the bathing towels, and the glowglobes, the burrowers: gene surgery and splicing, recombinant DNA—"

"Oldoch. You know that is rank heresy to me," Morix said, glowering.

"Yes, my lord. But, my lord, what is one more heresy to a heretic people? Sorry, sorry, sorry, I know you are neo-orthodox—I'm Machinist—"

"Enough, Oldoch," Morix growled, and gestured with his hand to dismiss the kennelmaster's errant words. "The ones we left behind are the true heretics. Now, tell me about this pup."

"Yes," Oldoch said, looking down. "He is the result of a sibling cross, from a line particularly strong in the bonding trait. It is too early to be sure, but he could be the one we have been looking for. Ilox is the alpha of his year-group; he lets no one eat and drink before him. A tough one, as you said you wanted for Phlarx. Come here, Ilox."

Oldoch took a step toward Ilox, and raised one hand to signal come. Ilox stood still, watching. One of his first memories was of Oldoch scooping him up from the dam and taking him to a low, cold, white table and laying him there to be touched and poked and injected by the vet. The kennelmaster was almost a head shorter than Morix, and his body fur was darker and coarser. Morix was the older: his muzzle was greying, as was the fur of his crest.

Ilox sniffed. One of them had wet fur; it was an odor no Lindauzi could hide, no matter how much deodorant was used. Ilox could smell the deodorant, too—dark and musty. Oldoch was getting nervous; Ilox could see him scratching under his neck and the sides of his muzzle.

"Come, Ilox," Oldoch said again and repeated his hand signal. His voice had gotten shaky and Ilox could see him retracting his claws so as not to scratch again in front of Lord Morix.

Ilox waited. He had played this game before with Oldoch and usually the kennelmaster didn't get quite so irritated. Oldoch's ears were lying close to his head and his nostrils were flaring, his crest erect.

"He thinks we are playing a game," Oldoch said, and quickly walked across the sand. Morix and the youngling followed a few paces behind. Oldoch cuffed Ilox sharply and then held him under both arms for Morix's inspection. Ilox twisted his neck to look up into Morix's eyes. They were dark and as hard and as cold as stones.

"Unfortunately, this particular pup still retains some of the aggressive tendencies dogs are noted for. But I believe he will make a fine companion pet for your son, my lord. Ilox is healthy, intelligent, and strong."

"I see," the other adult said dryly and motioned to the kennelmaster to set Ilox down. He then carefully examined Ilox, finishing when he ran a claw inside Ilox's mouth to feel his teeth and gums. Ilox hated the feel of fur in his mouth. He had bitten once, when it was Oldoch doing the examining, and he had drawn blood. Oldoch had backhanded Ilox, howling and cursing.

"Well, son, this one is to be your companion, as Sandron has been mine. My father gave Sandron to me when I was your age, and he has been with me ever since. This is the first of Sandron's get I've not sold. Here he is, the pup I promised you for your upright day. You heard what Oldoch said, and I have explained to you what the bonding trait is and how important it is to all of us—why we left our home and are here on an alien world. If this pup is as Oldoch says, if you and he can—well. Happy Upright Day, Phlarx."

Sandron? An adult male-dog, his sire? Ilox was puzzled. Few adult male-dogs came out of the house to the kennel. The guard and attack-hounds with their beasts came and went, but only very occasionally would a house-dog come near the kennel. Sometimes a tech came to puzzle over the brightly-lit and constantly moving circuitry Ilox had been told never to touch.

He had, once. It had taken him three days to recover, soaking in baths of burngel, with tubes inserted into various parts of his body, as he floated in a dreamy, drugged sleep.

"Aren't you afraid of anything?" Oldoch asked when he came to take Ilox back to the kennel from the house vet. "You could have been killed. I've spent too much time on you—artificial insemination, *in vitro* fertilization—to have you fry yourself. Are you listening to me?" Oldoch pulled Ilox's ears.

"Yes," Ilox had answered, pulling away and refusing to look Oldoch in the eye. Techs had removed a section of the kennel wall for repair and all he had done was touch the exposed circuitry. He was fine now, and he hadn't been hurt that badly. None of the other pups would even go near the circuits, which, as far as Ilox had been concerned, had just been moving lights. What was there to be afraid of? Even now Ilox wasn't scared; he just didn't want to get burned again. And besides the wall had been replaced.

Even though few adult male-dogs, except for the hounds, came to the kennel, Lindauzi did, male and female, and often, to look over the pups in the choosing pens or to examine one of the dams. Ilox remembered the kennelmaster once telling an overweight female Lindauzi that Morix's dogs had won gold more than once.

"He keeps the most impeccable genecharts I have ever seen,

and I have been a breeder practically since I stood upright. His kennels are the best. The dogs in this kennel are the most promising of what we hope for. We supply semen and ova for kennels all over the continent. The Crown Prince himself gets his dogs here." The Lindauza had taken a girl-pup and a dam. For her daughter and for herself, she said.

"Well, son?" Morix asked again, nodding his satisfaction to the kennelmaster. Oldoch practically sagged in relief.

Ilox looked at the Lindauzi youngling, who, he was sure, was at least a dog-year or two younger than he was. The youngling's fur was lighter and blonder than his father's. His muzzle seemed sharper and longer, and he seemed to be having a hard time keeping his fangs and claws retracted.

"A Lindauzi will come for you, Ilox," one of the nurse-dams had whispered to him when he was sick and she was leaning over him, wiping his hot forehead with a cool, wet cloth. "A Lindauzi will come for you and love you and care for you. The Lindauzi love us, little Ilox."

She had sung the words over and over, until he had fallen asleep.

Phlarx timidly raised his arm and touched Ilox's bare shoulder with one hand. Ilox flinched and pulled back, looking down at his shoulder at the sudden thin bright red line.

"Phlarx, retract, retract! How many times have you been told to retract your claws in greeting? You walk upright, you are not a baby in the nursery. Why can't you remember that—it should be like breathing. You've hurt your pup, see? Kennelmaster?" Morix shook his hand in Phlarx's face, all five claws extended, and the youngling jerked back, shielding his eyes, his throat.

Ilox felt something cool pressing on his shoulder. He looked to see a line of the white woundcream slowly dissolving into his skin, drawing closed the rip as it disappeared. The kennelmaster returned the tube into the belt at his waist and nodded back to Morix.

"Listen to me, Phlarx. Ilox is not a toy. He is not a ball for you to toss or a model airship for you to fly around your bedroom. He is a boy-pup: intelligent, feeling, and capable. This is no mean gift I am giving my only male child and heir on his upright day. If he is to be your companion, you must take especially good care of him and look after him and love him, and he will love you. Do you understand?"

"Yes, Father," Phlarx muttered, glaring at Ilox.

It's not my fault, Ilox thought. He remembered, though, a nurse-dam telling him it was always the dog's fault. *Lindauzi are smarter, quicker, more clever.*

He looked up at Morix, who laid a hand on Ilox's head and drew him to his side. Ilox pressed his head against the Lindauzu's broad palm, liking its feel as Morix stroked his fair hair.

"He's young, kennelmaster, he will learn. He will take good care of Ilox. Print out his genechart for me; I will explain it to Phlarx so he will know producing such a pup is no easy thing. And I will tell him again why this is so important."

"Yes, Lord Morix, the Search, now the Project," Oldoch said and dropped to all fours in the traditional Lindauzi gesture of respect.

Ilox let Morix take his hand, and, after the two adults finished up the arrangements, walked with Morix and Phlarx out of the choosing pen, through the kennel, and out onto the wide plantation lawns to where the aircar was parked. Ilox watched Phlarx out of one corner of his eye, wondering what it would be like to be with the youngling. Where would Ilox sleep, in Phlarx's bed, or on the floor? The nurse-dam had always said to be chosen as personal companion was the hope and dream of all dogs. Would they play together as he and Arxes had? *(Oh, he had forgotten to say good-bye. . . .)* Would any of the dams he knew come and see him? Ilox felt Phlarx watching him as they walked, and when they got into the aircar, he sat down by Phlarx in the back.

They stared at each other as Morix ordered the car to start and then fly over the plantation to the family house. The car slowly lifted as it hooked into the continental traffic net. Kinsella, the Vaarchael family plantation, was beneath a major flight path between the east and west coasts so that there was always a steady stream of vehicles of one kind or another overhead. Morix glanced back once and then turned to a workscreen filled with the twisted shapes of Lindauzi script. He spoke softly, the screen's glowing letters shifting and moving in response to his voice.

"I'm Phlarx," the youngling said, turning toward Ilox with an open hand and retracted claws. All his teeth were hidden, the Lindauzi equivalent of a smile. Ilox smiled back and put his own hand on top of Phlarx's. Ilox's hand was small, pale, and almost hairless in comparison. When Phlarx closed his fingers, Ilox's hand almost disappeared. He squeezed back.

I think I like him, Ilox thought. No, I do like him. The nurse-dam had been right about Phlarx as well; Phlarx liked him, too.

"I like you, Ilox," Phlarx finally said as the aircar moved in and out of traffic, the thick green lawns spreading out below them, divided into lanes and paths by white, pink, red, and orange flowers.

"I like you, too," Ilox answered. Does he love me, though, like the nurse-dam promised? She had never told him what love meant, where it was, what it looked like. Had she loved him when he was a baby-pup holding him to suck on her teats? Had she loved him when he had grown inside her, making her belly big? He wasn't sure if the nurse-dam who had told him about being chosen by a Lindauzi was the one who had borne him. Arxes didn't know and none of the others in his year-group did, either. Maybe being liked was enough.

Ilox looked again at Phlarx, who was staring outside, and repeated the nurse-dam's song to himself: *A Lindauzi will love you, and you will love the Lindauzi*. He could remember the rest of her song now—words about the heart-bonding, the link, but he still could not decide what she had meant. Was love this intense, almost instant liking?

He would find out what love was. Of that he was sure. As they sat there in the back of the aircar, his hand in Phlarx's, Ilox could just feel, barely, Phlarx's body vibrating, and he could hear, very softly, a rumbling, coming from deep in the Lindauzu's throat. And although Ilox was close enough to Morix that he could reach out and touch him, it was only Phlarx Ilox felt: the prickling, tingling, the heat, the uncertain happiness, the fear—everything— was Phlarx and Phlarx alone.

Phlarx woke before anyone else. Today he was going to get a pup. Father had promised when Phlarx had his seventh upright day, he could have a pup. Just like Tyuil, his sister, who had gotten a girl-pup, Nivere, on her seventh upright day.

The wall was just becoming translucent, letting in the first of the morning light when Phlarx got out of bed. He brushed his fur in front of the mirror, making sure no little tufts stuck up anywhere. Father always said the first thing anybody should do in the morning was brush his or her fur. He had made Phlarx go back more than once when he had forgotten or had done it too quickly.

"Unbrushed fur means you don't respect yourself. You are my son: the Viceregal heir. You have Imperial blood; some day you will mate into the Imperial family. . . ." Phlarx shook himself. Father's words always became jumbled together in his head. It made it hard for him to think.

Phlarx looked at his fur brush. It was a snarled nest of his blond fur. He laid it where the menial could find and clean it. He looked back into the mirror. No tufts were showing. Good. He bared his fangs: yellow and clean.

He was the first one at the table for the morningmeal. Where was everybody? Father? Mother? Tyuil? Phlarx sighed and squirmed in his chair.

Mother came in first. She nodded at Phlarx as she sat down, pressing her hand into the palmsign by her seat. Phlarx sat on his hands and looked down at the table. Mother always wanted him to be still and quiet.

A house menial brought in Mother's morning drink in a cold frosted cup. Phlarx dug his claws into the chair. Where was Father? *When* were they going to the kennel? Eating was going to take forever.

"Phlarx. Retract. Be still. I'm tired of replacing chair seats because of you," Mother said, sipping her drink, the ice clinking. She did not look at Phlarx when she spoke. The Lady Ossit stared at the wall behind him, her eyes dark and distant.

"Yes, Mother."

After an eternity of sitting still, Father finally came in, followed by Tyuil and Nivere. His sister lightly ran her claws through his crest. At least she understood. She and Nivere whispered together until a glare from Mother silenced them. Then the four trays were herded in by the same menial. Finally, morningmeal started. Phlarx ate as slowly as he could. Mother said eating fast was eating like a four-legged animal. Did he want to revert, forget he had a name, run howling in the dark, eat meat raw and dripping with blood? Did he?

"No, Mother."

Phlarx still finished eating before everybody else.

"Well, Phlarx. I see you are ready," Father said, speaking for the first time. Phlarx flinched at the sound of his father's voice. He really had tried to eat slowly.

"Yes, Father."

"Come," Morix said and stood.

With one quick glance at his sister, Phlarx followed Father out into the hallway, to the lift, and down and out into the garden. *What will my pup look like? Like Father's dog, Sandron?*

"Now, son, I want you to understand, as much as you can. You are my heir; some day you will be Viceroy and rule this continent for the Prince, from the sea to the Great River. You must lead; you must be a Promulgator; you must understand the significance of what is happening to you today. The time for the culmination of the Project is near—must be near—the Project for which we left Lindauzian. I was born right before we left. . . ."

Phlarx said nothing. He was just glad Father kept walking. He had heard Father's boring speech about the Project and the Search and the fleet crossing space, leaving the homeworld, a thousand times. Well, maybe five hundred times. What he hadn't heard from Father was just what it all meant and he was afraid to ask. Phlarx kept hoping Father would tell, but Father seemed to think Phlarx knew what the Project was, what Lindauzian had been like, what the civil war had been about, all of it. Phlarx and his sister were Earth-born and all they knew of snowy, distant Lindauzian came from memory blocks, school lessons, and sermons in the temple. There was little mention of Lindauzian at home; talk of the homeworld only made Mother even more dour and silent.

Father kept talking until he saw Oldoch at the garden gate. Behind Oldoch, still in the morning air, was the aircar. Oldoch was the kennelmaster. He took care of all Father's dogs, especially those bred to be pet companions. Phlarx didn't like the dark-furred, short, lower-caste Lindauzu. At least the other adults spoke to Phlarx when Father was around; Oldoch looked right through him.

Oldoch and Father talked as they got into the aircar. They talked as the car flew over the plantation to the kennel, which was at the far end. They talked as they got out of the car and walked over the green lawn. They talked as they walked through the kennel to the choosing pen, a hush spreading around them, nurse-dams shushing babies, grabbing toddlers to make them be still. Phlarx paid little attention to their words which fluttered over his head like Oldoch's waving hands: bonding traits, gene complexes, empathic links, my Lord Morix this, my Lord Morix that. Instead Phlarx concentrated on walking slowly, keeping pace with Father and Oldoch. The son of Lord Morix did not go tearing around like some animal.

Phlarx knew before Oldoch said anything which pup was to be his. The pup stood facing them in the middle of the choosing pen, his arms across his chest. Fair hair and skin. Blue eyes. Phlarx felt scared and nervous and excited and almost happy; his ears and crest drooped. Would this pup like him?

"Come, Ilox," Oldoch said, and gestured with his hand. He glanced nervously at Father. The pup didn't move; he just watched them.

"Come, Ilox," Oldoch muttered and repeated his hand signal. Shaking his head, his fangs extended, he strode across the pen to slap the pup sharply. He then picked him up under both arms and turned to face Father. Phlarx winced at the pup's pain. He stared at the pup, who was ignoring him, looking first at Father, then at the kennelmaster.

Father nodded for Oldoch to set the pup down and, as Phlarx watched, examined him, checking his ears, teeth, nose, feet, and hands. The pup looked only at Father and Oldoch.

Phlarx couldn't stop looking at the pup. He wanted to stroke the pup's arms, scratch behind his ears, chase him across the choosing pen. He wanted the pup to look at him.

"Well, son, this one is to be your companion, as Sandron has been mine," Morix said when he was finished with the examination. "My father gave Sandron to me when I was your age, and he has been with me ever since. This is the first of Sandron's get I've not sold. Here he is, the pup I promised you for your upright day. You heard what Oldoch said, and I have explained to you what the bonding trait is and how important it is to all of us—why we left our home and are here on an alien world. If this pup is as Oldoch says, if you and he can—well. Happy Upright Day, Phlarx."

The pup—Ilox—was finally looking at Phlarx. Phlarx's body quivered. He raised his hand to touch Ilox's bare shoulder. Ilox flinched and pulled back. *Oh I hurt him, he's bleeding, I didn't meant to. . . .*

"Phlarx, retract, retract! How many times have you been told to retract your claws when greeting someone? You walk upright, you are not a baby in the nursery. Why can't you remember that —it should be like breathing. You've hurt your pup, see? Kennelmaster?" Father shoved his hand in Phlarx's face. He instinctively pulled back, covering his eyes and his throat. Phlarx knew how sharp Father's claws were.

"Listen to me, Phlarx," Father said angrily as the kennelmaster applied medication on the cut. "Ilox is not a toy. He is not a ball for you to toss or a model airship for you to fly around your bedroom. He is a boy-pup: intelligent, feeling, and capable. This is no mean gift I am giving my only male child and heir on his upright day. If he is to be your companion . . ."

All he ever does is talk at me. I bet he starts talking about the Project again.

"Do you understand?" Father asked. "Do you understand how important this is for you and for all Lindauzi on this planet?" Father asked, a deep rumbling the backdrop for his words.

"Yes, Father," Phlarx muttered, glaring at Ilox. *He's not going to like me, I know he isn't. Why can't Father just shut up?*

"Get the aircar ready, Oldoch," Father finally said. "I have work to do and I am sure Phlarx wants to get his pup home."

"Yes, my lord," Oldoch said.

Father walked with the kennelmaster out of the choosing pen, back through the kennel, and out to the aircar, discussing the necessary paperwork for the pup. Phlarx walked to Father's left, Ilox to his right. *Father's letting him hold his hand. He's never let me. He's watching me, I feel him watching me.*

The aircar was waiting just outside the long low kennel building. Phlarx and Ilox got in the back. Father grunting, climbed into the front.

"Access: traffic net, Vaarchael plantation overlap. Destination: Vaarchael house. Go," Father said as the aircar rose slowly into the air. Father nodded to Phlarx and Ilox and then turned to the workscreen in the navconsole. "Access: Population. Birthrate, reversion rate, suicide rate, Earth . . ." Father spoke softly, playing his hands across the workscreen, words and numbers rising from the screen's green depths to glow before him.

"I'm Phlarx," he said, and turned toward the pup, his hand open, palm up, claws retracted. Phlarx also lifted his head to expose his throat. He covered his teeth with his lips. Ilox smiled back and laid his hand on top of Phlarx's. Phlarx closed his hand over Ilox's. *He's mine. Nobody else's. Just mine. He's going to like nobody else but me. And I'm going to like just him.*

"I like you, Ilox," Phlarx said, holding tight to Ilox's hand. He had never held a pup's hand before, or any dog's hand, for that matter. Such smooth skin. Absolutely no hair, no pad, really, and so small. And instead of claws, dull, stubby hard growths. The pup's skin felt cool against Phlarx's hand pads.

"I like you, too."

Phlarx didn't let go of Ilox's hand until the aircar landed in front of the gate into the family gardens. He was afraid that if he did that, this new something between them, a soft shining link, would be shattered, as if it were made of fine glass, so fragile that one tap of a hammer would destroy it forever.

When the aircar stopped just outside the flower-covered walls of the palace of the Viceroy, the Vaarchael family house, Ilox was stunned by its massiveness. The high walls made even the Lindauzi look small, and almost every Lindauzi adult was at least three or four heads taller than the tallest adult male-dog Ilox had seen. The walls were sheer smooth red stone. The house was separated into several different big blocks connected by glass bridges. The bridges were transparent, and Ilox could see dogs and Lindauzi inside, moving about.

Phlarx and Ilox followed Morix through the wall gate, which dilated when Morix placed his open palm on a hand-shaped spot. When Ilox stepped into the inner garden, he gasped. There had been nothing like this at the kennel—masses of flowers, more pink, and red, and other colors: blue, yellow, orange, and colors Ilox had never seen before. The air had a rich smell, and for a moment, when Ilox first inhaled, he felt light enough to take to the air himself.

"Phlarx, take Ilox to the hounds' quarters and tell the alpha there to house-imprint him. You want him to be able to go wherever you go, so the house has to know him," Morix said, looking down at his son and Ilox. He stood with his arms crossed over his chest and both ears erect, a stance which Ilox would later learn meant approval and satisfaction.

Ilox held tightly to Phlarx's hand after they left Morix and made their way through the garden, past more flowers and fountains of light and water, until they came to a smaller, rectangular building, around which were parked personal flyers. Ilox had seen them sail over the kennel countless times.

The alpha hound was taller than any male-dog Ilox had seen in the kennels. He was as big as he was tall, and he picked up Ilox to take him inside for the imprinting. Ilox wondered why the alpha didn't smile and seemed so grim and tight, but he was afraid to make any noise around the alpha, let alone ask him any questions.

"Press your body, your entire body, into this screen, pup, and once it adjusts to your shape, don't move. You'll feel it move, but don't you move. This won't take long."

The alpha then inserted several glowing tubes into various places on Ilox's body: his temples, his groin, his chest, and his back. Ilox then pressed into the screen and felt it move and change as it fitted itself to him. The white screen grew around him until Ilox was completely enclosed, the white screen-flesh becoming a translucent grey. He wanted to cry out, but his mouth wouldn't open. Where was Phlarx? Why didn't he stop this alpha from hurting him? There was a sudden intense pressure, and the screen, giving off odd sucking noises, peeled itself away from his body. The alpha slapped the screen to make it finally let go; then he started pulling out the tubes.

"There. Now the house knows you," the alpha said, and picked Ilox up and set him down beside Phlarx. "Run along now," he added, and then waved them away. The alpha clearly had things far more important requiring his attention than coddling the pet of the son of the Viceroy.

Ilox took one quick look around the hounds' quarters before following Phlarx out. Mostly rows of beds, laser pistols, places for clothes, tables, food storage units, cooking consoles. But in the back, on shelves, inside long glass cases: skulls. Row after row after row of sightless, toothy skulls. Big, medium-sized, baby-sized. Ilox wanted to ask why they were there, but before he could get up his nerve, Phlarx came back for him and took him outside.

That night, Ilox slept beside Phlarx in the same bed. Phlarx pulled him close and held him across his chest. Ilox slept in the new clothes Phlarx had given him. He had never worn clothes before and had been astonished at how soft and warm the cloth felt against his bare skin. He had stood in front of a mirror, stroking the cloth, tracing and retracing the lines of his body.

"I look so *different* in clothes," he had said to Phlarx as he pulled one tunic over his head to try on the next. Phlarx had just laughed and handed him the next tunic, a dark red one, without sleeves, which he told Ilox was the proper wear for ceremonial occasions in other family houses. Then Phlarx slipped the family collar around Ilox's neck. The patterns were the same as the family mark just under Ilox's collarbone: three silver bars and a dark red half-moon. Hanging from the collar was a silvery circle, marked with Phlarx's and Ilox's names.

"There. Now everyone will know you are mind and nobody else's."

Do you belong to me, too?

But Ilox had said nothing as he pulled the next tunic over his head. Much later, he got up and padded across the thickly carpeted floor to stand in front of the mirror again. Ilox placed his hand on the mirror and a dim light came on, illuminating him in a faint pool of white, cut out of the darkness. He stared into the mirror and watched as his hands touched again every part of the tunic.

Ilox learned how to read when Phlarx did. It was a simple matter, and, although neither one admitted it, Ilox learned far more quickly and far more easily than Phlarx did. Phlarx was soon asking Ilox for help with the assigned readings given every day by the teacher, an elderly male whose fur was yellow-colored and thin. There were patches on his elbows and knees. He was so old his muzzle and crest were completely white. Writing was much harder. No matter how tightly Ilox gripped the stylus, the marks strayed across the deskscreen.

"You don't have claws, Ilox," Phlarx said. "This stylus is made for a clawed hand, not those funny little things you have on your fingers. Wait, I'll write it for you." Phlarx absently raked his claws on the wall, and then he took the stylus to rewrite the sentence Ilox had just tried to write.

Even after Morix brought him styluses made especially for pup hands, Ilox still wished he had Phlarx's claws. He wanted to be able to carelessly scratch his fingernails on a wall, to retract and extend them as he needed to. He wanted to be like Phlarx: taller and stronger. Dogs just weren't as strong. Even though he was finding out things he could do and Phlarx could not, because he was smaller and shorter, Ilox still wished he were like Phlarx. After a time, it was reading that gave Ilox again the sense of strength and sureness he had felt as the alpha in his year-group. Phlarx, once he had satisfied the teacher, was simply not interested.

Even so, Ilox found he needed to be better than Phlarx, at least in reading. If he had been asked why, he could not have explained why, but he knew he had to be. Maybe it was because in the kennel nursery, Ilox had been the strongest, the smartest, the alpha pup, and here, in the Vaarchael house, Phlarx was the strongest and he was in charge. Ilox knew he could never be stronger than Phlarx, but being smarter — maybe that was better. Ilox took a secret pride in being able to read easily words Phlarx stumbled over.

"Well, at least I can say them better than you," Phlarx had said, laughing. "Come on, try saying *brulyndrrthxt* again. . . ."

Ilox had tried to get his tongue around the name of the white, pink, and red flowers, but he could only sputter out the last syllables. They had both laughed and Ilox had gone to read the rest of the botany text out loud. Phlarx had sat back in his chair, his eyes closed, listening.

"Don't you want to read some?" Ilox had asked.

"Why should I bother reading all that stuff, Lox? My father is the Viceroy of the eastern half of this continent. I'll always have someone to read for me — I'll always have you," he added and ran his claws through Ilox's thick fair hair, something he knew Ilox liked. "Come on, let's go down to the pool and swim. You can finish reading this later and tell me about it."

Ilox was never able to understand why Phlarx didn't want to read. Words for Ilox were like food. He ate them, he swallowed them whole, and wanted another serving as soon as possible. Now, instead of getting up at night to look at himself in the mirror in his new clothes, Ilox slipped out of Phlarx's warm grip and got up to read. He read aloud in a whisper, savoring the sounds of the words in his mouth, even words like *brulyndrrthxt,* words he just couldn't say, words no dog could say. The teacher had told him it was impossible, his mouth was the wrong shape and he had no muzzle or fangs. He still kept trying.

But more than the words themselves, it was the stories that drew Ilox out of his bed at night. Until he read the stories about Lindauzian, the Lindauzi homeworld, he had not known the Lindauzi had come from another place, from one of the stars in the night sky. Ilox had not known that some of the brighter and bigger moving lights he saw in the same night sky were Lindauzi shuttles going to and from other Lindauzi plantations or the Lindauzi cities, or to an even bigger light in the sky, the space station orbiting the Earth.

Once Morix found Ilox up late at night, reading a long story about an ancient war on Lindauzian, between the northern and southern continents, and how Choxin luEliaan, and his Iani, Volian, had saved the north.

"What are you doing, pup? Why aren't you in bed?" Morix said, startling Ilox, causing him to jump. Ilox guiltily slapped the screen and it went black, the letters and video of the story fading away.

"I was just reading a story—one for school, and the teacher told Phlarx to read it, and I . . ." Ilox feared Morix. He knew the Lindauzu would never hurt him; Ilox was too valuable a dog. There were, however, other ways to punish overly inquisitive pups. Ilox had not forgotten seeing a house-dog shoved into an isolation cocoon. Inside, it was total darkness, and worse than that, there was no sound, no feeling. Nothing. It was as if your body had been taken away. Once Phlarx had let him get inside one. Ilox never wanted to again.

There were, Ilox well knew, Lindauzi who *did* physically harm their pets. He had awakened before Phlarx just that morning and had wandered down into the garden. To his surprise, as the garden was usually empty early in the morning, there were Lindauzi everywhere, talking in loud voices; someone Ilox couldn't see at first was yelling. When Ilox finally pushed his way through, he saw a skinny red-furred Lindauzu inside a restraining net. He was screaming and snarling. Blood glistened on his fangs and claws and spattered his fur.

"There's another one," the red Lindauzu screamed and lunged at Ilox, pushing against the net, trying to rip it apart. "Let me at him, let me at him—"

A laser bolt seared the air, and the red Lindauzu dropped to the ground, his words lost in high shrieks of pain, all the louder as everyone else was abruptly silent, their words cut in half by the sudden red beam.

"Stay there, pup! Don't move! You, another net, now. Call a medic, move." It was Morix. He stood across the garden, gesturing with his laser pistol to house menials. Ilox, more afraid of Morix than the crazed red Lindauzu, locked his feet in place. Morix stepped forward as the menials rushed about. In five minutes, another net was in place, and a medic had shot two or three tranks into the red Lindauzu. The crowd surged back at another gesture from Morix, and Ilox saw there was somebody lying on the ground beside the now sleeping red Lindauzu. An adult male dog lay in the wet grass, covered in blood. Claw marks shredded his back and both ears had been ripped off.

Fear. That was what Ilox felt from the Lindauzi around him: dark, restrained fear, so much of it he felt choked. He watched them watch Morix as he continued giving orders: take the body; now that he's sleeping, take the red Lindauzu, now, hurry. The Lindauzi were afraid—of the red one's sickness. That was it. Ilox could hear them muttering: *it could have been me, you . . .* Two middle-caste Lindauzi, teachers perhaps, whispered above Ilox about feral reversion, regression, atavistic fevers, and how this was the first reversion in a long, long time. I thought we were safe, finally safe, one said. The breeding reports, the first signs of true bonding, I thought we were safe. What was Morix going to do about it, firing off a laser was well and good, but that doesn't stop reversion, was the Project really working, would Morix tell the Crown Prince in Umium, how much time was *really* left? And what a waste of a good dog, a companion. . . .

"Ah, hush, this one is Lord Morix's," one of the Lindauza said, the older by the white fur of her muzzle. She looked down at Ilox, and then at a nudge from her friend, backed away. Both Lindauza lowered themselves to all fours, as Oldoch and other lower-caste Lindauzi had to the Viceroy countless times. Dogs never did; instead adult dogs lay flat on their stomachs.

"Go back inside, Ilox. Go find Phlarx. You shouldn't be here;

you shouldn't be seeing this." Morix had made his way across the garden after the red Lindauzu and the dead dog had been carried off in an aircar.

"Go, now," Morix repeated, and Ilox turned and ran back inside. When Morix spoke that sharply, Ilox moved as quickly as possible—as did Phlarx. When Phlarx forgot, on Ilox's third day in the house, to program Ilox's meals, Morix's words had been even sharper and blunter.

Ilox looked up at Morix from the deskscreen. With the screen's luminous glow gone and the windows opaque, there was almost no light in the room. There was only a thin red light around the door and the bed. Morix's eyes had glowed green, reflecting the light from the screen; now Ilox could see only a body-shape in the darkness.

"Phlarx should be reading these stories, not you. They are not your stories. They will only clutter your brain with things you do not understand. Go to bed, pup, now."

Ilox went, but he did not immediately fall asleep. He lay very still, listening first to Morix's footsteps as he left the room, the door opening and closing behind him, then to Phlarx breathing beside him. Phlarx stirred and rolled over, throwing out an arm across Ilox's chest. Ilox turned and looked at Phlarx. Phlarx's ears were pressed close to his skull.

"What are you dreaming about, Phlarx?" Ilox whispered. Whatever it was, it was making him angry or upset and it wasn't from any story. Why did Morix think stories would bother anybody, let alone him, Ilox wondered. Very little seemed to make Phlarx upset, Ilox thought as he carefully lifted Phlarx's arm off his chest. Things that made Ilox tremble barely seemed to faze Phlarx. When Ilox had rushed back from the garden and told Phlarx of the dead dog and the screaming red Lindauzu, Phlarx had shrugged it off.

"They'll lock him up for feral reversion, regressive behavior, and dog abuse," Phlarx had said carelessly. "They'll probably defang and declaw him, too."

Ilox had stared at him. *I'm shaking. I just saw somebody dead, and you're acting like I just told you the sky is blue.* Ilox couldn't figure it out. What *did* upset Phlarx, though, was his father. Phlarx visibly cowered when Morix came into the classroom to stand behind the two of them. Then Phlarx's ears drooped against his head and his crest went limp.

"Are you dreaming of your father, Phlarx? Is he yelling at you?

Is he speaking to you in those cold words? He just spoke to me that way," Ilox said and rolled over, his back to Phlarx.

It wasn't fair. Ilox liked to read; Phlarx didn't. What did it matter to Morix if Ilox read? They were just stories, stories about a place that was so far from where Ilox was he could not imagine the distance. Beyond the moon. Another star. And Phlarx had never been there and didn't seem to care about the place where his father had been born.

"Father says he dreams of Lindauzian, misses Lindauzian, but he was a baby, how could he remember? I like snow, but not all the time. Mother says it would take years to get there and those that stayed behind—if any of them are still alive—don't want us to come back, anyway."

It was Lady Ossit, Phlarx's mother, Ilox knew, who missed Lindauzian the most. She was older than Morix and truly remembered the homeworld. She spoke of it very little, or anything else, for that matter, but Ilox knew when she was remembering being a youngling on Lindauzian. Her eyes became unfocused and her lips curled down to conceal her fangs. Then a deep, low rumbling started in her throat and she started to sway, very slowly, back and forth.

"What's wrong with your mother?" Ilox had asked the first time he had seen her swaying and rumbling. They were walking back to Phlarx's room after school and had to pass by the old nursery, rooms no longer used as Phlarx and Tyuil were too old. Standing in the middle of the room, surrounded by climbing mazes, clawing posts, sand pits, and rock caves, was Ossit rocking back and forth.

"She's remembering Lindauzian, what it was like, what she misses. Don't bother her. I did once, she slapped me across the room and she didn't retract her claws."

Ilox wanted to ask her to tell him the stories in her head, what she was seeing, and where she was in her reverie. Then, maybe, he would be able to really see the places in the stories Morix didn't want him to read. There were vids with the text, but somehow it wasn't the same.

"Why can't I read as much as I want," Ilox whispered again. Because he was a pup, he thought, just a young pup, only seven-and-a-half years old, that was why. Ilox closed his eyes and started to repeat as much of the story as he could remember, his lips moving without sound, the way Lady Ossit's body moved.

* * *

"Phlarx."

It was Father. His low rough voice rumbled out of the com-screen. Phlarx instinctively drew back, one hand slightly raised to block his father's words before they bruised his face. *What have I done now?*

"Yes, Father."

"Where is Ilox?"

Phlarx glanced uneasily around their bedroom. He was alone. It was early morning and raining. The walls were still opaque. Only a faintly barely perceptible glow showed the sun was out.

Ilox had been amazed at the walls.

"The walls don't look clear from the outside. The same red stone all the time. But here, inside the house, the higher the sun is up, the more translucent they become. Why?"

Phlarx didn't know and he didn't care. Father didn't have time to answer. The teacher said it was something only an engineer needed to be concerned with, not the Viceregal heir. Ilox would have to be satisfied knowing the inner house walls were photosensitive. Now get back to work on Lindauzi grammar. Ilox kept trying to ask more questions, despite the teacher's irritation.

"Ilox. Your pup. Where is he?"

"Uh, he's not here," Phlarx said, desperately listening for a clue in Father's voice as to what he had done. *Everything I do is wrong.* "He sometimes gets ahead of me. He likes to do that, look around." Where was Ilox? Had Ilox done something wrong? The first time Phlarx had awakened to find Ilox gone, he had been sure the pup had had enough and run away. Phlarx had him housepaged and searched for by menials. They had found him riding up and down the outer lift.

Where'd you think I'd gone?

I thought you left me.

"Phlarx, I know he is not there. He is here, with me. I found him in the school room. Come here." The comscreen went blank.

The room was silent, except for Phlarx's ragged breathing. He was afraid. Father was angry with him. He looked back at the comscreen, into his green reflection. His ears were flat, his crest limp.

Phlarx walked slowly out of the room, his toeclaws catching in the carpet. He stopped to sharpen his fingerclaws in the hallway, and then walked even more slowly, his fingerclaws trailing along the wall the way Ilox did. Ilox loved to leave a glowing pink trail in the red.

Phlarx wished he could walk even more slowly.

Father stood in the middle of the school room, his hands

behind his back. Ilox sat in a chair beside him, examining the palm of his left hand. The wallscreens were on. Phlarx recognized the words of a homeworld story. The teacher had told him to have it read by today. Until seeing it on the school wallscreen, he had completely forgotten about it. A holographic map of Earth's solar system graced the center of the room. Another wallscreen: equations. Also to be done by today.

"Yes, Father."

"Ilox was here, since before daybreak. Doing your work. Lindauzi work done by a pup."

Father spoke in hard little words: Phlarx was lazy, Phlarx was the Viceregal heir; he had obligations and duties; Phlarx had let Father down. He would be the reason the Project failed, and did he have any idea what that meant to every Lindauzi on Earth—

"I didn't tell him to come here—"

"He's right, Lord Morix. I came here all by myself—"

"You. Pup. Go to your room."

Ilox ran out.

Father's fangs dripped saliva. He growled, low and deep, from his chest. His erect crest and ears were bristling. When he moved his hands, his claws cut the air.

"No son of mine will have his work done by anyone, especially a dog. You are a Lindauzu. My heir. You let your work be done by somebody else."

"But I didn't tell him to."

Phlarx jumped back, throwing up his hands. He felt just the tip of Father's claws.

"Make no more excuses. You will do all this work. All of it. No son of mine will be lazy and stupid. Reversion isn't always becoming violent. No morningmeal, no noonmeal—no meals at all until you are finished. I will tell your teacher to check your work and have you do it again and again until it is correct."

Phlarx stayed in the school room until long after the noonmeal. When he had completed the last of the equations for the third time, he left, not waiting for the teacher to tell him it was finally correct. Phlarx didn't care. Even though his stomach hurt from being empty, he wouldn't go to the family meal room—not if he would have to sit there and look at Father's face.

I hate him.

At the door of their bedroom, he slowly pressed the palmsign. Was the door always this slow? When he was inside and it had closed behind him, Phlarx finally felt safe.

He stood in front of the door, breathing hard.

"It's too sunny in here," Phlarx said, and slapped the darker square in a multicolored stripe by the door. Its colors went from white through shades of grey to night-black.

The walls dimmed. The edges of everything in the room became less distinct, more rounded. Colors shifted, became more muted.

"Phlarx?"

Ilox sat cross-legged in the middle of the bed.

"Yes."

"I've been waiting for you. I've got some food; Tyuil snuck it out for you. Was it really horrible?"

"Yes, it was." Phlarx covered his face. "I hate him. I really hate him."

"Oh, Phlarx."

Phlarx sat down beside Ilox, his words coming in a rapid monotone: "I hate him, he never listens to me, he's never really touched me. He doesn't care what I think, what I feel. I'm just the Viceregal heir, the only son of Lord Morix. I hate him."

Phlarx drew back his head and howled.

"It's all right. I'm here. We're here. It's all right."

Phlarx lay his head in Ilox's lap. He let Ilox scratch behind his ears, the top of his head, under his chin. Phlarx closed his eyes and let one hand rest on Ilox's knee.

It wasn't long after, when Ilox was exactly eight, that he received the Blessing of the Iani.

"The Iani, they are in the old stories with the Lindauzi, the stories from Lindauzian. Another people, tall, with long fingers—fingers like mine—and short noses, like mine, right? But they are all gone, aren't they? What's this Blessing for?" Ilox asked Phlarx the morning they were to go to the Madaanic Temple. They were finishing up morningmeal together in Phlarx's room, having been told by Morix not to eat in the family meal room. The Lady Ossit was not well; she wanted to rest before going to the temple.

"The Iani are all gone. They died out before Father and Mother were born, back on Lindauzian. I don't know about this blessing. There aren't any in the stories about the Iani and the Lindauzi we read for school. It's something Father says is very important to the Project and don't ask me about that either. Father says he will explain it when I am older and not to ask him now. Mother just shakes her head. But we have to go, and you have to wear this tunic," Phlarx said, apologetic. He didn't like going to the temple. The priest always talked too long about things Phlarx didn't understand. It was hard to stay awake, and if he did fall asleep, his father would be more than a little angry.

"You have to go. I have to go. Are you ready?" Phlarx asked. He put their morning dishes on a floating cart and shoved it out the door. A house menial would come by eventually and take it away.

"I'm ready," Ilox said. "Where's the temple?"

"At the eastern edge of the plantation. We have to fly there. Father said he was leaving right at the eighth hour," Phlarx said, glancing at the time line above the door.

There was no one in the temple except for the Vaarchaels and the priest. Morix and Ossit stood to one side of the dais. Tyuil and her pet companion, Nivere, stood opposite. The priest stood alone in the center of the dais. He was completely white, as were all members of that caste. His eyes were pink. The priest walked slowly, his body was stiff, to the edge of the dais, to face Phlarx and Ilox. Ilox realized, as he watched the white Lindauzu walk, that he was old.

"Phlarx, Ilox," the priest said in a gravelly voice. He waited until they had walked up from where they had been sitting in the first row of chairs facing the dais. The chairs radiated out in concentric circles, with the dais at the center. When they were standing on the first step up to the dais, the priest raised his arms and the light changed. Glowglobes, which had been clumped around the walls in the circular room, rose up to a point half-way between the priest's head and the apex of the domed roof, where curved beams came together to make a many-pointed star. Between the beams the roof was golden, as if filled with light, movable light that dimmed and brightened.

At a gesture from the priest, Phlarx and Ilox stepped up onto the dais and followed him until they were in the middle. The priest spoke again, this time in a language Ilox had never heard. As if in answer to his words, a black shadow formed behind the priest. It wasn't the priest's shadow, as it was skinnier, with long splayed fingers and toes. The shadow, Ilox realized, was about as tall as the alpha hound who had imprinted him a year ago.

"We ask for the bond, heart to heart, mind to mind, soul to soul. We ask that this pair may be the ones to restore what was lost, to bring us the hope we have been so long without. . . ." the priest chanted, and then changed to the strange language again. He laid his hands on Phlarx's and Ilox's heads and spoke again, asking for the blessing on this pair. Each movement he made was repeated by the shadow, even to touching their heads.

When the shadow touched Ilox, at first he felt nothing, but then, lightly, lightly, the tips of the long fingers. He felt a sudden chill and a deep sorrow. He shuddered, and Phlarx shuddered at the same time. Then the priest threw back his head and howled. As if they were a chorus, Morix and Ossit both howled.

"May this pair be the ones who will bring the Project to final, glorious fruition. May our long exile of the soul and body be over. May this pair be the ones," the priest repeated, and raised his hands. The shadow disappeared and the glowglobes moved back to their original places. The Blessing was done.

Ilox saw Sandron, Morix's companion pet and Ilox's sire, up close only twice. The first was a few weeks after he had been brought into the house. Phlarx had to go to Umium with his mother and no amount of pleading and begging from either one to let Ilox come had moved the implacable Ossit.

"I am getting new clothes, new boots, for you, Phlarx. And I want to go to Umium; I am tired of being here on Kinsella. I am going for myself as much as for you. I do not want to have to look after Ilox and you both. If Ilox needs something new, you must get it for him here," Ossit said, standing in the doorway of their bedroom, her arms closed across her chest. Ilox was sure she didn't like him. When Phlarx had first taken Ilox to her, she had barely glanced up at him from her deskscreen. She nodded, retracted her fangs momentarily, and then shooed them off.

"Your dog stays here, Phlarx. Your father and Sandron can look after him. He is Sandron's pup, after all. Let's go." Ossit had no companion pet of her own. Ilox wondered, as he watched them through the wall, what it would be like to be hers. He couldn't imagine Ossit running her claws through his hair or scratching him behind his ears the way Phlarx did.

For that matter, Ilox couldn't imagine Ossit scratching Phlarx behind the ears.

Ilox didn't stay very long by himself in the bedroom. It felt empty, and he thought if he spoke out loud, his words would sound hollow and small. Ilox knew where Morix was: in the huge Viceregal office on the top floor of the house. Sandron would be there. Phlarx had told him Sandron was always there. He even slept there, in a small room inside the office. Sometimes Morix slept there as well.

"He doesn't say much to me, Lox," Phlarx had said. "It's Father he always talks to. He watches everything Father does and he follows him with his eyes around the room. You do look a little like him, just a little."

Ilox stopped to look in the mirror just before he left the room. Sandron. His sire. His father. His father who looked a little like him. Phlarx and Morix looked alike—same blond fur, tufted ears, same short muzzle. Phlarx even walked like Morix, his arms swinging by his side. Would Sandron's hair be the same yellow-white as Ilox's? Would their eyes be the same blue? Would Sandron like Ilox? The nurse-dams never spoke much about sires. Ilox ran his fingers through his hair and smoothed his clothes and walked out into the hall.

There was a lift that would take him straight to the Viceroy's office; it was at the far end of the hall from their room. Ilox loved to ride it because it was all glass and exposed to the outside of the house. The plantation spread out from the house in ripples of deep green and brown. The other plantation buildings—the hounds' barracks, the flyer and airship hangers, the aircar garages, the kennels—all seemed to be growing out of the earth along with the trees. Fields, now fallow for the coming winter, were just behind the barracks. Phlarx had told Ilox mostly food for dogs grew in the fields they could see from the lift. Lindauzi ate mostly meat: cattle, sheep, and pigs raised in the interior of the continent. The few fruits and vegetables Lindauzi did eat were grown on the other side of the house, in long, low buildings, with few windows. Ilox had been inside one once; it was cold and grey and the plants were cold and grey.

Just before the lift reached the top of the house, Ilox could see even wider fields beyond those growing dog food. These far fields were brown now. The thick-leafed tobacco, loved as a delicacy by the Lindauzi, had long since been harvested.

This time, instead of taking the lift, Ilox decided to walk the spiraling walkways which linked the different levels of the house. He walked as close to the glass walls as he could. The Lindauzi he met nodded and absently patted Ilox on the head. All the dogs he met were adults. Most were intensely focused on whatever job they were doing: herding one of the floating food trays or laundry carts, pushing a carpet cleaner sucking at the dark tufts of Lindauzi fur which always seemed to be everywhere. One female stood in front of a panel of the glass wall. She was scrubbing away claw marks left by Lindauzi babies. Only a few smiled and nodded at him. No dog spoke or patted him on the head.

It was Sandron who greeted Ilox at the office door. Ilox timidly placed his hand on the palmsign and stepped back to wait as the door changed from white to yellow. It opened with a whoosh, and Ilox was staring up at an adult male dog who was staring down at him.

Sandron was tall, and his hair was as fair and as thick as Ilox's. Sandron's eyes were the same blue. To Ilox's surprise, Sandron's body was heavy and thick. Ilox looked down at his own stringy body; how did anybody get so fat?

"Yes? Are you lost, pup? Why are you here? How does the house know you for the door to present the welcoming color?" Sandron demanded.

"Uh, uh—the Lady Ossit sent me here. I'm Ilox. . . ."

"Ilox?"

"Let him in, Sandron," Morix called from inside. "It's Phlarx's pup. Ossit has taken the boy to Umium and I promised him I would look after his pup. He's one of yours, by the way, Sandron. Can't you tell? Look at that hair, those eyes. I saved this one for Phlarx for his seventh."

Sandron stepped back then, and let Ilox come inside. The carpet was a deeper red than anywhere else in the house and so thick Ilox could feel himself sinking each time he took a step. There were low tables, each one with a glowglobe floating above it, making islands of bright light. One ball drifted toward Ilox and positioned itself above and behind him, casting a yellow circle around him. Ilox wished he could keep one of the round creatures a touch away at night. With just the tip of his finger, he knew a glowglobe would become bright and warm. Ilox loved holding them, rubbing them on his face.

Morix's office was dark, even though it was morning. Morix sat behind a huge wide desk and was surrounded by banks of screens displaying charts and maps and figures.

"Take him over there, Sandron," Morix said as he turned back to a wallscreen showing a map. Ilox wanted to look and ask where the place was that the map showed; instead he let Sandron lead him into a smaller room.

"Here's a desk you can use to practice reading and writing. There, I turned its screens on. You've already started school with Phlarx, haven't you?" Sandron asked, speaking quickly, and looking back over his shoulder toward Morix.

"Yes."

"There are some toys over here. A food dispenser. Relieve yourself over there. And the floor will make a bed when you lie down. There is no reason for you to bother Lord Morix or me, pup. I think one glowglobe will give enough light." And Sandron left.

Ilox stared after him. Evidently being someone's sire meant very little, if anything at all. A sire wasn't the same as a father, then. Even though Phlarx was scared of his father and Morix was very tough on him, Ilox had more than once seen Morix give his son a special look. Sandron had barely glanced at Ilox.

He watched as Sandron walked back into the office to stand behind Morix. Morix turned and spoke quietly to the adult dog, pointing to the screen in front of them. Sandron bent down to look, and Morix absently scratched Sandron's head and kept talking. Ilox wished the Lady Ossit had let him come along. He wished Phlarx were here with him. Ilox looked away from Sandron and Morix and sat down before the desk and told it he was ready. A picture appeared in the screen directly in front of him, and as Ilox bent down to look, the glowglobe lowered itself with him. He could just hear its almost inaudible humming.

The second time Ilox saw Sandron close up was when he was nine. It was a scream that called Ilox back to the top of the house. It shook both Phlarx and Ilox out of a deep sleep. The scream was filled with so much profound pain that Ilox cried out himself. Phlarx knew immediately who it was.

"Father. Something has happened to Father." Phlarx jumped out of the bed and ran down the hall. Ilox ran after him. The screams that followed beat against them as they ran.

Morix was in his office. Ossit was already there. She was cradling Morix in her arms, stroking his fur and crooning softly. Four other Lindauzi stood around uncertainly and two dogs, house menials, a male and a female, were at the door. Ilox and Phlarx pushed past them to stand just inside. Tyuil and Nivere were already there.

"I told you, Morix. I told you and told you: it will never, never work. These creatures aren't the Iani. The Crown Prince is wrong. No, no, don't tell me how close the Project is, or about Phlarx's pup. These creatures aren't the Iani. Yes, I know they are both large primates—an accident of evolution, a cosmic joke at our expense. We should have stayed on Lindauzian and accepted reversion. This is our punishment, Morix. Do you hear me? Do you hear me? . . ."

Lady Ossit stopped her relentless stream of words, words it

seemed she had been saving forever, when she saw Phlarx and Ilox in the room.

"Get them out of here," Ossit growled, low and deep in her throat. "Get them out of here *now*."

Tyuil took them away, but not before Ilox heard what Morix was saying: "He's *dead*, Ossit. Sandron's *dead*. He's gone. I came up here and I found him in his bed, cold and still. He wasn't so old, not for a dog. I'll never have another dog. Lord Madaan, Lady Aurelian, protect him. . . ."

Ossit's voice began again: "Do you hear me? We should have stayed on Lindauzian and accepted reversion. . . ."

For days afterward, it was as if the house had been caught inside a cold black fog. Everyone, Lindauzi and dog, walked about with eyes cast down and cheerless faces. No one saw Morix for a long time. Late at night, Ilox would awaken and when he stepped out in the hall, he heard Morix wailing, a wordless noise rising and falling in the darkness.

It was the Lindauzi mourning song, a wordless prayer to Lord Madaan, who, with Lady Aurelian, had called the first Iani out of the trees and the first Lindauzi out of the caves, and had placed hand in paw, paw in hand, and bound them, heart to heart, mind to mind, soul to soul. Then Madaan taught the Lindauzi to walk erect and Aurelian taught the Iani to walk on the ground and forsake the trees.

Ilox had heard this story and the mourning song in the Temple. He wanted to ask the priest who taught dogs to walk erect, and why weren't dogs in *The Book of The Forest?* He wanted to ask what was a metaphor and a symbol and why did Morix and Ossit speak of the temple stories that way, as truth revealed in fiction. He wanted to ask if what he had heard Oldoch say was true: had the Iani bred the Lindauzi the way dogs were bred, but Phlarx always made them sit in the back and leave right after the last blessing. And asking Morix and Ossit in or out of the temple was out of the question.

The priest came to the Vaarchaels on the fifth night after Sandron's death. Ilox saw him, a white flash against the pink walls as he rode up the walls to Morix and Ossit's chambers. There was no wailing the fifth night.

A month after Sandron's death, Ilox saw the Lady Ossit kill herself. No screams awakened him; rather he just turned over and was awake. Had someone called his name? Phlarx? No, Phlarx was fast asleep, flat on his back, his muzzle in the air. Ilox got up carefully and stepped out into the hall. There was no one there. A dream, a bad dream, he told himself, and just as he turned to go back to bed, he saw her, a sudden shadow, running down the hall. The Lady Ossit? Was he still dreaming? Had she been standing at their door? Ilox hesitated, looked back at Phlarx, and then ran after her, afraid to call out her name, but knowing she had called his name and she had been standing at their door. She had called his name, repeating it over and over and over.

Ilox caught up with Ossit on the walkway between the third and fourth levels of the house. He stopped on the third floor landing and looked up to see her halfway up the walkway. She had opened one of the glass panels; Ilox could feel the rush of the night air, a quick cool stream on his face and bare arms and legs. Did she see him? He didn't know. He didn't call her name or ask why she had called him. Not the Lady Ossit.

"So, it's true, our promised one is empathic enough." The Lady Ossit turned from the open panel. Ilox could just see her yellow eyes like dim lights in the dark. "But I can't hold on any longer; I am too tired. Tell them that, Ilox. I am too tired and I feel it, just there at the edges, a darkness in which I won't be able to think, to speak, to know my name. Tell them, Ilox."

Then she climbed up and stood on the edge of the open panel and jumped. Ilox heard her body strike the ground three-and-a-half levels below.

Phlarx and Tyuil did not weep for their mother. The Lord Morix did not keen the mourning song. Her ashes were scattered over the tobacco fields on the second day after her death. For a long time afterward, Ilox would dream of her falling and the open panel and the hard sound of her body as it hit the ground.

It was in the winter of his eleventh year that Ilox saw his first wolf. The family had left the plantation for its annual ocean vacation, flying east for an hour until they were over water. Ilox never tired of looking at the sea: vast and at first green, then blue, then grey, its surface rising and falling like the beating of his own heart.

Several Lindauzi families from Kinsella and neighboring plantations had built villas on a small offshore island: graceful, low white houses that seemed to grow out of the earth. All were built close together in the center of the island, in the heart of a thick maritime forest. Carefully kept paths led to the beach. Ilox loved running down the path to the sand and out into the surf, shouting at the sudden cold shock of the water. Once they had come when it was snowing—delicate flakes falling from a heavy grey sky.

Phlarx let Ilox run in the sand and water for hours, watching him from a balcony at the far end of their villa.

"Run, pup," Morix had said the first time they had taken him to the island. "I know the plantation house is sometimes not big enough for you. Let him run, Phlarx, until he is tired."

Ilox had taken off down the steps without looking back, leaving Phlarx standing there with his father and sister. It had been a cold day with a rough wind, but he hadn't cared. Ilox had run and run and run.

When the airship landed on this trip, and the menials had carried everything into the villa, Phlarx let Ilox go alone down to the beach.

"I'll be there in a while. We can play this new game Father ordered from Umium . . . you go run first."

Ilox took off. When he got to the beach, he ran straight across the sand into the water, falling and laughing as an icy wave slapped him in the face. He stood up, shaking the water from his hair, and looked around. He gave no thought to wearing cold wet clothes. Lindauzi fabric was always water-repellent and self-heating, adjusting to the body and air temperature.

"I have the entire beach to myself. There's nobody here anywhere. Just me: Ilox." A damp wind was moving through the marrow grass and the sea oats. He shivered and shook himself again and started walking on the hard wet sand. His feet crunched on the litter of broken sea shells, and he shoved his hands into his pockets and pulled his cloak closer.

Ilox picked up and discarded sea shells as he walked. All of them seemed to be broken and fragmented—glistening bits of dark blues, oranges, and creamy whites. He wanted to find what he called a horn-shell. Phlarx had found one the last time they were at the beach, and Ilox loved the low honk it made.

After walking and stooping and tossing shells into the water, Ilox found himself out of sight of the path back to the villa. He turned back then and ran back to the dunes and scrambled up to the top and stood and looked about. Then he set off, walking on a winding path which led up and down and in and out of the stunted trees of the island forest, to the mainland side of the island. The path came out at a small cove. The dark water did not rise and fall as it did on the seaward side; its ripples were only weak echoes of the waves slapping the sand.

Was that a boat out there on the water? Ilox wasn't completely sure, since he had never seen any Lindauzi use a boat, but he and Phlarx had floating toys they played with in the pool, and those were called boats. Who was in the boat? Ilox walked down to where the sand met the water to get as close as he could.

There were two in the boat. They weren't Lindauzi. They were dogs.

Two dogs. A redhead and a blackheaded one. Two adult male-dogs. Dressed in fur. Were they pretending to be Lindauzi? Whose villa had they come from? To whom did they belong? Ilox watched as the long wooden boat came closer to the beach with each stroke of the long sticks the two dogs were pushing into the water. The red dog stood up to throw out what looked like a great spider web into the water. It was the black dog who spotted Ilox and grabbed the webthrower's arm, pointing and talking. The web was quickly pulled in, and they started rowing the boat toward the sand. Ilox watched, as after several strong strokes, the web-thrower, and then the black dog, jumped from the boat and started pulling it until the hull scraped on the ground.

Ilox took another step closer. Part of him wanted to turn and run as fast as he could the other way: back down the path, up and down the dunes, pound across the sand, up the steps, the balcony, and then be safe with Phlarx. Another part took another step toward the two dogs dragging the boat farther up out of the water.

When Ilox took the next step closer, one of the dogs looked up at him. Ilox froze as the black dog poked the red dog, who let go of the boat and stood, his hands on his hips, facing Ilox. They were shorter and skinnier than the house-dogs. Their faces were covered with rough hair. How could any family let their dogs look like this? Or be here, alone, with this boat?

The red dog held up both hands, smiling. He gestured toward the black dog, who repeated the red dog's open hands gesture and smile. Ilox took another step and waited. Both dogs took another step closer. Now they were only separated by a space as wide as Ilox and Phlarx's bedroom back on the plantation.

The red dog's body was narrow and long, and his eyes were green. When he smiled, he showed missing and broken teeth. The black dog was broader and one eye was missing and a scar stretched across one cheek. His skin was darker, a brown color, and his hair was a thick mass of tiny curls. Both were dressed in clothes made of coarse black fur. Around each dog's neck, where Ilox wore his collar, were necklaces, made of long yellow teeth that Ilox was sure came from no dog or Lindauzi mouth. Ilox stopped moving closer when the space between them was as wide as their boat was long. They stopped when he did, and waited.

"Who are you? Where are your Lindauzi?" Ilox finally asked after a long silence. The two dogs looked at each other, and then the red one spoke and pointed to their boat. Ilox only understood one word: Lindauzi. He barely understood that; the dog's mouth seemed barely able to get around the word.

"Lindauzi? They are back there," Ilox said and pointed the way he had come. "Are you lost? Have you lost your Lindauzi?"

The dogs shook their heads, still talking and pointing to their boat. The red dog said "Lindauzi" again and gestured with his hands as if he were pushing the word away. Then he pointed to Ilox and to himself, the black dog, the boat, and then the water. He pointed at the web and then pressed his hands together to make a waving motion, then he pretended to eat something. Then he spoke again, repeating all his gestures.

They want me to go in the boat. To get something—food? Where would we go? How would we get food? I've never been in a boat. And their words—why do they sound like noise?

Both dogs stepped closer to Ilox. He stepped back, wishing he hadn't wandered off by himself. They pointed yet again to him, themselves, the boat, and the water.

"No, I can't go with you. Phlarx is back there, and . . . I can't. Leave me alone!"

Ilox bolted. He tore across the sand. Down the path. Up the dune until he was at the crest. Then he looked back, panting. The dogs were walking back toward their boat, shaking their heads. The black dog looked back once. Ilox watched as they dragged their boat back into the water.

"Did they stop their boat just for me? Just to ask me to go for a ride?" he asked Morix that night.

"You met wolves, Ilox. Wild dogs. They kill dogs like you. Running away was the right thing to do; I knew you were smart. Good pup."

That was all he said. Wolves. Dogs who were wild and bad.

Much later that night, Ilox awoke suddenly, as if his name had been called over and over again. The voices—it had been the two wild dogs, the wolves, but how could they be in here, in their bedroom? How did they know his name—he hadn't told them. There was no one in the room except for him and Phlarx. Ilox heard nothing except for the steady sound of Phlarx's breathing.

"But they were right here. They were right there, at the door."
Ilox got out of bed and first looked in each corner of the room,
touching the walls lightly to briefly call up the inner lights, soft
and dim and pink, like small flowers pushing back the dark and
then out, and back into shadow.

No one was hiding in any of the corners. No one was outside
the door. And there was no one in the hall or on the balcony. Ilox
kept looking. Down the lift to the great room, then through the
library. Then outside, shivering in the raw winter cold.

Ilox kept looking until he was in front of the hounds' quarters,
wondering why he had come here, of all places, in the middle of
the night. Except for the alpha who had imprinted him four years
ago, Ilox had very little to do with any hound. Their flyers came
and went, they stood guard outside the plantation force fields, and
if any hound even recognized Ilox's existence, it was only as the
companion pet of the master's son, a young dog to be watched out
for.

Ilox saw the flyers returning before he heard them. It was a
clear night, and the half-moon made sharp shadows, as if they
were cut out of black paper. First one flyer, then the next flew
across the moon and over the silver-gilded villa and then down,
across from Ilox at the far end of the hounds' quarters.

Ilox was alone in the middle of the green lawn, half in shadow,
half in moonlight. Short twisted trees, transplanted from the island
forest, grew here and there in the lawn. He didn't know if the two
hounds even saw him standing there. Ilox didn't want them to see
him, so he stepped deeper into the shadow and watched.

The two tall hounds climbed out of their flyers, their bodies
silhouetted, the moonlit metal of the laser pistols on their hips
shining as they moved. One hound reached back into the flyer and
pulled out two heavy objects, one in each hand. He handed one to
the other, and as he turned Ilox saw what the hound had pulled out
of the flyer.

Two heads. The head of the red dog and the head of the black
dog. Their necks had been cauterized with the lasers; no blood
dripped into the lush green grass.

Their eyes were open.

Interchapter 2

Millennium Minus One Year

Transmission received by Lindauzi observation satellite, local time, 31 December 1999. Transmission interruptions are local in nature, as the spread of the second stage viruses has disrupted such routine operations as electricity, telecommunications, food deliveries. . . .

Good evening. This is National Public Radio in Washington and All Things Considered, Friday, December 31, 1999; I'm Susan Stamberg, sitting in for Noah Adams, who is ill. Happy New Year, almost, sort of. I had thought to talk about how this is the Millennium minus one year—that it is almost *the beginning of the 21st Century, and how all the parties that are being planned for this evening will just have to be repeated next year when it really will be the Millennium and so what: why* not *do it twice? I had thought to talk about the kinds of parties and where and who and with what. How many fireworks, how much champagne. I was going to go on about the Y2K computer scare and how at least the scare got us to fix all those lines of code to read 2000 and not 1900 and nothing will happen—probably. And I even spent time collecting all this information and I really do have it all here.*

Really. And so what.

Something has *happened, something that puts Y2K worries and fears to shame.*

This New Year's Eve, one humanity has been waiting on for two thousand years, isn't turning out as we hoped. Most of the big Millennial parties have been canceled. There won't be a huge mob in Times Square this year. Midnight mass last week at St. Peter's was televised and devout Catholics were urged to stay home. There won't be a party on the Mall in Washington this year. There are rumors that John Paul II is ill. Dick Clark won't be hosting his Rockin' New Year's Eve anymore; he's dead.

Everybody everywhere is being told to stay home and watch the fireworks on television. Being in a huge crowd just isn't safe New Year's Eve 1999.

And Noah doesn't have a cold or the flu or a 24-hour virus. Noah hasn't sprained his ankle or broken any bones. Noah doesn't have a migraine or even a hangover. Noah is dying. He isn't in a hospital; he's at home. All the hospitals in Washington are overflowing, and Noah is too sick, the doctors tell me. Being hospitalized won't do him any good.

It's the plague, the virus, the return of the Black Death, The Disease, capital T, capital D, super-AIDS, apocalyptic flu.

I want to tell you Happy New Year and mean it, and I can't. I'm scared. I have never been more scared in my life and . . .

Chapter III

Caleb, 15-17 October 2155

WHEN CALEB WOKE UP, HE COULD TELL IT WAS night. The air had turned cool and the shadows had filled up the Strong basement, turning the tangled iron frames, rods, poles, pipes, and chairs into grey and black shapes. He lay still for a long moment, his head thick and heavy with sleep, wishing he could just stay right where he was, not get up, not do anything but sleep and sleep. When Caleb finally rolled over and sat up, he was surprised to find himself stiff and sore. Why did he smell smoke? He ran his fingers through his tangled hair and pulled out bits of twigs, leaves, and cobwebs. He smelled his hands: the smoke was in his hair.

What am I doing here? I should have been home a long time ago. Aunt Sara is going to kill me.

I am so hungry.

Caleb sighed. He'd better go home, no matter how late it was. The tunnel would be the quickest way. Caleb tried to see into the tunnel, but it was even darker than the basement. At least in the basement he could see shapes. In the tunnel he wouldn't be able to see his hands or his feet or what he was stepping on. He would only be able to go by the touch of his fingers on the wall. But

Mama had made him memorize the tunnels—he *could* get back by just touching the wall.

Take care of Davy, Caleb. Take care of your brother.

Davy should be asleep now, Caleb thought, curled up in the skins and furs in their little space. Davy should be down in Jackson asleep. By himself.

Caleb stood and set off into the tunnel. He had to get home right away. Something was wrong and he knew he should know what it was, but he couldn't make himself remember. It was as if he were hiding something from himself in another room and had locked the door to that room. And he had always been able to remember everything, always. What was wrong with him tonight that he couldn't remember?

It took Caleb only a few minutes to get through the short tunnel, from where he had slept in the basement of one wing of Strong, to the basement in the other wing. The entrance into the long tunnel that would lead him back to Jackson somehow looked even darker, so dark it was as if the blackness would swallow Caleb up. And even though he still couldn't find the key to the locked room, he knew entering the long tunnel would make him remember and Caleb wasn't sure he wanted to.

Take care of Davy, Caleb. Take care of your brother.

It wasn't long after entering the long tunnel that Caleb found himself touching book spines and stepping from one broken asphalt chunk to another. It was when Caleb smelled smoke that he remembered. Smoke smell filled the tunnel, heavy, thick, close. And with the wood and paper smoke smell, riding on its back, were others: burnt hair, charred meat. When he came to the entrance of the main Jackson tunnel, which led directly inside, the smell was replaced by smoke itself, dense, smothering smoke. Caleb had to step back, coughing, covering his mouth. Then he took a deep breath and went on.

Caleb walked slowly, coughing, his eyes burning. Even though he had slept, he felt heavy and tired and sore and stiff. He was so hungry his stomach hurt. Each step felt weighted. Caleb had to make a conscious effort to place one foot in front of the other, keep one hand on the book spines, the wooden and metal shelves. When he was halfway there, he knew he should have heard voices, soft and low, muffled by stone and metal. And he knew he should be able to see the wavery flicker of coronas, like smoke made of light, yellows, whites, blues, and the babies, like great fireflies. Most of the grownups should have been outside by the fire, but a few stayed inside each night. The very old and a few other men and women stayed to watch over the ones too little to sit up and listen to the stories and songs.

An old woman should be singing. Caleb remembered how it had been just—last night—he had stood in the back, behind all the others, hidden in the darkness. Not even a flicker of firelight brushed his face. But tonight, he heard no voices, soft, low, loud, or noisy. He knew there would be no old woman singing, no small crowd to hide behind. The tunnel was silent and for the first time he could remember, its darkness pressed against him. It was almost a relief to see just ahead, where the tunnel opened into the Jackson warrens, the pale shadow of a fire, a fire that was burning where no fire should be.

Caleb stood still, each foot on a separate asphalt chunk, the fingers of his right hand touching a fat, thick book wedged into a shelf of other fat, thick books. He tried to read the letters on the book's spine, but there wasn't enough light. He was scared and didn't want to go any farther. *I'm always scared, I am so tired of being scared. Papa is never scared.* Caleb hated being scared. He hated jumping at shadows and unexpected noises. Once he had found himself standing naked and alone at the edge of a creek bank, a rope swaying back and forth from an overhanging tree branch. He was about twenty feet above the water; to Caleb it looked to be about two thousand feet above. All the other boys were swimming below and laughing and calling him a halver fraidy cat. *C'mon, fraidy cat. Scared little halver. Jump, jump. Are you too scared, little halver?*

Caleb had turned and run then, feeling sick to his stomach and hating himself for running, for being scared. Now his stomach still hurt and he was still scared, but he had nowhere to run. Caleb stepped out of the tunnel and into Jackson. Here and there about the room, dying fires sputtered with only a few flames and wisps of smoke. Smoke filled the room, a trapped grey fog. Books were everywhere: burnt, shredded, torn, charred, ashes, pages like snow. And directly in front of Caleb was a body. Caleb looked down to see a woman lying on her back, her torn tunic exposing her breasts. Her head was gone. It had been cleanly cut from her neck, severed with one sure stroke by something very sharp and hot. Caleb held his stomach, trying not to throw up at the smell of burnt flesh. She lay in a great pool of dried blood, her hands open, her arms outstretched, as it she were trying to grab something out of her reach.

He stepped over her, and through the mess of books, his feet tracking blood on the white pages. Another body, another headless woman, blocked the doorway into what was a main corridor, lined with living spaces. Behind her were still more headless bodies, piled in crumpled heaps, arms and legs gesturing at odd angles, blood everywhere. The floor seemed to have been painted in blood. Even the walls looked as if they were bleeding. Caleb heard nothing: no crying, no moans, no calls for help.

He stooped to look carefully at the woman blocking his way into the body-filled corridor. What was her name? He should know who she was. A deertooth necklace lay in blood where her head had been; Aunt Sara wore Mama's poptop necklace. This woman wore bracelets made out of black wires and rings of copper wire. *I've seen those bracelets. Every morning.* It was Martha. She and her husband, Jacob, lived in the space directly across from Caleb and Davy. He stood up and looked around; it was going to take a long time to find Davy and Aunt Sara.

"I have to do this," Caleb whispered; somehow speaking out loud seemed the wrong thing to do. "I have to find them." He didn't want to. He wanted to sit down in the blood and wail. He wanted to throw up the little he had in his stomach. He wanted to turn and run and run and run, and never have to smell burnt flesh again.

Take care of Davy, Caleb.

For the first time in his life, Caleb wanted to tell Papa to shut up.

A baby's headless body lay a few feet ahead of Martha's. Naked and on its stomach. Caleb laid one hand briefly on the baby's back: soft skin, like Davy's had been, but cold. He stepped over fallen metal shelves, deerskins, bearskins, flattened styrofoam bowls, and stray arrows and spears. Littering the floor everywhere, and crunching beneath Caleb's feet were name-stones. Just ahead was the main room, where the iron cauldron had bubbled and cooked over its fire, the changing aroma of its stew making the air rich and pungent. The cauldron had been overturned. Stew and blood mixed together on the floor, sticking to Caleb's feet as he crossed the room, stepping over more headless people: one man, two, three women, a boy, two girls, a third girl. . . .

It was the combined smell that did it: Caleb threw up the little he had in his stomach, in dry heaves that seemed to turn his stomach inside out. He pressed himself against the nearest wall, gasping, sweating, telling himself he had no time for this, he had to find Davy. *OK, enough, no more, let's go, what was Davy wearing? He was asleep, he doesn't wear any clothes, but he had time to get up. His favorite calfskin tunic?* That seemed to stop the heaves. Focus, Caleb thought, keep moving. His and Davy's sleeping quarters were off the next corridor. Just get past these next bodies and keep moving.

He had to step on a man and a woman to leave the main room. It wasn't like stepping on mud or thick grass or piles of animal skins. Yet it was something like all of them: the soft, yielding flesh, backbones, and elbows like pieces of wood.

Now, just a bit more: down the corridor, left, and left again. More bodies and more bodies. If he could just see somebody's face, anybody's face: eyes, mouths, tongues, ears, hair. Papa said they keep the heads in glass cases. *Davy's head, Aunt Sara's, his cousins, staring sightless from a shelf. . . .*

Maybe he should start counting again.

A woman's head lay on the floor where Caleb had to make his first left turn. It must have been dropped when the hounds left. Her name was Ruth. Ruth's eyes were still open, a startled brown. A knife with a carved handle lay between her and a man's body. John the hunter had such a carved knife. John had a scar on his left arm.

Little things Caleb saw every day, things he had never thought about more than once, were now beacons, markers, calling out names unmistakably in the silence. A birthmark. A broken finger. A favorite walking stick.

Another left. There was Aunt Sara. Behind her were his cousins. Aunt Sara wore leg bracelets made of thick red curly wire. Caleb wished he hadn't wished her head to explode. Their bodies were scorched. They smelled like meat going bad.

Davy was where Caleb thought he would be, in their family space. He was sitting up against the wall, a bowl in his lap, waiting for Caleb to spoon out Davy's share. There were hunterbeast claw marks and tongue welts on Davy's chest, arm, and legs. He hadn't had the chance to get dressed.

Davy? It's me, Caleb.

Jacksoners always buried their dead in graves as deep as a man was tall in a small, tree-filled hollow not far from the white columns. His aunt and cousins were too heavy; Caleb could carry only Davy to the little hollow. Caleb found the gravedigger's tools: a mattock and a shovel. The metal heads were old. They were shiny with a patina of years of use. The oak handles had been replaced many times. These particular handles were new. The wood was rough in Caleb's hand as he dragged them down to the hollow where he had left Davy's body. He chose a spot surrounded by other graves, low mounds of earth now thick with weeds, leaves, and broken branches. Caleb didn't want Davy to be alone.

Before he started digging, he ate. He went back into Jackson to find the pantry: strings of dried apples and peaches and pears, strips of dried meat, the maize saved for both next season's seed and to be ground into flour. The smell of maizebread baking in the squat iron pots was one of Caleb's favorite smells. Davy had liked the white, blue, yellow, and purple maize kernels. He played with them, making pictures and writing the words Caleb was teaching him. Caleb took everything he could carry, filling up two of the leather sacks he found hanging just inside the pantry. He ate slowly, sitting besides Davy's body. Mama had said once to eat slow after he had been sick. Give his stomach time to get well, she had said.

Caleb dug for hours until he realized it would take him forever to dig a grave as deep as Davy was tall. His back ached. His hands were blistered. Sweat burned the blisters. At first light, he stopped digging. The grave wasn't as deep as it was supposed to be, but it was deep enough. No animal would find an arm sticking out and dig Davy up. Caleb carefully wrapped his brother's body in the light brown doeskin that they both had slept under, and then eased the body into the grave. He had seen bodies wrapped for burial before; Davy's didn't look right; it was too short without Davy's head. Next, he sprinkled two or three handfuls of maize kernels on top of the skin. Finally, he filled the grave. When Caleb was done, the sun was up and he could see his shadow, new and fresh, cut from the morning light. Then he gathered newly-turned maple leaves, bright yellow in the center, with fire-red-orange stains at the edges, from the trees in the hollow and covered the grave until none of the raw earth was visible. He left the mattock and shovel lying where he had dropped them when he had finished covering Davy.

"Ashes to ashes, dust to dust. I give back what was given. Please hold Davy close, in the palm of your hand. Take him to the promised land of milk and honey, the summer country on the other side of the golden river. Ashes to ashes, dust to dust," Caleb said, reciting what the elders said whenever any member of the tribe was buried here. In the hollow of graves, he thought. Old,

old words, his mother had told him once, remembered from the time before the Arrival.

Caleb stepped back. He rubbed his stomach and swallowed. He was more tired than he could remember being, and very thirsty, and he wanted someone to tell him what to do next. He wanted Mama and Papa. Caleb wanted them to hold him close against their bodies and stroke his hair and rub his back. Caleb wanted to sit close beside his father. He wanted it to be night and for his father and him to be sitting around the fire with everyone else in the tribe. He wanted to lean into his father in the dark, for his father's arms to take him in, his father's hands to muss his hair. Caleb wanted to smell his mother's hair fresh after she had bathed. He wanted to feel her hand lightly brush his face, pull his curly hair back behind his ears. He wanted to hear his name in his mother's and his father's voices.

He had been so angry at Davy when Mama died. After all, if Davy hadn't been born, Mama wouldn't have died. Now, though, Caleb wanted Davy, too. He wanted to feel his little brother's hand in his. He wanted to hear his little brother turning and moving in his sleep. Caleb wanted to hear his name in Davy's voice.

Caleb brushed away the dirt and leaf bits from his tunic, his legs, and his hands. He ran his fingers through his hair, thinking he would like to go down to the creek and swim, as he and Davy had done three or four times a week during the summer. The water was probably too cold, but still, he wanted to go swimming. Now he knew he would be brave enough to take that rope and swing high and out over the creek and let go and fall, fall to hit the water and then down, down, to the creek bed, cold and muddy and quiet. Instead he gathered more maple leaves, the reddest he could find, and added them to the ones already on the grave. Red was Davy's favorite color. He knelt down by the grave and carefully placed each leaf, one by one, on the earth.

Caleb found a place to sleep inside one of the tunnels. He curled up with his leather sacks of dried fruits, grains, and meat. He knew there was probably more food in the pantry and that he should go back inside Jackson for it, but he couldn't. Crawling through the broken stones and twisted metal, walking through the corridors, the dried blood, the cold bodies — no. Caleb cringed and curled into a little ball. *Papa would have gone back. . . .*

He didn't sleep well at first, even though he was exhausted. It was daytime for one thing, and he was just inside the tunnel and it wasn't dark at all. Davy had always been an arm's length away. Caleb had liked watching Davy sleep. His little brother had slept on his back, with one arm across his stomach, the other flung behind his head. To his surprise, he missed Aunt Sara's loud voice, as she argued with his cousins. And Caleb still missed the sounds of both his parents sleeping as well, even though it had been four years since Mama had died. Mama and Papa had slept on the other side of the open metal walls, behind a skin Papa had hung. Sometimes Caleb had heard them talking in low, muffled voices, their words lost in the skin.

After Mama's death, neither Caleb nor Papa had slept very well for a long time. Caleb would lie awake listening to Papa turn over and over, rearrange his furs and skins, sit up, sigh noisily, and eventually get up and walk away, his footsteps soft in the dark. Once Caleb followed Papa, padding behind him, a shadow among shadows. First, Papa had gone to check on Davy, who slept with a wet-nurse, the cradle at her side. After laying his hand on the baby's head, Papa had gone outside. Caleb found him sitting on Jackson's front steps, just past the white columns.

"I knew you were behind me. I heard you. I've heard you awake at night, but I haven't known what to say. Sit down beside me, son," Papa had said and Caleb sat down in the crook of his father's arm. "It makes it easier having you nearby; I guess I should have told you that. She made it easier when I missed Phlarx. That was hard; I couldn't even show my grief, let alone speak of it." Caleb leaned into Papa.

It was Papa who came for Caleb the night Davy was born.

"Wake up. There's someone I want you to meet. Wake up."

Yawning, Caleb took Papa's hand and went with him to the healers' room. Caleb loved the place because of its rich smell of herbs and roots, some hanging in nets from the ceiling, others loose, like so many apples on shelves, or in baskets on the floor. Caleb could see Aunt Sara at the far end, sitting in a low chair. She was rocking a cradle. He followed Papa around two sleeping patients, hunters gored by wild pigs, to where she was sitting.

"Here he is, the person I want you to meet," Papa said, and knelt by the cradle.

There was a tiny baby inside, with red skin, no hair, a wrinkled face.

"Who is he?" Caleb whispered.

"*Your brother, David. Davy.*"

Mama had told Caleb that morning that today she was going to have her baby. Here was the baby, where was she?

"Where's Mama?" Caleb asked, his voice a little louder, as he tried to see all of the room at once.

"Haven't you told him?" Aunt Sara asked sharply.

"Now I will, Sara," Papa answered, his head bent down over the baby. His voice had suddenly become slow and heavy. "Your mother's dead, Caleb. She died giving birth to your brother. Mary's dead."

When Caleb woke up and climbed out of the tunnel, stupefied by sleep, he could tell by the sun that it was late afternoon. He had slept almost the whole day. Caleb's head felt clogged, as if he had a cold. *Papa would be up before me. He always gets up before first light, in the grey time, when the sky is not blue and not black and the stars are vanishing one by one. Sometimes a white shadow of the moon is still in the sky. I would sit up and slip out from under the furs, dress, and go up and out into the morning, passing men and women stitching skins together with those iron sticks Mama had been afraid I would stick in my feet. Or some would be scraping a skin or grinding corn or nursing babies. Everybody who was awake would be doing something. I would find Papa, and Davy would be with him and he would see me and Papa would and . . . But they wouldn't be there at all. It's late afternoon, almost evening, morning was hours ago.*

The tunnel entrance was an old window, the glass panes and wooden frame long since gone. The window opened into what Caleb called a brick pit: a square made of four brick walls and a cement floor sunken into the earth. The tops of the brick walls were just above Caleb's head. Jacksoners kept the pit clean of leaves and branches. Aunt Sara had made Caleb clean it out more than once. Now, Caleb thought, the pit would fill up with leaves very slowly, another thin layer, fall after fall, until they would be deeper than Caleb was tall. Caleb did not want to get out of the brick pit. If he did, he would be facing the broken white columns, the ashes of the garden, and where he had been and what he had done the night before. Instead Caleb opened up one of his leather sacks, pulled out a handful of dried apple slices and stuck a few in his mouth.

I don't know what to do.

I don't know where to go. I'm scared. I need someone to tell me what to do. Boys in the tribe become men when they are thirteen. There are only eleven wooden beads on my life-necklace.

The apple slices were almost too dry to eat without water, but Caleb forced himself to keep chewing. Finally he swallowed. He reached into one of the sacks again and pulled out a dried strip of meat. Now that would be like chewing one of the bits of plastic lying around everywhere or a piece of wood. He put the meat back in the sack. In a little while, he would have to go and find some water.

"But I don't feel like drinking or eating," he whispered, not sure why he was being so quiet. There was no one anywhere near to hear him. Or was there? Yes, everyone in the tribe was dead. But the Footwashers? The Covenant-keepers? The Footwashers' burrows were at the end of Tate Street, across Market and Friendly, not very far at all.

If I can find Papa, then everything will be all right.

"The Footwashers (especially the Footwashers) and the Covenant-keepers think Jacksoners are heretics and not followers of the True Faith. We are only suffered to live because of our humanity. The Footwashers go out of their way to avoid the contamination of Jackson. Of course we see them from time to time, scavenging, hunting, but that's about it," Papa had explained.

The Covenant-keepers were more tolerant, Caleb remembered, and gentle. Jacksoners and Covenant-keepers had even married each other before. But the Footwashers were closer, not far from where Caleb had spotted the airship. Maybe now it wouldn't matter if he were a Jacksoner, and a halver, too.

When Caleb had crossed Friendly and stood in front of the house of the Footwashers, he stopped and went no further. The Lindauzi had been there as well. Long ago they had shot the cross off the steeple. Now the entire roof was gone and the brick walls were charred and broken. Smoke hung over the building in a thin grey haze. Caleb breathed in the odor of charred and cooked and rotting flesh. Burnt hair. Inside there would only be headless bodies and blood. He let his breath out slowly and then walked away. He found the same thing at the house of the Covenant-keepers.

Father Art in Heaven really must be angry.

Caleb spent what was left of the afternoon and the early part of the evening trying to visit all the places he had been to with Papa, places where they had scavenged in old houses and buildings.

"Maybe some of the others got away," he kept telling himself. "Everybody can't be dead. Somebody had to have gotten away."

He found no one. When it was too dark to look anymore, Caleb found himself back on Tate Street, in front of a building, a store building Papa had said, which was one long room, with its opposing walls two rows of metal drums. Here and there a drum would still have a door, hanging by its hinges, a few intact. Each door had a little window and inside Caleb knew were mouse nests, cobwebs, and rabbit dens. The front of the store once must have been mostly glass; now there was the metal door and window frame. Just outside someone had set one of the drums to catch rainwater; Caleb leaned over and dipped his hand into the dark, leaf-littered water and drank and drank. The water wasn't fresh; there had been no rain for several days, but Caleb thought it was the best water he had ever had, and besides, it was too far and too dark to go to the creek. After washing his face, Caleb went inside to stand beside one of the drums. He had only done this once, could he remember? Ah, there, there: the tiny mice minds, food, mostly, they were thinking mostly about food. There, just a touch, fear, and out they came, climbing on top of each other, squeaking and squealing, a quick brown spurt of little bodies, and the drum was empty. Then Caleb crawled inside to nestle down in the leaves. He took a few more apples, a strip of meat, and a handful of corn from one of his food sacks and ate slowly, chewing and thinking. This time he had no trouble falling asleep.

Caleb was running, running in Jackson, in a Jackson with endless corridors and turns and shelves and books and walls of skin and fur. Where was Davy? He had to look at each body, turn them over, try to recognize their clothes. His hands were covered with blood. Blood was everywhere: the floor, the shelves, the books, the skins, furs, the ceiling. He wanted to run the other way, up and out, but he couldn't. Caleb had to find Davy, he had to see his brother's body and be sure. There. That body, a man, did it move? Had the hounds missed somebody? Caleb tried to speak, to ask, but he had no sounds. Where had his voice gone? His tongue was still there, he could feel it touching his teeth, the roof of his mouth. If he could just speak, maybe somebody would answer. If there was sound, there would be life. And Davy—wait. Behind him, a noise. A human noise? Which way did he run now, away or to? Caleb tried to move, but he couldn't—his feet were mired in blood, thick fresh blood, warm blood . . . the soundmaker was getting closer, its claws were clicking on the floor. . . .

Caleb woke up and turned and banged his head on the metal drum wall. There *was* a sound and it was outside. Caleb grabbed his sacks, climbed out of the drum and ran to the storefront. Standing in the doorframe, he looked out in a night that was no longer dark, but lit by the huge search lights of two Lindauzi airships and the smaller beams of the hounds' flyers. What were they doing? What did they want? Everybody was dead; they couldn't possibly know Caleb had survived.

Up the hill and on the right from the drum store was a building made of pink and orange bricks. Like Jackson, it had white columns and multiple terraces of steps that led up into where there had once been a glass wall. Inside were high once-white walls and even higher ceilings and broken skylights. A gallery, Papa had said, a place for art. Paintings, pictures, like the one of Jackson. Where are the pictures, Papa? Gone, son, I don't know where. Across the street from the gallery was an old church, made of darker brick. Tall trees pressed against the church, and vines crawled over its dark brick.

Caleb watched as the flyers took positions above and around the church and the gallery. At the same moment, each flyer shot quick bursts of white fire balls into the church and the gallery. When the balls struck the pink and orange and dark-red bricks they seemed to pause for a moment, and then bloomed into great flowers of fire and light, hungry flowers eating at the brick, melting it, bringing down the walls. The trees burst into huge torches of flame, burning away what was left of the darkness. Caleb wondered if Papa knew the Lindauzi name for the fire balls. He had told Caleb the name for what the hounds were doing: wolf cleansing. The burning of the buildings was to be sure no more could ever live here again.

The church and the gallery swallowed in fire, the flyers moved down the street to the next buildings. Two buildings at a time, on both sides of the street. More fire balls, more bricks and stones and metal melting, falling.

I have to get out of here.

Caleb ran, asking Father Art if just this once He would not be angry — hadn't He been angry enough? He raced down the street, the fires behind him, jumping over tree branches, asphalt chunks, whatever the dark shapes were, he didn't stop to look. A falling brick struck him hard in the leg and he fell headlong into a wash of leaves.

"I can't be hurt, I don't have time," Caleb gasped and pulled himself up, not looking at his leg, not looking back. He couldn't run anymore, but he walked as fast as he could. His leg hurt, his chest ached. Where were his sacks? Gone, lost, back in the drum store, no way to go back and look, the hounds might be there by now, the drum store might be on fire. Where was he going? Tate led to Market, then to Friendly. But there weren't any Footwashers anymore who could hide him down in their burrows. Quick, down this side street, what was its name, Carr, and he fell again. This time Caleb lay still, breathing hard, hoping the pain would go away. Caleb could hear the fire behind him, roaring, almost as if it were laughing.

Caleb made himself get up. He limped back to Tate. He had to know where the hounds and their fire balls were. There, silhouetted in the flames, were the airships. They weren't coming this way, maybe Father Art had heard his prayer after all. He watched as the airships moved toward Jackson's broken tower. He couldn't stay here; he was sure the hounds would burn everything around Jackson and the Footwashers and the Covenant-keepers. The fires had been started at the edge of what had been Jackson territory. If he went back, up Tate, through the fires—would he be in a place where the hounds weren't burning? No, Tate Street itself was on fire: the dry leaves, the pine needles, and the broken branches had made the street into a hot river of flame and smoke. The trees on either side of the street were burning, the rotten remains of the houses—everything was burning. The street had become, Caleb thought, something like what Hell must look like. And there, in the bright night sky, he could see the two airships and the flyers around Jackson's broken tower, throwing fire balls as if they were playing a game.

Back up Carr, Caleb thought, down Mendenhall, over Spring Garden, through the brambles to Lee. Where will these names go now, Caleb thought. There is nobody left to use them, attach them to a place. Jackson, Tate, Friendly—everything had become empty words. Well, I will remember them, Caleb told himself as he walked slowly, biting his hand so he wouldn't cry out loud. His leg felt wet. He touched it and then tasted blood and sweat. He was bathed in sweat. Even though the fires—no, it was all one fire now—were a block over, the air was hot and heavy with smoke. It was getting harder and harder to breath. Fire started to fall around him, the leaves smoldered and then exploded into smaller fires. Caleb kept walking and walking. He crossed Spring Garden and pushed his way through the brambles at the end of Mendenhall. Briars tore at his skin, branches slapped him in the face, cob-webs caught at his hair. Finally he got through. Caleb stood on Lee and looked back at the fire which seemed to fill the sky. He remembered a story as he stood there, a story he had heard once, about the First Man and Woman, Adam and Eve, in their garden. They had been bad and forced to leave and humanity had been bad ever since, so bad that Father Art had sent the Lindauzi to teach humanity the final lesson. The Flood hadn't been enough.

"Father Art told Adam and Eve never to return," the storyteller said, after shaking his head over the evil of the current generation of Adam and Eve's descendants. "If you try to return to this garden, there will be an angel guarding the way, armed with a flaming sword." Caleb knew what swords were from the King Arthur and the Knights of The Round Table stories Papa and Mama had read and told. He and Davy had played King Arthur with sticks for swords.

Caleb walked for what seemed like a long time on Lee, until the white glow of the fire receded and a few of the stars reappeared. This street, he thought, would take him to the Big Road, and on the other side of the Big Road, across the jumble of a broken bridge, was the Mall, where he and Papa had gone over a year ago and had spent the night. The Mall was the biggest place Caleb had ever seen. There were stairs everywhere, the railings laced with crawling vines dangling to the floor. Tall spindly trees grew toward the broken skylights that brought in shafts of light to form yellow pools here and there. Glass crunched underfoot wherever they walked. From the skylights to the yellow pools, the sunlight formed white pillars filled with slowly turning dust motes, lost dandelion seeds, maple wings.

"These stairs," Papa had told him as they walked up the funny Mall metal stairs, "used to move up and down. People just stood still and let the stairs carry them. I saw people doing it in the Lindauzi memory wall."

"These stairs used to move and carry people?" Caleb had begun to wonder just how many of Papa's stories were true and how many were made up. "Why don't they move now?"

"There is something, a power—like lightning is a power that splits up trees and starts fires—it made everything work before the Death and the Arrival. It's gone now, son, at least it is for humans. But I saw the memories. People like you and me and Mama and Davy just standing still and letting the stairs carry them up to the *next level. They weren't wearing clothes made out of skins like we're wearing. More like what Lindauzi humans wear. This big place,"* Papa *had said, and spread out his arms as wide as he could, "was filled with people."*

"Hellloooo," Caleb *had shouted, his voice echoing in the silence, bouncing in the empty spaces, floating in the white pillars of light.*

The Mall was a long walk from Jackson, Caleb remembered, but then he had the rest of the night to get there. He could stay there until he figured out how to find Papa. And there was food cached there, left by the tribe for those caught out at nightfall. Not that the food hidden there did Caleb any good now. He wished he hadn't dropped his food sacks—but they were probably burnt up now, and even if they weren't, there was no going back. He would just keep walking, Caleb thought; there was no point in trying to sleep. At least now the fire's roar was harder to hear, and the light against the sky seemed almost beautiful. He would be safe at the Mall, at least for a while and then he would go east, the way Papa had went. Caleb was sure Papa was alive, or why else had he had that dream—was it a day? two days ago?

Never mind, Caleb thought, best to keep walking. Not think about a dream or being hungry—his stomach was growling again —or being thirsty or his leg hurting. Keep walking. It wasn't for some time that Caleb noticed his feet were making crunching noises. Bird eggs—no, too many. Caleb looked down. Acorns. Acorns everywhere.

"There's always something to eat, Caleb. Even in the dead of winter. There are roots you can dig up—I'll show you where to find them—and if you have a bow and arrow, there are rabbits and cats and squirrels," Papa *had said to him once. "You just have to keep your wits around you constantly. You can't slack up for a moment, son; you always have to be on guard—"*

"Now, Caleb, don't let your father impress you with his foraging skills. I taught him everything he knows, including where those roots are," Mama *said laughing. Caleb looked from one to the other. His mother leaned over to gently tweak her husband's nose. Papa laughed and shrugged his shoulders.*

"Yeah, she's right, son. What would a Lindauzi-raised human know about surviving outside?"

Caleb knelt to pick up the acorns, ignoring the pain in his leg. Don't eat them green, he remembered his mother saying. *Roast them in a fire. If you eat them green, you'll be sick. And they taste better roasted; some of the bitterness is gone.* I had a piece of flint for fire, Caleb thought, but it's back in Jackson. Papa used both flint and a magnifying glass, and he had taught Caleb how to use both. But the glass was gone; Papa had taken it with him when he had gone on the scouting trip from which he had never returned.

Even with the moonlight it was hard to tell, but Caleb thought all the acorns looked at least a little green. Well, if this was all there was, did Caleb have any choice? He squeezed two acorns together in his fist, cracking them against each other. Caleb picked out the shell bits and then gingerly tasted the acorn meat. Bitter, really bitter, Caleb thought, and spit the acorns out.

Now he felt even hungrier. Well, maybe just a few acorns would be all right. He picked up a few more and cracked them in his hands and chewed and swallowed the meat as fast as he could. Maybe Mama was wrong; maybe the green ones were OK. Caleb ate and ate, trying not to remember what else she had said about acorns. Thinking about Mama made his throat feel closed and tight.

I need to look for water. Both Mama and Papa said there was usually a little water somewhere left by the rain. It might be dirty, but it would have to do if you were really thirsty. I am really thirsty.

There had been no rain for several days, but Caleb found just enough to take the edge off his thirst in the bottom of a big metal bucket sitting beside two yellowish-brown half-circles. A sign behind the cracked half-circles read M DONALD's. Caleb wouldn't have touched it any other time; it felt gritty going down. His stomach started hurting then, so much that he had to sit down in the middle of the street, in a pool of moonlight. Caleb bent over double, pressing his hands against his stomach, hoping to press the pain away.

A Lindauzi airship passed overhead, low and for a moment hiding the moon, as Caleb threw up. He tried to look up when he was in the airship's night shadow, wondering briefly if they could see him being sick below them on the ground. His stomach heaved again, and Caleb didn't care if the Lindauzi saw him or not.

Mama, I want Mama, my stomach hurts. Papa, where's Mama? She's dead, Caleb; I told you she was dead, remember? Here, let me wash your face. It'll make you feel better.

Caleb lay still in the middle of the street, his cheek against the rough asphalt, his hands still clutching his stomach. He felt hot and dry, and he wanted to go somewhere and lie down and sleep. He wanted something to drink; he wanted to be somewhere inside and not alone in the moonlight.

Mr. Donald's place, Caleb thought, when he finally stood,

careful not to put too much weight on his left leg. He and Papa had scavenged there once. They had brought home sacks of yellow styrofoam bowls and straws he and Davy had played with in the creek, squirting water at each other. The bowls had been shared with the rest of the tribe, a treasure grudgingly accepted from the hands of a Lindauzi-raised man.

He stopped to pick up a long stick before he went inside Mr. Donald's place, to dig through the trash and scare the mice and rats out. Caleb had seen what could happen to a sleeping human left alone in a rat-infested place. Then he remembered: *if I can call them out from those metal drums, I can do it here.* He could still use the stick; if he was lucky, he might be able to club one of them with his stick, even though rat meat was better cooked than raw. Ah, there, there, just like before: the tiny minds, bigger, there were no mice, only rats, tough, almost mean, food, mostly, they were thinking mostly about food. There, just a touch, fear, and rats swarmed out of the piles of cups, bowls, straws, plastic rings, big, grey and brown rats, almost the size of kittens. For a moment Caleb was surrounded by rats, a living, moving river of rats. Then they were gone, before he had time to think about clubbing one with his stick. Just as well, he thought. He wasn't sure his stomach could handle raw rat meat.

There were coins everywhere beneath the trash. Countless old coins: dull brown-red and silvery-grey. Jackson hunters used them to make arrowheads. Some swore by the red ones, others by the silvers. Women bored holes in them and looped the coins together to make jingling bracelets, anklets, and necklaces. Papa had once tried to explain to Caleb what coins had been used for before the Arrival, but his explanation was foggy. Caleb just couldn't understand why someone would give food and clothes in exchange for coins. And whose faces were on them, anyway?

Chieftains. Chieftains before the Arrival, had been Papa's answer. Caleb scooped up a handful of the coins and poured them from one hand to the other, feeling his eyes get wet and his throat get thick. Why did Papa have to leave? It wasn't fair; he needed Papa.

Rubbing his eyes, Caleb, using the bowls and the straws, built a small fence in a semi-circle facing the counter. Behind the counter he found some tall metal cups and set them around where he was going to lie down. If the rats came back and knocked them over, he would hear and wake up. When they were in place, Caleb felt safe enough to curl up beneath the counter. He was so tired.

*   *   *

Bright mid-day light, broken by the holes in the ceiling, woke
Caleb up. For a moment, he wasn't sure where he was or when
it was. Not Jackson, the caves — Mr. Donald. And how long had it
been since the hounds had come. Just three mornings ago? Caleb
shook his head and held his stomach. He was starving and thirsty.
There's always something to eat, he thought, and slowly got up.
Outside, he limped out into the street, and looked in both directions. Empty brick buildings with hollow eyes, vines up and down
the walls, like worms crawling out of a skull. Leaves and pine
needles and broken branches piled up in drifts as high as Caleb's
waist.

*"Did a lot of people live on this street, Papa?" Caleb asked when
they were walking home from the Mall, their sacks filled with little
things they had found. Caleb couldn't wait to show his mother the
clear glass cups they had found. She loved to fill them with water
and hold them up to the light. He had found something for Davy
as well, a tube with bits of colored glass inside. When Caleb held it
up to the light and turned it in his hand, it was as if the tube enclosed a flower that bloomed and changed each time he moved his
hand.*

*"People didn't live in stores, son. They lived in houses. All these
buildings on this street, I think, were stores. They came here for
things, things to take and use in their houses. They would give the
coins to people in the stores and then go to their houses. I saw them
doing that in one of the Lindauzi memory walls on the station."*

*"How is a house different from a store? These sort of look like
those brick houses past the Footwashers."*

*"Caleb, we've scavenged in houses before, remember?" Papa had
said. "And we talked about the differences between houses and
stores. Anyway, houses are . . ."*

Caleb yawned and stretched and then took a step forward. *Oh,
God, my leg. It hurts.* Caleb immediately sat down on the curb and
pulled off his boots, unlaced the knife strapped to his right calf,
and then looked over his legs carefully. There was one long jagged
cut on his left leg. It was dark red, and it was tender to his touch.
The dried blood felt crusty. It was going to hurt to walk. But his
leg could have been worse, he thought, as he carefully strapped
his knife on and then pulled on his boots. At least he had had his
boots on. *You will wear boots outside of Jackson, do you hear me?
You will wear them or you will be one sorry little boy.*

"Yes, Mama," Caleb said as he stood. "I'm wearing boots."

The only clouds in the sky were high streaks, as if someone
had dragged his hand across the blue and ripped it open so that

it showed the white underneath. When suddenly Caleb found himself in shadow, he looked up, startled. A Lindauzi airship—the same one as last night, the same one that had destroyed Jackson? The airship was directly overhead, at the height of the pine trees growing between the buildings. As Caleb stared, the bottom of the airship opened.

A one-man hound flyer dropped out to hover beside the ship. After a moment, the flyer moved down and out, then toward Caleb. There was a abrupt explosion of light, and pine needles and leaves a body-length away burst into flames. Another explosion. Fire burned on Caleb's other side. Another and Mr. Donald's was on fire.

Caleb bolted. The flyer was just behind him; the airship, just above.

I've got to keep running; I can't stop. Quick, an alley. They can't follow me in there.

The laser kept spurting flames to Caleb's left and right, forcing him into a narrowing fire-shaped path.

If I could just run faster, if I hadn't been sick, my leg, it hurts hurts hurts . . .

Caleb ran into the alley, into its shadows between two crumbling walls, a space so narrow he knew the flyer could not make its way in. If he could just get out of range of the lasers, he'd be all right and with the fire and the smoke, maybe the hound would lose him. Up, over a heap of old cans, ohhh—The rusting metal gave way beneath Caleb and he fell, the metal cutting at his bare upper legs, his arms, tearing at his tunic. Blood was all over everywhere. *No, I can do it, go, go, go. Where to run, where was the flyer?* There, he could hear its high whine—it was—there it was, hovering at the alley entrance.

He had never been so scared in his life. The hound was going to kill him, cut off his head, and stuff it in a case.

The alley opened up into another street and Caleb could see yet another alley, with more rusty cans—if he could get inside them, maybe the hound would go away. Maybe the cans would muffle the sounds of his heart.

Caleb started walking slowly, coughing from the smoke, his left leg throbbing, the other cuts aching, blood sticky on his clothes, on his fingers. He kept one hand on the wall and every few steps he looked back at the flyer hovering there. Why didn't the hound just burn him down? Maybe the hound was going to let him go. If he could just make it out of this alley, across the street, hide, he'd be all right. His gut heaved again and Caleb leaned into the wall, puking, his body shaking. He felt dizzy, so dizzy. When he looked up, the flyer was gone. *Thank you, Father Art, thankyouthankyouthankyou—*

Loud trumpeting cries. Heavy bodies running on the ground, beating the pavement beneath big broad feet. The beasts. They had let loose the hunterbeasts.

One more run, just—

Caleb froze. There, standing very still in the alley entrance, was a hunterbeast, staring at him. Its black eyes drilled holes into Caleb's chest, cutting through his torn tunic into his flesh, through his lungs, his heart, his bones. Caleb wouldn't have been surprised if two laser beams shot out of the creature's eyes. Its spiked tail twitched back and forth behind it, stirring up a little flurry of leaves. The fire was behind the beast; Caleb could see it had spread beyond Mr. Donald's house; soon that side of the street would be nothing but fire. The morning sky was filling with great clouds of smoke. The beast took one step toward Caleb.

He couldn't move. He wanted his legs to take off, but he couldn't. It wasn't because the big cut on his left leg had reopened or that there were the scrapes and gashes from the barrels. Could he push the beast away, touch it with fear, like the rats and mice— no, Caleb couldn't move, could barely think. Terror had completely eaten him up. It was all Caleb could do to close his eyes.

The hunterbeast took its time walking to Caleb. Its heavy feet crunched the leaves. Something wet brushed against his legs, sniffed at the blood. The beast was smelling at his legs, his buttocks, up and down his back.

If I move, it'll kill me. It'll rip off my head and carry it back to the hounds. It'll tear off my head. It'll eat me. . . .

"Be very still, pup. If you try to run, the beast will rip you apart." A hound, it had to be a hound, talking in American, his mouth giving the words funny shapes and sounds. The hound spoke again in the growls of Lindauzi, ordering the beast away. Caleb could hear its claws scraping the pavement.

Caleb's legs gave way then, and he slumped to the ground.

"Sit up, pup," the hound said, again in American, and to Caleb's amazement, he felt the hound's hands under his armpits picking him up. He opened his eyes to look into the hound's face.

No lasers? The beast had been called off, maybe. . . .

"I was hoping you'd be able to run. Let me look at your legs, be still. How did you get so cut up?" The hound shoved Caleb on his back and then knelt down to start roughly examining Caleb's legs.

"If you move, that beast will kill you. You hear me? Be still, or I'll break your arm, understand?" The hound squeezed Caleb's arm so hard he cried out, and then went back to poking at the cuts.

"Ohh, that hurts," Caleb said, finally finding his voice. He spoke in the snarling Lindauzi speech.

"Lindauzi? You speak the civilized tongue?" The hound cried out in shock in the same language. "How could any wolf pup have learned Lindauzi? I'll have to call the ship."

The hound sat up, and keeping one hand on Caleb, pressed a place behind his ear, and became very still. He stared down through Caleb, straight into the earth. Then he spoke very rapidly in Lindauzi, and for a moment, his hand on Caleb relaxed.

"I said: don't move," the hound snapped when Caleb tried to shift himself out of the hound's reach. "Where are you going to run, bleeding and cut like you are? Answer me, you damn wolf pup. Get up, they want you. Get up."

Caleb made it to his feet and then he threw up again. He started crying, but he didn't care. He hurt all over, he was sick, he felt dizzy, he was hungry and thirsty. He threw up again and couldn't stand up anymore. Everything hurt too much.

"Filthy, stinking wolf," the hound grumbled, his boots covered with vomit. "If they didn't want you, I'd take your head right now." The hound kicked Caleb in the side, stepping back quickly when Caleb threw up again.

"I hate you, you misbegotten kennel-dregs," Caleb gasped in Lindauzi, wondering if he was going crazy saying such things to a hound. But he didn't care. Now the hound would kill him. It didn't matter.

The hound jerked Caleb up to his face and then slapped him, a hard backhand splitting Caleb's lips. More blood trickled down Caleb's chin.

"Just shut up. Shut up." The hound dropped Caleb back into the leaves and stepped back. He pressed behind his ear again and cocked his head, as if listening.

Caleb retched again, another dry heave, mostly blood and spittle. He covered his face, hating himself for letting the hound see him cry.

"Well, you are a lucky pup. I just got my orders. The Viceroy thinks a Lindauzi-cursing wolf-pup would be the perfect novelty to send to the Prince in Umium. You were going to be beast fodder. I was going to let him chase you; he needs the practice," the hound said in American, nodding his head toward the creature who was nosing in the leaves behind him. As Caleb watched, it shot its paw out quickly and scooped up a rat. The beast ate it whole, in one gulp. Behind the beast the fire was getting louder and bigger, the smoker blacker and thicker. It was getting harder to breath.

"I'm to fly you to Umium myself now—a wasted hour. Get up. Oh, never mind," the hound muttered and picked Caleb up in his arms to carry the boy against his chest. Caleb craned his neck to look up at the hound's face again. The man was very tall, as all hounds were supposed to be. Hounds were bred for speed, endurance, cunning, and size, his father had said. Hounds were supposed to be able to run a day and a night and never tire. Only the racers, bred for the great arenas, with long, long legs and broad chests, could outrun hounds. But only in the arena, never for the long haul.

The hound carried Caleb out of the alley and into the street, only to step back from the heat of the fire that was now burning almost the entire block facing them. Caleb could feel the heat slapping his face and he started coughing again, even though it hurt to cough. The sky was filling with smoke. Little trails were crawling across the street, igniting leaves and dried wood and pine needles. Caleb could hear beneath the fire's crackling mice squeaking and running into the street, their feet like leaves pushed by the wind. The hound whistled sharply and the beast followed, pushing close to the hound, sniffing at Caleb's dangling feet. Another beast joined the first, snuffling first at the hound's legs and then made little wet licks of Caleb's blood. The second beast's breath was wet and warmth on Caleb's skin. The hound whistled again, a higher note, and the flyer, hovering in the middle of the street, floated until it was a few feet away and at the height of the hound's chest. Caleb closed his eyes.

The hound heaved Caleb into the back of the flyer and told him to be still. He then spoke sharply to the beasts in Lindauzi, telling them to wait for the airship to send another flyer down, and to go hunt, find food, go, go, go, and the beasts took off running. Caleb found himself lying across a seat made out of something soft, yielding to his body's weight. Above his head was a clear dome, made, he supposed, out of either glass or plastic. He could see the tops of the buildings nearest him, and the smoke from the fire. The air was hot and close. Part of the dome was open, and the hound pulled himself up and over the side of the flyer and into the seat nearest Caleb.

"Here, put this on all those cuts. It'll stop the bleeding and close the wounds, kill any infection," the hound said and handed Caleb a thin tube. He showed Caleb how to squeeze the tube so that a warm white creamy thickness came out that rubbed into his skin. And to Caleb's amazement, the white cream did stop the bleeding, close the wounds, and ease his pain.

"Now, spray this on yourself. It's an hour to Umium, and your wolf stink is making me sick." The hound handed Caleb a bigger tube with a dent at one end. Caleb turned it over and over and looked back at the hound.

"Never mind, stupid pup, I'll do it," the hound muttered and jerked the tube from Caleb's hand. The hound pressed his thumb into the dent. The spray felt cool on Caleb's skin. He wondered how wolves smelled. Caleb remembered Papa had told him the Lindauzi called all humans outside their cities and plantations wolves. And he remembered Papa telling him Lindauzi smelled when they were wet.

"Now, don't bother me. Don't say anything. Just look out the window—oh, here, eat this, it'll make your stomach feel better," the hound said and tossed Caleb another tube, which when Caleb squeezed it, oozed out a bright yellow, sweet-tasting cream. And his stomach did feel better. "Now be quiet. I could be back in my barracks now, but I have to take a wolf pup to Umium." The hound shook his head.

The hound pressed something and the dome closed over their heads. Then he ran his fingers over the multi-colored panel in front of him and the flyer rose into the air. Caleb sat back against the soft seat and watched the hound as he made the flyer work. The hound's skin was pale and smooth, the same color as Papa's. His ice-blue eyes were like stones worn round and smooth in the creek. The hound's hair was red.

Caleb turned away from the hound to look out in the enormous blue sky and at the old city spreading out below him. He could see the fire, like a huge, bright flower, blooming in a spreading cloud of black and grey smoke. They flew over the Big Road and then over the Mall. Caleb wished he was running down the Road, his feet barely touching the earth, running where his father had walked, running to wherever his father was. The hound banked the flyer to the left and then sharply up, throwing Caleb back in his seat. Now he could see nothing, except the sky.

Good-bye, Davy. Good-bye, Mama.

Caleb wished he had put more maple leaves on Davy's grave. He knew the wind would blow most of them away, or maybe, if the fire kept blooming, the leaves, the trees in the little hollow — everything would burn. Ashes to ashes, dust to dust.

How am I going to find Papa now?

Caleb squeezed himself into a corner, as far from the hound as he could get. He felt very tired and sleepy. His arms, his legs, the cuts — the hurt was gone, replaced by a slow drowsiness. His head was so heavy. . . .

"Wake up, pup. Look down there," the hound said after he had shaken Caleb. Caleb followed the hound's finger to see the shining domes of a Lindauzi city, looking just the way Papa had said. The city was on three islands at the mouth of a river running into the sea. Caleb gasped. He had never seen anything so big as the sea. *Papa was right; it goes on forever.* The sun shone on the water and the city domes.

"That's Umium, the biggest city on the Earth."

Caleb said nothing as the flyer started to descend and the domes and the river and the sea came closer and closer.

Interchapter 3

Arrival

Transmitted from the royal flagship, via Lindauzi observation satellite, local time, 1 January 2001, noon, Eastern Standard Time, English language version:

We interrupt regularly scheduled programming for this special announcement.

Please do not be afraid. We are not hostile. This is not a prank or a joke.

I am Corviax, commander of the Lindauzi star fleet, speaking to you from high Earth orbit. As is obvious to you, I am not human. I am, in your terms, an alien. We know of the crisis afflicting your species, the terrible disease now ravaging your world. We learned of this disaster through routine scanning of the radio and TV transmissions from your world and diverted our journey to offer you our medical assistance.

Please do not be afraid. We are not hostile.

We ask all air defense systems to stand down. We are not attacking your planet; we are here to render assistance and help in fighting the plague. Tomorrow, at this time, noon, Eastern Standard Time, Lindauzi shuttlecraft will land in the following cities: in North America, Toronto, Quebec, Ottawa, New York, Washington, Atlanta, Miami

. . . in South America, Bogotá, Caracas, Rio de Janeiro, Brasilia . . .
Please do not be afraid. We are not hostile.

We are here to render assistance and help in fighting the plague.

Please be forewarned that if our shuttlecrafts are attacked, we will respond defensively and will make every effort not to cause loss of life.

Please do not be afraid. We are not hostile. . . .

This announcement will be repeated every hour on the hour for the next twenty-four hours. No one is in danger; please remain calm. . . .

Chapter IV

Ilox, 2138-2140

WHEN ILOX WAS THIRTEEN, PHLARX WAS SENT TO Umium, the Lindauzi planetary capital, for school. There was no question but that Ilox would go with him. The week before they were to go, Ilox was taken alone by a house-dog to the plantation dog clinic and left there with the Lindauza vet whom he usually saw only briefly, twice a year, for a physical and annual inoculations.

"You are a healthy growing pup, Ilox," she would always say as she examined him through the medscreen, which seemingly removed his flesh, layer by layer, down through skin, blood vessels, internal organs, connecting tissue, to his bones. Ilox could see, on the monitor, his own heart beating, his own lungs breathing.

This time the vet did not ask him to step into the medscreen or the bodyglove. Instead, after he undressed, she asked him to lie down on a white table like the white table the kennelmaster had examined Ilox on years ago. It felt cold to his bare skin. The vet carefully inserted various glowing pink and orange tubes into Ilox's chest, groin, and head, and then checked the data on the medcoms surrounding the white table.

The vet didn't stop talking the entire time Ilox was with her. "There, everything seems normal—just a routine check. So, you're going to Umium with Phlarx. You are excited, yes. I know I would be if I were you; I remember my first trip there—beautiful, absolutely beautiful. I was born here on the plantation—and so were you, so were you, I remember when you were born —and this is home, but still, Umium, the capital. They say it is almost exactly like Emium, the capital on the old world. That's what my parents told me—they were children on Lindauzian . . . Now, spread your legs, there, and let me fit this on your penis. There, not too tight, good. Now, let me just put these restraints on your arms and legs, don't want you jumping around, there. This won't take but a minute; you just lie still while I take this semen sample. Most dogs seem to like it. Try to be still, Ilox, I knew we would need the restraints. There, there . . . good, good, the more the better. Done. You can put your tunic on now, no, that's it, you can go. That's all. Now, let me just save this data into your medfiles. . . ."

She smiled and touched the dark blue-faceted stone hanging on her chest. She turned away from Ilox, to the medcoms, muttering to herself. Lord Madaan's stone, Ilox thought, as he slipped his tunic back over his head. Morix and Ossit wore one. And just last week, Phlarx had been given one in temple in a brief ceremony, from the white-furred priest. Almost every adult Lindauzi wore such a stone. Ilox could remember only a few who did not, such as Oldoch, the kennelmaster.

"He's a non-Madaanic. Father told me that means he believes the way of the machine should be applied to all life, not just to creatures like the hunterbeasts and the towels. Even to Lindauzi and especially to dogs. I think that's what Oldoch believes," Phlarx had said when Ilox had asked him.

"Oh, I almost forgot," the vet called out. Ilox looked back over his shoulder into the clinic. She stood at the white table, peering into her compad, her fingers busily working. "Airsickness medication. If Lord Morix were flying straight to Umium, you probably wouldn't need them, but since he is inspecting the Viceroyalty, a lot of up and down, over three days, you might. I'll send some over tomorrow. Press the dermic on your side immediately upon takeoff and leave it there for the first day. You'll be a little sleepy while in the air, but that's all. Run along now," she said, still looking into her compad, the claws of her free hand drumming the table.

Ilox stood at the door, his hand on the palmsign. Then he shrugged his shoulders and went out. He leaned against the wall, which glowed red and pink in response to his body weight and heat. Did she know he had been doing just what her machine had done when he was alone? That not even Phlarx knew? That he was trying to see female dogs naked? That when he and Phlarx had gone swimming with Phlarx's sister, Tyuil, Ilox had to hide himself until the hardness went away? He had wanted to touch her companion pet, a female older than Ilox. Nivere. With breasts and . . .

This time, though, with the machine, its tight glove close and wet around him, had been the most intense Ilox had ever felt. Ilox wanted to tell Phlarx about how he felt when he saw Nivere, about how he felt when he touched himself, about how he felt now. He couldn't. *Phlarx doesn't even seem to know Tyuil is different. He would laugh and scratch my head.* Ilox stood there, leaning against the wall outside the vet clinic, the wall glowing behind him, until he heard his name called out on the housecom.

By the fastest Lindauzi aircraft, at high altitude, the trip to Umium from Kinsella was around forty-five minutes. The larger airships, built for size and strength, and not for speed, made the trip north in almost two hours. The Viceregal air yacht's fastest time was an hour and half. But not this trip.

"Father wants to show me the Viceroyalty or something like that," Phlarx had grumbled as he and Ilox finished packing the morning they were to leave. "It's going to take us three days to get there. Three days. We have to go to every major plantation, to Tarian, to Osium, even to Narmius. . . ."

Ilox nodded, only half-paying attention to Phlarx's complaining. He had heard the litany of Lindauzi cities and plantations before, and couldn't quite understand why Phlarx wasn't excited to be going to all the different places. He was — to see other places, new, strange, unfamiliar. Kinsella was Kinsella, he knew every corner of the place, and he had never been anywhere else and now they were not only going to the planetary capital, the biggest city on Earth, but to a half-dozen others, from the Great Ocean in the east to the Dividing River in the west, to the Warm Sea in the south and the river's mouth, and the cold plains in the far north. The city of Narmius was the farthest north, on the shores of an enormous lake. Ilox couldn't wait to go. His things were packed; it was Phlarx who was dawdling over what to take.

And complaining the entire time. "Why do we have to go south? Hardly any Lindauzi live there — it's just a research station, it's too hot for Lindauzi, just wolves, that's what I heard—"

Ignoring another familiar complaint, Ilox picked up his bags, placed them on a floater and pushed everything out into the corridor. And saw Lord Morix heading in their direction.

"Uh, Phlarx, you'd better hurry. Your father is—"

"Phlarx. Are you and Ilox ready? The yacht crew is waiting, so is the priest."

Phlarx stopped in mid-grumble.

"Be on the roof in ten minutes."

Phlarx was suddenly able to make up his mind what to take.

The yacht didn't leave the roof of the Vaarchael house until a Madaanic priest came onboard to bless its flight. Phlarx told Ilox that the white, thick, bushy-furred Lindauzu had walked up and down the corridors, rode the lifts between the decks, went in and out of cabins, clutching his blue stone. In each place, the priest asked Lord Madaan to share His presence and protection.

Ilox listened groggily as Phlarx talked. It was hard to focus on Phlarx's words. The airsickness medication made him feel as if he were never quite awake. Phlarx's words had spaces between them. Listening and watching him tell about the priest, Ilox thought, was like watching Phlarx swim and talk in thick water.

"Then the priest told Father the trip and our time in Umium would go well, and he left. And we took off after that, about twenty minutes ago. We'll be at the Warm Sea research station in about an hour and a half. Are you listening to me, Lox?" Phlarx said when he had finished telling the story about the priest. "You might as well be asleep for all the fun you are. Your eyes are open, and that's all. How long before that stuff wears off? Our room is bigger than Tyuil and Nivere's, Father's in . . ."

Ilox looked up at Phlarx with half-open eyes. They were in the sitting room of their suite. Phlarx stood at the port, staring at the receding ground below, describing how everything on the ground was getting smaller and smaller, the plantation houses looking like tiny pink and red cubes. Ilox lay spread-eagled on a low couch that had folded out from the wall. He felt as if he were floating above the floor.

"In about . . . two hours, Phlarx, it . . . wears off in two hours . . . after we get to the station," Ilox said, pushing his words through heavy layers of sleep.

"Are you going to miss the entire flight being sleepy-headed?"

Ilox nodded and closed his eyes, Phlarx's words falling together in a soft jumble of blurred noises, as if his head were wrapped in

a thick cloth and flies were buzzing around him. It was better to
dream:

*Instead of an airship he and Phlarx were on a starship. Phlarx
wanted to play hide-and-go-seek. Ilox didn't want to; he felt foolish
to be running around the great ship, the stars close outside, playing
hide-and-go-seek. They had played the game when they were very
little, in and out of the many rooms of the family house. Thirteen-
year-olds didn't play hide-and-go-seek, Ilox had said, over and over to
Phlarx, but Phlarx kept insisting, grabbing Ilox's hand, taking him
down the lift, dropping, the two of them, down, down, down . . . The
dream shifted, and Phlarx was gone and Ilox was in the center of an
enormous room, surrounded by Lindauzi, red, black, white, grey,
yellow-furred Lindauzi, all trying to touch him, stroke his hair . . .*

Ilox sat up, breathing hard. He shook himself, trying to shake
off a warm prickly feeling in his skin, just as he had felt as a child
when a Lindauzi was near. Ilox ran his fingers through his hair,
to try and comb out the dreams from his brain. There. Where—
oh, on an airship, going to Umium, to school, he and Phlarx. No,
not there first, where was their first stop? Somewhere south, by
the Warm Sea, Phlarx would know. Where was Phlarx? The little
sitting room was empty. Outside, through the port, Ilox saw only
a bright white-blue sky. Why had he dreamed of a starship, and
all those Lindauzi trying to touch him? And where was Phlarx?
Did he want to play hide-and-go-seek? Ilox shook his head and lay
back down on the couch, his head still thick. Phlarx was probably
playing somewhere on the airship. If he weren't so sleepy, he
would be, too, despite the game being a child's game. *Phlarx is
younger than I am. Our years add up to the same number, but his
are longer than mine. It's taking him more time to be older. I have
to remember this, not let the drugs take it away, this is important. . . .*

On the third and last day of the trip, the yacht made five stops,
at a succession of small plantations, each one closer to Umium
than the last. When the yacht took off the fourth time, Ilox was
airsick, throwing up his breakfast in the observation lounge.
Phlarx carried him back to their cabin and carefully pressed the
dermic against Ilox's side. He waited until the drug began to take
effect, and gently laid Ilox on the couch.

"I'm sorry . . . I got sick . . . my stomach . . ."

"We will be in Umium by nightfall. Sleep, Lox."

Sometimes, Ilox thought, Phlarx is older than me.

Ilox didn't know where he was. The airship? At home on Kinsella? Umium? The room was large, large, with a great high ceiling, like the temple dome, arching way overhead, and clear, above he could see clouds like hurried animals moving, jostling each other. He had to run, run somewhere, as fast as he could, before, before what? Ilox didn't know, he just had to run. Then, a Lindauzu, a Lindauza. More Lindauzi, filling up the huge room, and they were all chasing him, trying to touch him, get close to him. . . .

"Come on, Lox, wake up. We're there, it's time to get off the ship. I thought that airsickness drug was supposed to wear off. Feel better? Wake up."

Phlarx was shaking Ilox awake. Ilox pushed Phlarx's arm away, and sat up. He felt bad. His skin, what was wrong with his skin?

"I don't feel good," Ilox said softly, knowing Phlarx wasn't listening, that he was looking out the port again. The white-blue sky was gone, replaced by the faint pink of tall buildings, the odd light of the city forcefield dome. How could he be sick, now? The ship had landed; he couldn't be airsick. Besides, he felt different. His skin prickled, like it had when he was little, and the way it had three days ago, but worse. This hurt. He was sweating. The heat came in flashes, sharp, quick, then gone, leaving him tired and shaky. Then the heat again.

"Are you awake? Ready to go?"

"Yeah, I'm ready. Let's go—what about our things?"

"The menials will take care of that. Come on, Father and Tyuil and Nivere are outside waiting for us. We have to go to some reception at the Prince's palace tonight, and then school tomorrow, remember?"

Okay, maybe it's just new Lindauzi, more Lindauzi, more heat. It'll go away.

The next heat flash came as Ilox and Phlarx walked down the ramp from the airship to the roof of the imperial palace. Ilox gasped when they stepped away from the ship and he could see the city of Umium all around. The palace of the Crown Prince, a huge triangular building, was in the exact center of the city. Ilox could see nothing *but* city: the tall building cubes, red, orange, pink, the shining causeways between them, high over far-below streets, the glass outer lifts rising and dropping. And the palace itself, the entire plantation of Kinsella could fit into the leg of the triangle on which they had landed. Just ahead Ilox saw Morix and Tyuil and Nivere standing by a lift, waiting for them to drop down into the building's unseen heart. A small handful of dog menials and lower-caste Lindauzi servants, from the yacht and the imperial household, waited to one side.

Ilox felt a quick wave of fire that made him gasp and wrap his arms tightly around himself.

"What's wrong, Ilox? Are you going to be sick again? The palace roof isn't going to move, I promise. There they are, let's go," Phlarx said carelessly, pointing to where the others were waiting.

"Wrong? Nothing. I just felt something," Ilox answered and followed behind Phlarx across the roof, walking on a path of brightly colored stones.

Ilox became ill when the lift reached the ground level. The prickling intense heat became even hotter when he stepped out into a garden. The heat crawled over his skin as he tried to walk. Ilox wanted to tear off his clothes, scratch away the heat, throw himself into the nearest fountain, anything to alleviate the heat and the itching. Then the headache began; skull-pounding, hammering pain that beat Ilox to his knees, screaming.

"Father! Father, Ilox, he's really sick!"

"What happened to the pup? Quick, call a medic, hurry!"

"Ilox, can you hear me? I'm here, I'm here . . . "

The words around him were like hard stones, bruising his ears, cutting his skin. He tried to push the noises away with his hand, but it was like pushing away very persistent flies. Ilox thought he felt Nivere's touch on his arm, cool, delicate, and soft. But her words and Phlarx's and Tyuil's and Morix's, the medic's, all became a black jumble that swallowed him.

And for what seemed like a long time, Ilox floated in the jumble, drifting, bumping into odd shapes and forms and colors. He kept trying to find Phlarx. Phlarx was nearby, Ilox could feel him, close, but where was he, why couldn't he touch Phlarx? There were too many others, without faces, without names, just hands, touching, touching—

Phlarx?

I'm here, I'm right here, squeeze my hand, hold on, I'm right here.

Where are we, where are we going?

To the space station. They want to put you in quarantine . . .

Quarantine? What's that? Phlarx, I'm scared, don't let them hurt me—

Just hold on, Father says it's going to be all right, just hold on. . . .

Ilox stayed on the space station for two long years.

The first year was as if he were swimming in thick, soupy water, struggling to keep his head up, swimming as hard as he could, trying to find bottom to stand on, a branch to hang onto, anything. There were times when Ilox felt he had reached land, but a wave would slap him back into the black, thick water. Sometimes it was all he could do to just float. If he slipped, and fell below the water, Ilox knew he would be lost: his self would leach away, a chunk here, a piece there, until there would be nothing left. Interspersed between water and land there were moments of light: bright, almost hot light, and shining voices, glowing faces. Thousands of faces. Or just one face would coalesce out of the mob, and that one face was usually Phlarx's. Once it had been Nivere's.

"Is he awake? Can he hear me? Lox? It's me, Phlarx. Can you hear me?" Phlarx's voice was the first voice Ilox was sure was real after he had found himself swimming in the dark soup.

Where is he? Why can't I see him, touch him? Phlarx?

"We are bringing him to full consciousness for the first time since he became ill. We have to be very careful, even here on the station since he is so sensitive—"

"I just want him to hear me, know I'm here," Phlarx said.

"He should. After all, it's you he's the most sensitive to, it's with you the bond has been. . ."

There, it is Phlarx. That shadow is shaped just like him. . . .

"Lox?"

Phlarx stood above Ilox, beside his bed. Ilox lifted one hand slowly to touch Phlarx's face, then his arm. *The same soft fur. Phlarx has just brushed it. I bet his comb is tangled with hair.* The gesture took all of Ilox's strength. Phlarx's face dimmed, returning into shadow. The brightness faded.

"Ilox?" It was one of the research medics, another shadow to Phlarx's left.

"Yes."

"Do you feel the heat? Is your skin still sensitive?"

"I feel Phlarx," Ilox whispered. Why did they keep asking him questions? Why didn't they just leave him and Phlarx alone?

"No heat at all?" the medic asked.

"Just Phlarx."

"How does Phlarx feel?"

"He's afraid for me. He's glad to see me, he's missed me, and he's really scared. I'm scared."

"Can you feel him, Phlarx, his fear?" the medic said, turning to Phlarx who with one hand gripped Ilox's closest hand and with the other, stroked Ilox's hair, his forehead, his face.

"Yes, I feel him. He's going away, though, he's . . ."

The brightness was gone. The faces blurred into the murkiness of the watery shadows; the voices merged into the sound of the shadow's liquid currents. Ilox drifted on his back, staring into an empty dark sky.

There were Lindauzi everywhere: tall, dark, light, red, black, brown, yellow, white. There were the very old with silver-streaked fur, white muzzles, and dark yellow teeth. Only a few were young. Ilox was surrounded by them. He stood in a small circle of pulsing light which kept him just beyond their reach. He could smell them, feel their breath.

Their hands were open, their sharp claws extended. The circle was drawing into itself slowly, the light contracting and receding until it brushed against Ilox's skin. The light sparked and hissed when it touched him.

Ilox grew smaller and smaller, and the separate faces became mouths, eyes, wet fangs. The light oozed into his skin, into his body, and he glowed. Ilox filled up with light, he was light. . . .

"Ilox. Wake up. Wake up, Ilox."

Ilox stared up into a blond-furred Lindauzi face. The glow-globe behind the face cut a circle out of the room's shadows.

"Phlarx? Where's Phlarx?" Ilox said slowly and carefully. It felt like it had been a long time since he had talked about anything. His tongue ached and his throat was dry and sore.

"Note: first response is a request for the bond-mate, even after weeks in a drug-induced coma. Testosterone levels have increased. Other physiological changes indicate sexual maturity. . . ." The blond Lindauzu went on and on, speaking into a small voice-recorder. Two other Lindauzi made careful notations in their compads. Ilox turned his head, and felt something give a slight pull on his temple. He reached up to feel one of the plastic tubes. Tubes were in his chest, his sides, his stomach, and his groin. Each was filled with a ruddy sparkling fluid that moved in rhythm with his breathing, with his heart.

"Where am I? Where's Phlarx? We were in Umium, on the palace roof. Why isn't Phlarx here?" It hurt his throat to talk.

"Note: anxiety over absence of bond-mate—"

"Where's Phlarx?" Ilox croaked. The pain in his throat was killing his words. He wanted to hit the blond Lindauzu, but he was too weak to lift his hand. Why wasn't Phlarx here, and where was he? Wait, Morix—had it been Morix? The medics?—someone had said to take him to Umium Station, the space station. He was on —in—in the space station and the world was turning below. Ilox wished he could see outside, see the Earth— Oh, his head still throbbed. At least the prickliness and the heat were gone, well, almost. The tips of his fingers were warm. And, yes, the dreams lingered, like ghosts flickering in his thoughts.

More ghosts than I can count, so many, so many.

"The medication to alleviate his physiological responses to his psychic sensitivity is working, although slowly. Dreamtapes indicate he still senses multiple Lindauzi presences. In his body extremities, he still has heat sensation. . . ."

"I said: where's Phlarx? He's supposed to be here." Talking hurt, and why didn't this Lindauzu just answer his question?

"Note: continued agitation," the blond Lindauzu, his fangs protruding, said. "Phlarx is planetside, in Umium. He will be here in three standard days."

"I miss him," Ilox said and closed his eyes. He had never felt so tired. Why couldn't they all go away and let him sleep? But if he slept, would the dreams come back, and the heat, and the skull-beating headaches—

"Can you stop my dreams?" Ilox said as loud as he could. "And my throat's sore. It hurts to talk."

This time one of the other Lindauzi, a brown-furred Lindauza, heard him. She nodded, her fangs retracted. She pulled another tube out of the wall and brought it to his mouth.

"Drink this. It'll soothe your throat," she said.

The blond Lindauzu turned off his voice-recorder and glared at her.

"His throat is dry and sore. Someone is not monitoring *all* his physiological responses," she said shortly, glaring back.

"Oh, very well. I think we have enough here to make a hypothesis for the causes of his reaction. He is entering puberty—and now is in puberty, thanks to the medications. His sexual maturation caused certain hormones to be released at a greater level. In tandem with this, the growing maturity of his bond brought on heightened psychic awareness. Together the two produced his reaction to Lindauzi psycho-emotional needs, even though they have been suppressed and sublimated since the Extinction—"

"Treatment?" the brown Lindauza asked, interrupting.

"Hormonal injections, pain-sublimation drugs. In a few months he will be fine. Then we can start breeding experiments using his semen. . . ."

Talk, talk, talk. Ilox sighed.

Phlarx did come in three standard days, along with Tyuil and Nivere. The brown Lindauza scientist brought them into Ilox's room. She made several adjustments to the tubes, checked the medscreens, and made notations in her compad. Phlarx, Tyuil, and Nivere stood in the doorway behind her, waiting.

"Phlarx," she said, and gestured for him to come into the room. "Just Phlarx right now," she added before Tyuil and Nivere could step forward. "Just a moment."

"Is he all right?" Phlarx asked. Ilox was asleep. Phlarx let one hand rest on Ilox's arm. Phlarx wanted to pull out all the tubes and pick Ilox up, but he was afraid the scientist would send him away. His father had explained over and over again how important Ilox was to all the Lindauzi on Earth. Ilox's genes could be their salvation and the vindication of their faith.

"Without the bond, we are dying as an intelligent species— reverting to how we were before the First Bonding. Your pup's genes hold the promise of breeding dogs who will be able to bond as completely as my father's generation did with the Iani.. And by the recreation of those bonds, the civil war we fought on Lindauzian, the long journey across space, our exile here—all will be vindicated. We can return to the homeworld, bonded, and save even those heretics who chose death and reversion. Do you understand, Phlarx?"

Phlarx understood all right, but he didn't care. He had heard his father's speech before, over and over and over. Phlarx could recite the entire story, line by line: the Plague, the Extinction of the Iani, the Grand Argument and Debate, the Civil War, the Journey of The Search, and the Exile, and the Project. Phlarx looked from one scientist to the other, hoping they wouldn't try to tell him the same story. He wanted Ilox back. He was tired of these scientists and his father telling him what he could and could not do with Ilox. The blond scientist made it quite clear he expected his instructions to be followed explicitly.

"He is getting well. As soon as he is physiologically an adult, he will be completely well," the brown scientist said, looking up from her compad. *Now she is going to ask me if I understand, if I know how important this all is.* Phlarx inwardly groaned.

"Then why is he so skinny?" Phlarx asked quickly, hoping to avoid a repeat of his father's story. Ilox looked tired; there were dark circles under his eyes and his face was thin and drawn. "He doesn't look like he is getting well," Phlarx said, feeling his crest rise, not enough, he hoped, for this veterinary scientist to notice. What was her name, anyway? Ostiga?

"He will gain the weight back. You know you have a very valuable dog here, Phlarx. If we can breed others from him successfully, with his psychic sensitivity . . ."

Phlarx looked down at his feet and sighed. His crest drooped. She was going to repeat the same old story. And he had just heard it yesterday in temple. Phlarx was tempted to recite the words with the vet: how Lindauzi were dying younger, fewer were being born, then the Plague, the Extinction, and the rest.

"Umium was built to mirror Emium," Morix had told him after their return from taking Ilox up to the station, "and to be the home of just as many Lindauzi. My father, your grandfather, said when he was young, Emium was so thick with Lindauzi and Iani you couldn't move on Holy Days. When we left, one house in three was empty. And there are houses here in Umium that have never been filled. . . ."

Talk, talk, talk.

"I said you can wake him now, Phlarx," Ostiga said. Phlarx looked up, startled and embarrassed. How long had she been waiting for him to pay attention? But then everyone knew the Viceroy's son wasn't quite the heir the Viceroy wanted.

"Now?"

"Yes. Go ahead. Touch his face, call his name."

Phlarx laid the back of one hand on Ilox's face. With the other, he smoothed back Ilox's hair, twisting a strand of it around his claws. "Ilox? Wake up, it's me, Phlarx."

Ilox didn't respond.

"Call him again," Ostiga said.

"Ilox. Please wake up. Ilox, it's me, Phlarx." Phlarx took Ilox's hand and bent down beside his head. "Lox? Wake up."

"Phlarx? I looked for your face in the crowd. There were so many others. I couldn't find you." Ilox spoke so softly that Phlarx could barely hear him.

"You found me, I'm here," Phlarx said.

"Yeah, you really are," Ilox said, and reached up with his free hand to touch Phlarx's face.

"Tyuil and Nivere are here, too. See?" Phlarx said and pointed behind him. He looked at Ostiga, who nodded, and then Tyuil and Nivere came into the room to stand beside Phlarx.

"Everybody's here," Ilox whispered.

"How do you feel, Ilox?" Ostiga asked. "Any heat in your fingers? Headache?"

"Just a brush of heat, barely warm, in the tips of my fingers. And my head, if I move it, hurts a little. But not like before. Can I get up?"

Phlarx looked at Ostiga hopefully. Ilox certainly looked better now that he was awake. Much better than he had months ago when they had first brought him up to the station. This was the second time Phlarx had seen Ilox awake since that afternoon on the palace roof. Had that been a year ago? Phlarx had come for other visits, but each time Ilox had been asleep, turning fitfully and crying in his dreams, the pink-filled tubes pulsing and glowing all around and in him.

"You may sit up. Phlarx, you and your sister may stay for an hour or so. Then I'll come to take you back to the Umium shuttle. I don't want him to tire out. He is much better, but he is still very weak."

"When can he come down to Umium to be with me?" Phlarx asked.

"I can't let him go back. He could get sick all over again; you've been told how valuable his genes are. When you return to Kinsella, he can go planetside then."

It seemed as if Ostiga had just left when she returned to take Phlarx, Tyuil, and Nivere to the shuttle docks.

"I'm sorry, but you have to leave now. I think you will be able to come back in a month, Phlarx. I am sure he will be much stronger then."

Phlarx watched as first Tyuil, then Nivere said good-bye. *Why was Nivere taking so long? What was she saying to Ilox that she didn't want anybody to hear?* Phlarx felt his fangs starting to protrude. *She's just a girl-dog. Ilox is mine. He's always been mine.* Nivere touched Ilox briefly on his face with the back of her hand and then walked away to stand by Tyuil. Phlarx scowled at her, then bent over Ilox.

"I'll be back in a month, the vet told me I could. She said you'd be much better then. We can explore the station together," Phlarx said, his hands curved around the bed rail.

"I'll be here," Ilox said, and they both laughed.

When Phlarx got to the door, he stopped. Ilox just fell asleep.

I felt him slip away. Phlarx looked around the room, feeling he had to know this place where Ilox had spent so much time. It was a hospital room and a laboratory. Monitor screens covered the wall, which fed the tubes in Ilox's body. Phlarx could see, on the screens, inside various parts of Ilox's body: his heart beating, his blood flowing in his veins. His brain, his lungs, his bones. Another wall was a workstation for the veterinarians: more monitors, compads, memory blocks. The wall behind Ilox's head was a mural of Umium and the last wall was more screens and charts and graphs and a door into what looked like offices. A glowglobe floated above Ilox's head, its light having dimmed when he fell asleep.

"Time to go. He's asleep," Ostiga said.

"I know," Phlarx answered and followed her out.

It took six more months before Ilox was truly free of his psychic and physical pain. Each month he grew stronger and the pain receded. There were relapses, when the heat burned inside his skull again or the dreams returned, coupled with headaches that felt like loose balls rumbling and banging around in his head. But, never again did he feel the pain he had felt on the palace roof in Umium.

Phlarx came, at first once a month, then, as Ilox got stronger, once a week. At the end of the six months, the vet said Ilox could finally leave his room. To celebrate they decided to explore the veterinary research ring of the station together: up and down and all around each level, the observation deck, the hydroponic gardens, the no-grav gym, the station library (from which they got chased out).

"I have to stay here until you finish school in six months," Ilox said. They were in the no-grav gym, floating high above the floor. He was glad they had ended their exploration tour there, roaming the station had tired him more than he thought it would. But it had felt so good to walk and walk and to climb and even run through the gardens and to just stand and watch the Earth spin below. They had watched the day move over the land, a bright wave chasing the night. Umium had shone like a nest of jewels in the night-shadow.

"I know. They're afraid you'll get sick again. And they want to start breeding experiments," Phlarx said. He was floating on his back with his eyes closed.

"Tell me more about school," Ilox said and closed his eyes as well. He didn't want to talk about the breeding experiments.

Ostiga and the blond Lindauzu, Idimber, had said that as soon as he was strong enough they would start collecting semen. Letting him go exploring with Phlarx no doubt meant they would start right away. Ilox both hated and liked the machine, which was the same as the house vet had used down on Earth.

"It's all right. Not much to talk about—just like school in Kinsella, except more people and busier. It'd be more fun if you were there. Sometimes it's really hard. The teachers get mad at me if I don't do well because I am the son of a Viceroy and have imperial blood." Phlarx yawned. "I get tired of hearing that. Some of the others laugh at me because I have a planter accent. You were always better at school than me, Lox," Phlarx said.

Ilox said nothing to that: it was true. He opened his eyes and stretched and scratched behind Phlarx's ear. It was something he remembered from his dreams. Another creature, with long, long fingers and taller than an adult dog, an Iani, had come out of the crowds. Ilox had not been able to see the Iani's face; it had been dressed in shadow. Lindauzi lowered their heads to it and the Iani scratched and scratched, behind too many ears to count. The scratched Lindauzi made rumbling noses, their eyes closed, lips curled.

Phlarx's eyes were closed, his lips curled, he rumbled.

"You've never done that before," Ilox said as he continued to scratch.

"Done what?" Phlarx whispered.

"Rumbled, like you're doing now."

"Are you sure? I feel like I have, maybe I dreamed it," Phlarx said, his voice slow and slurred, as if he were talking in his sleep.

Ilox kept scratching.

One month before Phlarx finished his schooling in Umium and one month before Ilox was to finally leave the station and go back down to Earth, to Kinsella and Phlarx, Ilox found himself alone one night in the station library. He had only been allowed to enter the library a few times on Kinsella, as Morix thought such places were wasted on pups: the stories aren't yours, go on back to your room, pup. Remembering Morix's look and his extended claws and fangs, his erect crest, made Ilox hesitate before entering the library on Umium Station. He was sure some Lindauzi— Ostiga or Idimber—or any of the other vets and techs would come along and ask him if he were tired or needed to rest or it was late, shouldn't he getting back to his room? Was he supposed to be about now, shouldn't he be in bed? Or wasn't the Earth beautiful from so high above?

There must be something in the library they didn't want him to find, Ilox had decided after his third or fourth attempt had been thwarted. And tonight, with all the vets in conference and the techs doing data analysis, was the best and perhaps the only time he would have to find out what they didn't want him to know. He was supposed to be in his room. But two days before, they had finally removed all the night monitors and disconnected the medscans. For the first time since Ilox had come to Umium Station, the Lindauzi wouldn't know exactly where he was. He could tell them, he decided before venturing out, he was just going for a walk to the station's central core, to the no-grav gym. He did have pretty much free run of the station, having become, more or less, its mascot.

Free run of the station except for the library in the central core.

There were only a few Lindauzi out and about in the research and clinic section, where Ilox's room was. Those that weren't in conference were, Ilox thought, probably at dinner in the habitat ring. Even so, when he passed the first Lindauzi, a tall, blond-furred Lindauzu, who looked too much like Morix, he froze, not knowing whether to try and press himself into the shadows behind a wall support or to run. The Lindauzu only nodded his head and kept on walking, intent on whatever he was studying in his compad. *Deep breath, count to ten, fifteen. There, close to the wall, hand on the metal, boy, I wish it was like in Kinsella and would turn pink at touch, act normal, there, the lights just dimmed for night, now, walk slow.*

Besides, what would the Lindauzi do? Put him out the airlock? Not their great dog hope — or so Ilox had overhead Idimber say to one of the station priests.

Ilox shook his head. He didn't want to think about that.

There was no one on the lift down from research to the central core. Just Ilox and the lift's almost melodic humming and its close walls of warm pulsing light. When the lift had dropped to spoke-level, it shifted from *down* to *forward*: a pause, jerk, another pause, then movement. Ilox wished again, as he had the first time he and Phlarx had roamed the station, that there were windows of some kind in the spokes. He wanted to see the station and the stars and the moon turning all around and above and below him, the great dodecagonal central core, the ascending levels of rings, turning as the spokes that punctuated them turned. Core (library, temple, administration, operations), research/hospital/laboratories, habitat and gardens, then docking and cargo/observatory. All of which Ilox and Phlarx had explored. The month before Phlarx was to come and take him home was going to last forever. The lift stopped again, after pause/jerk/pause, started ascending, this time, Ilox knew, up into the core to the library, which filled one entire level of the dodecagon.

The station library looked like the house library on Kinsella, except bigger. The memory walls, arranged in interlocking star patterns of five walls, created a huge maze. Each wall was a separate component of memory and record, seemingly random lights shifting, receding and approaching, until the right touch and command were given. Ilox couldn't see the other side of the library, or even the library's tall windows, which separated the walls into panels of glass and steel. Here and there were low tables and chairs—low for Lindauzi, Ilox knew he would need a small ladder to sit down. There were faintly luminous lines on the floor, of different colors, leading to one cluster or another. Nesting on the ceiling were glowglobes, like huge luminous bunches of grapes. There were no Lindauzi, at least not any Ilox could see. Ostiga had said all the vets onstation were going to be at the evening conference and the techs were either in labs or eating, depending on their shifts. Perhaps there was a stray astronomer, but nowhere near Ilox.

He and Phlarx had stepped inside once or twice on their explorations, but Phlarx had never wanted to stay and any vet already there made sure they both left.

"It's just a library, Lox," Phlarx had said the last time they were shooed out. "Just like the one at school and the one back home. Come on, let's go to the gym or the pool."

Just a library, Ilox thought. He remembered the few times he had been in the house library and the even fewer times he had been allowed to use the library. It had been a wonder to say the right command and watch as words, pictures, and numbers floated up as if they had been hidden in deep water.

Ilox knew he could lose himself for days in any library. Phlarx, on the other hand, would be and usually was absolutely bored after five minutes in the library. Ilox shrugged and looked carefully around outside; the corridor was empty. He stepped back inside and pressed the palmlock, closing the door behind him. There, for at least a couple of hours the library was all his. Two hours, Ilox thought, was about the maximum time he could take, before somebody checked his room and started asking where he was. Idimber had said the conference would last about two hours. A glowglobe appeared over his head, dropping down from the nearest ceiling nest.

He wished Nivere, Tyuil's pet, were with him, right beside him, so close he wouldn't be able to not touch her. He would be able to smell her hair and her skin and put his hand there and there. Just as he had done in his dreams. Would she let him? Did she feel what Ilox felt? He had thought so the last time she had come with Tyuil to visit on the station. Ilox shivered — now was not the time to think of Nivere, although there were days and nights when he thought of nothing else.

"Where do I start? I guess the first one is good enough," he said to himself, and followed a pale blue line to the nearest memory wall. He knew the Lindauzi could tell the walls apart and that the colored lines meant different subjects, but what he didn't know. Phlarx could never remember and always had to check the directory panel that marked the edge of each wall. There were rows of colored lines in the panels, matching the floor lines. Ilox touched the blue panel line: ah, there, dog anatomy. Well, there were a lot of vets in the research section, after all. White-and-blue, physiology. White-and-dark-blue, neurology . . .

It was in the third cluster, the fourth wall that he saw was yellow-and-blue, dog history. History. Dogs had a history before the Lindauzi? The pictures Ilox saw were unlike any he had ever seen. No dogs had ever looked like that in any house he had ever been inside. Such strange, strange clothes and they were alone; there were no Lindauzi.

A long text appeared to the left of the images. When Ilox started reading, he thought it was just a story, an old, old story, but the more Ilox read, the more it was apparent that this was history, this had truly happened in the past. A history of dogs before the Lindauzi.

Ilox knew the Lindauzi did not come from Earth. And he had guessed, after meeting the two wolves at the beach, that there had been a time when there had been just wolves. But not like this. Not with cities and airships and strange wheeled things on the big roads. And were these people dogs or wolves? To Ilox they looked the same. The still image before him was that of a city — not a Lindauzi city with its enormous buildings, arched and curved, the great blocks stacked one on the other, the translucent dome, but a dog city. A dog city with tall buildings and wide streets and wheeled groundships everywhere. And dogs, dogs, dogs. Or were they wolves? Tall, fat, skinny, old, young. And there were no Lindauzi.

Ilox glanced up at the clock line, at the top of the memory wall. He had been in the library just under an hour—time to finish the history? He felt just the faintest prickling in his skin. There were Lindauzi nearby, probably somewhere on the far side of the library. If they came over here, what he would say? Could he hide—

Never mind, he would think of something. "End still data, begin continuous image flow," Ilox said, and waited. There, live-action. Now, the dogs—were they getting sick? There were less in the streets, and they looked tired, unhappy, and yes, ill and dying. The dead lay in what Ilox thought were city gardens—huge trees, green lawns, even a lake, a stream—where the other dogs brought the bodies in and dumped them, set them on fire. Bodies and bodies and more bodies.

Image-shift: In the sky above the tallest of the city's tall buildings, there were Lindauzi airships slowly descending, as if they were floating, like gargantuan leaves. When the landing gear extended, they became enormously heavy birds. The image divided to show both the descent of the airships and the dogs in the streets. Their wheeled vehicles, the small personal ones and the large transports, the dogs walking—everything became still. Everyone and every thing became very still, looking up and waiting. In one corner of the wall, another smaller inset image appeared, of a Lindauzu. Was it the Crown Prince—no, this was Prince Orfassian's father. Ilox had seen Corviax's picture on Kinsella, in the Temple, in various places on the station, and of course, by the library's entrance. Corviax had only recently died, Ilox remembered, just after he had been brought onstation. The Lindauzi had worn green armbands and howled and muttered in little huddles and knots and keened for days.

Beside Corviax's picture was a long text, unfolding downwards like a dropped scroll.

"They knew the Lindauzi were coming—the Prince told them, said he was going to help them. Dogs were sick—all over Earth they were sick and the Lindauzi said they would help. They let the Lindauzi come."

Could the dogs have stopped them?

Ilox shook his head; he had no answer to that.

The huge airships settled in the middle of the city gardens,

fields, open-air arenas. For a long time, according to the chronom-
eter ticking away in the bottom of the image screen, the ships just
sat where they had landed, like great birds, their wings drawn
close to their bodies, heads tucked in. They waited in city after
city (were there ever so many dog cities?): cities of white dogs,
black dogs, brown dogs, yellow dogs, and cities with dogs of all
colors. The dogs came to the arenas, the city gardens, the fields,
and they waited as well. Some even rolled out red carpets, a darker
red than Lindauzi houses, over the green grass.

After five days, in the city with the tall, tall buildings, in the
middle of a huge grassy lawn framed on one side by trees and the
other by a lake, the airship doors opened and the Lindauzi came
out. Ilox asked the wall to provide the audio then. Most of the
time he preferred the written text which kept scrolling down the
side of the image, but this time he wanted to hear.

It was a translation. Ilox could tell the words he heard did not
match the dogs' lips.

*I told you they were like bears, just like big bears. How in the
world did you miss seeing the one on TV—it must have been on a
thousand times in the last week.*

I don't know—big dogs, maybe. . . .

Not dogs. Cats, mountain lion-sized cats, maybe. . . .

No, you are both wrong. Bears. They are definitely ursine.

God, I hope they can help us, stop the plague.

They have to, I mean, advanced technology and all that. . . .

Dogs? Dogs calling the Lindauzi dogs?

Then the image shifted, and the Lindauzi were walking on the
same streets with the dogs, side by side. In and out of dog
buildings. Riding in dog vehicles. Visiting what could only be dog
schools. Standing silently in what looked like dog temples. Why
were there crosses on the tops of temples? And who was the dog
tied to the crosses, his face in pain, thorns smashed on top of his
head? Ilox saw his picture again, in multicolored windows, and
there was a baby and a woman as well in the windows. A family?
Before the man, and the baby, some dogs made cross-signs over
their chests. The wall memories had no commentary on who the
man and the baby and the woman were and why the man was tied
to a cross.

"He wasn't important to the Lindauzi," Ilox muttered, staring
hard at a the thorn-crowned dog. "I wish I knew his name." He
glanced up at the clock line: about one more hour. And so far,
none of the Lindauzi in the library had noticed him.

"Go," Ilox said and the image changed, to crowded streets filled with dogs. There was something wrong with what Ilox was seeing, and he stared for a long moment before he told the wall to continue. Dogs and Lindauzi were walking side by side. No dog ever walked side by side with a Lindauzi. Every dog, regardless of station, stayed one or two paces behind any Lindauzi. Even Ilox walked at least one stride behind Phlarx in public.

That was it. He told the wall to freeze the image and Ilox stared hard at the Lindauzi and the dogs on the street in the dog city. He focused on two in particular, a bearded dog wearing some sort of protective glass covering his eyes and a light-furred dark-crested Lindauzu, a young Lindauzu by the color of his muzzle and the height of his crest. The Lindauzu, of course, was much taller than the dog, but his head was bent as if he were listening intently to whatever the dog was saying—as if whatever the dog was saying really was important and worth hearing.

What happened? How did it happen? Why?

"Continue."

The screen split and Ilox watched as the airships rose out of the cities and landed again in the countryside, in meadows and grain fields and wide lawns. Dogs came and set up tents and lean-tos. They left behind empty houses and unmoving vehicles.

Why did they leave? Now they are living like wolves. . . .

Image-shift: There were more and more tents surrounding the airships, with small fires and clothing strung on ropes between trees. Behind the airships Lindauzi began to pile up huge reddish blocks, which Ilox recognized as Lindauzi housing components. Then the houses appeared, the same great houses he had known all his life, dwarfing the tents, making them look like mushrooms sprouting after a hard rain. There were fewer and fewer dogs in the cities and more empty houses with broken windows. Dogs in the cities looked sick and tired and frightened and still carried their dead to the city gardens. The tent-dwelling dogs who lived by the Lindauzi houses looked rested and fed and in good health.

Image-shift: Domes grew over clusters of the Lindauzi houses, shimmering golden in the sunlight. The domes were like great jewels scattered on the earth. At night, a new star shone, a tiny moon, the Lindauzi space station. Now dogs lived inside the domes with the Lindauzi, sleeping at the foot of Lindauzi beds and wearing Lindauzi collars. Outside, the dogs kept dying. There were more dead in the dog cities than living.

Image-shift: Sick dogs, refugees, from their corpse-filled cities, stood outside what were now Lindauzi cities. One by one, the dogs fell to their knees.

Image-shift: Dogs came upon the Lindauzi cities at night, armed with stones and spears. A few held what Ilox guessed were some sort of guns, like the laser pistols carried by the hounds. When the dogs attacked, they died. There was a sudden white light, freezing the dogs in place, arms raised to throw, guns cocked. Then they fell and lay still in the grass and dead leaves.

Image-shift: Dogs, no, now they were wolves, sleeping in their temples or in tunnels beneath their city streets, in caves, and in basements. Others were traveling, at night, in little armed bands. The little groups seem terrified and kept looking up into the sky. It wasn't long before Ilox saw what terrified the dogs: Lindauzi flyers dropped from behind clouds and set the earth on fire with their lasers.

Dogs killing dogs—no, hounds killing wolves.

Ilox's right hand rose up involuntarily to brush against the face of the hound in one of the flyers. He touched the hound's big hands as he fired lasers through the air, through trees, through flesh.

Image-shift: winter. The snow lay deep silent drifts. Trees bent and snapped beneath the weight of the snow. The snow and the wind blew around the city domes, and Ilox could see Lindauzi and dogs moving about in the brightly-lit cities, riding up and down lifts. Outside there were bodies in the cold, the wind slowly covering them in white—

Ilox looked up. His two hours were up. The conference was almost over and he had to be back in his room before Ostiga and Idimber came in to check. And hadn't that dark Lindauzu over there, across the library—had he seen Ilox and what Ilox was looking at? Was he walking this way?

"Clear wall, erase record request, reset." There, now, careful, unhurried steps, the door was just a few steps away—

"What are you doing here? Aren't you supposed to be in the research wing?"

Ilox turned around. It was the dark Lindauzu. He had seen him. He stood by the memory wall Ilox had been using, his arms crossed, his crest erect, fangs extended.

"School work. I had to look up a biography of Corviax's father, the Left Emperor."

Ilox took a step toward the door.

"You don't have any memory cubes."

"I have to try, uh, try and remember it—an oral report."

"You shouldn't be here by yourself."

"Ostiga said it would be all right."

"I'll speak to her, letting pups run loose on the station, in the library. Go on, now, go."

It was all he could do to not run the last ten steps to the door, the dark Lindauzu's scowl pressing close on his back. There, the door, and out, and into the lift-tube.

"Research, go."

I made it. I made it. Is he going to call Ostiga? But she did say I could go anywhere, she'll tell him that, it'll be all right.

Ilox pressed himself against the lift-tube wall, feeling its pulses against his skin, low, faintly warm, humming vibrations. The wall memories had to be true. They had to be. Did Phlarx know? Morix —Ilox was sure Morix knew.

And what do I do now?

That night, after Ostiga and Idimber had come and gone, Ilox lay awake in his bed, replaying what he had read and seen and heard, over and over and over again, trying to understand, trying to make sense of it all. He wanted desperately to talk to someone, but there was absolutely no one at all.

"Phlarx?" Ilox asked. "In school, what did you learn about how dogs and Lindauzi came to be living together? Did you learn that in school?" They were in the observation lounge of the shuttle taking them from the station down to Earth. The station looked like huge wheels within wheels, with connecting spokes and moving lights, flickering, glowing, winking on and off, changing colors. Phlarx had come up from Umium the day before, this time with his father. After a long series of what seemed like pointless tests and low, muttered conversations with Morix, Ostiga and Idimber had let Ilox go home. He was all right; it was all going to be all right.

"Came to be together? Dogs and Lindauzi have always been together," Phlarx said, still staring at the station.

"No, not always. The Lindauzi came from Lindauzian in ships, huge ships—I wonder where all those ships are—and found the dogs here. Dogs were already on Earth."

"Are you sure, Lox?"

"Never mind, forget I asked. How much longer will it be before we land? Do we have to stay in Umium long before going home to Kinsella? . . ."

*   *   *

They only stayed in Umium for an hour, enough time to leave the station shuttle and board the Vaarchael air yacht. By nightfall, they were at Kinsella, and in bed in the room they had both left two years ago. The bed wasn't the same, it was new and bigger than the one that they had slept in two years ago. But then they were both bigger, their bodies longer, lankier, bonier. Phlarx fell asleep almost immediately, but Ilox couldn't. As much as it felt good and right to be sleeping beside Phlarx again, doing so also made him replay for the thousandth time all he had seen a month ago, all the images that he couldn't stop thinking about. Finally Ilox slipped out of Phlarx's arms and went to stand by the window.

I'm fifteen, but I'm still a pup. The Lindauzi still pat me on the head or scratch behind my ears and tell each other what a good, good pup I am, and marvel over how well Phlarx and I get along, and maybe it's finally over, we're finally safe. But they don't hear anything I say. And if I asked them about what I saw — do all of them know? Phlarx doesn't, but Morix, Oldoch, Ostiga, do they know?

I have nobody to talk to.

All those bodies in the snow.

Interchapter 4

The Arrival, Plus Ten Years, 2011

Perhaps it was how Lindauzi smelled when they were wet. Or that you could never be sure whether they were angry or sad or upset: crest erect, down, fangs extended, retracted, claws extended, retracted—just which combination meant what? Oh, there had been and continued to be primers and broadcasts on Lindauzi body language, but Donna Radley could never keep it straight. She didn't want to; she didn't like or trust any Lindauzi. And she was allergic to their fur; it made her sneeze. The latter was particularly unfortunate for Donna, as she was in almost daily contact with the aliens. UN Press Pool liaison to the Lindauzi. The title had sounded pretty good, but more and more Donna felt like she was nothing more than a slightly glamorized PR person for the tall, furry beasts—the latter epithet one she kept to herself. It wasn't popular to speak ill of the Lindauzi, the saviors of mankind. If she could just get one of them to give her a straight answer, instead of all their double and triple talk about helping human-kind fight the plagues, restoring the torn social fabric, interstellar amity, and so on and so forth, blah, blah, blah.

Donna thought it was all bullshit, and that the Lindauzi were up to something.

"But, Donna, the *vaccine*—they *gave* us the vaccine. People aren't getting sick anymore, what's not to like?" Frank, Donna's on-again, off-again boyfriend, thought she was being paranoid. He looked at her over his coffee cup, his dark red hair falling over those green eyes Donna found fascinating, and shook his head. Frank was a UN reporter as well, the education beat. For the first time since the Lindauzi Arrival, schools, at least in the New York area, were in operation again. They were having lunch in Dalfinckey's, a little coffeehouse not far from the UN — and it had just reopened a year ago. There were about fifteen others in the tiny place, in little close knots at the polished blond wood tables. That there were so many in such a close space spoke a great deal to the growing sense that the worst was over, that being together didn't mean infection. She glanced out the wide front window: there were two men just walking down the street, in the middle of the day, laughing and talking. Last year, if there had been anybody on the street, Donna wouldn't have been able to see their faces for the surgical masks. She touched her own face: still a little odd to feel just flesh.

"I know they gave us the plague vaccine, Frank, but why? What's in it for them?" Donna asked, looking away from the two men and back at Frank. "And they just happened to pick up one of our TV broadcasts out there in space and took a detour from wherever they were going? C'mon, honey, there are holes a truck could drive through in that story. Yes, I would like some more coffee," she said quickly to the waiter who had seemingly appeared out of nowhere. Donna wondered if the woman had been listening. She was wearing a silver-and-white Human/Lindauzi Friendship button. Frank was right: she was paranoid.

"An advance emigration fleet, routine scanning — I thought you watched *Star Trek* reruns — typical behavior for your run-of-the-mill interstellar travelers," Frank said after the waiter had left.

"That's just it, Frank. Their story sounds like something off *Star Trek* — it sounds made up. The universe is a pretty big place — they just happen to be passing by our solar system? Give me a break. Do you want those fries?"

"No, go ahead, take them. It works the other way, too, Donnie, they had to be somewhere in space, why not nearby?"

"Why haven't they let any of us visit that space station they are building?"

Frank rolled his eyes. "It's under construction. It's dangerous. You reported that story yourself, after interviewing Prince Corviax."

"I know that. And they won't let us into those pink cube build-ings they are building out in Jersey and on Long Island. They were going to leave five years ago, but there just happened to be a plague outbreak in Europe the month before departure—and now they are building a space station. Frank, there are just too many unanswered or half-answered questions for me—what time is it?"

"1:15—where you gotta go?"

Donna shook her head again. "About the station: I think I asked Corviax one too many questions about it—I've been invited to go up tomorrow. I need to go do some prep work."

"To the space station? And you didn't even tell me? Donnie, you forgot, didn't you? You'd forget your head if it wasn't tied on. How you got to be such a good reporter, I'll never know—"

"I remember the important stuff—"

"A trip to the space station isn't important? You've been rant-ing on about all this paranoid stuff and you're getting ready to be one of the first humans in space in twenty years? You've got to stop this crazy stuff, you've got to. You tell me there is some mystery there and then you forget to tell me you were asked up by the head Lindauzi. Donnie, honey," Frank said, shaking his head.

"I'm sorry, honey, I was going to, really. I just found out about an hour ago, right before I left the office to meet you. I'm sup-posed to be at Kennedy tomorrow morning at 9—you know, where they converted part of the airport for their airships and shuttles. Oh, God, Frank, you are going to hit me, I just remem-bered—I asked and you can go, too."

Donna was glad that the French fries were small and that Frank didn't use a lot of ketchup. She did wish Frank would stop laughing so hard. OK, so she was forgetful. And maybe a bit para-noid about the Lindauzi. Maybe Frank was right: the Lindauzi were just a good and generous people, who, by the grace of God, were in the neighborhood when humankind was in its worst crisis.

It had all happened so gradually, almost carefully, as if the Virus itself was changing and growing, becoming progressively stronger. A few deaths here, there, in so-called marginal communities— male homosexuals, poor urban blacks, African villagers—in the late 1970s. In the 80s, the Virus was called AIDS, and the death count kept rising. Drugs were found that slowed it down, kept it at bay—the infected sometimes hung on for more than ten years.

We lived with it, Donna thought, AIDS was just a part of human life—and if you didn't know anyone sick, it was far away and somebody else. Safe sex, condoms, and of course there would be a cure eventually.

The mutations started appearing in the mid-90s. Instead of sexual transmission, air- or water-borne. A shift from the immune system to the respiratory system. Donna remembered the huge posters on the Carolina campus: SUPER-FLU: EVERYBODY NEEDS TO BE VACCINATED NOW. Rapid onset. Someone would feel a little bit sick in the morning and by nightfall, too ill to even try and get to a doctor—not that there were many doctors who weren't sick as well. The air became fetid and heavy with death, as people died in their beds, on the couch, on the bathroom floor. No one went out at night, rode subways, commuter trains. Malls depopulated. Anywhere large groups of people had once gathered were empty. Schools closed, universities sent students home. In the daytime, everyone who could find one wore a surgical mask. Donna remembered her next-door neighbors with red and blue bandannas over their faces. The president proclaimed martial law and armed masked troops were everywhere, shooting looters, carjackers, even the maskless.

But not everyone got sick. The big cities became dangerous places, but Donna remembered driving out in the Orange County countryside surrounding Chapel Hill and seeing healthy people, feeling safe. It was almost as if the Virus (no one called it AIDS anymore) was like a huge net of blinking lights laid over the earth. Where the lights blinked on, there was sickness and death. Where the lights blinked off, there wasn't.

The blinks were getting closer and closer together when the Lindauzi came.

Of course everyone loved the Lindauzi.

"We have to be at Kennedy tomorrow at nine A.M., Frank—you can come, can't you?" Donna asked. *I don't want to go up there alone.*

"Can I come? Can I come? Is the Pope Catholic? Miss out on one of the biggest stories since the Arrival and the Vaccine? Donnie, I mean, really. Honey, I will be there, cameras and recorders in hand. Space station here we come," Frank crowed. "Here's looking at you, kid," he said, lifting up his coffee cup. "Besides, it should be a hell of a ride."

*   *   *

Once the Lindauzi shuttle pilot said they could relax the seat locks, Frank couldn't sit still. He wanted to see everything on the shuttle, look out every window, take picture after picture of the waning Earth below and the waxing space station ahead. Both views, Donna had to admit, were spectacular. The Earth was beautiful: aquamarine blue, deep green, ruddy browns, the clouds like swirls of frosting. And the space station. Yes, it did look like an enormous bicycle wheel, but that was such a cliché, Donna thought. Every science fiction story she had ever read described space stations as bicycle wheels, hubs, spokes, rims. A man-made, no, Lindauzi-made star? A space starfish? A beautiful silver and grey and white starfish caught between the Earth and the Moon?

"Donnie—come here, you can see the night down on Earth, in Asia, I think, and the cities, like, like little glowing jewels—c'mon, Donnie, don't just sit there. We have this entire shuttle to ourselves and you are just going to sit there the whole time?"

"Coming, Frank," she said. Donna got up, sighing, knowing Frank wouldn't leave her alone until she came and saw the Asian night. Donna wished she were enjoying all this as much as Frank was. But the empty shuttle bothered her—weren't there other UN reporters, Europeans, South Americans, Asians—who should have been asked to be the first to tour the station? And UN officials—nobody from the Secretary-General's office? They were all coming later, Corviax had said just before takeoff; this was an advance trip, to make the station more familiar to the public. He had refused, again, to answer her questions about the station, telling her she would find a lot of her answers on the station, wait, be patient. Yes, but where are the materials coming from for this station—there aren't any huge mining and metal refineries working on the Earth, not so soon after the Virus and the Vaccine? The Moon, I told you that, Miss Radley, the Moon. The Moon—where— We will talk later, please, be seated. . . .

"It is beautiful, honey," Donna said, looking down at the Earth in shadow. Frank put his arm around her and squeezed. She squeezed back, thinking they were going to be on again, and maybe this time it would stick. Standing there beside Frank, she decided not to tell him her worries and suspicions again—at least not until they were home. And maybe this trip to the station would put it all to rest.

"Let's just sit here and watch, Frank, we've got about an hour left, don't we?"

"Yeah, let me go get some coffee. Be right back."

Or not to rest, Donna thought, still watching the Earth. There were just too many unanswered questions. Where were the materials for the station coming from? The Moon—or the Lindauzi fleet? And if it was the Fleet, as some thought, did this mean the aliens weren't planning on continuing their emigration anytime soon? Why were the Lindauzi offering genetic counseling to human parents? Just good will, Frank would have said, but it seemed like too much good will, Donna thought. And if you made a map of the outbreak of the Virus in the 90s, didn't it look awfully regular—as if there were some sort of unseen pattern? She had showed Frank her map and her graphs and he had just shaken his head, and told her she was really, really paranoid. Had she considered seeing a therapist? How effective was the Vaccine anyway —people were still dying, just not in such dramatic numbers. Or were they? Why were there so many mechanical failures in the communication satellites lately? News blackouts in Russia, China, Japan—

"Here, six creams, one sugar, just the way you like it—sweet, and a little coffee with your cream. Whatcha thinking about?" Frank said and sat down beside her.

"Oh, what we might see on the station—those factories Corviax talked about, the low-grav medical centers, that stuff. Look, Frank, you can see those space cranes now, God, they are huge."

"Yeah, they look like real cranes—those long sharp beaks, dipping, moving. Wow. It looks like we are headed directly for one of them—the docking clamps—I do have all the *Star Trek* videos —must be right by them."

"We are on final approach. Please lock your seats."

"That's a different voice, Frank," Donna said, as she automatically worked the arm controls so that the seat would constrict around her, a gentle vise to hold her in.

"Huh, what are you talking about?"

"The Lindauzi that just spoke—he, or she—I can't tell male and female voices apart—somebody different from the pilot."

"Donna, so? Maybe it's a recording. I imagine the pilot is kinda busy right now. God, look at that crane move—it must be moving a hundred tons of metal—look at that huge sheet, a wall, you think?"

"You're probably right. We're just about there—doesn't that crane look taller than the Empire State Building and the World Trade Center combined? And that metal wall or whatever it is . . ."

*   *   *

We interrupt this program for a special UN news bulletin. Two UN correspondents, Press Pool Liaison Donna Radley, and Education Reporter Frank Hawes, were killed in a tragic accident in space this morning. They were on a special assignment to the Lindauzi space station, having been invited there by Prince Corviax to make an advance report to the Secretary-General prior to official visits next month. Apparently the pilot of their shuttle became suddenly ill and flew off-course directly into the path of a construction crane. Death is believed to have been instantaneous.

Chapter V
Caleb, 17 October-25 December 2155

PAPA HAD TOLD CALEB STORY AFTER STORY ABOUT the Vaarchael family house and Kinsella, the plantation. Most of them were about Papa and Phlarx, his Lindauzu. Papa had told Caleb about the great Lindauzi city of Umium; he had told Caleb about Umium Station, practically another city in the sky, going around and around the Earth. Caleb had, however, grouped Papa's Lindauzi stories with the old fairy tales of magic carpets, winged horses, and sword-wielding princes and golden-haired princesses. Wonderful stories—and Caleb remembered every single one, every word, every change in inflection, or shift of eyebrows—but still stories, make-believe.

Now, below Caleb, beneath the golden domes, at the mouth of a great river by the ocean, was the Lindauzi city of Umium. It was almost too much to take in, to believe was real.

"It's the biggest city in the world," the hound repeated in a dry voice, in his funny-sounding American. "It's where the Crown Prince, the grandson of the Emperor, lives. Even Lord Morix himself must walk on four feet before the Emperor's grandson. Someday the Prince will take us all to our true home, Lindauzian. You're a lucky wolf-pup—you're a gift to the Crown Prince, a novelty, a Lindauzi-cursing wolf. . . ."

Caleb stopped listening to the hound, letting the man's words become background noise. Beneath the domes, drenched in their golden light, were buildings three and four times bigger than the Mall, made of the Lindauzi pink-and-red blocks. Flowers grew everywhere — in vines down the colored walls, in carefully laid out gardens; even the trees were in flower. Here and there, between the buildings, the flowers, the trees, fountains rose and fell in showers of water and light. The deep rich green grass looked as smooth and as soft as the black bear skin that Caleb knew had burned along with everything else in Jackson. The hound spoke into the main panel of the flyer, and to Caleb's surprise, the dome just ahead became wavy and loose, like golden smoke, and they flew in.

Father Art? Please listen. I'm almost inside this Lindauzi city. I know you won't be able to hear me inside. And, Papa, I need to look for him. Will You help me? Father Art, hold me in your hand, close to your chest, close to your heart.

Causeways of glass and metal connected the buildings: no stone paths cut through the grass. Inside the causeways, which looked like huge tubes, Caleb saw what had to be Lindauzi, and yes, they did look like great bears. And beside them, behind them, carrying, pushing: humans. Just like Papa had said. At the heels of the Lindauzi.

The Lindauzi and their humans were in the air as well. Flyers of every shape and size filled the air, ascending from and descending to the roofs of the buildings as the dome opened and closed. An airship even bigger than the one that had destroyed Jackson flew overhead, casting a dark shadow on Caleb and the hound.

"Look, wolf, there's something you will never see back at Kinsella — that big ship, there, going up. A shuttle to the space station," the hound said, pointing.

No, I'm sure I would never see such a ship in Kinsella, since I have never been there, you four-legged scum. But still Caleb looked as the red ship rose in a great arc. He knew where the station's path was in the night sky. Papa had pointed it out to him more than once.

"You can see the entire world from up there, Caleb. It's beautiful — blue and white and green, shining with sunlight."

Where is Papa? Will I find him here in this Umium place? Is this Morix the hound keeps talking about the same one from Papa's stories? Phlarx's papa? What am I going to do? What will I tell Papa when he asks me if I took care of Davy?

The hound landed his flyer on the roof of a great house, clearly the biggest building in Umium. He touched down so lightly Caleb wasn't sure they had landed until the hound told him to go ahead and get out, and not to go anywhere, to stay right by the flyer while he took care of some things.

Caleb took a few steps away from the flyer, just to show the hound *he* couldn't tell Caleb what to do, and looked at where he was. The hound hadn't landed far from the roof's edge; Caleb could see the city fanning out below. All but a few buildings he could see were in shades of pink and red. Didn't they ever get tired of the same colors?

Caleb looked behind the house, out to the sea. Far out in the water, on a little island, stood the statue of a very tall woman who held a torch in one hand. She was a human woman, not a Lindauza. Caleb wanted very much to know where she had come from and who had built her on the island and why.

The Lindauzi must love flowers. There are even flowers growing on that lady out there, curling around her torch; at least that's what it looks like. The air was heady and rich with the perfume of the flowers which were growing everywhere: up and around the linking tubes, the arches, down the walls. *I guess this is the house of that Emperor's grandson, the Crown Prince. I wonder if he's like the princes of the old stories, with a sword and a shield. How can I be given to anyone? What's going to happen to me?*

Papa tried to explain once.

"Do you own Max, son?" he had asked.

"Own him? Own Max?" Caleb had echoed, puzzled. "Well, he is my dog—yeah, he belongs to me. Is that what you mean, Papa?"

"Yes. The Lindauzi think of their humans the same way you think of Max—as their dogs. They call humans who aren't theirs wolves, remember? Wolves are wild."

"But I'm your son. Do I belong to you?"

"Belong to me? You don't belong to anybody but yourself, son. Nobody but yourself."

But Papa was Phlarx's. Am I going to be the Crown Prince's?

Caleb shook his head. The Lindauzi could think what they wanted. He would never belong to anybody.

All the rooms in Jackson would have easily fit onto the roof of the great house on which the hound had landed, with room to spare. Other flyers were parked here and there, and one landed and another took off as Caleb watched. A Lindauzi climbed out of the last to land and walked away with long purposeful strides.

Caleb wanted to see him up close, to put a real face to all the stories, but he only saw the Lindauzi's back and soon that was even out of sight.

The roof was a garden. Tall slender trees and bushes with delicate lacy leaves were enclosed in stone boxes. Caleb had never seen such trees: they were like none that grew anywhere near Jackson. The nearest tree's bark was silvery-white and shiny, so smooth and so shiny that Caleb wanted to stroke its trunk. The tree's deep burnished gold leaves—the gold of the water Caleb had seen from high in the air—were shaped like ten-pointed stars.

"I said not to go anywhere. Wolf, wait for me." The hound yelled at Caleb when he walked toward the trees, his hand out to pluck a leaf, to stroke the trunk.

He can't tell me what to do. His monster beasts aren't anywhere near, dirty four-legged butt-sniffing idiot. Yell all you want.

The bark was as smooth as Caleb had thought, but the star leaves didn't feel like oak or maple leaves: they were thicker and leathery. Caleb crushed one in his hand and watched it uncurl and smooth out as it had been before.

"I told you to stay put, wolf," the hound said and jerked Caleb away from the tree. The leaf fell heavily to the ground, not the lazy descent of the leaves knee-deep on Tate Street. "These aren't Earth trees, you little shithead. They're from the home world and some of them are fatal to dogs and wolves. Stupid."

"I am not a dog or a wolf. I'm a boy, a human boy. Don't call me a wolf. My name is Caleb Hulbert, the son of Ilox and Mary," Caleb grunted as he tried to twist away from the hound's grip.

"Huu-muns? There aren't any such creatures on Earth. Just dogs, wolves (and there are very few of *them* left), and Lindauzi. At least here on Earth, anyway. Now, come on. I am to deliver you to the house kennelmaster; he will present you to the Crown Prince. Then I can get out of here and back to Kinsella."

Max is—was a dog. Not me, you fur-faced jerk.

Keeping his grip tight on Caleb's forearm, the hound made Caleb walk across the roof. They passed more of the silvery trees and then a tree with flowers the size of Caleb's head, with wavy, feathery fringes. Some of the other trees had branches wiggling and twisting like snakes, and a few were covered with fragrant flowers whose scent was so heavy Caleb gagged and choked as they passed. Caged birds, for the most part, set silent and melancholy, even as their neighbors in the next cage, tiny, furry animals, squeaked and screeched. The cages were made of bars of light, vibrant and shining.

There's just too much. There's just too much to see, to hear, to remember. Papa's gone, Davy's dead. Aunt Sara, everybody in Jackson. I haven't even finished crying and here I am. That was two—three?—days ago? I can't even remember exactly how many days had passed since the hounds had come to Jackson. I am so so tired. I want Papa—

The hound hurried Caleb through the roof garden into a grove of silvery trees. In the middle of the trees was what Caleb thought was a little house, a hut, dark red, and set apart from the pink stone everywhere else. Above the little house the trees made a canopy of leaves, a darker silver, made luminous with almost pure white sunlight.

"Open," the hound said and the nearest wall seemed to slide apart. "Now, inside," the hound said and taking Caleb by the arm, led him through the new door.

"Down." The floor dropped, followed by the entire house, like a stone. Caleb pushed against the wall, his hand stuffed in his mouth. *I will not cry out, I will not let them know I am scared, I will not cry out. . . .*

When the little house stopped dropping, the hound and Caleb faced the beginning of a dark passageway that reminded Caleb of the shadowed passages in Jackson. There were four other passages, two on the left, two on the right. The hound, still holding Caleb's arm, stepped in the corridor directly facing them and slapped his free hand on the wall, which glowed a warm pink in response, a light that followed them as they walked, as if a halo of roses were trapped inside the stone. In just a short while, they turned into another corridor, then through wide white doors into, the hound said, the kennel offices. Four or five Lindauzi stood just past the doors, one at a green screen (what was that machine —com, computer, now he remembered), the others over its shoulder. Directly over their heads were bright, glowing globes suspended in the air. Caleb saw more of the floating lights all around the room. Around them were more computer screens and consoles, tall tables, then a glass wall—were those babies behind the glass?—

One of the Lindauzi turned around and looked directly at Caleb.

Caleb held both hands over his mouth to push down a scream. It was the first time he had ever really seen a Lindauzi face to face. Even seeing the back of the Lindauzi on the roof hadn't been enough. All the stories were true: tall, very tall, yellow fangs and claws, covered with fur, snouts or muzzles, not noses, dark golden eyes. Part of Caleb wanted to run as fast and as far as he could, but the hound never let go of his arm. Another part wanted to run the other way, to the Lindauzi. *What is wrong with me?*

"You're hurting me, let me go," Caleb yelled, surprised at finally finding his voice and that he could still be pretty loud. He didn't know where he would go if the hound released him; he just knew he would go.

"I said: shut up," and the hound clamped one hand over Caleb's mouth and then yelled himself when Caleb bit into his palm. By then the Lindauzi were hurrying across the room, their heavy boots and toeclaws thudding on the floor. Caleb became very still when they were upon him and the hound: furry black shadows out of his nightmares, out of all the whispered tales around the Jackson fires.

"Hound, what is this all about? Can't you see we are working? Why are you bringing this pup here? You are from House Vaarchael, the Viceroy's house; I see by your family mark. What are you doing here in the imperial palace with this strange pup?" the tallest Lindauzi said. Caleb thought it was male, by its dress and the deepness of its-his voice. His fur was black and his fangs, shining in the overhead light as if they were polished, protruded.

"My lords," the hound said, releasing Caleb and dropping to the floor to lie completely flat. Caleb thought the hound must be crazy. He held himself very still.

"My lords," the hound said again, raising his head when the tall black-furred Lindauzi nodded, "the Viceroy has sent me with this wolf-pup, a pup who speaks the civilized tongue and yet has until this morning lived in the wilds as an untamed beast. My lord said he was sending a message—"

"A message?" the tall Lindauzi said and turned to a shorter, red-furred Lindauzi beside him. "Chlavash, what do you know of a message from Kinsella?"

Chlavash sputtered, said he knew nothing but he would check right away and hurried off. When he returned, he held in his hand a small clear cube, which he quickly gave to the black Lindauzi.

"Well. What does the Viceroy have to say to the kennelmaster of the imperial palace," he said, and squeezed the cube until it glowed and turned smoky-white, its edges blurred and loose. They all waited as the cube re-arranged itself into the shimmering head of another Lindauzi who started to speak in formal, somber tones. The Viceroy.

"Well. So you can speak the civilized tongue, pup," the kennelmaster said after the white smoke image had finished speaking and the head had transformed itself back into the little cube. "Tell me your name."

"Caleb Hulbert, son of Ilox and Mary."

"It's true, a wolf Lindauzi-speaker. You have done as your lord asked, hound, you may go. We will take the pup and prepare him for presentation to the Crown Prince."

The hound left hurriedly, not looking back. Caleb watched him go, and when the white doors had closed behind the hound, turned to the three Lindauzi who formed a semi-circle facing him: the black tall one, the shorter red, who watched him, his head cocked to one side, and a blond-furred one.

All Caleb's clothes were taken away and destroyed, even down to his name-necklace, with his eleven years of beads. Caleb protested when the red Lindauzu cut it off, but the Lindauzu only rubbed his head and told him to be good. Then the Lindauzu took him to a cage whose bars were a lattice of light—light which Caleb now knew was unyielding and would repel him, making his skin hot and red. The light-lattice hummed as the birdcages on the roof had hummed.

His neck felt funny without his necklace and Caleb kept touching it, rubbing his skin where the necklace had left a faint circle. He didn't mind not having his clothes, casual nudity had been an everyday thing in Jackson. He had seen almost everybody naked at one time or another. But the necklace—how would he remember his age? And Papa had put on each year's bead himself. Caleb wanted to shake the light-bars and demand the red Lindauzu bring it back, but even to get close to the light made his skin too warm.

Caleb spent the night in the cage, curled up on a foam pad in the corner. He wanted to sleep, but couldn't. He kept remembering and remembering and remembering. There were a handful of other boys in the cage with Caleb, all of whom were much younger—no more than four or five, maybe six. Davy's age, more or less. They ignored Caleb and slept tangled together in a nest of pads.

After trying to sleep first on his left side and then his right, on his stomach, by counting backwards, Caleb finally gave up and rolled over on his back. He wished Papa would come and tell him a story—the soft sounds of his father's voice in the dark would always put Caleb to sleep. If Papa were here, Caleb thought, he

would ask him to tell a story about the summer country, the country where there were no Lindauzi and humans were safe, a story
Papa had learned from Mama. *It has white sands and a blue-green
sea and the sky is blue-white. When the waves come in, they make
long ribbons of foam on the beach, tumbling, falling, like houses
falling down. The sun burns hot in the sky and it is never cold there;
there is never any snow. To go to the summer country, first find the
great river in the middle of the land, the river that divides the land
into east and west. Follow the river all the way to the sea and then,
in a ship with wide sails, go southeast across the sea, past one green
island and another, until at last, you see more land, land like this,
bigger than any island. That land is the summer country. Sunlight
will dance on the water and the sand beneath your feet will be warm.
There will always be fruit hanging on the trees, fresh and sweet,
fruits whose names you won't know. You will never want for good
things to eat in the summer country. . . .*

When Papa told Caleb the story late at night, Papa's voice had
been low and soft, and each word had, in its undersounds, rest,
sleep, rest, let go, rest. It would be so dark in the family's space
in Jackson that Caleb could not see more than the outline of his
father's face, but that was enough. Now, here in this cage, Caleb
could not recreate the sounds of Papa's voice, and the words of
the story weren't enough. The cage was in a room the size of one
of the big stores at the Mall, and there were other cages, above
and below, and across, rows of cages, and some were empty and
some held children of different ages, boys and girls. Each cage was
made of the same humming light-lattices, a hard light, luminous,
and a green-tinged yellow. The humming seemed to bore in
Caleb's head; it didn't help to try and sleep under the foam pad.

*Papa, why didn't you come home? I wouldn't be here if you had.
Where are you?*

The next morning, the red Lindauzu, Chlavash, had to shake
Caleb awake.

"Get up, you need to be cleaned up, wolf, before you see the
Crown Prince today. Clean and well-dressed," Chlavash said as he
herded Caleb, groggy and yawning, down a corridor to a small box-
like room. "Step inside here."

"I know how to bathe," Caleb protested, but Chlavash ignored
him as he fingered the controls on the wall. The Lindauzu
stepped back and the door winked shut. Caleb thought water
would come out of the ceiling, but instead the room suddenly
filled up with a hard, fast wind that picked him up, wrapping itself
around him again and again and again. He was too terrified to

scream; Caleb just closed his eyes and wrapped his arms as tightly as he could around himself. When the wind subsided, his entire body tingled, and he had never felt so clean. The door winked open and Chlavash took him by the arm and led him out, and down more corridors, past a nursery, a toddler room, another with some of the boys who had been in his cage, labs, then a room with mirrors and clothes.

When Chlavash had finished dressing Caleb, the Lindauzu let the boy see himself in one of the mirrors. Unbroken mirrors of any size were a rarity in Jackson, and the few the tribe had were kept hidden away, being considered just as sacred and as precious as styrofoam cups and cans of Coors beer and books. Each family did have at least a small piece of an old mirror, and the Hulberts, being Readers, had several pieces, but none were big enough to see more than one's face. Caleb had, of course, seen almost all of his body when he looked down into the creek, but not like this. In the creek, his image was wavy and blurred, bleeding away at the edges with the current. Chlavash's mirror was as tall as the Lindauzu and clear and sure and unmoving.

The clothes Caleb saw on his body were unlike any he had ever seen—no furs, no skins. Caleb wore a dark blue tunic, all of one piece of cloth from his neck to just above his knees. The tunic's color made his eyes even bluer. A black belt at his waist. Soft grey leather boots on his feet. A grey cape around his shoulders. Everything felt soft and smooth. He looked so different, as if he should have a new name and not be Caleb Hulbert, son of Ilox and Mary. His dark brown curly hair was brushed and his olive skin shone from just a touch of an aromatic oil.

Caleb sniffed at his new smell.

"So you won't have a wild scent," Chlavash said, clearly pleased at how Caleb looked.

But Papa will still recognize me, won't he?

"Well, wolf, let's go meet the Crown Prince. When you see him, you will lie flat on your stomach, you will not look him in the eye—"

"I told you my name is Caleb," Caleb said, turning from the mirror to look up at Chlavash.

"Your wolf-accent is hard to understand, and your wolf-name is meaningless. Let's go. The Crown Prince is waiting. Do as I told you."

I won't lie flat on my stomach and I will look him in the eye if I want to. I think.

Chlavash took Caleb's hand and they walked through what Caleb thought was a maze of corridors, until they came to a set of rounded doors, which slid open when the Lindauzu placed his hand on a black circle. Inside was a small round room with a red floor. When the doors closed and the room began to rise, Caleb realized it was like the little house he had ridden down from the roof. He pressed himself against the curved sides, closing his eyes.

"The Crown Prince is looking forward to adding you to his collection," Chlavash said absently, peering down at his finger claws. "He loves to collect curious things," he added as he started to groom his chest fur, plucking out tangles and knots.

"What is this we are on?" Caleb asked, partially opening his eyes.

"This? On? Oh, you mean the lift—it carries people between floors; it's powered by machines. . . ."

Machines? Except for Lindauzi aircraft the only machines Caleb knew were mostly rusting scrap metal or marvels in stories. Crown princes belonged in the old stories, he remembered, and castles. Surely this great house was like a castle, and it had a prince, so it must be a Lindauzi castle. *I wonder if he will carry a sword and be girt with mail, have a winged helmet. . . .*

The actual meeting, after Caleb's mental wanderings, was something of a letdown. Chlavash led Caleb into an enormous room with a high, high ceiling. The pink stone of the walls was broken by tall windows, glowing with sunlight. Caleb could just see the rest of the city of Umium spreading out below and the sky, the blue wavy from the shield dome. Between the windows were pictures on cloth, in rich, vivid colors almost as bright as the sunlight. Caleb tried to figure out what the cloth pictures were about, but they were of unrecognizable things and Chlavash gave him no time to stop and look.

There were Lindauzi all over the place, sitting in front of computer screens and consoles, lights moving and rearranging before them. A huge globe turned slowly above one computer: it showed the entire Earth, just the way Papa said it looked, round and blue and white and green. Just like the globe that had been kept in Jackson, except there were no lines and words for the old human countries and cities. America had been the name for this part of the world, Caleb thought. Chlavash and Caleb walked through the middle of all the computers and the Lindauzi until they came to another door, which, this time, did not dilate or wink or slide apart. It seemed to be much older, and was made, Caleb saw, of wood, a dark carved wood. One of the prince's curios. Chlavash reached for a dull golden handle and simply pulled the door open.

wonder if the culling my father initiated — so many dead. Enough. Let me examine your teeth. Strong heart. Strong legs. Yes, he'll do fine. I'll enter him in the games this summer. Please send my thanks to the Lord Morix and tell the kennelmaster I want this one ready for the games here. That will be all," the Crown Prince said, and waved his hand at Chlavash and the door.

"Oh, yes, let me hear you curse," the Prince said, just before Chlavash opened the door.

"You miserable four-legged motherless whelp," Caleb blurted. Chlavash inhaled sharply. The Prince laughed.

"Excellent, even though your accent is atrocious. Who taught you?"

"My father."

"Where did he learn the civilized tongue?" The Crown Prince sat down at his desk and flicked on his screen.

"Kinsella. He was a throwaway. Could I ask you about Morix—"

"A cull, I thought so," the Prince said, looking intently at the figures appearing before him. "Thank you, Chlavash."

Caleb went out ahead of Chlavash, who closed the door behind him.

Caleb had stood very still while the Crown Prince had examined him, liking and hating the curious sensation of the royal claws on his skin. He tried to understand what the Prince had said; it reminded him of another Jackson story:

It had been at night by the fire, in front of the white columns. He sat by Papa, leaning against Papa's sure strong weight. Aunt Sara had closed her book and sat down. Another woman, Margaret Mary, stood immediately to begin her story. Caleb could not see or remember her face. She was on the other side of the fire — a shadow, a voice behind the flames and smoke. He closed his eyes when she began:

Before the Lindauzi came, we were free, to come and to go as we pleased, and no one owned us but ourselves. We walked the world and it was ours — the earth, the sky, and the sea. Our ships sailed above the clouds and below the waves; the earth yielded to our plows . . . Before the Lindauzi came, we walked on the Moon. . . .

Then another faceless voice, a man, picked up the story.

In the last years before the Millennium, the Disease, the Sickness, the Plague came, bringing with it choking fear and panic and closed doors and empty streets and death, death, death. There was no room in the hospitals; bodies were left by the road, in the

"Your Highness, Prince Orfassian, I come with a gift
Viceroy of Eastern One," Chlavash said and dropped to
"Lie on your stomach, like I said," he hissed to Caleb. "D

"No."

"I said—lie on your stomach," Chlavash growled and
up to yank Caleb to the floor.

"Cease, Chlavash, and stand upright yourself."

Caleb turned in the direction of the new voice. A Li
who looked a little shorter than most of the others had st
from behind a solid black desk, which seemed to be made
rock. This Lindauzu wore what Chlavash had told Caleb
blue Madaanic stone on a silver chain around his neck. H
older than any Lindauzi Caleb had seen so far. His muzz
grey and the crest down his neck and back was also grey a
The Lindauzu, like every Lindauzu Caleb had seen, was
chested and wore black leggings, and when he stepped out
behind the desk, Caleb could see the familiar high boots, with
truding toeclaws.

Chlavash stood slowly and with lowered head presented
Prince with the same cube he had retrieved for the kennelma
After watching and listening to the same message, the Pr
nodded and came over to inspect Caleb as he stood by Chlav

"A wolf-pup. A wolf who speaks Lindauzi, found down so
in the ruins of—what was the name of that place near Kinse
What was the name used for that region, Caro, Call, no matt
the Prince said, and dismissed the old name with a slight gestu
Greensboro, Carolina, Caleb thought. *Easy enough words to
member.* "And my Lord Morix sends this pup to me as a gift f
my collection of curios. Well, let's see what we have here."

Morix? The Morix in Papa's stories?

Caleb stepped back when the Prince touched him, recoilin
from the feel of the claws on his skin. *Don't touch me, I don't wan
you to, but your fur, it looks so soft.* Caleb froze, having no ide
what to do.

"It's all right, pup, it's all right. He must have a Lindauzi-bred
parent, a cull, perhaps. Even so, they have always been like this
ever since our arrival, afraid, not wanting and yet wanting. We
have bred for the wanting, the knowing, and in his generation, it's
finally becoming predominant. The Lord Madaan willing, it is not
too late—but never mind, such things are not your worry,
Chlavash, and certainly not this pup's. Perhaps this one doesn't
have a tamed parent—the potential has always been there. I

*park, on the beach, and there was great lamentation and wailing and
cries for help across the Earth . . . And the tall red Lindauzi ships
came from the night's stars into the heart of our cities. They had
heard us, they said, in their ships traveling between one sun and the
next, they had heard us, and came to help. . . .*

*They were kind and gentle and good and so wise, and they helped
us, slowed the dying, and they loved us. They loved us. . . .*

Another voice:

*The dying will only end, they said, if we came and lived with
them in their great red houses. Come and live with us, and let us
love and care for you. And we did. We left our ships, our fields, our
houses, for love of the Lindauzi. We left our books, our paintings,
our songs, for love of the Lindauzi. And so that no more would die.*

Another voice:

*But a few of us didn't love, couldn't love, wouldn't love the Lin-
dauzi. Better to die than be kept, to leave our ships and fields and
houses and books and paintings and our songs. It would be better to
die.*

Another voice:

*A man would stop his car and leave it by the road. A woman
would stand up from her desk and walk out the door for love of the
Lindauzi. We laid our lives at their feet for love of the Lindauzi. . . .*

Another voice:

*But some of us have never loved the Lindauzi. We will never take
the collar. . . .*

There followed a time for Caleb that was like a long grey dream,
which gave him little time to think about himself and even less
time to mourn for Davy and worry about would he ever find his
father. The memories and the tears did come, as sharp and as
clear as broken glass, but only in isolated moments, late at night
or early in the morning or between things, when Caleb was waiting. None of the Lindauzi ever understood why his eyes welled
up: Was the pup hurt? Had he been hurt? Was he sick?

"It's Papa and my brother Davy, I miss them—"

They dismissed his words. No dog knew its sire and dam, and
only a short time was spent with its litter-mates. What was there
to grieve? Now, if the dog's Lindauzi died or was hurt, well, that
was another matter altogether. And besides, there were important
things at hand for this pup. He was being trained to compete in
the summer games.

The kennelmaster made Chlavash personally responsible for

Caleb's training. "Remember, that he belongs to the Crown Prince does not guarantee an automatic gold. The judges are scrupulously fair. A gold medal for this pup is honor for the Prince and wealth for you. This is your first solo training job, Chlavash."

Caleb trained every day with Chlavash in the kennel gymnasium. He learned how to walk: back straight, eyes forward, hands at his side. He learned how to turn so that the lines of his neck would be accentuated. He learned how to show the lines of his body and the muscles in his legs and his back. He learned how to walk naked and clothed since he would compete both ways at the game. Caleb practiced tricks with hoops and hurdles, climbing and swinging on bars, and he dove and swam. Some days they practiced outside, on the palace roof, beneath strange trees of which some were from Earth and some from Lindauzian or other worlds on which Lindauzi had once lived.

He could not tell one day from another. Every day beneath the city dome was the same and the days had no names or numbers that Caleb could remember. The trees had no fall colors, no leaves dropped off to drift to the ground. They were always green or silver or golden or white and the flowers always bloomed. Once or twice Caleb caught a glimpse outside the city, across the river: bare, grey, and cold. Was it November or December? Caleb wasn't sure and even though Chlavash told him over and over, Caleb could never remember the names of Lindauzi months. Caleb wondered, too, as he ran or swam or jumped or climbed, about the human Lady festooned with Lindauzi flowers on her tiny island in the sea. Once Chlavash took Caleb to swim in the ocean, but the water was freezing and Caleb couldn't see the Lady anywhere.

"But why, Chlavash? Why am I doing this? Why do I have to walk naked in a big circle in front of Lindauzi judges? Why do I have to run and jump over those little fences? Carry that torch? And do those tricks on those bars?" Caleb asked one morning some two or three months after his arrival in Umium. He especially hated the bar tricks. At least today they were training on the palace roof and Chlavash had Caleb running a long course through the trees, in, around, back, circle upon circles. They had taken a break at the roof's edge and Caleb was trying to see past the dome outside: was it raining? Was that lightning in those clouds out over the sea?

"I miss rain. I'd rather be caught in it than do these stupid exercises over and over."

"Dogs don't ask such questions, Caleb (Caleb had insisted the red Lindauzu learn his name and had won when he simply refused to do anything unless Chlavash did). You belong to the Prince. He wants to win gold with his tamed wolf in the summer games. You will be the one and maybe the last wolf there—especially if the next wolf eradication is done on schedule—but who knows if that will happen—there is a new outbreak of reversions, a fever this time. Never mind. Come, let's go down to the pool, I want you to swim now. Here, wipe off with this towel while we take the lift down."

Caleb took the towel and let it wipe off his sweat. The first time Chlavash had put one of the semi-living creatures on him, Caleb had screamed. Chlavash had taken him to the pool for the first time. It was in one huge room, one level below the kennel, and was surrounded by a tiled deck and platforms at different levels. Balls of various sizes lay here and there—for training coordination, Chlavash had explained. They had the pool to themselves.

"Only dogs swim here," Chlavash had explained. "Lindauzi don't like having wet fur."

Because you smell so bad when you do.

Caleb swam for an hour, using slow, sure strokes. Then he floated on his back, staring up into the pink-and-white ceiling.

"Time's up, Caleb. Here, use this to dry off," Chlavash had called, holding out what appeared to be a thin, furry irregularly-shaped white cloth, about as long as Caleb was tall.

It moved when it touched Caleb's bare skin, a slow, sucking crawl.

"Caleb! Come back here, I should have explained, I forgot you have never seen one before. It's all right, the towel won't hurt you. Caleb!"

Chlavash explained when Caleb walked back, warily, from behind the nearest platform. The towels were alive and they weren't. They moved in response to body heat, feeding on moisture and the tiny flakings of skin that were shed every day. Towels, the hovering glowglobes, the burrowers living even farther below, hauling waste, were all creatures, genetically engineered for particular purposes, the Lindauzi had brought from their home world. Towels kept you dry.

"Made? How do you make something like this towel animal?" Caleb had asked.

"Breeding, gene surgery, DNA splicing."

"Huh?"

"Never mind. It won't hurt you. Just let it dry you."

Now Caleb liked the way towels caressed his skin. He didn't tell Chlavash what he let the towels do at night.

"Wolf eradication? What do you mean?" Caleb asked as the lift dropped. There, dry. He pulled the towel off and let it drop to the floor and pushed it away. It whimpered and tried to wriggle back toward him, but Caleb pushed it away again. After the second push, the towel bunched up on the floor and sniffled, occasionally sticking out a pseudopod or two.

"Here we are," Chlavash said when the lift stopped and its doors opened. "Don't leave it there—you know how badly they smell when they die." Towels, if not in contact with either other towels—seeing a tank of the writhing creatures once had given Caleb nightmares—or any living flesh, died and rotted. "What did you ask me about?" Chlavash asked as they started walking to the pool. He had a compad in his hands and was busily making a note on Caleb's training progress.

"Wolf eradication."

"I don't know why I bother answering all your questions," Chlavash said, looking up from his figures. Caleb waited and said nothing. He had been watching Chlavash for the past few weeks and was sure the Lindauzu was more than a little anxious for Caleb to do well in the games. Caleb was also sure the Lindauzu liked him and liked talking with him, but only when they were alone. If Caleb asked Chlavash any question other than the very routine when another Lindauzi was present, the red Lindauzu ignored or laughed and said something about how clever pups were.

"Wolves are nuisances and pests. They occupy valuable land needed for expansion and they destroy things—Lindauzi crops, plantation fields, flyers. They steal pups, kill hounds. The Lindauzi have been on this world for over one hundred and fifty orbits and still large territories in the optimally inhabitable zones are unused—because of wolves. They have to be eradicated—or should be. But it is being delayed—I forgot your swimming clothes, never mind, swim naked, here we are, (and there's the kennelmaster) give me the towel—with this new reversion fever there aren't enough Lindauzi to supervise the hounds to do the continental eradication the Prince wants. Now, swim—oh, hello, yes, kennelmaster, he is doing well. . . ."

The kennelmaster had been waiting to talk with Chlavash at the pool. Caleb stepped away from the two Lindauzi, stripped,

and eased himself into the pool. He wanted to ask what a reversion fever was, but Chlavash wouldn't respond with the kennelmaster present. Caleb started swimming on his back. That way all
he could hear was the water, the faint sound of the pool's pumps.
*This fever, I hope it makes them all sick, so sick they will never be
able to kill any humans again. The Lindauzi want to hunt them
down with their hounds, just like the Jackson hunters killed the deer,
the rabbits, and the possums. But they aren't going to cook the meat
and tan the skin. The Lindauzi want to just kill them.*

The fever wouldn't stop them. The airships would come out of
the sky, with their attendant flyers around them like angry wasps
with laser-stingers of fire. They would find the humans in the
ruins of the old cities, in burrows and warrens beneath the streets,
in caves in the hills, in huts by the sea. Would even the Summer Country be safe? These were the places where the stories
said humans still lived, free from the Lindauzi. Jackson had
been such a place, and the Covenant-keepers and the Footwashers had lived in such places. These weren't just old tales
passed down, but told by wandering story-tellers, links between
one tribe and the next, immune from tribal hates and distrusts,
promises in the shadows of the burrows that they weren't alone.
    The airships would blast open the burrows and burn down the
hovels. And the flyers would fly low over the ground, shooting
down those who tried to run. Then the beasts would be released,
to continue the killing, to be sure no one, not even a baby hidden
behind a fallen door or a rock, remained alive. Then, when all
were dead and just the fires burned, sending up dying trails of
smoke, the hounds would take the heads.
    No one would be left alive.
    Caleb's dreams came back that night: the fire, the blood, the
screams, the headless bodies, and the great force-field sack of
heads rising up in the air. And the search for Davy in the shadows
and the smoke and the sticky blood. Carrying the body out and
down the steps, wondering what his face would have looked liked
dead. Laying Davy on the ground as he dug the grave. Wanting
to touch Davy's face.
    Chlavash came the third night of the nightmares at the re-
quest of the kennel night attendant. Caleb was making noise and
keeping the others awake.
    "That pup has screamed and cried three nights in a row. Then
he wakes up and he does not sleep; he just sits. See? The way he

is sitting now, in the corner of the cage. He will not be ready for the games if this goes on, Chlavash. He will be too sick."

Chlavash nodded and dismissed the attendant, a grey-haired dam, and pressed the control to release the light-lattice. Caleb did not look up as Chlavash crossed the cage floor. Caleb's cage wasn't in the huge room where he had spent the first night weeks ago, nor did he share his cage with other pups. The favored pup of the Crown Prince now had a special private cage, a room all his own immediately below Chlavash's own quarters.

"Caleb? Caleb? Why are you crying? The night-attendant said she thought you were having nightmares."

"Go away, killer."

"Killer? I have never killed any living thing," Chlavash said as he eased himself down on the floor by Caleb. He wrapped his long arms around his legs and leaned his head toward Caleb.

"Lindauzi and Lindauzi hounds killed my brother, my family, my tribe, took Papa—killers, killers, *killers*." Caleb threw himself at Chlavash with the last word, ripping at his fur, jerking his crest.

"What? Caleb?" Chlavash grabbed Caleb's arms, flipped him around, and held Caleb against his chest until the boy was still. Caleb tried to twist away, but it was no use. He sagged, spent, completely empty.

"Tell me about your dreams, tell me why you are crying, why you can't sleep. Tell me why you tried to hit me, called me a killer. I didn't kill your litter mate, your sire, your dam. I have never killed anybody. I am only Chlavash, your trainer," the Lindauzu said and chucked Caleb's head with his chin.

His fur is soft and his arms feel like Papa's felt when he hugged me, when Mama hugged me, nobody's touched me since, nobody, he's a monster, a killer, they hunt us down . . .

"There, there, Caleb-pup, it's all right, it's all right," Chlavash said in a low deep voice and slowly began to rock back and forth, back and forth.

Caleb woke up alone. He thought it was dawn, by the grey light in the room. There were no windows in Caleb's cage, but always after the light turned from black to grey, Chlavash would come with breakfast.

Where is Chlavash?

Caleb shuddered, remembering what had happened last night: the nightmares, crying, and Chlavash holding him, rocking him, like a baby, like he had rocked Max.

What am I supposed to do? Papa, tell me what to do. You lived with the Lindauzi and they threw you out. You said you would have run away if they hadn't thrown you out first.

He rolled over and stood, stretching, and then pulled on his exercise breechclout. Chlavash said he was growing, and if he didn't protect himself, he could get hurt. Kicking at a drowsy towel, Caleb paced back and forth in the room. Chlavash would be there soon with food and drink and then off to the gymnasium or the pool or the roof park. Practice, practice, practice. And he was just a boy in an enormous Lindauzi house.

"Caleb, you can do anything you want. Remember that," Papa said. "You can do or be anything you want. The only limits you have are those you set yourself."

OK, Papa, but I'm scared.

"Being brave doesn't mean not being scared. Being brave means going ahead, even though you are scared."

There was a noise out in the hall. Chlavash, talking with the dam who watched him at night. Caleb knew just how Chlavash walked, the way his toeclaws scratched, the huffy way he breathed. *He needs to exercise, not me.*

All right, Papa, I'll figure something out. I promise.

Interchapter 5
2061

From the Journal of Corviax luOrfassian laSardath luCorviax Alerian, Crown Prince of Lindauzian, Heir to the Left Throne, Supreme Commander of The Search Fleet, the 60th local year since the Arrival, 11 Flowermoon 11453, Lindauzi reckoning,

Fifty local years have passed since the inception of the Project. Sixty local years since the Arrival of the Lindauzi on this planet. Whether today is actually 11 Flowermoon 11453 Lindauzi reckoning is open for debate among the astronomers on Umium Station. And does it matter? I will not see Lindauzian again.

I am old. My muzzle and crest and the tips of my ears are white. I was young when we left Lindauzian and middle-aged, if the years in sleep aren't counted, when we found these star-cousins of the Iani. Sixty years we watched and waited, released the plagues and now there have been sixty years more. It is harder to concentrate, to write this takes much longer than it did before. The medics say it is a residual effect of the sleep viruses; I say it is old age.

It is probably both.

I am tired.

I will not see the Project's end. I will not see the salvation of my species, the recreation of the bond: heart to heart, mind to mind, soul

to soul. I do not know how many more years, local or Lindauzi (there is little difference, a matter of days) I will have.

Orfassian—I wonder if he has the same hardness of vision? There is more culling of the star-Iani to be done—can he order the release of more plagues, knowing only one in five will receive vaccines? Can he continue the pogroms?

The bond is here; I know it. Already they become our companion pets—just as we once were theirs millennia ago.

We must hold on, resist the allure of reversion. I know it has its own appeal: to let go, to give into to the dark, to release the burning light, to drop the weight of intelligence. Reversion nibbles away at the edges of our consciousness, frays our souls.

I have wanted to yield myself.

Orfassian must be strong.

These star-Iani must become even lonelier, need us even more. New plagues—for their own pets—are ready.

There. I have sent the order; they will be released.

I am so tired.

But my vision lasts—Lindauzi and Iani, stronger together than alone. Heart to heart, mind to mind, soul to soul.

Chapter VI
Ilox, 2140-2142

I HAVE NOBODY TO TALK TO.
 I dream of those bodies in the snow.
　　But there was Nivere, another dog—another human, Ilox thought. Older, seventeen to his fifteen, and female, but who else was there? They were the only companion pets on Kinsella. Morix had never replaced Sandron and Ossit was dead. There were hounds and menials of one kind or another, and the pups bred in the kennels, bred to be companions, yes, but sold by the age of seven.

　　Would Nivere talk to him? She had to listen, she had to.

　　And there was the *other* thing: her body, his body, wanting to touch her, growing hard when he thought about touching her, and the *other* dreams—

　　Never mind, Ilox thought as he sat in the window, Phlarx asleep across the room, the night sky still black. *I will talk to her, tomorrow, no, next week, Phlarx said he and Tyuil were going alone with their father to that city in the far north, by the lake.*

Ilox and Nivere both watched Tyuil and Phlarx and Morix board the family air yacht early one morning a week after Ilox and Phlarx had returned from Umium Station. Phlarx had not wanted

150

to go to the north, Ilox had only been home a week, why couldn't Ilox go?

"It is one day and one night, Phlarx, and this is a family matter and you must go with your sister. Ilox will be fine," Morix had said, clearly irritated. "I told you this before Ilox came home. I will not discuss this farther. Grow up, Phlarx."

"It's all right, it is just one day and one night," Ilox had said, echoing Morix, to Phlarx that morning, as they lay in bed, Phlarx idly playing with Ilox's hair. "You'll be home tomorrow after morningmeal."

"I know, Lox," Phlarx said, not looking at Ilox, but at the long strand of bright hair in his claws. "I know."

The outer door to the yacht closed, clinking shut and sealing. Then there was a hiss of smoke, the legs retracted, and slowly, almost clumsily, Ilox thought, like the bumblebees in the gardens, the yacht rose in the cool morning air.

"I wish we were going with them," Nivere finally said when the yacht was at the height of the nearby trees. "But we can't. Dogs are dogs and Lindauzi are Lindauzi."

"Why is that, do you suppose," Ilox said slowly and carefully, not looking at Nivere, but at the yacht which was turning and extending its flight wings. He gulped—now or never. "Why are things so that dogs must always do what Lindauzi say? If I could show you something about dogs and Lindauzi, something that, well, it would make things look different, would you come and look?" *Please, please.*

Nivere was silent for a long moment, until the air yacht was out of sight. She stared at her fingers as if she had never seen them before. Finally she turned and looked at Ilox. "You're crazy. You know why dogs always do what the Lindauzi say. It's just how things are."

"But, Nivere, it hasn't always been that way. I can prove it. In the library here, I can show what I found in the station library: old memories of when the Lindauzi came to Earth. They haven't always been here; we were here first. Just dogs—humans, that's our real name—nobody else. Then the Lindauzi came and everything changed. I can show you—tonight, after eveningmeal."

Even though the Vaarchael house was pretty much theirs, and no menial would argue with the companion pets of the children of Lord Morix, something told Ilox that they shouldn't just walk into the library. This investigation had to be totally secret: no menial should be able to casually mention to Morix she saw

Nivere and Ilox roaming among the memory walls. And definitely no Lindauzi. Ilox knew the white-furred plantation priest sometimes would be in the library. Explaining their presence to a priest —no.

"Well?" Ilox said, watching Nivere. She said nothing for a long, long time. She ran her fingers through her thick black hair, smoothed her clothes, re-scrutinized her fingers.

"I'll go with you, Ilox, but only to show you that you're wrong," she finally said.

"Fair enough."

After the eveningmeal, being very careful not to be seen, stopping once when a floating tray drifted by, Nivere and Ilox crawled through an air duct grate just outside Nivere's room, which was one floor up and over from the library. The grates were for house menials to service the huge tubes that laced through the house like veins and arteries, pulsing with warm and cool air. In a few minutes, cobwebs and dust on their faces and clothes, they were at the grate Ilox knew was up on a library wall. He eased the grate back into the duct and then started to back down the wall service ladder, a series of rungs from the grate to the floor.

Nivere slipped once coming down the ladder. For too long a moment, she swung back and forth, barely gripping the rung. Finally she managed to swing herself back and get both hands on the handrails. Ilox was above her, clenching his teeth, choking back any words. There was nothing to say or do; there was no way he could have helped her.

"You know, if this were a house for dogs, you wouldn't have slipped," Ilox said when they were both standing on the floor, the open air duct above their heads. Glowglobes that had been clustered on the ceiling were dropping down above them.

"What are you talking about, a dog house?"

"This house, except for the rooms we sleep in, was not made thinking about us. Think about it, Nivere. Look at these handgrips, the rungs," he said.

"So?"

"They aren't made for hands like ours. They are made for Lindauzi hands, hands with retractable claws. The controls on the lift are for claws, not fingers like ours."

"But why should they be for dogs? Dogs aren't supposed to climb up and down in here—and we really shouldn't be in the library at all. Why did I let you talk me into this?" Nivere said, frowning at Ilox. "I should just go now, before we get in trouble."

"Wait. Please, you said you would look at what I found. You'll see. That wall cluster, we'll start there," Ilox said quickly and took her hand and led Nivere across the room before she could change her mind. She watched as Ilox laid his hand on a dark circle on the first wall of the five in the cluster. The circle changed color when he touched it. Then a menu appeared, with a list of questions to be answered to initiate a memory search.

"Voice or manual?" The question came from the wall itself, in low Lindauzi tones.

"Voice," Ilox said. "Earth, Continent One. Time: Before the Lindauzi Arrival. People: native inhabitants. Chronological. There, now the wall will think a bit and sort the data. Nivere—think. The beds are always too long for us. No dog could fly an air-car because we can't make the necessary sounds for voice-operation. How many times have you asked Tyuil a question and she just didn't understand. They don't think the way we do. Ah, here it is. A dog city, Nivere. No Lindauzi anywhere. New York, I think."

Ilox and Nivere spent hours reading and watching the pre-Lindauzi memories. He took her through the years of the sickness, the deaths, then the Lindauzi Arrival, and what he called the Change when dogs (humans, humans, humans, we must use that word. We are *not* dogs) lost their world to the Lindauzi. Then Ilox called up even older memories of a time long before the Lindauzi Arrival.

"See, we walked on the Moon; we made the spaceship that traveled there. And those big skinny airships, with the long wings—dogs made those, dogs—humans—made those and flew them everywhere. They took everything away from us—"

"Stop, just stop it. Do you know what you are saying, Ilox?" Nivere screamed. "The Lindauzi love us, and we love the Lindauzi. You love Phlarx, I love Tyuil, and they love us, you know that. They would never hurt us—"

"Tyuil and Phlarx didn't do this badness in the past, I know that. But if Tyuil died, they would put you down. What happened to Lian when old Ahain died? The old priest before this one? Do you remember?"

Nivere nodded her head dully, and pressed back against the wall behind her. They were sitting with their backs to one wall, facing another. In front of them was a frozen image of a dog schoolroom. A dam stood in front of the room, writing in strange letters on a green board. Pups were writing on rectangular white sheets, sitting at what looked like wooden desks. Ilox looked at Nivere and she turned her face away.

Lian had not been much older than Nivere was now and had come from another kennel. When Ahain had died, Lian had cried and cried and cried; he refused to eat, to drink. Ilox found the older dog in the house gardens, on a stone bench, his face in his hands, rocking back and forth, moaning.

"Eat, Lian, please. Here, I brought you some bread. Please." Ilox had begged, but Lian didn't stop rocking or moaning. The next day the house vet came for Lian. It was done very quickly. Lian was still sitting in the garden, still crying, still refusing to eat. Ilox saw Lian and the vet from the window in Phlarx's room. The vet pulled a dermic from a kit on her hip and pulled back Lian's head and pressed the tip of the dermic to his neck. Ilox remembered when she had done that to him, how cool it had felt and his surprise at the sudden intense warmth in his neck, and how quickly the warmth faded.

She held the dermic against Lian's neck for a long moment, and then pulled it away. He went limp and slumped in her arms. Very gently, it seemed from the window, the vet laid Lian's body on the bench and then signaled to two menials who came out and carried Lian away. Ilox watched as they carried the body to the recycler.

"Remember? When a dog's Lindauzi dies, we are always sent to Lord Madaan and the Forest with them."

"Yes," she said dully, "I remember. I don't want to believe any of this. I mean, I came here because I was sure you were wrong, that you had made a mistake or made it all up. And I came because I wanted something to do while Tyuil was gone; I didn't want to be bored waiting for her all day. These records in these particular memory walls are true, they are history records—see the label there. Over there, fiction. But they love us, and we love them. I am so, so confused."

"I don't know what to do, either, but I had to tell somebody else. It was too much to know by myself."

"Everything I ever believed is wrong, Ilox. I wonder what else they lied about—we need to come back and find out, don't we?" Nivere said.

"We can't come in the daytime, Nivere, not and stay and look up stuff. No dogs are allowed to do that. Morix would be furious."

"Then we come back at night. After Tyuil and Phlarx are

asleep. We'll time ourselves to be sure we get back before morning. That's what we will do."

Ilox smiled, glad he had convinced Nivere to come back and that now it all seemed to be her idea. It didn't matter; now he wasn't alone. They probably wouldn't get caught. That a pet might leave their Lindauzi in the middle of the night, crawl through an air duct, sneak into a forbidden place, and then do such forbidden things as read and watch forbidden records was unthinkable. No Lindauzi would ever suspect a fifteen-year-old boy and an seventeen-year-old girl to even think of such things, let alone carry them out.

They sat very still for a long time, side by side. Their glow-globes were so close together over their heads that the light created a half-moon around them. After forever Ilox reached out with his left hand and very gently and very slowly and carefully placed it over Nivere's right hand and squeezed. She looked at him and smiled back.

Will she let me touch her again? I have wanted to do this for so long it hurts.

Without letting go of her right hand, Ilox very slowly turned her face with the side of his right hand. *It's like everything we are doing is underwater, slow, soft, in thick air.*

"I saw in the dog—human, we have to remember and use that word, at least between us, we are humans—in the human records, adults do this. And I have seen a few adult menials do it, too," he murmured.

"Touch like this?" Nivere said, her voice equally soft and low. She touched Ilox's face then, tracing the curve of his jaw, the folds of his eyes, the shapes of his lips.

"Yes. And I saw them do this." Ilox placed his mouth on hers, once, gently, and pulled back.

"Yes. I caught two menials doing it, but they did it longer—like this," she said. Nivere put her mouth over Ilox's and moved her lips over his. "They got caught—the Lindauza, it was Ossit, was really mad."

"The Lindauzi don't touch mouths, do they?"

"They rarely touch each other. Just us. No, not there, not yet. It makes me feel too strange," Nivere said.

Ilox shrugged and put his hand back on her face. As she had done, he traced her lips, her ears. He kissed her again.

Nivere kissed him back, parting his lips with her tongue.

"What, oh what are we doing to each other?"

"I don't know," Ilox whispered, shifting his weight to alleviate the pressure in his groin. He was afraid to ask her to touch him there the way he touched himself, the way the vet's semen sampler had touched him.

Ilox and Nivere stayed in the library until it was almost light. They kissed and touched each other's faces and held hands for a long time. Then they slept.

Ilox woke first, to his groin ache. There's something else, he thought. Would there be more memory-images of humans together like this somewhere? They would just have to look.

"Tomorrow night, after midnight, we'll come back," Nivere said, standing and yawning.

"I'll meet you at the duct near your room," he said and got up to follow her up the ladder. Both climbed up very slowly and carefully, making sure they had a tight grip on each bar before going up to the next one. It was a long fall to the library floor.

"Can't you *ever* feel them, Nivere?" Ilox whispered the next night, his voice low in the dark. They had been in front of one of the memory walls when, at Ilox's sudden insistence, they had torn across the room, scrambled up the ladder and through the open grating.

"You feel them right now?" Nivere had asked when Ilox had demanded they run.

"*Now*. Lindauzi are just outside—if they catch us—come on," he had said and grabbed her hand. The images on the wall vanished behind them, responding to his urgently hissed command. Ilox hadn't wanted to leave either; the pre-Arrival dog (he gave up on using the word "human," he kept forgetting to say it instead of dog) memories they had been watching had been about interpersonal behavior: male and female, male and male, female and female, young and old. Male and female was what they had wanted to see. And being with her and watching the male and the female touching, Ilox felt like he was putting his entire body directly into wall circuitry again. Just being close enough to touch her again—

At least she believes me now about what happened when the Lindauzi came to Earth. How they changed us.

A dim light glowed beneath them, shining up through the grating. Ilox had just set it back in its place. He peered through the metal crossbars at the three Lindauzi huddled together before one wall. Not the wall that he and Nivere had been standing before. What were they doing in the house library so late? Morix, a priest, another priest.

"Feel them? You've asked me that a hundred times, Lox; no, I can't feel them, see them, or hear them. Not when they are just outside the library, out in the corridor. Not when they are in the next room. I can tell, sometimes, how Tyuil feels—especially when she is really happy or very unhappy. Times when she seems to want me the most. But now, no, you know I couldn't tell the Lindauzi were coming to the library. What are you feeling? What do you feel when you feel them?" Nivere asked, leaning back against the metal wall, her breathing finally slowing down. She closed her eyes and pressed her hands against her face and then through her dark coarse hair, each movement slower and calmer than the one preceding it.

"At the worst, when I first got sick, it was like they were inside my head, pushing me. I burned all over. Now, it's just a sudden prickling, a flush of heat, except for Phlarx," Ilox explained. He sat back against the wall beside her after checking one more time to see if the Lindauzi below were leaving—not that it mattered if he looked. Ilox would know when they left.

"The vet on Umium Station explained it to me when the drugs finally took effect. We're being bred for an empathic bond with the Lindauzi. It's always been part of us, but raw, unenhanced, hit or miss, latent. The vet said it was like experiencing something in a dream. Well, it woke up in me. I'm one of the first to fully manifest this latent trait. Its manifesting has something to do with my body changing from a boy to an adult. Now that I'm older, I don't need the drugs anymore, but they don't think I would ever be happy in Umium. So many Lindauzi, all wanting that bond, but it's meant for just one dog and just one Lindauzi. You know, I can almost tell what Phlarx is thinking now. It's what they want from us, Niv; that's why I spent the last two years on the station."

"I missed you, Lox," Nivere said, and stroked the side of his face with the back of her hand. "Can you sense when they leave?"

"Yes, oh, yes. Did I miss much in Umium?" he asked plaintively, taking her hand in his. "Ah, there, they're gone, Niv," Ilox said, pulling away from her to look down through the grate. "The last one has left—see the glowglobes dimming. I don't think they will be back tonight. Come on." He and Nivere climbed hastily down the ladder and waited impatiently for two of the clustered glowglobes to sense their presence and drop down to be their personal haloes. Then they crossed the room and made their way through the maze of walls.

"Planet: Earth. Time: Pre-Lindauzi Arrival. Native records, native interpersonal behavior, male and female, voice and motion program, begin from where most recent query was stopped."

They were soon seeing what they wanted to see: adult dogs, males and females, touching each other, as Nivere and Ilox had touched each other, but there were ways they hadn't learned, ways Ilox had guessed about, but had not been sure of. Now they knew.

This is the end of our childhood, the last bit of our innocence. Ilox held Nivere's hand. He could feel her excitement; it matched his own. Their two energies merged: twisting like two bolts of lightning lacing together in the sky. He turned to her then, as he started to pull his tunic over his head, and laughing, for no reason either could later explain, they tumbled to the floor in a tangle of clothes, arms, and legs.

Ilox awoke first and sat up. Nivere was still asleep and he carefully covered her with her tunic. Was this love he felt for her? It felt akin to what he felt for Phlarx, but only akin. Why was it different? Why did no dogs do what he and Nivere had just done? Or did they? Or was it just the Lindauzi machines, like the ones the scientists had fitted over his penis, over and over again. It was all a puzzle, a giant puzzle. Still something was missing. Something else about the Lindauzi and the dogs. And the tall, long-fingered ones in his dreams. The same tall, long-fingered ones in the Madaanic Temple, the Iani and their Death. *We were alone, then they came, and now . . . I'll figure it out. But when I do, what then?*

Ilox had hoped once they returned to Earth and the Vaarchael family plantation that things would be the same as they had been two years ago, before going to Umium and the station. Just him and Phlarx, and Tyuil and Nivere. Well, maybe not quite the same. Ilox and Nivere had met several more times in the air ducts above the library to practice what they had seen in the memory walls. Neither had told Tyuil or Phlarx. Somehow both knew what they were doing was not acceptable behavior for any dog, male or female.

"But don't the wall memories say this is how dogs made pups?"

Nivere had asked once when they were lying together in the air duct, lazily stroking each other. "Are we making a pup inside me?"

"Yes, the pups grow inside the females and make their stomachs bigger and bigger. We saw that," Ilox answered sleepily. "But the house vet said I would be bred when I came back from the station. And the station biologists and geneticists said my semen samples would be used in breeding experiments. But the Lindauzi only want dog pups when they want dog pups, so they put something inside; see this little scar there, inside your thigh? Here it is on me. The skin's a little tougher there. They put it in me after taking all their semen samples on the station. Whatever is inside stops pups. We didn't make any."

Why did the Lindauzi fix dogs to have pups only when they wanted them to? And why had Ilox never seen any adult male and female dogs doing what he and Nivere had just done together? The Lindauzi adults did. Ilox had seen a few Lindauza big with unborn children. Ilox felt sure he and Nivere would be able to easily figure out the mystery of dog-pups if they kept exploring in the library.

It was as easy as Ilox thought it would be, although he had to find the answers to the questions alone, and he had to wait longer than he wanted to find them.

"I'm going away, Lox," Nivere told him three weeks after they had begun their nocturnal activities. It was late afternoon and they were in the bathing pool swimming slowly in the warm water, the underwater glowglobe lights rippling across their bodies.

Ilox stopped swimming to tread water. "Away? Where? Why?"

"Tyuil is to be mated this month, to Orvelth, the son of the Viceroy of the northern region of the continent. That's why Morix took her to that city up north—to make the final arrangements. I'm to be mated as well, with his companion. We will go north to live. Lox, I don't want to go," Nivere said and began swimming for the side.

Ilox followed her, swimming underwater with strong, sure strokes. He surfaced to find Nivere sitting up on the poolside, a towel drying her hair.

"They took out the pup-stopper in my thigh this morning. I heard the vet say yours will be taken out next week. I don't want to go, Lox."

"We were going to keep accessing the memory walls here. Find out everything," Ilox said, hanging to the edge of the pool deck, water dripping down his forehead. He wanted to reach up and touch her, but she stood up before he could climb out of the water.

"I know. But I can't stay here now," Nivere said and walked off, the water in her thick black hair glistening beneath the glowglobe following her.

Tyuil was mated with Orvelth in the Vaarchael family temple on Kinsella in an informal ceremony. Ilox listened patiently to Phlarx tell him over and over how they were to behave. He knew Phlarx had to sit and listen, without speaking, without moving, while Morix gave the same instructions.

"We'll sit behind Father," Phlarx said, "and we'll have to wear red-and-silver tunics with white sashes. . . ." Ilox sat at the deskcom in their room, idly playing a game: hunterbeasts chasing criminals through deserts. This was the third time Phlarx had told him where they would sit.

"Should we dress now?" Ilox said, interrupting Phlarx before he could start the fourth repetition.

"I guess so."

Morix had gone ahead with Tyuil, and for the first time, Phlarx and Ilox were allowed to fly alone in an aircar to the temple on the plantation's eastern edge. Phlarx had been practicing, and somewhat to Ilox's surprise, flew the car perfectly, landing only with one or two bumps in the green lawn surrounding the temple. Forming a circle around the lawn were tall flowering trees whose silver-white blossoms were redolent with a tingly fragrance. The temple was rainbow-colored. It sparkled and shone in the sun, a half-sphere of changing light and color. Then, as they walked across the lawn from the aircar, Ilox saw the temple was a mirror faceted like the jewels Lindauzi wore around their necks. It reflected the silver-white flowers, the lawn, even the colors the Vaarchaels and Ilox were wearing. All the times he and Phlarx had had to come here and he had never noticed the temple was a mirror.

The temple's interior, unlike its shining outside, was cool, dark, and close. Thick metal ribs came to a point in the ceiling, forming a multi-pointed star. This time, instead of gold, grey was the color between the ceiling ribs. Tyuil and Orvelth, their fathers, and their companion pets, stood beneath the star on a raised dais, facing the priest.

All the chairs were in concentric circles, expanding out from the dais. Glowglobes clustered around the star and made a ring above the dais.

"You two sit here," Morix said, pointing with a stiff arm to two chairs behind him. "Pay attention and be quiet," and he sat down directly in front of them.

"Yes, Father," Phlarx mumbled as he sat down, the small pride he had had from his first solo aircar flight dropping away like winter Lindauzi fur on a hot summer's day. Ilox brushed one hand briefly across Phlarx's arm and then sat down beside him.

"What do we do now?" Ilox whispered as softly as he could into Phlarx's ear.

"Nothing—sorry, Father, we'll be quiet," Phlarx said quickly and Morix, after a hard stare, turned back around. Ilox looked at Phlarx sheepishly and turned to watch the dais.

The glowglobes encircling the dais began to rotate, going faster and faster, until they made a giant circle of light. Then the priest stepped forward.

"Orvelth, offspring of Omas and Varlax, companion of Gort. Tyuil, offspring of Ossit and Morix, companion of Nivere . . ." the white-furred priest began the ceremony.

Behind the priest a shadow was forming. *I know that shadow, the tall long-fingered ones.* The shadow grew until it was just shorter than the priest, then it fused with the priest's shadow, subsuming it.

"In the name of Lord Madaan, offspring of God, companion of Aurelian, offspring of God . . ."

When Aurelian's name was said, the long-fingered shadow darkened, becoming an opaque black. It seemed to acquire texture and substance.

"Bless this union . . . Tyuil, Orvelth, mated, your bodies joined," the priest said. Then he blessed each companion, and the ceremony was over. The priest and his shadow raised their hands in a final blessing. When that was done, the shadow was gone, as if it had been turned off.

Ilox didn't see Nivere again for a long time, not until his seventeenth birthday. She left with Tyuil for the north immediately after the ceremony. Ilox found himself almost as much alone as he had been on the station. Phlarx was gone for most of the day, training with his father in managing the plantation and in the duties of the Viceregal heir.

Ilox had, most days, long stretches of time to prowl through the library files from the deskcomputer in his and Phlarx's room.

He went from reference to reference, hunting down clues and bits of fact. But three mornings a week, veterinary scientists had Ilox report to the Viceregal research labs for more experimentation. At least Phlarx had to go through the experiments with him.

"He is the one you are linked with," a biologist explained in rather bored tones once. "Now that you are past the confusion of the onset of your puberty in Umium, he is the only Lindauzi you can truly perceive. You can sense other Lindauzi are near, but it is only Phlarx's emotions you can read."

The two of them, once Ilox sensed Phlarx had come, would be placed in separate rooms and a researcher would have Phlarx watch visual recordings of scary stories, funny stories, sad stories. And across the building, Ilox would have to tell another researcher what Phlarx felt and the gist of what he was seeing.

Ilox grew very tired of the endless questions, all at best echoes of the questions he had answered and re-answered on the space station. At worst, the questions were exactly the same. Why did he have to keep telling them over and over what Phlarx felt?

"Make them stop this and leave me alone, Phlarx. I don't like it."

"I can't. Father says this is my duty to our species."

He was even more weary of them taking semen samples. Oh yes, it felt good, but the tiredness and emptiness he felt after each sample was taken grew monotonous. If they would just let him ask the geneticist or the veterinarian or the biologist questions about dogs and Lindauzi, and dogs before the Arrival, but each time Oldoch, who was supervising the research, merely made a notation on his compad and walked away to check on the pregnant females kept in the next room.

"I don't like you," Ilox muttered after each sample was taken, glowering at Oldoch's retreating back. "I didn't like you when I was little, and I don't like you now."

Ilox asked Oldoch if he could see the females his semen had impregnated, or at least see the pups. The kennelmaster refused.

"None of your concern," he said shortly as he stalked off with another sample. "Why would you want to, anyway?"

Because they're part of me, fool.

He tried, late at night. He went to the kennel and tried to find a way in to the nursery. There were just too many doors between the outside and the nursery which didn't know Ilox to let him pass. He found himself stopped in a dark hallway, wondering what the females and the pups looked like. Thinking about Nivere. If she were growing bigger in a cold city by a shining lake in the north.

Ilox finally did sort out why and what had happened so long ago and when the Lindauzi had come to the Earth in their great starships. And he began to understand why he and his semen were so important. He did not find out everything until just before his seventeenth birthday. He was only able to use the deskcom in his and Phlarx's room sparingly, as Phlarx, to Ilox's surprise, began to use it when he returned from working with Morix. Ilox always helped him, fidgeting until Phlarx finally gave up and went to sleep.

Then he sat down alone and placed his hand on the screen and whispered to the computer to start where he left off.

On the station and with Nivere in the house library, Ilox had learned that dogs had had the Earth first, before the Lindauzi came. And the Lindauzi had helped the dogs to fight the plagues and epidemics that were everywhere on the planet. But the Lindauzi hadn't stopped there; the Lindauzi changed the way dogs lived. They took the dogs from their own cities and houses and brought them to live in Lindauzi cities and houses.

But more than changing the houses the dogs lived in from theirs to Lindauzi houses, the Lindauzi changed the way dogs lived with each other. Males were separated from females. Pups from their dams and sires, to be raised in kennels. The pre-Arrival ways of mating and bearing young were eliminated. Only Lindauzi-controlled breeding was allowed: artificial insemination, stud males, surrogate mothers. The Lindauzi bred dogs according to a master plan, stressing certain characteristics, culling others.

These certain characteristics were what Ilox's semen contained: empathy, sensitivity, strength, intelligence, endurance.

Empathy was the most important.

Some years later, Ilox would want to tell his first-born son what empathy and empathic bonding meant and the story he learned those late nights in his and Phlarx's room, hunched over a deskscreen.

He would have already told his son bits and pieces of the story, a little here, a little there, but never the complete tale from beginning to now. He would want to wait until his own son was a little older, had seen a few more things, had more understanding. His son would be so much younger at any age than Ilox himself was. Like Phlarx, who always seemed younger.

It was, when it was completely put together, not a terribly complicated story, although Ilox at first thought it was. But the story was simple, after all.

Once upon a time, an intelligent species evolved on a far distant planet. They learned, over thousands of years, how to go from one world to another and how to live on these different worlds. On one such far planet, this species found itself alone and cut off from all the other worlds, with no way to travel in space. They had gone too far to go home. So they built cities and farms and temples. And they were lonely. They took their pets and began a long, long breeding project, a controlled evolution, until one day, on this far world, there were two intelligent species, living in a harmonious symbiotic relationship. Each complemented the other; each had certain characteristics and talents the other did not have but needed. It was love, it was need, it was two halves of one whole. The two species formed life-pairs, with a more intense bonding than each had within their own species for reproduction. Indeed, mating, same-species bonding, over time, became subordinate to the interspecies life-pairs. Yes, each species reproduced, but fulfillment came from the other species. This was not what the original species had planned—intelligent companions had been their long-ago dream, an end to their loneliness. This bonding was different, more, and better, and so they hid their old past, and it was as if the two species had always, always been together.

Then the two species came to the point in their mutual evolution when they were again looking up past their sky into their heavens, to their three moons, to the nearby worlds circling their star. Ships were built to travel from one world to the next, and, of course, these paired species went together.

It was on the fifth world of their solar system that they found tragedy—a bacterial virus, alien to each—harmless to one species, lethal to the other. In one generation's time, where there had been two, there was now one. One species with its soul cut out, its heart dead. And the irony: it was the original species that died, the descendants of the long-ago travelers stranded, who had created the second. The second, now the only species, knew if they could find no other race for the life-pair, the soul-bond, then they would follow their symbionts into extinction. Not quickly, from an alien disease, but slowly, over years and generations. Without the lost others, fewer and fewer of the Lindauzi would be born, and the long years of their lives would decrease. In the end, they would revert to their nonsentient animal ancestry, and thinking and reasoning would be lost.

Most of the Lindauzi accepted their coming reversion, the slow loss of intelligence, but not all. They fought, the two sides, the Accepters and the Dissenters, at first with words, and then with weapons. Cities burned, died. Parents turned their backs on their children, children turned their backs on their parents. And the Dissenters, having won the right to choose, left, to go on a search for another species to replace the one that was lost. This was the driving force that pushed the Lindauzi to the stars, and eventually to the third world of a relatively obscure star.

The Dissenters observed, collected data, specimens. This new species, this Mankind, Humankind, as it called itself—so like the Iani. The DNA, almost, almost—there was enough latent potential, a promise for the future, that if this Humankind, now the dogs of the Lindauzi, could be bred and changed, that then the old symbiosis of the heart and mind and soul could be regained, and each race would be the stronger for it. But not all the dogs and there were just too many for only a million Lindauzi. The diseases . . . and the breeding, and then, if Lindauzi could hold on and wait; if the dogs would let themselves be dogs.

"They killed us and said they had come to help. Then the Lindauzi just took over and starting making dogs into what they wanted, what they needed. We weren't asked. And from me, they are going to get the genes for their life-pairs. And all that we had, as a singular, distinct people, is lost. That's why they took away our sex, so we could give that to them. That's why I never knew Sandron or my birth dam. And we aren't becoming their equals— are we?"

He knew from the memory walls that dogs once had mothers and fathers, brothers and sisters, lovers, and families, homes, places of their own, and pets, too.

We had little four-legged animals for our pets. And the Lindauzi killed the pets, just like they killed us. The Lindauzi put special poisons in the air; most of the little animals died. Then we couldn't love our pets; we had to love them.

All, everything, taken from them by the Lindauzi, so they could give it all to the Lindauzi.

Tomorrow Tyuil and Nivere will come home. There will be a banquet. I will be expected to make Phlarx happy. And I want to. But this.

He found himself shaking and sobbing. *I loved them, I still love Phlarx. But it's all lies. They didn't ask; they just came and killed and the few of us left, they took us from ourselves.*

Tyuil returned to Vaarchael with Orvelth and her new child the next day at noon. It was a cold day in the middle of winter. Ilox had gone to the top of the house, to the window just outside Morix's office, to watch for the airship to come. There was glass between Ilox and the sky, glass and then the golden force field, but still he knew it was winter. The gold of the force field could not hide the heavy grey clouds of the sky and the wind in the trees just outside. It was snowing. Ilox shivered involuntarily, even though the temperature in the house was always the same.

Ah! There they were. Ilox watched as the dome changed from its glassy solidity into a wavy gas and the airship passed through, flying just over the house itself. He turned to watch as it landed on the lawn on the other side of the house. *Nivere is there. She's with Tyuil. Does she still feel as I do? Will she still want to touch me?*

Ilox didn't see Nivere until nightfall at the family dinner table. She sat across and down, between Tyuil and her mate, Orvelth. Ilox ate slowly, waiting for her to look at him, wishing she would look at him. When she finally did, Ilox knew. It was as if a spark, a bit of fire, passed between them. He sat up straight, clenching his fists together. Ilox looked toward Nivere once more when the housedogs brought out the dessert, a cold sweet bread, with bowls of an even sweeter sauce for dipping. She looked up, and Ilox followed her eyes: an air duct. *Of course, I'll wait for her there tonight.* He felt an almost painful aching in his groin.

The house had never felt more still than it did that night. Ilox slipped out of bed carefully, lifting Phlarx's arm and then gently laying it on the bed. He breathed in and out in long, deep breaths and then went out into the hall and headed for the dining room. She would be there, he was positive, waiting for him.

He walked silently in the hall, the thickness of the carpet swallowing up the sounds of his feet. Ilox didn't, as he had ever since coming from the kennel to the house, run his fingers on the wall for light. Tonight, he knew, was a time for darkness.

Nivere waited for him just outside the dining room.

"Where will we go? Into the air ducts?" she said, whispering.

"No, not this time. In the library. I have things I want to show you." Ilox took her hand, feeling once again the sudden surge of energy in his loins, spreading throughout his body. They found an almost private place in the middle of the maze of memory walls.

"Do you want to first see what I found out or . . .?" Ilox asked and laid his hand on her cheek. Once she had been the taller. Now he was. Ilox gently pulled her to him and placed his mouth on hers, as they had seen in the wall memories, as they had done themselves over and over.

They undressed slowly, their bodies bathed in the diffuse white-golden light of the glowglobes. They touched each other even more slowly, so slowly, each touch almost painful in the denied longing it released. *How could they take this from us? Yes, yes, and again yes.*

This time Nivere awoke first. When Ilox opened his eyes, he looked up to see her face above his, her hand stroking his bare chest. He smiled and pulled her down to kiss again.

"No, let's wait. I want to see what else you found out. Show me the memories," she said, laughing, and sat up.

"Oh, OK," he said, groaning, and reached up to touch the wall. "You won't like them—the Lindauzi did terrible things—"

His hand stopped at the wall. He became very still. Ilox felt a faint flush of heat, a prickling in his skin. A faint pulse throbbed in his head.

"Lindauzi. Nivere, get up, GET UP. Run!"

"Lox? What?" Nivere said drowsily.

He shook her. "Get up. There are Lindauzi just outside. They're coming in here."

A door opened, a shaft of light cut across the room. In response to the door and the Lindauzi presence, glowglobes came down from their roof in a rush of brightness. Ilox stood up, pulling Nivere with him. There were three Lindauzi walking toward them, their toeclaws clicking on the floor. Ilox recognized them: the Lord Morix, Oldoch and the house medic.

Ilox did not see Phlarx again. Morix wasted no time. He didn't even allow Ilox or Nivere to dress. He had the kennelmaster drag Nivere and Ilox, naked, into a small room at the far end of the house, close to the dome. Ilox could just see, through a layer of glassteel and the darkness, the snow falling. Falling so heavily that everything seemed to be white.

"I caught them, just as they are, smelling of sex. They were watching dog history in the library. Ilox, Nivere, how could you?

Ilox, you, especially you. You are my son's. You have the gene complexes . . . and to regress, to bond with this female." Morix was furious. Every fang was exposed. His ears and crest were flat, and his eyes hard and cold.

"I don't understand, my lord. We tested and tested Ilox and all his pups carrying his genes. . . ." Oldoch said helplessly, ringing his hands.

"Put them all down, every one of them. And this female, too. Send word to the station to do the same. Erase all their records in memory. Now," Morix growled, pacing back and forth.

Put down Nivere? No. . . .

The kennelmaster called for the vet. She came within minutes and acted quickly, just as she had done when old Ahain had died and left his dog alone. Before Nivere had a chance to cry out, to lift her hands, the vet pulled out a dermic and pressed it hard against Nivere's neck. Seconds later, she slumped over.

"Call the house menials. Take the body out," Morix said and then turned to Ilox, who stood very still. Ilox wanted to touch Nivere one last time, one last caress, but he dared not move. When the menials came, he started crying, hard, heavy aching sobs that came out of his chest.

"Be quiet, pup," Morix snapped and slapped Ilox across the face, throwing him against the wall. Ilox tasted blood on his lips, felt it warm on his face.

"Well. Kennelmaster. Medic. Vet. What are we to do with Ilox? Put him down as well? He's flawed. All his promise gone; so much for my praise and fame at the Imperial Court. Did you know the birth rate is down again? The reversion rate is rising? This pup was the last great Lindauzi hope. Now we have to start the Project again. I would put him down now, but he's my son's and his sire was mine. I can't."

Phlarx!

"Put him out then," Oldoch the kennelmaster said, glancing out the window. "He has some chance of surviving outside in the winter, very little, but some. You can tell Phlarx he took ill suddenly and we will choose him another pup."

They aren't going to talk to me at all. Not even a single word. And I can't; it's as if my mouth was locked. Phlarx!

Phlarx woke up.

Ilox? Where was he? Not in bed, not at the deskcom, something Phlarx thought Ilox to be obsessed with. Not anywhere in their bedroom.

"But I heard him. As if he were right beside me, at my ear."

Phlarx got out of bed. Glowglobes dropped from the ceiling to follow him out the door into the hall. He turned left and took a lift down. Then another left, heading for the far side of the house, nearest the dome. He felt as if he were being pulled by a violent storm down into its eye. There he would find Ilox, who was in trouble, who needed Phlarx.

Phlarx started running. Ilox was getting farther and farther away.

Ilox, wait for me!

"Phlarx. What are you doing here, out of bed in the middle of the night?" Father said when Phlarx finally stepped, panting, into a little room in a part of the house he rarely went to. Father, the house medic, the house vet, and the kennelmaster were there. All four turned to look at Phlarx at the same time.

They look so guilty.

"Phlarx. I might as well tell you now rather than later. Ilox is dead. An accident. The menials just took his body away. I didn't want you to see him," Father said quickly, glancing at the vet, the medic and the kennelmaster.

Ilox.

Phlarx howled.

"But I still feel him here," Phlarx said, shaking off the howling. He pointed to his head. "He can't be dead. You're lying."

"A vestigial trace," the medic said in soothing tones. "Let me get you something to make you sleep," he added and stepped toward Phlarx. He took him by the arm and started walking him out.

Phlarx stood still and shook off his hand. He looked at Father, knowing that if anybody knew what was going on, Father knew. Father had turned away and was speaking earnestly to the vet in such a low voice that all Phlarx heard were dark sounds.

"He's busy, Lord Phlarx. Come on, let's go back to your room. It'll be all right," the medic said, taking his arm again. He gently tugged at him. Then, gently against his arm, he pressed a dermic. Phlarx let the medic take him from the room.

There were no good-byes, farewells, good lucks. The hound brought his flyer down until it was hovering just above the snow, making a blue shadow on the white. He opened the back hatch and pointed.

"Go on your own two feet, pup, or I'll throw you out. Hurry, I've got other things to do."

Ilox stepped out into the snow, instantly drawing himself in from the sudden harsh cold. He cupped one hand around his genitals, and spread the other across his chest. The flyer shot straight up into the air and was gone, the sound of its ascent swallowed by the wind.

He was surrounded by the winter. His feet, fast losing feeling, were up to his ankles in snow. The wind blew snow in his face, in his hair. Ilox could see nothing but grey and white and black — snow, trees covered in snow, and the shadows of the trees. He could hear nothing but the wind. Ilox could discern no path, no walkway, nothing — just more trees, dark and uncertain behind the snow. His teeth chattered so hard he thought they would break.

One foot, one step. The other foot, another step. Doesn't matter which way. Just one step, then the next. Faster and faster to stay warm. Keep the snow out of my eyes. Hug myself, hold in the warmth. Think about Nivere, Phlarx . . . don't think at all, just look for a place to get out of the snow. There's got to be a place I can get out of the snow and the cold.

Phla-a-r-x-x.

Chapter VII
Caleb, January-May 2156

PAPA HAD NEVER SEEN A REAL DOG BEFORE COMING to Jackson. The only creatures he had seen, besides the hunter-beasts, were birds and rabbits, squirrels, mice, moles. The Lindauzi permitted only small Earth animals inside their domes. Even outside, on the grounds of the Vaarchael plantation, Kinsella, there were mostly small animals. Once Papa had seen a deer from far away. But it had run, its white tail a disappearing flag, before he and Phlarx could get close enough to really see it.

There were two large Earth animals the Lindauzi kept in their laboratories, bears and big cats, sometimes tigers, sometimes lions, or cougars.

"The Lindauzi are fascinated with bears and big cats," he had told Caleb. "I think it's because they sort of look like both and feel some sort of kinship. I didn't even know they were Earth animals until once, when I was out hunting and saw a bear and a mountain lion. Magnificent creatures. But they didn't scare me as much the first time as did seeing a dog."

Papa saw his first dog shortly after Mama had rescued him from the snow. He was just beginning to learn American and was having a hard time making his tongue shape his way around the new sounds: Cu-uh-up. Wah-teerh. Mai-ree.

For a good while, especially when Mama had to go out, Papa would just sit in a corner of the great room, where the cauldron was constantly simmering over an always-tended fire. Papa would watch and listen, repeating the sounds he heard from the women minding the cauldron: kairuttss. Unyunns. Nife. Poetaytoes.

He was certain the women were watching him as well, and beneath the sounds of the fire and the bubbling stew, the slicing of the vegetables, when their backs were turned, Papa was also certain the women were talking about him: too tall, too blond, too fair. *His eyes are so blue. Too blue, if you ask me. What in the world was Mary Hulbert thinking to bring this Lindauzi-bred human home? She should have just left him to die in the snow; we'd all be better off.*

Those sounds Papa made into words first, much more quickly than others.

It was a totally new sound Papa heard one afternoon in the great rooms, loud, insistent, almost musical, but rough. Not human, not Lindauzi, and there was no pattern to it, not that Papa could tell. Not long after the new sound, the noisemakers themselves came. Animals: small, four-legged animals with floppy ears and muzzles and fangs and sharp teeth. Fangs. Furiously wagging tails. Noisy, loud, repeating one sound, one note, over and over again. A montage of colors: brown, white, black, red, solid, spotted. The creatures were shaggy, smooth, and rough. How many there were, Papa couldn't tell, but there were just too many, and one of them, then two, then three, were sniffing around Papa's groin, his hands, his feet. Licking his legs. And behind the little monsters, dogs—no, men, *men*—laughing and shouting, calling for a bowl of whatever was in the big pot.

"Get away, beasts, get away," Papa had screamed in Lindauzi and ran. Little hunterbeasts? Papa knew what hunterbeasts were trained for. Shoving and elbowing, Papa ran out of the room, shoving aside some frightened women, knocking soup bowls out of their hands. Behind him some of the men shouted—to stop? Come back? He had no idea, he just ran. Another man tried to stop Papa at the entrance leading down into Jackson, but Papa knocked him down and kept running. The monsters only got louder and louder.

He hid in Mama's room under her furs and skins. She found him there, buried. He heard her, her feet soft on the cold floor. Papa shivered, his teeth hammering like mallets on stone.

"Ilox? Ilox, it's me, Mary," she had said gently and peeled off the skins and furs. Papa rolled over and sat up. He almost screamed when he saw what she had in her arms, one of the loud beasts, a very small one, but still loud and still one of the beasts.

"It's all right, she won't hurt you, don't run. She's just a little puppy, a little dog. Puh-pee. Dawg."

"Puh-pee. Dawg," Papa had repeated, looking back and forth between Mary and the little beast. He made no move to get closer to Mama and her little dawg.

"See, she won't bite. I want you to touch her. You've never seen a dog before, have you? I have always heard the Lindauzi hate dogs and killed most of them, and the cats, too. There are shelves of books on dogs in the library—there must have been millions once. Give me your hand, Ilox. There, see, she won't bite."

The beast's head felt warm and soft under his hand. When it touched him with its wet tongue, he jumped back quickly, but when Mama laughed, Papa touched the soft head again and let it lick him.

"Now, hold her, put your hand under her bottom, your other hand here. There. I'm sorry you got so scared when the hunters and their pack came in; I just don't know all that you don't know."

"The Lindauzi and the dams held us like this in the kennel nursery," Papa had said. Mama look puzzled at the last two Lindauzi words, so Papa explained. "A place where little pups, babies, are kept. Where they are bred and born. They were kept there until a Lindauzi came for them, picking them out of the choosing pen, sometimes to be companion pets, like I was. Or to be a menial."

"A pen? You were kept in a pen? Come on, let me show you something. Let me show you the dog pen here."

Papa followed Mama outside after they both wrapped themselves in furs. It was February and bitter cold. She took him to a little stand of trees not far from the white columns where there was an enclosure built out of logs and old wires. In front of the logs-and-wire was a shed made out of rocks and bits of old machines. The shed was built against Jackson's wall. The enclosure was filled with dogs of all sizes, and more were running back and forth, in and out of the snow.

"Some are down below. There's an entrance to the tunnels under the shed; it can get awfully cold at night. Most of them sleep inside, in the tunnels, in the winter. Was your pen like this?"

"In a way, but much bigger and enclosed, by, uh, hard light, and it was never cold," Papa said, fumbling with his words. There were things he just couldn't explain.

"They treated you like a dog. All of you, like dogs," Mama said, her words short and clipped with anger. Papa knew why she was so angry, at what had been taken away, at what had been lost, at the price he and all the other humans had paid for the Lindauzi's needs.

"That funny Lindauzi word for human. I can't say it, but now I know what it means: dog. Like these dogs, here. Listen to me, Ilox," Mama said, grabbing his arm and turning him to face her. "These are dogs. This little bitch-pup you are carrying is a dog. You are not a dog. You are a human, a man. I'm a woman. Do you understand? Dogs are animals; you are human. All this," she said and she gestured to include the snow, the trees, the earth, the sky, "was ours before they came. A human world."

"I told her I knew, I understood, Caleb. And I told her what she had said confirmed what I had learned from the memory walls," Papa had said at the end of his story. "Never forget this. Never."

I won't. And I won't forget how you learned to be a human, by watching and listening in corners, or how you learned what the Lindauzi did, and that you were scared, of what you knew and what you didn't know. I can do it, Papa. I promise I will find you.

In the mornings Caleb trained and practiced for the summer dog games. In the afternoons he was left to his own devices. He practiced reading and writing and Lindauzi, and he explored the imperial palace. It was the biggest house, the biggest building Caleb had ever seen, even bigger than the Mall. If he walked instead of taking the lifts, which worked horizontally as well as vertically, Caleb was sure it would take him almost an entire day to walk from the inner gardens and fountains, through the long corridors, through all three wings. The palace was three-sided, a great triangle (unlike most Lindauzi houses, which were cube_) and it seemed to have endless corridors and turns and twists. Dark red carpeted stairs, pink walls that glowed to the touch, fingers leaving trails of rosy light. Great causeways between the sides of the triangles, translucent glassteel walls and transparent floors above the high arcs of water and light from the fountains. All the doors in the palace opened like an eye winking or like water after a stone had been dropped in. For the first few days, when he had the chance, Caleb went in and out of the doors, just to see them open and close.

Chlavash worried, at first, that Caleb would get hurt or in trouble when he explored the mazelike palace corridors and causeways. Or more to the point, Caleb thought, as he listened to his red-furred trainer talk, Chlavash was afraid Caleb would get *him* in trouble.

"You are the Prince's dog. You have special privileges. Don't abuse them — understand? I don't want to have to explain to the kennelmaster or even the Prince why . . ."

Caleb nodded, not listening. He understood. Be a mouse, be a smart mouse. After all, if the Lindauzi really think I am a trained dog, and not one of their companion pets, they won't pay too much attention to me, even if I am right beside them.

And, of course, they didn't. Not even the Crown Prince, the one whom the Lindauzi had to approach on four legs and who was acclaimed as the son of the Lindauzu who had led them on the great search across space, to save their species and find more Iani, the son of the Lindauzu who was sure humans could become what they had lost. Or so Chlavash had told Caleb once, finishing another story Papa had begun just before he had disappeared. The Prince only saw Caleb as a stray wolf, a cull. Only the best, the brightest, the most empathetic had been taken into the Lindauzi domes.

Yeah, right.

". . . and the Prince is coming to see you this morning, his special dog. He wants to see how much you've learned. Others are saying he can't train a wolf, that only Lindauzi-bred dogs can be trained. Ah, here he is. My lord. On your stomach, Caleb," Chlavash hissed, and jerked Caleb down with him.

Caleb sighed and lay down on his stomach. He glanced up at the Prince: *He's just like Aunt Sara. Never wrong, always right, and everybody has to do what he says.*

After signaling for both Chlavash and Caleb to stand up, the Prince examined Caleb in a perfunctory fashion, finishing up with one claw inside Caleb's mouth, checking on his teeth, turning Caleb's head this way and that to see the lines of his neck.

"You have done well, Chlavash. The kennelmaster was right. And we will do well with him at the summer games. I am glad as these may be the last."

"My lord?" Chlavash said and motioned for Caleb to stand aside and strip and swim. Caleb took as long as he could undressing, so he could hear what the two were saying.

"We have always been small in number in here — only one million when the Fleet left Lindauzian, and eight per cent of those didn't survive the coldsleep viruses. Adapting to this planet, its hotter temperatures even in the polar regions, has taken a further toll. We have never been able to occupy the entire world. Our birth rate, always low, continues to drop. The last generation born is the smallest. Many choose not to mate—you have not, have you, Chlavash—others are sterile. And the reversions have never truly stopped—this new fever is only more of the same. The suicides are beginning again. And these dogs, these Iani cousins—we have had so many setbacks in the Project, too many almosts. I have canceled the winter pogrom—perhaps it would be better, if instead we looked for bright wolves such as this one here."

"Yes, my lord. There could be hope among the wild ones," Chlavash said, his crest drooping.

The Prince sighed heavily. "Perhaps. Let me see him swim."

Caleb dived into the pool, a clean sure dive that cut into the water with barely a splash. A naked fish, silent beneath the water, in a silent, still, safe world. He wished he could stay below the water forever, where no Lindauzi could touch him, where no Lindauzi could speak of him as a statistic, as if he could ever forget.

The huge globe that turned slowly just outside the Prince's private office fascinated Caleb. During his free afternoons, he would wander there to watch it revolve, the seas and continents and islands passing before him.

"*This Earth is round, Caleb. Like, like those plastic balls we found in the Mall. Stop looking at me like I am telling you another fairy tale. I've seen the Earth from space, from that bright light you see every night, the Lindauzi space station. The Moon is round, right? I told you why we could only see parts of it—the Earth's shadow. And the sun is round. Well, so is the Earth," Papa had explained once. Papa had even tried to draw what he had seen of the Earth's land and seas on one of the plastic balls, but the charcoal kept breaking and smearing and rubbing off.*

Chlavash showed Caleb where he was on the globe. The Lindauzu touched a panel at the globe's base, and a green light lit up on the globe at the edge of one of the bigger landmasses, Continent One—so named, Papa had said, because it was where the Lindauzi had first landed.

"Umium. And here is Kinsella, right near where they found you. See the yellow line? That's the flight path the hound took when he brought you here. This globe shows every Lindauzi city and plantation on Earth. See all the green lights?"

Caleb saw. And he also saw a part of the globe where there were no green lights, around the globe's middle bulge. When all the flight paths were lit up, the globe was crisscrossed with yellow. But only a relative few went over the nongreen middle.

What's there? How can I find out?

Chlavash would probably tell me, Caleb thought. The Lindauzu loved to talk and answer questions. But Caleb wanted to find out himself. The answers, he was sure, were on the globe itself—the Lindauzi loved to record data. And there were colored squares on the globe's control panel Chlavash hadn't touched.

Being a dog-mouse in a Lindauzi house, Caleb decided, was bearable. Especially being the Prince's dog-mouse. No one questioned him when he came and went and stood staring at the globe. No one questioned him when he finally touched the control panel and made the green lights and yellow lines come on. He had resisted Chlavash's making him learn to read Lindauzi, but now he was glad he had learned.

"Lindauzi populations, urban and planter. Aerial traffic patterns. Wolf concentrations," Caleb said softly, after spending a long hour puzzling over the Lindauzi script. He pressed the red square above the last words. Small red patches appeared, south and east and north of Umium, in mountainous areas. Just west of Kinsella—a very small patch—so a few had survived the last pogrom. Farther west in more mountains. Farther west, on an eight-island chain. Caleb watched as the globe turned, exposing more small patches of red. One winked out as he watched—one last pogrom? Still, the mid-section remained without lights of any color.

Caleb looked down at the globe's control panel again. He had been practicing his written Lindauzi just for this for days. Chlavash had wondered idly where Caleb had come up with such odd combinations of words, but he had written them out anyway. Sometimes Caleb thought the Lindauzu wasn't all that quick.

"Green, yellow, red, all on. And the last panel: Un-ex-plored. In— What is this word. Hospital? No hospital? Inhospital—oh, inhospitable. Let's see."

Caleb was rewarded with a band of purple covering the entire mid-section of the globe. *Unexplored, inhospitable—to the Lindauzi. And it's south.* Caleb traced his finger down the Great River that divided Continent One to the Warm Sea. And then island-hopped southeast to the northern shore of Continent Two. This is the way to the Summer Country, he thought. And the northern shore, the islands, the thin strip of land connecting One and Two were all purple.

So that story is true as well.

"Caleb, I have a surprise for you," Chlavash said one morning some time later. The Lindauzu stood in the doorway of Caleb's light-cage, which by now, by unspoken agreement, was left open. Caleb had been practicing Lindauzi script on the small deskcom Chlavash had given him at the Prince's suggestion. *Let's see how much a wild one can learn. Yes, my lord.* Caleb had known Chlavash was coming—a sudden awareness at the edges of his thought, something akin to Papa's sensitivity to Phlarx, he thought.

A surprise? A new game? More exercises, probably—Chlavash isn't original. Thank Father Art the Lindauzi didn't breed for mind-reading and speaking.

It was in the early spring. Or at least Caleb was fairly sure it was springtime, because when he walked in the causeways girding the palace, he had never seen so many flowers, in the inner garden and out in the city itself. The Earth flowers had bloomed, adding yellows, blues, oranges, purples to the constant Lindauzi shades of pink, white, and red. The sky Caleb could see was clear and blue; the winter grey was gone.

"Oh, a new game to learn?" Caleb said, not looking away from the Lindauzi story he was trying to read. He was sure now that Chlavash didn't pick up on voice tones, but he didn't want to push his luck.

"No, no. We are going on a trip today. The Prince thinks it would be good practice for you to participate in one of the continental dog games. Sooo, we are going south to Continent Two. An airship is waiting for us on the roof."

He really, really wants to take this trip. He sounds just like Davy when we went blackberrying or swimming in the creek.

"So we have to fly over the purple zone to get there, don't we?" Caleb asked when they got into the lift.

"Oh, one of the Prince's secretaries did say you had been playing with the globe's control panels. Yes, over the purple zone. It's too hot for Lindauzi there. There are wolves there, but who knows how many. There was talk, the Prince told me, when his father was alive, of a cleansing, but his father believed it was against *The Book of The Forest.* So, the place is ignored. Ah, here we are, and there is the airship. Let's go!"

Just like Davy.

The Lindauzu pilot was fairly short for Lindauzu and his fur was black. He barely nodded when Caleb and Chlavash came inside, the ramp closing behind them. It was a small airship with only four seats and four rest-pallets in the rear. Caleb sat down by a port and leaned back as the chair molded itself to his body. Chlavash kept talking about where they were going: Perium, the Lindauzi city in the far south of Continent Two.

"Just local games, for the southern part of Two. You should do very well and it will help you get a feel . . ."

Caleb nodded, paying more attention to watching what happened to the city dome when the airship had reached the dome roof. It was like the dome became water and not hard air, malleable and soft, just enough for the airship to slip through and out. Minutes later they were far above the golden city dome and flying down the coast, with the sea shining and brilliant on one side and the white sand and the green earth on the other.

"We're going to have to stop briefly at Tarian," the pilot growled, glancing back at Chlavash. "The Prince has a package to be delivered to his cousin there. Just down and up."

"But, but Tarian is down at the mouth of the Dividing River, in the south of One, it's out of the way . . ." Chlavash began, but the pilot, with his fangs extended, only stared hard at the red Lindauzu, and then turned around to the controls. The airship banked right then and the sea disappeared, and the pilot ignored any other attempts Chlavash made to talk and finally secured a hush wall.

"Four-legged oaf," Chlavash snorted and reached up for an ear insert which he carefully put in. "Tell me when we reach Tarian, Caleb," Chlavash said, reclining his chair and closing his eyes.

Caleb smiled agreement and turned back to the port. He had heard Lindauzi music more than once and he hadn't been impressed: somber and grey, metal sticks clanging on metal pipes, tearing paper, claws on metal. Nothing like the songs Jacksoners used to sing. Hymns, Mama had called them.

Why is old Chlavash so bothered if we fly to Tarian first? Caleb wondered. He was glad just to look out at the land below him, an under world of endless forest, deep, dark, green. Trees growing up and down mountains like ocean waves. Lindauzi plantations with their golden domes and square fields of regular rows. Blue river snakes. Broken places, old human cities and towns. But mostly forest, constant, forever forest.

Tarian was at the mouth of the Dividing River, and it was as big and as wide as the stories had said. They landed on the roof of a house overlooking the river and Chlavash said he could get out and look, but not to get too far away. Caleb walked to the very edge of the roof, through another maze of white and silver trees, until he stood just before a railing of light.

The river was enormous. Caleb stood and watched as the water, silent from the roof of the house, but which he knew had a liquid language of its own, flowed on and on. Chlavash had to call him twice: the pilot was going to leave with or without the Prince's pup. The pilot followed the Dividing River to its mouth, and out over the water. *Your mama told me the way to the Summer Country, follow the great river, Old Man River—the Lindauzi call it the Dividing River—down to the sea. Take a boat there, at the river mouth, and out in the warm waters of the gulf, a pocket of the sea—the Lindauzi call the gulf the Warm Sea—and then southeast and farther out, past islands, until you come to land again. There is the Summer Country: white sand, hot, hot sun, too hot for the Lindauzi, warm clear waters.*

"Chlavash, wake up," Caleb said and jerked at the Lindauzu's arm fur.

"Caleb. What is it? What do you want?" Chlavash said sleepily. How could he sleep listening to that music?

"Well, what is it?" the Lindauzu said again, after he had pulled out the ear insert.

"Remember the globe, in the Prince's offices. What would you call the water at the mouth of the Dividing River, the water we're over?"

Chlavash rubbed his eyes and yawned. "The Warm Sea. Why?"

Caleb ignored the Lindauzu's question. "Remember the purple zone on the globe—are we going to fly over it today?" he asked, his hand resting on Chlavash's arm.

"The inhospitable zone? I think so. I'd ask the pilot if he weren't so surly. Let me check." Chlavash flicked a claw across a panel in his chair's armrest and a light blinked behind the pilot's hushwall. In a moment, a small growl came out of the armrest: "Yes, what do you want?"

"Better manners to a member of the Prince's court family, for one thing, and for another, a confirmation of our flight plan: over the inhospitable zone?" Chlavash growled back.

"Yes, in about fifteen minutes, the northern coast of Two is where the zone begins. And I'm a member of the Prince's court family myself. Thank you." The light behind the hushwall blinked off and the wall became an opaque grey.

"I shall report him when we return—as an atavism. And you let me sleep, Caleb, you can see your zone in fifteen minutes. You won't see much, though, since it's almost all heavy jungle. Perium is an hour after that at this speed. Just in time for the noonmeal," Chlavash said, as he put his ear insert back in. He nodded his head slowly to the unheard beat and then closed his eyes, the chair reclining until he was almost prone.

Caleb kept his face against the port. He didn't want to miss anything. The inhospitable zone, the Summer Country, was a riot of green. Dark, dark, almost black greens. Shiny brilliant greens. Yellow-greens. Green-yellows. Vines, vines, tall, tall trees. The jungle's living dome was green, filtering down to the earth a green and diffuse light. Flashes of other intense colors, flowers, and was that a strange tree, grey and so skinny, one thin stalk that begin to break up as he watched. But before Caleb could get a second look, the pilot pulled back and then shot the ship straight up and up, until they were flying over a white sea.

But Caleb knew what the breaking grey tree was: smoke from a fire. Humans did survive in the Summer Country.

Like Umium and Tarian, Perium was a river city, built at the river mouth of another great river, in the far south of Continent Two. The pilot landed the airship on the roof of another great house.

"The Prince's residence when he visits Two," Chlavash said as they walked down the ramp, Caleb behind him, relieved to see the familiar silver and white trees.

They were met by the house kennelmaster, a short, fat golden-furred Lindauza. Her speech was unlike anything Caleb had ever heard in the imperial palace.

"A Two accent," Chlavash muttered, barely loud enough for Caleb to hear, "always sounds like the speaker is one step from regression. Well, Vanth, here is my winner of the Perium Games," Chlavash pulled Caleb forward and signalled for him to make the token gesture of respect, a quick drop to the knees.

"This one? He looks a bit small, don't you think, Vash?" Vanth said, dryly, putting her hands on both sides of Caleb's face and turning his head back and forth. Caleb stood very still, feeling the tips of her claws pricking his skin.

"Small, yes, Vanth luOrox, but he's tough. Well-trained, of course," Chlavash said.

"Of course. Well. We'll see. The games start today; you arrived just in time," Vanth said shortly. "Follow me. I'll show you where to take your tough well-trained pup."

"Caleb. My name is Caleb," Caleb said. *You old smelly rug.*

"Follow me," she said to Chlavash, waving away Caleb's name with one hand and showing the way with the other.

Vanth led Caleb and Chlavash to a large, large gymnasium, with a track in the center, with hurdles of various heights. Running lanes and pole vaults were at opposite ends of the room. In one corner was a pool, with three diving boards at various levels. In another corner were gymnastic bars and mounts. In the farthest corner, facing the seats, was an elevated promenade deck. The gym was filled with Lindauzi and dogs.

Caleb craned his neck upward—*just how high was the roof,* he thought. It seemed clear, as if the roof was an enormous skylight. He could see drifting clouds and blue sky and the sun, almost too bright to look at through the glass. He let Chlavash take his hand as they made their way through the crowds. Most of the dogs were pups, other competitors, he guessed, and Vanth was right, most were taller than Caleb. Many were as dark as he was, or darker. Only a few were as blond and fair as Papa. Some had to be companion pets, he thought, by the way they stood by their Lindauzi, leaning in to listen, laughing, talking back, being listened to.

Ringing the huge room were dog-cages, made of the familiar light-lattices. Vanth led Caleb and Chlavash to a cluster of cages behind the pool, where there was also a long table. Set in the wall was a bodyglove, and Vanth asked Caleb to strip and step into the glove, its almost-plastic flesh adhering to his, like the towels, molding around his body. When the glove released Caleb with a low sucking noise, she fastened a bracelet on his arm. To record data—heart, respiratory rate—and your performance in any event, she said.

"He swims first, in half-an-hour, so don't bother getting dressed. Swim, then follow the circuit to the promenade. Chlavash, questions? Good luck," she said and left.

"Just remember how strong you are and how much you have trained," Chlavash whispered to Caleb as they walked to the pool. "Don't forget, you've beaten every dog your age in Umium. Don't forget."

Always do your best, Caleb. Yes, Papa.

Caleb took his place at poolside and waited. A horn sounded, low and long, and the room grew silent. No one moved. Caleb saw a white Lindauzu walking toward the middle, beneath the brightest part of the roof. For a moment, when he raised his arms to bless the games for Lord Madaan and Lady Aurelian, his fur seemed to glow in the white-golden sunlight. Then, he left, chattering spreading behind him, noises rippling out in waves.

Caleb looked to his left and to his right at the other two boys who were swimming against him. Both were much taller and bigger. One was so dark as to be almost black, and his hair was in tight curls all over his head. His eyes were two black stones. The other boy's skin was a golden brown, only a shade or two lighter than Caleb's. The golden boy's hair was shiny black and pulled back with a cord.

I bet they never swam in a place like Buffalo Creek.

"Swimmers, mark." Another horn, higher and sharper, and Caleb hit the water cleanly, becoming a small brown fish.

They left Perium late at night and flew without stopping, high in the air, until they reached Umium and touched down on the roof of the imperial palace. Caleb wished there had been a reason to stop in Tarian; he wanted to see the great river again. The pilot only grumbled when Caleb asked and set course for due north.

"No reason, pup. The Prince's cousin didn't have anything to send to Umium," the pilot finally said. Caleb watched as, in the directional screen, a yellow line grew out of Perium's green light, up Continent Two, out across the sea, and then up the coast of One to Umium, a large green light at the top of the screen.

"Be there in about three hours. Go make yourself comfortable and don't bother me."

Caleb watched the night sky for a time through the port, the stars burning in the dark. Once, far away, he saw the white flashes of lightning.

"There you are."

Caleb turned to look up at Chlavash who stood by him, peering out in the passing blackness. "The Prince will be pleased, Caleb, at how well you did in the games. First in swimming, third in the hurdles and the races. A tie for second in gymnastics. Best of Breed. Very well indeed," Chlavash said sleepily and leaned down to scratch Caleb behind his ears.

Caleb let him, hating and liking how it felt. He liked being touched, but he hated this scratching. *It's the way I scratched Max and he liked it, too. Best of Breed. I hated feeling their eyes on me, and having to walk this way, that way, turn on that foot, this foot, now, take off your clothes, flex, pose, turn again. Then that judge, that old Lindauzi, touched me, all over my body. And I felt him: he was so lonely, he was dying of loneliness. It's easy to push out Chlavash, but all of them, I couldn't.*

Chlavash walked back to his chair and closed his eyes as the chair reclined. Caleb watched Chlavash from the port until he was sure the Lindauzu was asleep, breathing slowly in out, in out. Then, carefully and as quietly as possible, Caleb walked over and scratched behind Chlavash's ear. The Lindauzi stirred and shifted his body, but he didn't wake up. He shrugged his head and turned and Caleb could see by the way Chlavash's crest lifted and his fangs retracted that he liked being scratched. And there was a rumbling, deep down in Chlavash's throat.

The Prince was pleased.

He was so pleased that he gave Caleb outside privileges. Now in Caleb's free afternoons, he could wander in the Umium neighborhood nearest the palace. Wasn't Caleb a lucky pup?

Boy.

All Caleb had seen of Perium was the huge gymnasium and arena. Of Tarian, the house above the river. Of Umium itself, only what Caleb had been able to see from the roof, the windows, and the causeways. It was like a garden out of the fairy tales, with soft, soft green grass everywhere, like cloth beneath his feet. And flowers: Caleb had never seen so many flowers, of every color, rich, deep, bright. The air around them was thick with perfume. But more than the flowers and the grass, Caleb liked the fountains. They were magic: light and water and color, rising and falling in glistening glimmering showers and arcs, waterfalls, spouts, geysers. Sparkling, iridescent, glowing. *Let there be light, and there was light, and the light was good. Once upon a time, there was a fountain of sunlight and moonlight and starlight.*

Caleb went from fountain to fountain in the gardens that surrounded the imperial palace. He wanted to strip and swim in the water, in the light, with the colors playing across his skin, blue, yellow, white, green, red. But he only stood in front of each fountain and watched and then listened, his eyes closed, imagining swimming in the light.

All around Caleb in the gardens were Lindauzi and dogs. *Humans. If nowhere else but in my own head, humans.* The dogs all seemed to be busy at something: herding the floating trays the Lindauzi used for carrying food and drink, toys—anything needing carrying; tending the few Lindauzi younglings; tidying the velvet green grass so that all the grass was the same height. No dog, except for Caleb, seemed to be just walking and looking. Some of the Lindauzi were, though, enjoying the spring and the afternoon. Picking flowers, having their dogs spread out food on the grass, trailing their claws in the fountains. Others were passing through, intent on whatever they were thinking, wherever they were going. No one, dog or Lindauzi, paid any attention to Caleb. It was as if being the special pet of the Crown Prince, in training for the coming summer games, meant being invisible.

He walked all over Umium every afternoon for several weeks, to each end of the island on which the main part of the city was built, to the rivers that made the island on three sides, and down to the sea, at the island's southern end. In the southern end, there was another park, a small one, right at the sea's edge, with smooth grey and white stone paths in the grass. From a little stone bench beside one of those paths, Caleb could see the human woman, the Lady, standing alone on a much tinier island, her torch high in her hand.

Caleb wanted to swim out to her, touch the edge of her long dress, and, then, from there, keep on swimming, floating on his back, farther and farther south, until he came to the Summer Country.

Could I swim under the dome? I wonder if it goes all the way down to the river bottom, to the sea floor. I wonder if the Torch Lady knows. I wonder if she knows if Papa is still alive—no, I know he is, I would have felt him. Like I felt those Lindauzi in Perium. He isn't dead in my dreams, he must be alive. In my dreams I can still see him. I can't see Mama or Davy, just their voices, their crying. I see Papa. Father Art, are you listening? I tried to pray to you in that Madaanic Temple, but I wasn't sure if you could hear me there. If any god who lived there, a Lindauzi god, could hear me—

There was a mouse, no, two, three, skittering across the stone path right in front of Caleb. Remembering how he had been able to touch the edges of Max's mind, collect enough thought to understand the dog, Caleb closed his eyes and *touched* a mouse mind.

fearfearfearnomove

The other two mice disappeared into the grass. Caleb got up from the bench and knelt down to carefully pick up the last mouse, small, grey-flecked brown, fear-frozen. He closed his hands around its little warmth, the rapid beating of its little heart.

I won't hurt you, see, nothing to fear, nothing to fear.

fearfearfearfear

The Lindauzi didn't much care for mice or rats, Caleb thought, as he stroked the animal's back, trying to sooth away at least a little of its fear. He knew they didn't kill them as they did cats and dogs, not with deliberation and intent, but they didn't want mice and rats in their houses. Palace menials were always setting traps, especially down in the kennels. But there were always mice. He had seen rats swimming before, in Buffalo Creek, but crossing Buffalo Creek wasn't the same as swimming beneath a forcefield dome and then out a long ways to the Torch Lady. So, how did the little rodents get into Umium?

Where are you from? Can you show me how you got inside this city?

fearfearfearfearsafedarkness

Out, did it know the way out, beyond, outside? Could it remember?

Caleb carefully put the mouse down on the ground and watched as it bolted, still mindscreaming its fear. It disappeared in the grass as the other two had, but Caleb kept his touch as long as he could. Down, the little mind went down, and then it flickered out, like a tiny candle being snuffed.

Interchapter 6

2138

From the Journal of Orfassian luCorviax laThanath luOrfassian luCorviax Alerian, Crown Prince of Lindauzian, Heir to the Left Throne, Supreme Commander of The Search Fleet, the 137th local year since the Arrival, 9 Rainmoon 11530, Lindauzi reckoning.

The Prince is dead; long live the Prince. Yaya, keeper of the Project, the arguer with Death, yaya, long live Orfassian.

Yayayaya.

I have been reading too many dog stories. My father had an extensive library of dog stories, recordings, broadcasts, and he never stopped reading, listening, watching, hoping, I think, to understand, find the key, the right link to accelerate the Project. And I watched and read and listened with him. So, today, when the medic came to tell me Father was dead, I remembered.

I have not keened the mourning song, cut my fur, broken my claws. But then, such grief is only for the companion, not a father or a mother or a same-species mate. My father taught me this — seek no real love in body-relations, only in the bond. The body only follows instinct: sex, procreation, parental protection. Love is in the mind, the soul. I asked him if he loved his own father and he told me, yes, for a time, and it weakened him, it hurt him, and in the end, it wasn't real. There are some Lindauzi, he told me, non-Madaanics, who seek love in the body. A sign of reversion, regression, of the resurgence of instinct over the mind.

I have only sadness for my father. The Iani who made us bred too well for me to find grief in my father's death. I have no companion, nor did my father. He would not take one, not until the Project was fulfilled and the true bond was re-made, heart to heart, mind to mind, soul to soul. My mother was only his mate.

I take no mate, not until the Project is fulfilled.

The Project is now four generations old. At least two generations more, perhaps three, before fruition, so the scientists tell me. The controlled breedings, the cullings, cultural eradication all continues. The latter is the most successful, I think. The civilization that was here, that they made and made them, is gone. Pockets persist, but the planetary culture is gone and ours has replaced it.

I ordered, to mark my father's death, the release of more viruses. We will, of course, provide a cure, in time. I have ordered a new pogrom, here on Continent One, to further reduce the wild ones, the wolves. There are some who want me to use bombs and lasers to cull, burn out the wolf colonies in the inhospitable zone, but these some are a few and were old when they came to Earth and remember the war my father fought against his father.

Hounds do the reduction in the pogrom, we don't. Those who want more direct killing by Lindauzi forget The Book of The Forest and that we must be able to stand before Lord Madaan and Lady Aurelian and say our hands did not kill or release the bombs or aim the laser. The hounds kill, the viruses kill—and they kill the weak, the ill, the stupid. These are necessary deaths.

I am rambling, as did my father in these journals. Enough. Yayayaya.

Chapter VIII
Ilox, July 2155-June 2156

FOR DAYS AFTER HE LEFT JACKSON, ILOX COULDN'T forget the look on his eldest son's face when he asked Ilox if he could go with him.

I should have taken both him and Davy. They're all I have left. And God knows, Sara hates us all. But she's scared of me. Nobody's scared of an eleven-year-old and a four-year-old, even if they are halvers. At least we'd all be together now. But if something happens on this trip, there would be nothing left.

Please, God, let them live.

The Lindauzi pray to Lord Madaan and Lady Aurelian—were they God's messengers to them? Or did Madaan and Aurelian come from another god, a god who doesn't listen to the prayers of dogs? I wonder if Father Art and His Son are at Madaan and Aurelian's side? Or do they see only Father Art's back too? I wish Phlarx had taught me how to pray. Mary did. And to read the Bible. Do the Lindauzi know we have a Bible, a book thousands of years old?

Mary. Nivere. Phlarx. Yes, I loved him, too. But—was that love lessened because? Oh, I know he didn't know. But the Lindauzi, their race knows. Making us their symbionts, their constant companions. But not quite. Something hasn't quite worked yet. Maybe we can't make the same grade as the symbionts who died, the Iani who

*left the Lindauzi so empty and so alone. We're just second best, good
enough for pets but not good enough for the full partnership.*

*After all, I did love a dog, another human. Me, the flawed
breeder.*

Yes, I should have taken Caleb and Davy with me.

Ilox walked east from Jackson on the Big Road. He knew
where the Lindauzi were. He had known all the long years since
Morix had thrown him out of Kinsella, where Phlarx was, and as
an echo in his head, a vague memory in his dreams, he knew how
Phlarx was feeling. Always.

The first few days after Mary had taken him from the cold and
the snow had been the worst. Phlarx's grief had almost consumed
him. Ilox had cried and cried. Mary had held him, rocking him
back and forth, neither one knowing more than the other's name.
He had cried for Phlarx so hard his body shook. And Ilox knew
that in the Vaarchael house Phlarx was crying as hard.

*I guess his father gave him another pup. But I never stopped feel-
ing him miss me, like a feather touching my skin, a faint brush
across my arm. The hurt for both of us never really went away. I still
miss him. I don't know. We may be second-best Iani, but not Phlarx
and me, heart to heart, mind to mind, soul to soul.*

Now he knew the Lindauzi were coming. He had known before Ezra had met the Footwasher hunter at Buffalo Creek, but
Ilox had also known no Jacksoner would ever believe him. He had
sensed them as a stronger, darker, closer presence than before,
and their hounds who would do the killings, a shadow before the
darkness, a shadow being driven by the darkness. Ilox's skin
prickled with the touch of heat. There was a barely perceptible
ache in his head.

Ilox had the Big Road to himself. Except for the occasional
deer and wild cattle he surprised grazing in the trees between the
lanes, the birds, and a fox or two, Ilox walked alone, stepping in
and out of the broken chunks of asphalt, between the occasional
heap of metal which had once been a car. He walked at a fast clip,
knowing he had little time to find out just where the Lindauzi
were and get back before they came to Jackson with their airships
and hounds, their lasers and their hunterbeasts.

*I know they are coming here; I feel them pointed this way, but
I can't sense when they will come. Just sometime later.* He had left
Jackson early in the morning, but after the first day he walked at
night. A Covenant-keeper hunter almost killed him the second
morning.

"I heard you before I saw you, thought you were some deer. 'Bout ready to shoot, then I saw yer face. Boy, you sure are a big fella. I don't recall ever seeing a man your size," the Covenant-keeper said, staring up at Ilox, his bow now safely slung over one shoulder. The Covenant-keeper was a small, fair-skinned man with shaggy black hair. He was a head shorter than Ilox. They sat companionably on what both guessed had once been a cement support for a bridge over the Big Road. The bridge and the other supports all lay around them: broken, cracked slabs, huge shattered hunks, grey and green, as honeysuckle and kudzu grew over and around.

"We call this Forty-Eighty-Five Road. Ya know, from the old signs. Or the Big Road. Boy, ya sure are a big fella," the Covenant-keeper said again.

Ilox nodded. He knew the red, white, and blue signs the man spoke of. Two of them were kept in Jackson amongst the other sacred relics. Some of the relics, like the signs, he understood. But other things even Mary hadn't known. Like the pieces of soft plastic shaped like fat fingers, with hard plastic rings at the end. Oh well.

"I'm a Jacksoner. I'm a scout. We've heard from the Foot-washers that they've seen signs of Lindauzi movement this way—"

"A Jacksoner? The only Jacksoners I have ever known are short and dark, and yer big and fair. Well, whatever. Moving this way, eh? This'll be news tonight at the prayer-fire. A Jacksoner?" the man repeated, cocking his head to one side.

Ilox smiled. He knew what the Covenant-keeper was thinking but was afraid to say aloud: *the Lindauzi grow humans big, bigger than any humans outside of their domes. Tall men and women. I wonder if this fellow—he says he's from Jackson, but Jacksoners are brown and short. I've got to be careful. Lindauzi grow humans different. The hounds are human, or they used to be; now they hunt us down. Can't let my guard down.*

Ilox and the Covenant-keeper ate together from the dried meat and fruit Ilox carried in his pack. The Covenant-keeper brought down a rabbit and they cooked and ate that as well, slowly turning the gutted animal over a low fire. Then the Covenant-keeper went on, and Ilox stayed in the rubble of the fallen bridge. That was the last time he walked during the day. Another hunter might not be so charitable to a man who was too tall and the wrong color.

It took a week of night-walking to reach Lindauzi territory. Ilox had thought it was nearer, but then he remembered that his last trip from Kinsella had been thirteen years ago and in an airship, and in a snowstorm. A hound's flyer could make that trip in forty-five minutes, the air yacht, an hour and a half. But land measurements?

"I learned tenstrides along with Phlarx, so many between the house, the barracks, the kennel. But from Umium, or even to the next plantation—I never did. Jacksoners measure long distances in time: a day's walk, a week, an hour. Shorter ones, with the old foot and yardsticks," Ilox told himself as he walked. He smiled at the sound of his own voice.

If anybody heard me, they'd think I was crazy, talking to myself.

Ilox knew he was in Lindauzi territory when he saw the distinct hazy yellow glow of a Lindauzi force field. It formed the perimeter of a plantation. According to the old sign that was still standing, the plantation occupied the site of a place called Durham. The city limits sign was almost covered in kudzu, but Ilox pulled away the vines to sound out the name: *Dur-ham, the City of Medicine.* Odd, no Lindauzi had pulled up the sign and melted it down. Or that no humans had taken it, to be stacked in some underground room as another memory of what was. He flicked his fingers against the rusted metal and a piece fell off. Now Dur-ham was the *City of Medic.*

It was just after midnight when he came to the plantation. There was a half-moon in the sky and the air was still and warm. Other than the crickets and the flutter of an occasional bat, Ilox heard nothing. He cautiously touched the force field, feeling it give slightly to his touch. Ilox couldn't see the house or the hound barracks: nothing but trees and fields of tobacco ready to be harvested.

He felt the Lindauzi who lived there: slow, dark-colored presences, still and quiet in their sleep. Only a few, a male and a female. The female was not well: he sensed a weak whisper of life. Ilox rubbed his head. The headache was getting worse. His skin was beginning to crawl with heat, just like before.

Phlarx?

Yes, just a faint, faint presence, but Ilox knew it was Phlarx. The awareness was too familiar, too much a part of who Ilox was for him not to recognize it. He slipped to his knees, still pressing against the force field. *It's been thirteen years. I still miss him. There's been Mary, and Caleb and Davy, but I still miss him. Morix was wrong: he said they had failed when they bred me for their emotional symbiont. Phlarx? Is that you? Do you feel me too?*

It struck Ilox like a bright white light flashing in his eyes. He covered his face, and his body shook, but Phlarx was there, groggy from sleep, and bewildered. For the first time, they could hear each other in their minds. Before, when they had been children, Ilox could only sense how Phlarx felt. Was this some gift of maturity? An unexpected fruit of Lindauzi breeding? It didn't matter.

Ilox? I told myself you were dead. It's been so long, so long. Where are you? Phlarx's voice rang in his mind, clear and sure as if the Lindauzu were standing beside him.

"I'm here," Ilox whispered out loud, holding his head. "Just outside the force field of . . . I don't know whose plantation this is, but it's the last one before wild country. Off the Big Road. Do you know where that is? *I'm supposed to be a spy for the Jacksoners. And here I am, on my knees, crying. Telling a Lindauzi where I am.*

The Vaarkens, our cousins. I know where you are. Do . . . do you want me to come? I've got another dog, Ilox. But he's never been able to be like you.

"But what about your father, Morix?" Ilox asked. "He was the one who sent me away. Did you know that?"

He never told me, but I guessed. He brought me the other dog the next day. He's not here. I run the plantation now. He is mostly in Umium now and is rarely here. Imperial business. I started taking care of the plantation a year after you went away. I am an adult now, Ilox, I am to mate in a year.

"But Morix will come home. What will we do then?" Ilox asked. *I'm thirty human years old and it's like all those years just vanished—blown away by a strong wind. I want him and he wants me.*

I will tell him you are mine and that you came back. I will tell him I'm an adult.

Do I sense fear in you, Phlarx? Does he still scare you? I don't care, just come.

"Come get me, Phlarx," Ilox whispered aloud, and sat back from the force field.

I'm coming.

Ilox wiped his face and leaned back against a tree. He felt very tired, as if the mental link with Phlarx had taken all his strength. A shooting star flashed in the sky. *It's early August. They come every year.* It was followed by another, bigger than the last, a longer whiter flame. The crickets sounded as if they were going insane. Fireflies. Leaves rustled, a branch snapped: A fox? A rabbit? A rushing in the trees, a deer?

Phlarx came in a personal flyer. He flew high above the Vaar-ken plantation force field; Ilox saw him as he came down: for a moment, a smaller, silvery metallic new moon. The flyer landed just beyond the trees, its leg supports thumping in the weeds. Ilox walked out beyond the woods and stood at the very edge of the clearing and waited as the flyer's roof opened and Phlarx climbed out. He was alone.

Phlarx stood by the flyer, his fur outlined in silver from the moonlight. Slowly and uncertainly, he stepped out to where Ilox could see him.

"Lox?"

"Yes, it's me."

Phlarx had grown taller in the last thirteen years. His arms completely enfolded Ilox.

For Ilox, it was like being a boy again. As it had been before he learned the lost human history, before he learned what the Lin-dauzi wanted and what they had done to get what they wanted. Before the years of marriage, two children, widowerhood, and having lived as an outcast among his own kind. All these things for a short time fell away, as easily as if Ilox were shedding clothes before swimming. There was just Phlarx when he woke up and when he went to sleep. For the first two weeks, that was all that mattered, and that Ilox could finally tell someone about his life, his children, Mary, about having no one to tell anything to.

"And then—I talk too much, Phlarx. You do have a plantation to run," Ilox said one morning the second week after he had come back. They were sitting at the meal table, just after eating. The walls were slowly becoming transparent as the sun got higher.

"I don't have that much to do, Lox, really. Just keep things running smoothly. You remember. Getting the tobacco harvested and prepared for the food-processing plants. Signing bills of sale for the kennel. Monitoring the household accounts like Mother did. Things of that sort," Phlarx said.

"Bills of sale?" Ilox asked, gently setting down his glass of orange juice. He had drunk it very slowly, savoring each sip. Jack-soners had stories about oranges and bananas, grapefruit—but they were just stories, fantasies of the years before the Arrival. He hadn't realized until the menial brought the juice how much he had missed that first glass every morning.

"You know. Father sells most of the pups from the kennel. He has an imperial reputation as a dog-breeder. That's where I got you, remember?"

Ilox remembered. He looked curiously at Phlarx over the rim of his juice glass. *Has he heard a word I've said for the past two weeks? Can't he even try to say the word human? Has he really been listening—or did he hear sounds and not words?*

"But where did you go? Why did you leave?" That had been Phlarx's first question.

"Phlarx, I didn't leave. Your father, the vet, the medic and the kennelmaster, they killed—yes, killed, Nivere and all the pups they had bred from my semen. Then they threw me out. Naked, in the snow. A woman found me."

"A wolf-bitch?"

"Listen to me, Phlarx. There are no dogs and wolves: only humans. And Lindauzi. There are few real dogs—canines—left. The Lindauzi have killed most of them. I am a man. I am a human; I'm not a dog."

"You stayed with this woman for thirteen dog—Huumun years? She was your mate?"

"The American word is wife, it means more than mate. I loved her, Phlarx."

"But didn't you miss me?"

"All the time."

"Then why didn't you come back?"

Phlarx's tone had been one of total bewilderment.

Ilox poured himself another glass of orange juice.

"Phlarx, I, uh, I, I'm not sure how much longer I can stay," Ilox finally said, each word heavy on his tongue. He peered down into the orange liquid as soon as he spoke. Ilox didn't want to see Phlarx's eyes.

"What do you mean? You're home. This is where you belong, here with me. You're my dog, this is your place. As Sandron was for Father, you are for me. I had my other dog put down because you came back."

"Put down? You had him put down because of me? Now I have his death on my head. Phlarx, don't you see? Haven't you been listening? I'm not your dog anymore. I'm your friend."

"What is this *friend*? That's not a Lindauzi word: it's wolf-speech. Of course you're mine. You were bred to be mine; Father told me that. Where are you going?"

"Nowhere. I'm just pacing. Listen, just listen, and try and understand, OK? Will you do that?" Ilox asked. He had jumped up from the table and was walking around the room. Through the now almost-transparent wall he looked down into the family gardens. At the door, he looked out in the hall, and finally, he stopped by a painting of Lindauzian, which hung on the wall behind the table. Then he turned back to Phlarx who was looking more and more puzzled. "Walk with me, Phlarx, and listen."

"All right."

Phlarx was hurt. Ilox heard the pain in every syllable the Lindauzu spoke. He felt it radiating from Phlarx in spreading circles of misery. Phlarx's eyes were dark, his crest was drooping. Ilox hurt too; he knew he was causing Phlarx more grief. Why didn't he just wrap himself around Phlarx, the way they had the first night he was back and every night since? Why didn't he let Phlarx hold him, scratch behind his ears, comb Ilox's hair with his claws?

It had been so much simpler when they were children.

Ilox and Phlarx walked all over the Vaarchael plantation. They walked throughout the house, up and down the ramps between floors, taking lifts from the lowest floor to the roof, and then down again and out into the family gardens. They walked down to the hounds' quarters where Ilox found to his amusement that the same alpha who had imprinted him twenty-three years ago was still there, although much older and greyer and grumpier.

They walked down to the vehicle hangars, where the Vaarchaels kept a number of personal flyers, different-sized airships, and of course, the attack-flyers of the hounds. Just beyond the hangars were the hunterbeast kennels; Ilox chose not to go in there. Then they went to the dog kennel and nursery and from there, out into the tobacco and vegetable fields.

Ilox did not stop talking as they walked: the light-furred Lindauzu towering some three heads over the fair human man. Phlarx walked with his head bent down toward Ilox, his hands behind his back, his claws retracted, his crest down. Ilox talked with his hands as well as his mouth, making wide, expansive gestures, followed by small ones, close and tight to his chest.

He again told Phlarx what it had been like to live with the wolves, humans untouched by Lindauzi breeding and training. These were humans who were not bred to be racers in the great arenas or broad-backed menials or a bright, sensitive personal companion as he had been.

"They are just themselves, Phlarx. They remember what it was like before the Lindauzi came, when this planet was theirs and theirs alone. They remember the great human cities that were filled with people who served no one but themselves. They tilled this soil, flew in this sky— they even flew to the moon. And then the Lindauzi came," Ilox said, and sat down. He and Phlarx were at the very edge of the plantation in a part that was still wooded and not cultivated. He sat down on a log and looked up at Phlarx.

"Do you know your own history, Phlarx?" Ilox asked softly. *He doesn't understand. He just doesn't understand. I feel his bewilderment, his straining, his grasping at understanding. And I feel him falling short. I hear him saying this isn't right, that this doesn't make sense.*

"Remember when we went to Umium and I got sick and I had to stay up on the space station? You were supposed to study your family history, Lindauzi history and culture all that time?" Ilox asked again. He watched as Phlarx paced back and forth, his heavy steps smashing the grass and the tiny weeds. Phlarx's ears were down; this thinking was making him unhappy, Ilox realized. *I have always been the older and smarter one.*

"Yes, I remember. I didn't do very well because you weren't there to help me read. But I remember. We started all the way back when there was one species on Lindauzian and they were lonely and they made their pets into true companions, into bond-mates and there were two species on Lindauzian: the Lindauzi and the Iani. The two species were paired and lived together, one Iani to one Lindauzi, always. And the Iani died from a horrible disease. And there was a war, and then we went looking—"

"And you found us," Ilox said, interrupting, "but we aren't the Iani. You've been trying to make us into Iani, breed us into Iani, and it hasn't worked. You have pets, but you don't have partners. And you have *wolves*, who won't ever want to be pets, because they need to be themselves."

"Are you telling me you've become a wolf, you have gone feral?" Phlarx asked. He had stopped pacing and stood directly in front of Ilox. It was twilight, and the sun was below the horizon. Long shadows stretched out from the trees, making the grass dark. Phlarx's shadow fell across Ilox. Had they been talking all day?

"I'm telling you that I've learned what it means to be a human. I love you no less; I've missed you all these years, but not as Phlarx's pup. I've missed you as Phlarx's friend, who stands at his side. Not behind him. Do you understand? The Lindauzi killed humans, with diseases—did you know that? And those pogroms —those hounds killing. Only as your friend can I know all this and still love you. Do you understand?"

Phlarx was quiet, very quiet, for a long moment. Ilox could

hear around him the crickets insanely chirping. An airship passed overhead, silent, its shadow making the twilight even darker. Already he could see the first sliver of the moon, and the evening star. And was that the space station, a green light, passing overhead? Yes, Ilox was sure of it.

What is he thinking now? Oh, no, Phlarx, you can't. Not to me. Please, please, don't . . .

Ilox tried to run, but Phlarx moved too quickly. He grabbed Ilox around his chest and held him tight, one hand over Ilox's mouth, the other under his arms. Ilox struggled, but Phlarx only held him tighter.

"This is for your own good, Lox. I think the vets can cure you, make you well again. Make you mine again, as when we were little. Now let me get this dermic against your neck. There. The vet said it would take just a few moments."

Ilox slumped, limp and slackfaced, in Phlarx's arms. Phlarx gently shook him once, just to be sure the drug had worked. Ilox was out. Satisfied, Phlarx pulled a handcom from his belt and pressed it on.

"I'm on the eastern perimeter, section 4. Pickup. Have cocoon ready, call vet. That's all," and Phlarx slipped the handcom back into his belt. He laid Ilox gently on the ground and started pacing back and forth as he waited, looking up into the darkening sky every so often, until he saw the aircar coming down. Once it landed he laid Ilox in the back and then instructed the hound to return to the house, quickly. No time was to be wasted.

After landing on the roof, Phlarx had the hound carry Ilox to the lift and follow him to the veterinary clinic on the ground floor.

"Careful, hound," Phlarx snapped when they got out off the lift. "Don't let his head drop. You're dragging his feet—give him to me. Now go." Phlarx carried Ilox the rest of the way. The vet was waiting for him, standing behind a white gurney.

"Will this really work? Can he be saved?" Phlarx asked, his voice thick with anxiety and affection. He held Ilox to him, Ilox's head resting on his shoulder.

"Lay him here on this gurney, Lord Phlarx," the vet said. She was the daughter of the vet Ilox had known as a child, and was as young as he was. She wanted very much to please Phlarx, who was the Viceregal heir. A good residency with the Vaarchaels could win her a place in research centers on the space station, as it had for her mother. But still she did not want to make promises that might not be possible to keep.

"I will do my best, Lord. The intensive long-term cocooning

and subliminal therapy have been very effective in such cases in the past. You do know that it is still very common for such dogs to be simply put down," she said, cutting away Ilox's clothing to prepare him for cocooning. "Neutering has also proven to be effective in behavior modification."

"Father neutered Sandron. I remember how dull he was. I have often wondered if that didn't cause him to die so young. No, cocooning and subliminal therapy."

"Dogs don't live nearly as long as we do, even though their life-spans have increased in the past five or six generations. There, if you will hold him while I insert these tubes." She pulled from glowing masses in the wall several long equally glowing pink tubes, which she carefully inserted into Ilox's groin, chest, and temple.

"I do think, though," she went on, "that with the proper sub-liminal tapes there is a good chance of reconditioning Ilox. You said he is exhibiting the usual symptoms of atavistic regression?"

"Yes," Phlarx said, shaking his head.

"This one here, he was supposed to be the breakthrough, the first true symbiont, wasn't he? But he was imperfect, too indepen-dent, if I remember what Mother recorded," she said, as she monitored the various drug levels and body readings on a screen in the wall. Satisfied that Ilox was now ready for cocooning, she adjusted some of the readings and then started pushing the gurney through the air to a cocoon she had already prepared.

"Yes, Father said he was imperfect. That he presumed too much, and that even though he was ready for complete emotional symbiosis and could give it, he held back and wanted indepen-dence, not interdependence. We can read each other's thoughts now," Phlarx said, walking by the gurney, one hand, claws retracted, protectively on Ilox's stomach. *How did he get so hairy? The thoughts — we have achieved symbiosis — almost. This will fix it forever.*

"I wish we knew more about the Iani," the vet said. "In the years immediately after the Extinction and during the war, so many records were lost. There was so much confusion and dis-order. We just have, really, only the stories and a few memory records. And we know they altered the records to make it appear as if Lindauzi evolved independently. Here we go, lift him up and sit him down there. That's right."

Phlarx laid Ilox, still attached to the wall tubes, into the long black tank that the vet had pulled out of the wall as well. He watched as she adjusted the tank so that it molded itself to Ilox's body. Then the vet adjusted the tubes, still glowing, so that they went through the top of the cocoon. Then she sealed it, and after adjusting the wall readings again, she stepped back.

"Well?" Phlarx asked, spreading out his hands, claws extended. The vet stepped back again at the gesture. She knew the Vaarchaels were prone to sudden bursts of temper.

"Well, he has been cocooned and is on full life-support. The subliminal tapes are already started, feeding directly into his brain. I am going to run several programs, all designed to refocus his attentions to the bond with you. You said he formed familial attachments with wolves; these tapes should either erase those memories or push them so deep they will stay permanently buried. By spring you should have the dog you had as a child, except now, of course, he is an adult."

"Is there any chance for failure?" Phlarx asked. *Doesn't she know how important it is to me to have him back? I wonder if she has a dog of her own. I doubt it, or she wouldn't be so lackadaisical about all this.*

"This is not foolproof, Lord Phlarx. But the chances for full success are very good. You do understand, though, if the tapes do not work, then he will probably emerge from the cocoon insane and have to be put down?" The vet hated saying this, but she had to. Nothing but the complete truth, always.

"I'll never have Ilox put down, no matter what happens. Father told me he was dead and, even though I knew, deep down inside, he wasn't, I never did anything to find him. I'll always regret that. If I had, this would have never happened. When will he come out of the cocoon?"

"For good?" the vet said, as she and Phlarx started walking toward the clinic door.

"Yes."

"In the spring. He will come out of the cocoon in the spring."

Phlarx watched as the vet made the final adjustments to the cocoon. When she was finally satisfied, she left. It was then Phlarx stepped over to the housecom.

"Can you come now and bless him, most holy? He's in the cocoon," Phlarx said, looking into the family priest's white face.

After the priest said he would be right there, Phlarx broke the connection and sat down to wait.

O Lord Madaan, O Lord Aurelian, turn your gazes on my companion, my bond-mate . . .

Deep. Into the wet, cold darkness. Still, silent. As if he were swimming in a dark river. Under the surface of the river, below the skin of the water. Just above, there was light and warmth. Yellow light and green lights. Warmth.

Was he alone? Where was Caleb? Davy? Phlarx? Why were all three together in his mind? Mary? She was there, too, near, close, beyond the skin of the water. The four of them blurred, merged, grew together in one indistinct face.

Then, the voices began. Love, love, love. The Lindauzi. Phlarx. Love the Lindauzi. Be, belong, be touched, in your proper place. Every species has its place, its position. This is yours. Here, beside, in touch. Here, this is yours. Love, love, love, love. The Lindauzi. LiinnndaaauzzziiiPhhhlllaaarxxxxxLllloooooovvvvvveeee.

Forget. Lie still, float on the river. Above the water, out of the cold, in the yellow warmth and forget. Fffoorrrggeettt. Listen. Be still. This is where you belong. For the love of the Lindauzi. FortheloveoftheLindauzi. Forthe loveofthe Lindauzi. Fo rthe loveof th eLindauzi. Lie still, let the yellow warmth touch all of your body. Ilox, this is where you belong. Here. Phlarx, by his side. At his side. Together. Dog. Lindauzi. Dog and Lindauzi. Dog-and-Lindauzi. DogandLindauzi. On the same river, your hearts, your lives, skimming the water. Down to the warm sea. Tooggeetthheerr.

"Ilox? Ilox, it's me, Phlarx. Lox?"

The voice came very close to his ear, low and deep. Did he know this voice? He thought he was supposed to, but he couldn't remember. Who was Ilox? Oh, yes, that was his name. He was sure of that. Ilox slowly sat up shivering, and blinking. The light was so bright, it hurt. Why was he so wet? Why couldn't he remember anything after his name?

"Ilox, it's me. Phlarx, do you remember? Please dim the lights; they're hurting his eyes. Lox?"

Ilox turned in the direction of the voice and wiped his eyes free of some wet stickiness. Did he know this creature? What did he know? He knew he was Ilox. He knew he was wet and cold and that the bright light was now dim. And the voice said it was Phlarx. The low deep voice.

The voice had furry arms and it was picking him up, out of the wet coldness. Into warmth. Where? The voice had a face. With fangs. Fangs, sharp fangs? Ilox pushed, struggled, and tried to get away, but the furry arms were too strong and he was too weak. He clung to the furriness. Oh, he was so tired.

"Vet, how is he? He doesn't seem well," the low deep voice said, just above Ilox's head.

"I must be honest, Lord Phlarx," said another voice, but this one wasn't as deep as the one above his head. It was higher and lighter. "It doesn't look good. He is showing all the signs of cocoon psychosis. But it is too soon to tell. He's very weak, of course, and his muscles have atrophied. Ilox will need much care, Lord Phlarx."

"I will give him all the care he needs. Everything," the Phlarx-voice said, and Ilox felt his body enveloped in the fur. Oh, warm, close. Was this? Why did his mind start and stop? Why could he barely see? Where was the river he had been in for so long? Why couldn't Ilox make his arms and legs work?

Where was the sun? The yellow warmth? The different faces? The voices? And the days, the moon, time. River. Oh, so tired. Dark, warm, light. Sweet and down into the fur.

Ilox snuggled into the fur and the arms and felt himself be lifted and carried. Then, after a year, after a minute, after a millennium, Ilox was laid down to sleep.

Chapter IX

Caleb, Nox, and Phlarx, June 2156

"**T**ODAY IS THE FIRST DAY OF JUNE," CHLAVASH SAID one warm morning. "The planetary dog games begin in just three weeks, and I think you are just about ready."

Caleb looked up from his morningmeal of bread, fruit and milk. He was in a new cage, now, in the Prince's private apartment, near the top of the palace. Chlavash's rooms were nearby, one corridor and a few doors away. Caleb's cage was almost like a room. There was a bed, a bathing pool and fountain, a table and a chair, even a window that looked down into the palace's interior garden and out at the other two wings of the palace's triangle. And bars at the door. Retracted, of course, enough to let him pass in and out, but still there.

"How do you know it's June? That's the dog calendar," Caleb asked, thinking he had lost track himself months ago.

Chlavash kept talking, oblivious to Caleb's turning away. "I know it's June because when you get invited to a beer dinner party, the pre-Arrival calendar is used. The invitation I received on my screen today was dated 1 June. Are you almost done? I think we should just swim today. Nothing else. Just enough to keep you limber for the games. Are you going to eat that apple?"

Chlavash ate it in two quick bites, wiping his mouth with his hand. Caleb wondered if the seeds would make Chlavash sick. Mama had always said to spit them out, that he would get sick if he didn't, and besides, she wanted him to plant his leftover seeds. She had even gone and shown him the apple seedlings she had planted. He hoped Jackson's Coors and Tuborg Gold had made the Prince and his friends sick—as sick as dogs.

It had become something of a fad in the past month among Umium upper-caste Lindauzi to drink pre-Arrival Earth beer. The Viceroy of Eastern One had sent the Prince six-packs of Coors and Tuborg Gold, and after the Prince had served the beer at a dinner party, everyone wanted beer at their dinners and receptions. Caleb looked away from Chlavash into his glass, suddenly hollow in his stomach, despite the food. Coors and Tuborg Gold six-packs had been Jacksoner sacred relics, kept inside the glass case beside the Jackson's picture. He could just see some hound smashing the glass, and then stepping over a headless body to grab the precious things.

Caleb yawned. He had not slept well the night before, either. He had woken up more than once, three of the dreams sharp and still present, ghosts in his cage. In the first dream Papa was somewhere near and very sick. Papa needed Caleb and kept calling for his son to come and help him. He called for Davy and for Mama. Caleb had called back—*I'm here, where are you, tell me where you are*—and had gone running down endless pink corridors, his fingers leaving luminous lines on the walls behind him. But Papa couldn't hear Caleb. In the second dream, Morix and Phlarx had been between Caleb and Papa, guarding the door to the room where Papa was. Caleb had pleaded and begged with the two Lindauzu, but it was as if he had been invisible and inaudible. No amount of crying and screaming moved either to even look at him. *Papa had dreams about Phlarx, too. He told me. He told me he loved Phlarx, not the way he loved me, Davy, or Mama, but he loved him. He said he always missed him.*

In the third dream, he was in his cage, lying in bed. He sat up and ran his hand across the light bars of his cage. They glowed brighter in response to his touch; the longer he stroked the bars, the brighter they became until the cage was filled with light. Then he had called out, even though his voice made no sound: *Mouse.* There, at the cage entrance, two of them, tiny black lumps in the light.

foodfoodfoodfood?

No, not yet. Show me down out, then foodfoodfood.

The mice chittered back and then ran down the corridor. Caleb scooped up leftover apple and pear cores, and followed their little mind-fires down, down, down, to the last stop of the lift, to the very bottom of the palace, and old tunnels, human-made tunnels, a place Chlavash had never taken him, controls on the lift wall that Chlavash had never touched. Down and down and down, the mice ahead of him, *foodfoodfood.* Then, at the tunnels' entrance, he tossed the fruit into the dark, the mice's coronas glowing brighter as they ate.

He had meant to tell Chlavash about his dreams and see what the Lindauzu thought, but not after the beer story. And besides, Chlavash never seemed to quite understand or appreciate how much Caleb missed his family, how real and present was the grief. And like many Lindauzi, Chlavash had only a formal relationship with his own parents. Telling dreams was something you did with a friend, a brother, a parent. Chlavash couldn't qualify for the last two, and even after six months of daily contact, Caleb wasn't sure he qualified for friend, either. And if he told, Chlavash might kill the mice Caleb had managed to tame in the last few weeks and who did come to his cage for apple and pear cores, bits of bread. He had yet to follow them into their darkness, a place so dark that truly only their coronas would light the way.

"I'm done," Caleb finally said, satisfied he hadn't forgotten any of his dreams. "I'm ready. June first, huh?" As he stood, Caleb thought momentarily of telling Chlavash his twelfth birthday would be June seventeenth, but, no, why bother. Dogs never had a birthday or received a new stone for their life-necklaces. Caleb still found himself reaching up to tug at the necklace that was no longer there. Papa had known his birthday, but only by the Lindauzi calendar, and because he had pestered Phlarx to find out. Most dogs never knew.

Chlavash and Caleb set off down the corridor, heading for the lift to take them down to the pool. Chlavash kept talking the entire way, waving his hands, slapping them against the walls, squeezing Caleb on the shoulder.

"Nobles from all over the planet will be at the games. The viceroys of every continent are coming, with all their families. Lord Morix, and his son, Phlarx, from Eastern One, Lord Forgath, from Western—"

"Morix. Phlarx? Don't they live in Kinsella?" Caleb asked, as they stepped into the lift.

"You know that. The hound who brought you here was from Kinsella. The Lord Morix had you sent here, Caleb, as a gift for Orfassian."

But you never said Morix and Phlarx together, the way they are in my dreams.

"Has he been there for a long time?"

"Yes, for years and years. He is very old. He came here as a youngling from Lindauzian. The Vaarchaels will be among the first to arrive. They are bringing a large entourage — all sorts of servants. Phlarx is to be mated while they are here. Here we are," Chlavash said, and followed Caleb out onto the pool deck.

"Will the Lord Morix and Phlarx bring their family dogs with them?" Caleb asked he pulled his tunic over his head. The pool was completely empty. He stretched and then sat down and slid into the warm water.

"Of course. Why are you so interested in the Vaarchaels? Keep your mind on swimming. Ready, set, go."

Caleb kicked off from the pool wall, glad to be swimming and away from the constant sound of Chlavash's voice. All he could hear was the water against his ears and the sounds of his arms and legs, as his body cut through the water, up and down the pool, lap after lap. Finally he heard Chlavash telling him to stop, to get out of the water, was he crazy? Did he want to hurt himself before the games?

Caleb said nothing as he crawled out of the pool, his body shaking. He let Chlavash drop a towel over him and sat still as the warm creature snuggled around his body.

Caleb dreamed the first dream again, of Papa, that night.

Papa was wearing a black skin that was closer to his own skin than any towel. He tried to peel it off, to wriggle out, but he couldn't. All around Papa was water, a river, a wide rushing river, and he kept turning over and swallowing air, swallowing water, and the skin wouldn't let him go. Papa had no voice.

A week later, it was the second dream Caleb was having every night: running through empty corridors in the palace. He went from door to door, knocking, pressing the palmlocks, until he came to the room where Papa was. And Morix and Phlarx stood outside, crests erect, fangs and claws extended. They growled and snarled and bit the air when they saw him.

"My father is inside, he's sick, he needs me, let me in," Caleb would say.

Morix never spoke; he shook his head and slashed the air with his claws. Caleb would always step back, his hands in front of his face. It was Phlarx who answered Caleb. The younger Lindauzu stepped out in front of his father, every fang showing, his eyes, their golden luster dimmed, hard and dark.

"You can't have him, he's mine. He's always been mine, he was made for me. You're just the chance result of a sperm and an egg, go away, pup."

"I'm a boy and he's a man. He's not yours; he's not anybody's. Let me see him, he's my father."

"Father-son, sire-pup—" and Phlarx would tear the words out of the air, shredding them. "Nothing, chance, biology. It's the bond, the bond—"

"Let me see him."

"Go away, go awaygoawaygoaway. . . ."

Chlavash grew worried at the dark circles under Caleb's eyes and at how slow he was getting up. He ordered extra food for Caleb's meals, he let him practice less, and finally, at the end of the second week of June (Caleb had kept count with a marker on a leg of his table), Chlavash called for the palace vet, who said to bring the pup down to the clinic.

"I can't take any chances this close to the games. They start at the end of next week, you know. Nothing I have tried seems to be working. Maybe the vet can help you sleep," Chlavash said. "And you've become so quiet, no more questions, no, something is wrong."

After taking the lift down, they walked through the kennel to the clinic. *Tell Chlavash, tell any Lindauzi?*

They were stopped just before the clinic by the assistant kennelmaster. Caleb stepped back to stand by a long table as the two started talking. He idly picked up and put down the chains and collars on the table. He put a blue and gold one around his neck but it was far too big. For an adult, he guessed.

"Chlavash, it's about Issoth—you know her, the dam who has produced so many of the Prince's prize racers?" the assistant kennelmaster said, his hands pressed together, his claws touching at the points.

"Yes, I know which dam you mean—very fertile, multiple births —but this pup here is sick; I am taking him to the vet," Chlavash said impatiently.

"This won't take long. Her last pregnancy is not going well.

The vet has advised me that either she or the pup will not survive. I know what the general procedures are in such matters, but, well, you know I just started here, and I don't want to bother the kennelmaster. Confirm that I am making the right decision. Issoth is one of the Prince's prize breeders, you are now his head trainer, you have the wild pup, and she is in the clinic. . . ."

"Let me see her," Chlavash said. "Come on, Caleb. This won't take long, and we are going there, anyway."

Caleb put down the blue and gold collar and followed Chlavash down several corridors, through several nurseries, for two and three year olds, four and five years, infants in rows of incubators, being carefully tended by several palace dams.

The dam of concern to the assistant kennelmaster lay asleep in the veterinary clinic's infirmary. She was enormous with child. Caleb was sure if he touched her swollen stomach it would feel as hard and as unyielding as a rock. Around her were other beds, with a few other dogs here and there, attached to the wall monitors with lights glowing in patterns above them.

"Caleb, you wait here, and don't wake her up. Let me see her records—this is her ninth pregnancy?" Chlavash asked as he examined the sleeping woman, opening her mouth, palpating her breasts and her abdomen. She has to be drugged, Caleb thought.

"Yes, all successful to date. All but two were multiple births, good racer stock. But this time her heart rate is low, she has developed high blood pressure, and she has gone into premature labor twice. She is in a great deal of pain—or would be. I had her inoculated with a mild sleep virus," the assistant kennelmaster answered, reading from a comchart set into a medconsole attached to the dam's bed. "Here are her records."

"The fetus?" Chlavash asked and bent down to look into the chart.

Caleb wanted to touch her himself, feel the child inside her, but he stayed very still, and watched her breath. Mama had let him touch her when she had been pregnant with Davy. He had touched his brother's hard little foot through his mother's skin, and he had laughed and laughed, and had not been able to tell his mother what had been so funny.

"I see no reason not to follow standard procedure. Take the child and put her down. She won't survive this pregnancy and there's too big a chance she will take the pup with her. You will tell the kennelmaster?"

"Of course, and notify the Prince," the assistant kennelmaster said and signaled to a vet tech.

"Good. Come on, Caleb, let's go, the vet is waiting," Chlavash said, and took Caleb by the arm and led him away from the sleeping woman. Caleb looked back once, to see two vet techs standing around her, the assistant kennelmaster speaking to one, gesturing to the other. *Take the baby and put her down? That's it?*

The vet took tissue samples from various parts of Caleb's body, put him in the bodyglove for a complete scan, and then inserted tubes into Caleb's head for a special separate brain scan. All the time she was looking, the Lindauza hummed to herself. She was very efficient, no wasted motion, no wasted words. Caleb tried asking her questions, but the vet just grunted whenever he said anything. It was his body she was examining, not him, flesh, hair, bones.

"There, done. Chlavash, other than being tired for lack of sleep, this pup is in fine health. Stress nightmares, most likely. Include this soporific in his food; that will do it," the vet said as she pulled the tubes easily out of Caleb's head. She rolled them up and then slapped the wall and watched as the tubes were sucked back inside. "He's perfectly fine."

There was a big low table, made out of metal and wood, that was set up beside the cauldron in Jackson. The women cut vegetables there for the stew. When they were done, they'd collect the peelings, the scrapings, the useless stalks, and throw everything into the compost pile. Then they would wash their hands, smooth out their clothes, brush back their hair.

"This lift is up on the roof," Chlavash said, glancing at the controls. "We'll have wait a bit before it gets back down here."

Caleb watched the red light start to descend the linear controls, divided into smaller squares by yellow lines. Each square glowed pink in succession as the light dropped. He counted down, knowing the palace had fifteen floors and then the kennel and clinic, and then one floor below that, the pool. And below the square for the pool there was another square. Caleb shook his head and counted again. The bottom square was from his third dream; its light had come on when he had followed the mice.

"Chlavash—what's the bottom square for? What's down there?"

"What, oh, down at the very bottom. Storage, maintenance,

machinery, waste recycling. Burrowers live down there, monitoring the recycling. And old, old tunnels, or there used to be. I've never been there, but somebody said you could follow them all the way out, under the river—ah, here's the lift. You must be feeling better, you're asking me questions. . . ."

The dream is true.

Chlavash kept talking as they stepped inside. And Caleb knew he would keep talking all the way up to the fourteenth floor.

Caleb tried to figure out which part of his food had the soporific, but nothing tasted sleepy. It was there, of that he had no doubt. Within half an hour after eating, he could barely keep his eyes open and his head was falling against his chest. Caleb tried to stay awake, wanting to remember his dreams and knowing this drug would take them away, but he couldn't. Pacing didn't help, nor did jumping into the bathing pool and sitting under the fountain. When he fell asleep there, he slipped under the water and woke up, spitting and breathing hard.

He whistled for one of the towels and let the creature wrap itself tight and warm and close all around his body. With the towel still hugging him, Caleb went back to his bed and laid down. He felt as if he were falling down, sliding down, faster and faster, into a heavy and close darkness.

Caleb took the soporific for the next four nights and there were no more dreams about Papa, the black skin, the river, or about Morix and Phlarx, or about following the mice into the dark tunnels. Caleb ate his eveningmeal and fell asleep. Chlavash shook him awake, sat with him as he woke up and ate his morningmeal, and then the Lindauzu walked the yawning Caleb to either the gym or the pool for a day of practice. His twelfth birthday came and went. On the fifth night, the night before the nobles arrived from all over the planet and three days before the games were to begin, Chlavash stopped the soporific.

"You need to be alert and sharp, now that you are rested again."

Caleb's dream of Papa returned that night.

Papa stood at a window, his arms crossed on the sill. He wore only a jockstrap and wall tubes were fitted into his groin, chest and back. Papa moved very slowly, but not because of the tubes. Caleb watched Papa twist and bend the tubes, pull them out and then push them back in his skin. Papa seemed to have been given the same

drug Chlavash had given him. Papa moved slowly, as if moving in
sleep, below water. His blond hair had been cut close to his skull and
there was a red and silver collar around his neck.

Papa? It's me, Caleb.

Caleb stepped across the small room, across a floor thick with
grass, grass that rippled and moved beneath his feet.

Papa?

Papa wouldn't turn away from the window.

PapaPapaPapa. . . .

"Chlavash, I want you to point out the Lords Morix and Phlarx.
After all, if it wasn't for Morix, I wouldn't be here. Will you do
that?" Caleb asked the next morning. Caleb was standing in front
of a mirror in the kennel dressing room as Chlavash directed a
house menial in how Caleb should be groomed. Caleb had tried
to catch the eyes of the menial, but the man kept his eyes down.
He only spoke when Chlavash spoke to him and then only to say
yes or no. The menial reminded Caleb of Ezra the hunter in
Jackson, a dark man with long skinny arms and legs, thick, bushy
hair. Caleb wondered if the menial had ever been outside the
imperial palace in his life. He knew very few ever had.

"Well, Chlavash?" Caleb asked again, looking down at his own
bare, dusky-skinned body. At least he was allowed outside. The
menial was trimming the hair in his groin. Caleb wondered why,
since hair had just started growing there and he didn't have an
awful lot. Fashion, Chlavash had said. The prize pet of the Crown
Prince should be an epitome of what current taste said the
appearance of a well-groomed dog should be.

"Yes, yes, I will point them out to you. They arrive today. They
will be presented to the Prince and you will be there for the
ceremony. The Prince wants everyone to see his prize wolf pup,
and, probably Morix will ask about his gift. Menial, when you trim
his head hair, be sure the curves of his ears show. Yes, just like
that."

Caleb sighed. Chlavash would make the menial take all morning grooming him. First the hair, then oiling his body. Then trimming his nails to a specific length. And, as the final touch, golden
sparkleflecks in his hair. For some reason the Lindauzu felt it
would show off Caleb's supposedly feral nature. Then a dark blue
tunic, to bring out his skin tones. With a sash in imperial yellow.

The Kinsella hound had landed on the roof of the bottom wing
of the triangular palace, the nearest to the sea. The official greet-

ing of the Prince by his nobles was to be on the right wing, a part of the roof on which Caleb had spent little time. He and Chlavash took their places there just after the noonmeal, one tenstride behind the Prince, between two trees unlike any Caleb had ever seen. There was a slight wind and Caleb could smell the oils and scents on the Prince's fur. The two trees, according to the sign, were Avenian pseudotrees, carnivorous and semi-sentient. They moved constantly in the presence of warm-blooded creatures, their whiplike branches striking their light-cages again and again. Every now and then, between Chlavash's constant yammer, and the crowd noises, Caleb heard the pseudotrees, a low, guttural moaning. Any other time, Caleb would have been fascinated by the trees and would have been pestering Chlavash with endless questions. Not today. He kept his attention on the red-and-silver air yacht that was coming on its final approach.

"There they are, those are the Vaarchael colors. You can see your Lord Morix in just a few minutes," Chlavash whispered.

The air yacht landed, and the hatch opened, extending automatically into a long ramp. First the hounds emerged and formed two protective lines. Then a tall, light-furred Lindauzu stepped out, followed closely by another Lindauzu who looked remarkably like the first.

"Lord Morix. His son, Lord Phlarx." Chlavash said.

Where is he? He should be with them. He has to be.

"The Vaarchael kennelmaster. Their vet seems to be taking care of that dog. Yes, she has him on a leash, a prized companion pet, I presume," Chlavash said.

The vet and her charge stood behind the kennelmaster, waiting as Morix and his son approached the Prince to make the gesture of submission. When they were one tenstride from the Prince, they dropped to all fours.

Caleb stared at the dog the vet had on a leash. If he could just get closer and see the dog's face.

After Morix and Phlarx stood up again and spoke briefly to the Prince, the two Lindauzu stood aside as the rest of their entourage dropped to all fours. More greetings, and then all of them, led by Morix, started toward the lifts that would take them down into the imperial palace and their apartments. Another yacht was already descending.

The vet and her leashed dog walked directly in front of Caleb and Chlavash. It was Papa, but a different Papa than the one he had said good-bye to over a year ago. It was the Papa in his last

dream. *He's sick, he's hurt. But I still found him. I found him.*
Caleb had to put his hand over his mouth to not cry out. He
locked his legs to not run. He pretended to listen to Chlavash as
the rest of the Vaarchaels passed, and the next yacht landed.

Papa?

Phlarx stopped so suddenly the vet, who was right behind him,
leading Papa, ran into the Lindauzu.

Who said that? Who are you?

*I know you, Phlarx, from my dreams. Your dog, the human, he's
my papa.*

"Caleb, see the next yacht? With the blue-and-white markings?
That's the Vaarkens, cousins and neighbors of the Vaarchaels.
Both tobacco planters, imperial kin, and . . ."

One brief glance into the waiting crowd, and then Phlarx un-
tangled himself from the vet, soothed Papa, and then walked on
to where his father and the others waited. Caleb watched as
Phlarx took the leash from the vet and led Papa into the lift with
him, the vet behind them. The doors winked shut and they were
gone.

*So, how do I rescue him? Where would we go? There's no Jackson
to go back to—the Summer Country? The mountains north of here?
Papa has always dreamed of the Summer Country.*

The tunnels and the mice.

". . . now, that yacht up there, the black one with the stars, is
from Continent Three . . ."

*Just walk into the Vaarchael apartments and ask for him, let my
father go? But Lindauzi and humans come and go all the time, on
errands and business. And I wear imperial colors, I can go almost
anywhere.*

*I've come to take Lord Phlarx's dog for a walk. Yes, I will be
careful, we won't be gone long.*

And Papa will help me. He will wake up and tell me what to do.

Today and the next two days, Chlavash said, as they left the roof
later in the morning, were to be taken up with receptions, meet-
ings, banquets, and matings. Formal mating agreements were
negotiated and those negotiated the year before were performed.

"Your Phlarx's mating is to begin tomorrow, in the Prince's
personal temple. The first day ceremony is tomorrow morning."

"Oh?"

"Yes, it will be quite an event, with his body-mate the daughter . . ."

That night Caleb dreamed again of Papa and Phlarx.

The next morning Caleb woke early. He wanted to be out of his cage long before Chlavash came with his morningmeal. He washed his face and then pulled out two tunics, the dark blue with the imperial yellow sash from yesterday and the other Vaarchael red. He put on the red tunic and then, over it, the blue. He combed his hair carefully, wishing it was straight, like the hair of most the Vaarchaels' dogs. Papa's had been cut so close the curls were gone. In the pockets of the red tunic he stuffed some of the apple and pear slices he had saved from the day before; the rest he ate as he left his cage.

I wish I had paper or a compad. To say good-bye to Chlavash, tell him I won't be at the games. He wasn't so bad, for a Lindauzu. I won't miss the games, though.

All the Lindauzi nobility were staying in the left wing of the triangular palace, spread out over four floors. One floor up, a lift across the triangle base, turn, through the left wing, and then up, and he was there. Caleb stepped out into what seemed to be an indoor park, with potted trees and couches and floating trays filled with food and drink. The room was shaped like a diamond, a red diamond, the favorite Lindauzi carpet color, and corridors punctuated all four sides. Each corridor was marked with family banners. The red and silver Vaarchael banner was three or four tenstrides away, across the room. There were Lindauzi and dogs everywhere. Carrying things. Herding the trays. Talking, walking, reclining on the couches. One dog was carefully cutting dead leaves from the huge ferns which marked every corridor exit. One such fern was right by Caleb, a green guardian for the lift. Its papery filigreed leaves contracted when Caleb touched it.

He pulled the blue tunic over his head, and, after looking around the room, stuffed it behind the fern pot. He finger-combed his hair, reminded himself to breathe, and walked across the room and walked under the Vaarchael banner.

The mouse just slips through, in and out, close to the wall, under and over, smiling, nodding. The mouse is very careful to look busy and knows just where he is going. The few Lindauzi standing around the Vaarchael colors didn't even look at Caleb as he walked past.

The family vet was in the dining room, sipping her morning drink and gazing out the window. The view of the city was impressive.

"Lord Phlarx sent me to walk the sick one, Ilox," Caleb said, looking down at the floor.

"Oh? At least I won't have to do it while he is off at the temple being mated. Have I seen you before? You weren't on the yacht yesterday, were you?" the vet said and poured herself more morning drink. The ice cracked and popped in her cup.

"I rode in the back, with the other menials."

"I never bothered going back there. Very well. I will get him for you. It's time for his medicine anyway. Why the Lord Phlarx persists in this childhood fantasy of his long-lost pet, I'll never know."

Caleb watched as the vet palmed open a door and then followed the Lindauza inside a small room. Papa sat on a bed in the corner. The room had one window, the window from Caleb's dream.

"Here, Ilox, your medicine," the vet said and pressed a dermic against Papa's neck. "Here's the leash. Have him back in two hours." The vet checked Papa's pulse and temperature, peered into his eyes, and left.

"Papa. It's me, Caleb. We're going to the Summer Country. Papa?"

Papa blinked and rubbed his eyes, trying to focus on Caleb. He looked much older than when Caleb had last seen him. There was grey in his blond hair and wrinkles spread out from his eyes. He was still a big man, bigger than any Jacksoner, but his body was wasted and frail.

"Papa? It's me, Caleb. Get up. Let's go. This is our chance to get out of here."

Papa wasn't supposed to be sick, not now, not after Caleb hadn't seen him for a year. Papa never got sick; Papa was tall, strong, sure. He was the one to lead them out of the Vaarchael apartments, across the diamond room, into the lifts, and down to follow the mice. Caleb wanted to hand everything over to Papa. He wanted Papa to pick him up, hold him close, stroke his hair, and tell him it was all right, Papa is here now. *Come on, son, let's go. Not so fast, we have to look like we aren't in a hurry, Caleb . . .* Caleb stared at the silent groggy man with his slack face, his unfocused eyes. This wasn't the Papa he had walked away from Jackson to look for. This wasn't the Papa for whom he had figured out a way to escape Umium.

"Pup, take him for a walk. You're wasting time. If the Lord Phlarx comes back from his first day ceremonies and finds his precious Ilox hasn't been walked—here, let me do it." It was the vet, standing in the doorway. She took the leash hanging on the wall and hooked it onto the collar around Papa's neck.

"Now, walk him. A good long walk, and have him back in two hours, like I said," the vet snapped. "Go on. And be careful."

"I will. Why is he so sleepy?" Caleb said and pulled on the leash. Papa stared at Caleb, and scratching his head, got up. Caleb tugged at the leash again and Papa started walking behind him.

"The medicine, the sleepiness is only right after he takes it. Now go on."

That was it, the medicine. As soon as it wears off, Papa would be himself again. He was sick in my dreams, but now he will get well and everything will be all right.

"It will be OK, Papa," Caleb said first in Lindauzi, and then in American, as they made their way out of the Vaarchael apartments, busy with menials decorating for the second day of the mating ceremonies, hanging up glowing streamers and draping sparkling nets over the walls. Then across the red rug and the diamond room and equally-busy Lindauzi, but busy at what, Caleb couldn't tell. Papa had looked toward Caleb when he spoke in American—was it Caleb's imagination or did Papa look more aware at American sounds? Maybe the medicine was wearing off.

"Here's the lift, Papa. All we have to do is get on and press that bottom control right there. All the way down, Papa," Caleb said in American and sighed.

Wake up.

Caleb held his hand against the palmsign and waited. The wall glowed in response to his hand and the lift door opened. He tugged at Papa's leash and went inside. He pressed the corresponding inner palmsign and the door closed. Safe. He was almost weak with relief. *Not yet, this is just the first part.* "Here we go, Papa, down," Caleb said and pressed the bottom control and the lift began dropping. *Papa, I need you. I don't want to do this by myself.* Fifteen, fourteen, thirteen. Papa leaned back against the liftwall, his eyes closed. Nine, eight. Three, two, ground, kennel, pool. Sub-basement. The lift stopped, Caleb pressed the palmsign and the door opened.

"OK, Papa, here we are," Caleb said and tugged at Papa's leash. "Come on." Papa pressed his hands against the liftwall and stood upright. Caleb tugged again and Papa lifted his hand to comb back his hair, even though it was too short to need a comb, and then let his hand drop. Papa had done just that back in Jackson when he was thinking, as if finger-combing his hair would start his brain working more quickly.

"Papa? Are you awake now? Never mind, let's go." *He'll be all right, he has to be. He's going to take care of me.* Caleb and Papa stepped out of the lift and Caleb quickly turned around to send the lift back up. Then he looked around to see where he and Papa were.

This is the place in my dreams. The mice are here.

The nearest light came from the lift itself, the pink moving light that marked each floor, until it stopped at the eighteenth square. They stood on a square metal platform, about one ten-stride wide and one tenstride long. Just beyond the platform was a slab of cement: old, cracked, with chunks missing. The slab was human-made—how Caleb knew this, he couldn't explain—but the platform was alien, the slab was not. It extended in three directions. To the left and to the right it ran along a tiled wall; in front, half a tenstride until it stopped. A thin light of luminous green paint marked the slab's edge. Metal pillars, regularly spaced, lined the slab's front edge. On each pillar were signs. Caleb pulled at Papa's leash and walked forward, carefully stepping over the missing places in the cement, until he stood in front of one pillar.

"72 ST." Each pillar was marked with the same numbers and letters. To Caleb's right, on the tiled wall: CENTRA PAR. The tiles with the missing letters had long ago fallen off. Caleb was in the presence of age, of time—this place was older than Jackson. Humans had built this place long before they had piled stone upon stone to erect Jackson's columns and white tower. A step or two more and Caleb peered down into a long low pit, with metal bars on the pit floor. Like—tracks, train tracks, Caleb thought, remembering the old tracks on Lee Street, not far from Jackson. Old train tunnels. To the left was darkness, to the right, Caleb saw a single yellow light that was coming closer. Directly ahead was another platform, mirroring the one on which he stood. In the exact middle of the track bed someone had painted another luminous green line; the yellow light moved directly above the green.

Burrowers? What did Chlavash say about them? Recyclers? Waste? Yes, just like the mice, Max, beast-minds, they are beasts.

Not knowing how much burrowers might be like hunterbeasts, Caleb pulled Papa back until they stood in a small space beside the lift doors. The lift's interior light cast a faint red shadow on Papa's face. They waited as the light in the tunnel grew brighter and closer. Caleb could hear whatever it was now, a sharp hissing.

The burrowers were running an elongated flat car fitting snugly between the two platforms. There were two of them in the front, and behind them were stacks and stacks of black tanks and barrels, held onto the car beneath a force field. Caleb recognized the characteristic yellow shimmering glow. The two burrowers were male, and small, smaller than even the smallest Jacksoner adult. They were covered with a fine grey hair and their pale eyes were tiny and shrunken. Their car floated above the ground.

Job to be donejobtobedonekeepmovingkeepmoving . . .

And the burrowers and their car and tanks were gone.

Mouse. There, in the track bed, two of them, tiny black lumps in the light.

foodfoodfoodfood?

No, not yet. Show me sunlightwarm then foodfoodfood.

After Caleb helped Papa down from the platform onto the cold earth of the tracks, he unhooked the leash and threw it as far as he could into the dark. Then, taking Papa's hand, Caleb led him after the mice in the direction the burrowers had gone.

The 72 ST CENTRA PAR tunnel was quiet. Caleb could hear the sounds of Papa's breathing and his own, their feet on the earth, the whispery mice feet. There was a dull thumping he heard for a long time until Caleb recognized the beating of his own heart.

He heard other sounds the longer they walked: water, faint, slow, dripping on hard stone. Rumbling, clanking—burrowers, he guessed, in another tunnel. A faraway rising whine, above his head.

"Papa, hear that whining noise? Over us? What do you think it is? You grew up in a Lindauzi house," Caleb said. His voice sounded hollow and loose as he spoke.

Papa said nothing: but he flinched at the sound of Caleb's words as if they had stung him. At least he wasn't whimpering and crying and muttering to himself the way he had when they had climbed down off the platform. Like a pigeon, Caleb thought, remembering the pigeons that had nested in the ruins of the Jackson's Tower, black and grey birds invisible in the twilight, cooing, chirping. *Davy was scared of the pigeons because he couldn't see them at dusk. There were so many they seemed to be everywhere. He ran crying back down into Jackson the first time Mama took him there.*

It didn't take too many tenstrides before the pale pink lights and the luminous green of the slab were gone, leaving only the green on the ground. When the slab light was gone, the darkness was closer, and Papa started crying again. At least he wasn't so sleepy.

"Papa, is it the dark? We can still see enough from the green line, see, right at your feet. It's for the burrowers and their car, I guess. I can't make it brighter. Papa, talk to me. Papa, Papa." The last "Papa" Caleb shouted at his father, and Papa grabbed Caleb's arm, squeezing hard.

"You're hurting—take my hand. Let's keep walking—I don't want to lose the mice—they *are* gone. It's OK, I'm sorry I shouted; I can call the mice again. You're safe. We got away. Everything is going to be OK. Let me call the mice and we can go." He wished he could see Papa's eyes and see if anything was there at all. Or would they be just blue, a dark blue, as if he were looking into an empty sky. He stroked his father's arm with his free hand.

You should be holding my hand. What's wrong with you?
Mouse . . .

Ilox knew this boy-pup. He recognized the pup's face, a face he had seen a thousand times when he was in the dream-water, in the black skin. The face would reshatter and reform over and over. But he couldn't remember the pup's name. He looked and looked at the pup: carefully combed, dark, curly oil-scented hair, skin darker than his own. The pup's blue eyes. He had seen eyes like that before, eyes he had looked into often. And a hand, a hand on his face, and the eyes.

The pup wanted something from him. Ilox was sure of that. The pup was hungry for it; Ilox could feel him tugging in his head, and when the pup tugged on his leash, Ilox followed him. It was hard to think anyway; he wanted to sleep.

I don't have anything to give him.

As the lift dropped, Ilox leaned against the wall, his eyes closed. The lights, blinking as they passed each floor, bothered him. One more thing he knew he should recognize, but couldn't. Everything—all the answers, all the names, felt so close, as if they were just beyond a thin wall.

The liftwall was smooth and solid, cool to the touch. Ilox could find no way through it, around it, under it, over it. And there was a light trapped inside, a soft rosy glow.

The lift stopped, the door opened.

Phlarx where I can't boy-pup down lift all the lights flashing dark here Phlarx?

Ilox gripped the boy-pup's arms, crying, wishing he could tell the pup to take him back, he didn't want to walk anymore, but the words kept slipping away from his tongue. The pup used odd-

sounding words and stroked his arm. He showed Ilox the green
lines on the platform and in the pit, and gestured at the darkness.

But the dark didn't go anywhere.

The Crown Prince's Temple of Madaan was without question the
hugest on Earth. It was said to be far grander than those that had
been on Aven, Volis, Zachanassia, or any colony world. Indeed, its
only rival was the Mother Temple in Emium, on Lindauzian
itself. But then the temples on Aven, Volis, and Zachanassia were
empty, as were the cities around them. And who knew if anyone
survived in Emium, if weeds and vines weren't growing up the
temple walls. The black ribs supporting the Umium temple's great
dome rose to a burning apex, a miniature sun blazing directly
above the sacred dais. The panels between the ribs kaleidoscop-
ically shifted in color, golds, blues, reds, greens, purples, blooming,
expanding, contracting. The light in the temple shimmered with
the changing colors playing over, around, and through the seated
Lindauzi.

Phlarx stood in the center of the dais, looking out into the temple sanctuary. Xian stood to Phlarx's left. He looked at her out of
the corner of his eye: quiet, collected, looking down at her feet.
His sister Tyuil and her mate Orvelth sat in the front row, behind
the Vaarken cousins. To Tyuil's right were Xian's cousins and
grandmother. Directly below Phlarx and between him and Tyuil
were Morix and Xian's father and the Prince. There was no one
else. They were all waiting for the priest.

Xian, Phlarx thought, was beautiful. Red fur, scented with
tobacco oil, her claws and fangs polished to a high gloss. But, as
Morix had reminded him again that morning, beauty wasn't why
she was here. *Her mother was the daughter of Corviax's sister; this
mating meant an alliance with the imperial family. And her empathetic quotient was among the highest of her generation — offspring
could possibly be . . . The Project . . .*

Yes, Father. Where's the priest?

There he was. The Lindauzi in the temple all turned together
to watch, as if every head was pulled at the same time by the
same string. The priest's white fur shone in the moving light. *He's
walking with a cane. The Prince said a temple on Four was closed —
not enough white Lindauzi to go around of late.* Phlarx could hear
the toeclaws of the priest clicking on the floor. Xian cleared her
throat, raked her fur one last time.

Today we exchange blood and pain. Tomorrow the neck rings.

*The third day, the blessings and the vows. And on the fourth day,
with a little medical help, we should both be in heat, the exchange
of fluids—*

(Phlarx?)

The priest slowly walked up the dais steps. He turned briefly
to gesture toward Morix and Xian's father, who followed him up.
Then the glowglobes descended from the sun to form a circle of
light around the entire dais. The Iani shadows began to form.

*I remember this from Tyuil's mating. Ilox and me, trying to
figure out what was going on. He should be here.*

(Phlarx.)

"Phlarx luMorix laOssit Vaarchael. Xian luOarx laCambit
Darnelian. Today, the blood of the heart, the pain of life . . ." the
priest began. More glowglobes came down to form a smaller circle
around the three of them.

(Phlarx.)

"Stop," Phlarx said, speaking at first so softly that no one heard
him. "Stop," he repeated, getting louder and louder, "stop, stop,
stop talking. Stop. Now."

The priest closed his mouth, dropped his hands, the Iani
shadow wavered and grew blurred at its edges.

"Phlarx, what's wrong?" Xian said, reaching for his hand, her
claws extended.

"Stop talking, so I can hear. There. It's Ilox," Phlarx said,
pushing back her hand. "Something's wrong."

*Her claws are out. Why? Father said she was old, that she'd been
waiting. I've been waiting, too, but I didn't know it, and I smell her,
and I feel, I feel, oh I don't think we will need any medicine—*

(Where boy-pup know down way down lift all the lights lost
one line dark Phlarx? . . .)

The boy-pup on the roof.

"Stop? You can't stop now, Phlarx," the priest said angrily. His
fangs and claws were extended, his crest erect, ears flat.

"Ilox needs me. I can't stay here and do this. He's down in the
waste tunnels. Somebody's taking him away—"

"Phlarx. What are you doing?" Morix said, stepping forward
and under the inner light-circle. Just behind him was Oarx, Xian's
father, who looked to be in a blood-rage. Phlarx could just hear the
growl, low and deep in Xian's father's throat.

Phlarx instinctively stepped back. Morix was the angriest—no,
Phlarx thought, looking at Xian—she might be the angriest of all.
Phlarx took another step back, outside the inner lights, until he

was alone, facing all of them: the priest, Morix, Xian, and her father. The Prince stood and raised his hands, dropped them, shook his head.

"I told you. I heard Ilox. He's my companion, my bond-mate. That shadow of yours, priest, that Iani, it knows. You see, Father, you see, Prince," Phlarx said, turning to the Prince, "the Project worked, at least for me and Ilox it did—"

"It failed. He failed. You should have left him in the cocoon. You can't talk to the priest of Madaan and the Crown Prince this way." Morix snarled. To Phlarx's amazement, his father had raised his hand as if to strike him.

"I'm not little any more. Don't you speak to me that way," Phlarx snarled back, his eyes half-closed. Mating lust, anger, he didn't know what it was, but it was filling him. His fangs and claws were out. He growled and snapped at the air.

"Phlarx!" Morix started toward him, but Phlarx stopped him, slashing the air with his claws.

"The Iani knows. See! The shadow heard me. It's just the shadow of this old priest's memory from before the Extinction, but it knows. This mating—oh, I want it, I feel it, the want, but it's my body that wants. Not my heart. That's Ilox's, he has my heart, and he needs raarraaaaagghhhme," and Phlarx roared.

Xian reached for him. He flung her off the dais, knowing where his strength was from, that it wouldn't last. *My body will never know now.* Phlarx turned to face his father, not looking to see if she was hurt or moved or bled. He and Morix circled each other on the dais. Phlarx's ears filled with roaring, he knew the priest was yelling, Xian's father, even the Prince—everyone was saying or screaming or snarling something. Even Tyuil, but she was so far away. It was all noise.

Phlarx shook his head. He had to hear, he had to talk. "Father. Listen. Over and over and over you told me what it was all for, all our history, all that we did here. The weeding out, the breeding, all for this. You almost had it with Sandron, but not quite, remember? I have it, so let me go."

Phlarx jumped at his father, who fell backwards with a heavy thump on the dais. Phlarx pinned his father's arms and bared his teeth against his father's throat.

"See? I'm adult." Phlarx whispered into his father's face. He bit twice at his father's throat, his fangs stopping short of breaking the skin. Morix lay very still, staring directly overhead into the bright light of a glowglobe that had followed them down.

Phlarx knocked the globe away and stood. He looked at them all: his father lying on the floor, the priest, Xian's father, the Prince, Xian just sitting up, Tyuil, her mate. All of them seemed to have become frozen, with their eyes locked on him.

Ilox needs me. I've got to find a flyer and a city map. I've got to get out of here.

The tunnel walls were black bricks. Caleb idly touched them as he and Papa walked. He brushed his fingers against the bricks, half-wishing the Lindauzi had made the tunnels. Then each touch would create light. There were a few of the Lindauzi red and pink bricks stuck in here and there, but touching them brought forth no light. Caleb shivered. Above them, how far above he couldn't guess, it was June and summertime.

"Papa, will you tell me a story?" Caleb asked. "You always told me and Davy stories before you left. Why did you go away? Just to show the elders you could do it? They are all dead—everybody is dead. Aunt Sara, Davy, the elders. Can you hear me?" Caleb said. These were questions he had waited a year to ask; it wasn't fair Papa couldn't answer.

Papa had been silent since his plaintive cries when they had climbed down off the cement slab and started their walk. Now he walked obediently beside Caleb, his hand limp within Caleb's hand. Papa used to walk with his arms swinging, and talking and laughing. He'd point things out to Caleb, a bird, a fox, a funny-shaped cloud, quick, look, before you miss it, did you see it?

"You can hear me, I know you can," Caleb muttered. "Turn here, the mice went this way and so does the green line." They turned into a short Lindauzi-made tunnel, with only Lindauzi stones. This wall wasn't dead; when he brushed his fingers against the pink and red bricks, he left four streaks of light. Caleb kept his fingers on the wall until they were back in a human tunnel and its black walls.

When they were in the next tunnel, Caleb sat down, his back to the wall. "Let's stop for a minute, we've been walking really fast, I need to catch my breath. I guess I should give the mice some of these apple slices. Just for a minute," Caleb said, looking up at Papa who was pacing back and forth.

foodfoodfood?

Just a little, here, then sunlight, yes?

foodfoodfood

"Sit down, you're driving me crazy walking like that," and

Caleb grabbed his father's hand and yanked him down to the ground. Papa sat down heavily beside Caleb. He leaned over and pulled at Caleb's arm.

"What do you want? I'm sorry I jerked at you, but you're not listening to me." *Is he finally waking up? I can't believe I am talking to Papa this way.*

Papa rubbed his stomach and pointed to the mice and the apple slices.

"You're hungry. So am I. I have to save some for the mice, so we can get out of here. You're just going to have to wait until we get outside. I can find food outside, you and Mama taught me all that. I have about two more fruit slices—oh, here take one, and stop pulling at me. I don't have any more food!" Caleb yelled in Papa's face. Papa threw up his hands as if to knock back Caleb's words.

"I'm sorry, I'm sorry. I have to save what I have left for the mice," Caleb said in a much softer voice. "That's all I have. You'll have to wait until we get outside."

Papa pulled at Caleb's arm again and pointed to his mouth. He rubbed his stomach, as if to be sure Caleb got the message.

"Let's go," Caleb said and stood. *Now my stomach's growling. How long have we been down here? It can't be that long, it just feels like we have been down here forever. I wish I knew how long it's going to take to get out.*

sunlight out?

"This way, Papa. The mice are going this way." In a few minutes they were at another platform, 50 ST 8AV. *Twenty-two streets down. So we are walking south, the green line is going south. Maybe I don't need the mice; I can just keep following the green line—*

Papa pulled at Caleb's arm again and pointed to his mouth.

Phlarx always brings me food milk oranges bread fish meat food all kinds cuts slices spoons Phlarx brings me food hungry my stomach hurts it's been long I don't know I can't remember his name I know his face all kinds of food

Phlarx took one last look before running out of the temple. No one seemed able to believe he had forced his father to expose his throat and submit. Morix lay still and quiet in the middle of the dais, one arm covering his face, glowglobes attentively hovering over him. Xian (*oh, to touch her once, taste even a little of the heat of this fire*) sat on the floor where she had fallen and there was blood on her face, her mating robes. She held her right arm as if it were broken. Her father, standing by the priest, stared at Phlarx, his fangs protruding, dripping saliva. The priest had buried his face in his hands. Phlarx could see his father's chest rising and falling. The Prince, Tyuil, Orvelth, the grandmother, all of them, just stared at him, their heads turning as he jumped off the dais and ran up the aisle and out.

Ilox needs me. I've got to find a flyer and a city map.

The temple was in the exact center of the city, set in a great round grass lawn, rimmed by flowers and fountains. The personal flyers of Xian's father, Tyuil and Orvelth, and the rest were parked just past the circle of flowers and falling water. Hounds stood on guard by what Phlarx guessed was the Prince's flyer. Phlarx jumped into the first unattended one he came to, yelled imperial palace and go, and took off.

After dodging three or four other flyers and a spacebound shuttle, he was on the palace roof and running again, to the nearest lift. "Switch, manual to voice control, directory, city map room," he said, breathing hard. *Hurry up, computer, can't you go any faster, I've got to go, hurry.* "Tenth floor, bottom wing—go, now."

The lift door slid open and Phlarx charged out into the middle of several dogs herding float trays. The trays flew everywhere, throwing food on the floor, the wall, water and drink in the air, dogs on top of each other. The Lindauza who had been right behind the dogs pressed herself against the nearest wall.

"Out of my way," Phlarx growled, snapping with bared fangs. The Lindauza screamed and hid her face. "Atavism! Atavism!"

That's it. Now I can be shot down. No atavism shall be suffered to live, lest we all slip down to four feet.

"I said: get out of my way!" Phlarx knocked back the nearest dog, snapping its neck, never breaking his stride. Ilox was afraid, confused, hungry. And he was calling Phlarx's name. Phlarx had to find him. Why couldn't they understand?

One tenstride, two, turn, a half-tenstride, the Prince's offices, in, through a room with a great globe, then the map room. A huge model of Umium was in the center of the room, and mapscreens were on three walls, the third overlooked the river. There were a handful of Lindauzi scattered about, facing the model or one of the screens. Phlarx took a deep breath, exhaled, closed his eyes.

Ilox? I'm here, where are you?

Down below black tunnels

"You. And you, all of you, get out of here. I said: get out of here, now." He growled and then he roared. *If I am going to be atavistic, I might as well be it all the way.* The room emptied.

Phlarx stood before a mapscreen, listening intently to Ilox trying to tell the boy he was hungry.

"Map, show city substructure, key tunnels."

The mapscreen's image shifted to show a cross-sectional view of Umium. Below the lawns, the basements, was an amazing, complex system of interconnecting tunnels.

Ilox? Where are you?

Here. Right here, boy-pup here.

Phlarx stared at the tunnel maze. How could he ever find the right one? "My lord, some of the others said you were here, and needed some help."

"I thought I told you to—" Phlarx stopped. It was a librarian. Maybe he could help. *Ilox did this kind of work for me when we were—*

"Yes. Is there a map of just these old tunnels?"

The librarian, a short, grey-furred Lindauzu, looked at Phlarx curiously, wondering, Phlarx was sure, if he was the same Lindauzu who had just ordered everyone out.

"Could-you-please-show-me-the-tunnel-maps?"

"Here. See, how deep down they go, in the island's bedrock. You know," the librarian went conversationally, apparently having decided the others Phlarx had ordered out had been wrong. "I really think we need to fill in most of these old tunnels, they are so old and so dangerous . . ."

Phlarx ignored the librarian's soft prattle. He placed one hand on the screen, moving it slowly until he felt a twinge: Ilox. "There he is."

"Lord Phlarx. Lord Phlarx." He was being paged on the city-wide intercom.

"You're the Lord Phlarx, there was just something on the city newsnet—" Before the librarian could finish, Phlarx knocked him across the room. The librarian hit the map controls and there was a bright flash and the entire wall went blank. The librarian rolled off the control console and hit the floor with a solid thud.

Have I killed him? No, he's still moving. Never mind. Which way are they going? Down to the maintenance level, waste and recycling. Are they going to go there—where else could they go down there?

"Maybe I can catch them before they go into the old tunnels," Phlarx said out loud, ignoring the librarian's moans. The lift he had taken down from the roof was only a few tenstrides away. He paused before leaving the map room. The dead dog lay where it had fallen, but there was no one else, no other dogs with trays, no Lindauza to terrify.

This time Phlarx walked.

"Times Square," Caleb read aloud. There was, as there had been at every numbered or named place, another platform, but only the one where the lift had stopped had been lighted. The Times Square platform was larger than the others, and its cement floor seemed to stretch away forever, swallowed up by the blackness. He wondered what he would find if he went up one of the stairwells.

"Pa—" Caleb swallowed the last syllable. Papa might have known what was at the top of the Times Square stairs from all his prowling in the Lindauzi libraries. He might have seen humans going up and down the stairs, across the wide floor, beneath the bright lights and high roof. That was a different Papa. This one had eyes that couldn't be still and a tongue that made no sense.

Caleb pulled himself up to sit on the edge of the Times Square platform. Papa stayed down in the track bed, running his hand back and forth along the cement. It hadn't been long since they had stopped to rest before, but Caleb still felt tired. He was very hungry. Well, if he didn't need the mice, but could just follow the green line, why not? Caleb pulled out the last handful of fruit slices in his tunic and gave half to Papa. Caleb sighed; the little bit of food did nothing for either of them. Papa kept tugging at his sleeve and pointing to his stomach, which grumbled and growled. Swallowing saliva didn't help.

"Stop pulling at me," Caleb snapped and pushed his father's hands away as if he were swatting at flies on a hot summer's day back in Jackson. "That's it; I don't have anymore. You will just have to wait until we get outside. Come on, let's go—wait, Papa, be still, somebody's coming." Caleb leaned toward the darkness they had just walked from: a whistling noise? Had the Lindauzi sent somebody to look for them?

"Come on, Papa, up here, we need to hide, just to be sure," Caleb said. "Come on," Caleb muttered and jumped down into the track bed to push and shove his crying and whimpering father until he climbed up on the platform. Caleb scrambled up beside him, grabbed his father's hand and jerked him again, to get him to stand up. "Will you come on? They're close—" He had felt who was coming: burrowers, that same strange mind, *gotta keep moving, jobtodomovemove*

There they were. More burrowers driving another floater car. This time Caleb could see a glowing green line on the car bottom, matching the one in the track bed. And the glowing air, yellow and pale and white. More black containers and just two burrowers.

As the car passed, the burrower in the back stared at the Times Square platform and at Caleb and Papa. It locked its white-pink eyes with Caleb and it kept staring until the car was gone, taking its sound with it.

"It saw me," Caleb said. "Let's go, Papa."

Phlarx stood at the edge of the 72 ST CENTRAL PAR platform, the lift doors open behind him, washing everything with its pinkish light. Everything was the platform and its green line, the tunnel, and two cracked staircases. Phlarx was panting, extending and retracting his claws.

"I'm too late. They're somewhere inside all these old tunnels. The librarian was right, we should have closed them off," Phlarx said, his first sentence repeating itself: I'M TOO LATE, I'M TOO LATE, I'MTOOLATE, louder and louder until he started roaring again, biting and slashing the air with his claws.

Don't ever do that, Phlarx. That's feral behavior. Mother, her voice dull and flat. She never touched me. Never. The dog-nurses did. I remember one with soft hair and eyes the color of Ilox's. Her hand scratching me behind the ears. My mother Ossit watched with her hands at her side. I tried to feel sad when she killed herself; I couldn't. Now, Morix touched me all right, a backhand across my face, a slap, a toss. And Ilox, who really touched me—oh, how I hurt him when he came back. He's down here somewhere with that boy-pup and he's hungry and he's scared and he doesn't like the dark and he's tired and he wants me.

Phlarx ran his claws through his crest and walked back to the lift. He stepped back inside and pressed roof. The doors clicked shut, and the lift took off, rattling a little this time, as it ascended. *Father, Xian and her father and her grandmother, the Prince—I bet everybody who was there is going crazy about now. Well, they will never look for me at the recycling depot. Not right away, anyway. Maybe I have enough time.*

He was sure that was where the pup was taking Ilox. He closed his eyes and saw again the mapscreen of the old tunnels and there, glowing like a tiny yellow star, where Ilox had first called him from. And he hadn't stopped: there was another yellow star. Another. They were headed south, following a burrower path. To the depot. Ilox's thoughts, his unvoiced calls, were making a string of yellow stars.

I'll be there at the depot, when they get there.

"Phlarx where?"

The boy-pup kept pulling at his arm and making him walk and walk fast. And no matter how many times Ilox told the pup he was hungry, the pup wouldn't give him any more to eat. Ilox was really hungry and thirsty; Phlarx never missed feeding him.

"Papa? Did you say something?" the pup asked, yawning. Ilox thought the pup was very tired. If Phlarx would just come, then the pup could rest. Phlarx would take them out of this cold, dark, damp place, feed them, warm them up.

"Too dark Phlarx light Ilox . . ." There had been someone else who brought light and food and warmth. Where was she? "Mary has food. Mary?"

Ilox rubbed his stomach again and pulled on the pup's sleeve.

"Mary? That's Mama, do you remember Mama? Do you remember me? Caleb. I'm Caleb. We've escaped from the Lindauzi; we're running away to the Summer Country. Papa?" the pup asked. He was very excited now, his tiredness gone. He kept repeating Caleb and pointing to himself.

"Caleb?" Ilox turned his head to one side. In his dreams he remembered there being another one with Caleb, smaller.

The pup took Ilox's hand and laid it on the top of his head. This was something Ilox knew he had done before. In his dreams, this pup, and the small one— He shuddered and the memory was gone, like leaves on water, washed away by the black river.

"Caleb, Davy, Mary. Gone. Everything, everyone, gone, gone," Ilox said, shaking his head. If he had just been a minute sooner, or a minute later, he would have remembered everything. The river current was just too strong.

The pup sighed and squeezed his hand and they kept walking, following the luminous green line.

Caleb's head hurt. His feet hurt. His stomach growled and gurgled. Knowing there was food outside was no help. He was sure he had been walking in the tunnels for the entire day, maybe even longer. Above his head, above the imperial palace, the golden city dome, was a black sky filled with stars and a white moon.

If only Papa would shut up, Caleb thought. If he would just shut up, being hungry and thirsty and tired and scared wouldn't be so bad. Or as bad, anyway. But Papa kept whimpering for food and drink, and he kept pulling on Caleb's tunic sleeve, regardless of how many times Caleb yelled at him or turned away. Papa wouldn't stop. Caleb wanted to hit him. Being in the tunnels made it worse. Caleb and Papa's voices echoed and bounced back from the dark walls. The slapslap of four feet. The dampness. The green line that went on forever.

Phlarx Phlarx Phlarx pup Caleb Ilox hungry tired darkness hungry stomach soft fur close warm

I hear you, Lox. I know where you are, where you are going. I'll be there when you get there, I promise. I'll be waiting for you.

"CHAMBERS ST. W BWY. WORLD TRADE CTR," Caleb read aloud. The green line had veered away at this platform, into a Lindauzi-made tunnel with its pink and red glow-to-the-touch bricks. This tunnel, unlike the others, wasn't level; this new tunnel went up.

"Papa, I think this is the way out," Caleb said, standing with his fists on his hips. "Come on, take my hand, let's go. At least you can't complain about the darkness—run your fingers on that wall —like this, see?"

"Ilox hungry Phlarx—"

"Shut up," Caleb said, and yanking his father's hands, started up the tunnel's incline. At the top, instead of yet another tunnel, they stood at the edge of an enormous open room. Hugh columns supported the high roof, made of a mixture of Lindauzi bricks, black stones, and sheer grey concrete. There were pulsing white nests of glowglobes here and there, filling the room with a soft ambient light. Beyond the columns Caleb could see doorways lining one wall, like a row of open mouths. The green line they had followed crossed the room's wide floor, and, beyond the columns, Caleb could see it dividing and forking into the various doorways. Above the doorways were words in the American alphabet. To Caleb's left and right, were other tunnel exits and more green lines, all leading across the room.

"P-A- PATH. PATH TRAINS TO NEW JERSEY. I guess

that's where we are going for right now, Papa, to New Jersey. Oh, look out, more burrowers and those cars of theirs," Caleb said and stepped back into the tunnel, taking Papa with him.

Three burrower cars came from the doors on Caleb's right. Without stopping or noticing the two humans, the burrowers flew over their lines and disappeared, headed for New Jersey.

"Let's follow them," Caleb said and, with Papa in tow, started out across the room to the New Jersey doors.

Father Art in Heaven. It's me, Caleb, down here below Umium. Can You hear me, under all the Lindauzi and their prayers to Madaan? Can You show Papa the way home? If You would just lay your hand on his head. Hold us both in the palm of Your hand, protect us from those who would harm us, above, below, beneath, and to the right and to the left, in front and behind. Amen.

The Path tunnel to New Jersey—Caleb picked the one in the middle—was not dark. More glowglobes, in clusters about five tenstrides apart—no, Caleb thought, *steps*, how many steps—a hundred. The wide tunnel floor was striped with the glowing lines, and every so often a burrower car would pass on either side, going so fast that there was a wind left behind.

About six hundred steps in, a burrower car stopped less than a tenstride away. Some of the black boxes must have slipped as the burrowers were very busy rearranging and moving the boxes about the car.

"Stand still, Papa, I want to see a burrower up close." The nearest burrower had no ears and the grey fur looked soft, like thick grass, close up. The creature had four fingers and four toes, both of which were wide and splayed and clawed. Its tail was curled around its waist, and to Caleb's surprise, the burrower was looking at him as closely as he was at it.

Caleb's burrower yawned, revealing rows of bright pointed teeth. Fangs. Then the car lurched forward in a flash of light and was gone.

"Let's keep walking," Caleb said. "We've got to be almost there. See, the floor is slanting up again."

As the tunnel's incline became more pronounced, it grew narrow and the lines merged. Finally there were just three thick lines and they were walking past burrower cars lined up, waiting to go through still more closed doors. The tall metal doors were opening and closing automatically, letting in three cars at a time. Each time the metal doors opened, Caleb caught a glimpse of huge and intricate moving machinery.

"We're not going in there. I bet there are at least a handful of Lindauzi in there. We can't be too far from the surface—is there another way up—there, Papa, see it—a lift and it's open and empty."

"Up swimming cold dark so dark—"

"Shut up and let's go. You know, this is almost too easy," Caleb said, but shrugged off the worry and led Papa through the waiting burrower cars, past all the black boxes and barrels and the quiet grey creatures, into the lift. Unlike the lift they had taken down from the Vaarchael family apartments on the fifteenth floor, there were only three level markers. Caleb slapped the top marker and the lift doors closed and they started up.

They stepped out into a Lindauzi office, much like the one just outside the Crown Prince's private office. Chairs, desks, pink carpet on the floor, computers, memory walls, glowglobes. This office was, however, empty. Caleb could see the blinking lights on the computers. And at the other end of the office, just past a ceiling-to-floor glass wall, was the night. Moonlight spilled in through the glass, staining the carpet. In the middle of the glass wall was a door. Where were they all? At the games, the weddings—gone home, since it was night? Never mind, Caleb thought, and yanking again at Papa's hand, led him through the office to the waiting doors.

A jumble of furniture, computers, a Lindauzi office, the boy's head —for the first time Phlarx was seeing through Ilox's eyes. His hunger and fear and now this. An office across the river, on the recycling plant's ground floor.

Phlarx opened his eyes. He sat in his flyer, hidden in the trees, just across the lawn facing the recycling plant office. Ilox and the pup would be out in a few minutes. He idly wondered where his father and Xian were looking for him. Not here, of that Phlarx was sure. He had been very careful to cut the flyer's link to the traffic net when he had left the palace. For a while, there was no way to trace him.

Caleb breathed in and out deeply, the air outside was sweet and warm. It felt good to breathe, to look up and see stars not obscured by a yellow dome. And it felt good to stand still, no matter how hungry and tired he was. For the moment, Papa was oddly quiet. It would be a little harder to find something to eat, Caleb thought, but never mind that. He and Papa stood on another

velvety green Lindauzi lawn, facing Umium and its golden dome
and the river encircling the city. It was but one tenstride—a few
steps—until the lawn just dropped off, down a sheer cliff, to the
river below. Umium's dome shimmered in the moonlight. Behind
them was the grey waste recycling building, making with the river
and the city, two sides of a triangle. The third side, across the
lawn, was edged with trees. There, cut in half by the moonlight
and the tree shadows, a flyer gleamed. Beside it stood a Lindauzi.

"Phlarx! Phlarx!"

Caleb jumped at the sound of Papa's voice. There was something in it he had never heard before, a lightness, a singular joy.
And when Papa first said Phlarx, his voice sounded the way it had
sounded in Jackson, clear and sure and true. The second Phlarx
was flat and dull.

"You were back, just for a minute—hey, where are you going?
Papa?"

Ilox shook off Caleb's hand and took a step out onto the lawn.
Phlarx was walking slowly across, his booted feet making no sound
in the wet grass. As he came out of the tree shadows, Phlarx
acquired a shadow of his own, elongated and distorted. He wore
a long black cape that dragged in the grass behind him, and his
head crest and ears were erect. He lifted his muzzle as if to sniff
the air as he walked. Two heads taller than Papa.

Caleb looked at Papa who had taken another step in Phlarx's
direction. His father's eyes were wide open; they seemed filled
with moonlight and starlight.

Phlarx was halfway across the lawn when Papa started
running.

"Papa!"

Papa stopped, almost falling, and then looked from Phlarx to
Caleb.

"Lox, it's me, Lox."

Papa buried his face in his hands and sat down on the grass.

Caleb ran after his father, knowing he had to get there before
the Lindauzu did. He placed both hands on Papa's bare shoulders,
wishing he had had the chance to at least dress Papa in a tunic,
not this jockstrap. He had seen both of his parents naked more
than once, but Papa in this red-and-silver thing looked too bare.
He wanted to cover his father's nakedness. Caleb ran his fingers
around the collar and found the release. There. On Papa's skin,
visible in the moonlight, was a red ring.

Caleb looked up at Phlarx who was standing a tenstride away.

"This is yours," he said in Lindauzi and tossed the collar at Phlarx. Phlarx caught, crushed it in his hands, and then tossed it behind him. Then he walked to an arm's length from Caleb and Ilox.

"You're Caleb, his pup, aren't you? You know, my father, my sister, my intended mate, her father, even the Prince—everybody is looking for me. Frantically, I imagine. Angrily, I have no doubt. Some even with lasers—once you are labeled an atavism, any Lindauzi can kill you. My father is probably speechless with fury. You know, Ilox was never scared of him, or at least not as much as I was. I have been, all my life," Phlarx said, and let one hand rest briefly on Papa's head. Then he sat down.

"I'm his son," Caleb said and stepped away to make the third point of another triangle, facing both Papa and Phlarx, and halfway between both.

"Where are you going? Where are you taking him?"

"I want to take him to the Summer Country," Caleb said, after waiting a long time to reply. He felt both Papa's and Phlarx's emotions; at first it was hard to separate and find his own. But, standing between his father and the Lindauzu, Caleb found his center, his strength, a strength, to his surprise, that surpassed both Papa and Phlarx. They were both so tired and scared.

"The Summer Country?" Phlarx said to the grass.

"It's an old human story, of a place where there are no Lindauzi and no Lindauzi come, with their hounds or their diseases. It's the purple zone on the globe in the Prince's office—or at least I think that's where it is."

"The purple zone? Oh, yes. The inhospitable zones—too hot for any Lindauzi. Or at least until we begin weather modification —we won't, though, not now. I remember my father talking to Oldoch once about that purple country. Oldoch wanted to burn them out, a few laser cannon blasts from the space station. Father was horrified, such impersonal death was against *The Book of The Forest*. How will you get there, Caleb? On foot, with a sick ma-un?"

"Yes, on foot, or I'll build a boat. I am not going to leave him here with you."

"But he's mine, Caleb," Phlarx said, finally looking back up. "Lox belongs to me."

"He is not yours. He's not anybody's. I'm not, you're not. Papa told me that: you belong to yourself and nobody else," Caleb said angrily. His stomach growled.

"If he goes away forever, I will die."

"I wish you would die. Look at how sick you've made him.

Look at him. I thought you loved him, he said you did, and you did this to him?"

"I do love him. I wanted it to be the way it was when we were younglings and together all the time. The vet said the cocoon treatment *might* work. It was supposed to make him forget you and the female."

"My mother, his wife. He loved her."

"Or the cocooning would make him like he is now. That was the chance I took. I lost," Phlarx said in a heavy, slow voice, looking now at Papa, one hand just touching Papa's arm. Papa looked up at the touch, first at Phlarx, then at Caleb. His head jerked from one to the other and then he began moaning, holding his head in his hands, rocking back and forth. Phlarx moaned back softly, rocking with Papa. A chorus, Caleb thought, like the mourners keening at a Jacksoner's grave.

Finally Phlarx stopped and looked up at Caleb. "The Lindauzi are dying, Caleb. We have been dying since we came here, we were dying when we left Lindauzian. Fewer and fewer younglings are born, fewer take mates, and the years of life grow shorter and shorter. Suicides, reversions—"

"I don't care. I DON'T CARE. It's not my fault; it's not Papa's fault. You just can't take him," Caleb yelled and grabbed Papa and pulled him up. Papa let Caleb pull him, but he kept moaning and held out one hand to Phlarx, who took it and held on. "Die, go on and die, and let him go. Leave us alone. He's my father—"

Phlarx dropped Papa's hand and stood. "I never cared for my parents; I hated my father. But Lindauzi aren't supposed to care for their parents or their children. Mating and whelping—instinct, honed, tuned, ritualized, but instinct. The real love, the only love, is for the other, the bond-mate. You can't possibly love him as I do. Ilox was all I ever had. He was the only one who loved me. After he left—after my father threw him away—it was his memory that sustained me. The bond, it only ends with death," Phlarx said, looking at the grass again, and whispering. "I can't lose him again."

"Papa talked about you. He said he loved you. Not the way he loved Mama or me and my brother, but he loved you. He said there were all kinds of love, so many kinds, and each was as real and as true as the others. He missed you, he dreamed about you. He said you were the closest friend he ever had."

"Ilox used that word, *friend,* when he came back. I don't really understand it. Lindauzi have no *friends,*" Phlarx said.

"Papa loved Mama and she loved him. He loved me, he loves

me. He loved you," Caleb said, not knowing what else to say to convince the Lindauzu that Papa couldn't go back to Umium or Kinsella, that Papa belonged to no one.

"You can't go to the Summer Country, the inhospitable zone, by yourself, with Lox. It's thousands and thousands of tenstrides from here."

"I'll walk. I'll build a boat, and I'll get there," Caleb said, his jaw tight.

"You'll die before you'll get there, and so will he. Something will happen to you," Phlarx said, shaking his head. "I can't let him die like that."

"He'll die here with you. Look at him. Is this the way he was when you were growing up?"

Papa stopped moaning and dropped back to the ground. He bent over to press his face into the grass and his back and buttocks were white in the moonlight.

"No, he wasn't. Lox, here, get up," Phlarx said and knelt down and picked Papa up and held him at his side, his free hand stroking Papa's head as Papa buried his face in Phlarx's chest fur. "I'll go with you to the Summer Country. Maybe it won't be so inhospitable. In my flyer. We'd better leave soon—they will figure out where I went—Father and the rest—and come for me. At least let me feed him, give him drink, and you, too. I know you are both hungry and thirsty; I have some provisions in the flyer."

"We are just going to go. Just like that? You're not going to argue anymore? This is it?"

"Yes."

And that was how it was. Both Phlarx and Caleb helped Ilox into the back of the flyer. Then they settled themselves in the front seat, and Phlarx found the emergency provisions stored beneath the navconsole. He fed Ilox as Caleb watched. Then Phlarx pressed his palm into the nav, waited for the lights, and after they blinked and glowed in response, he moved his fingers rapidly, until an amber light blinked.

"Course set. Ready? Let's go then," Phlarx said.

The flyer rose straight into the night.

Interchapter 7
June 2156

From the Journal of Orfassian luCorviax laThanath luOrfassian luCorviax Alerian, Crown Prince of Lindauzian, Heir to the Left Throne, Supreme Commander of The Search Fleet, the 155th local year since the Arrival, 12 Hotmoon 11549, Lindauzi reckoning.

Last night, after Morix told me about Ilox and Phlarx, I struck him hard, across the face. My claws were fully extended; I drew blood. I bared my fangs — I almost did as Phlarx did, there on the temple dais.

What a fool I have been, what a four-legged howling fool. Morix sent the reports in; I read them. The final reports said Ilox was an almost — not the real thing. That he had been culled — and now I find out the reports weren't even true.

I should have checked, flown to Kinsella, made Morix deliver his reports in person, inspected the damn pup myself. But the Crown Prince can't be everywhere; I must be able to trust those under me.

A four-legged howling feral fool.

The dog was flawed, my lord, Morix told me. Oh yes, he told me, his youngling and the dog were bond-mates — but not like we were working for. The dog loved a female, a female, Morix said, in understandable bewilderment. That was never a Project goal, you know that, my lord. The bond was to be total, complete, heart to heart, mind to mind, soul to soul. I didn't lie to you, my lord.

He is right and he is wrong.

But he loved Phlarx, didn't he, I said, feeling no satisfaction seeing Morix on all fours, dripping blood, his crest drooping.

Yes, but he found out what we did.

That was it, I think. The dog, Ilox, knew everything. And he wanted to have a choice to love. And he did choose, to love Phlarx and to love a female.

There was no place for choice in the Project.

We were so close, Morix wailed, keening the mourning song, so close.

Leave me, go, I said, go.

This morning the menials found Morix in the garden. I am sure he died on impact; from his apartment to the ground is fifteen levels. Xian was found dead in her apartment—poison.

Ilox and Phlarx, the only true bond-mates after one hundred and fifty-five local years, after five generations of controlled breeding, after culling billions of these people—with disease, with pogroms, after crossing light-years, a war. Enough. Ilox and Phlarx, heart to heart, mind to mind, soul to soul. And Phlarx cocooned him, drove his bond-mate insane to make him fit the Project's specification.

That little secret even Morix didn't know. Not until Ilox was removed from the tank.

What could I tell you then, my lord? The dog was insane—

And now Ilox and Phlarx are gone, disappeared. And Chlavash tells me my prize wolf-pup—what was his name?—is gone as well. Disappeared. I struck him, too.

I have been such a fool.

A true bonding, but a failure? Ilox chose to love more than Phlarx.

A failure.

We can hold on, perhaps for one, two, even three generations more here. Pulling in, abandoning cities, plantations, forced matings, artificial insemination.

I wonder how long they survived on Lindauzian. How long before the reversions and suicides and murders surpassed the living, the sapient? And what is there now, in the empty cities, in the hills, in the forest, wild, snarling animals, bringing down prey with their fangs and claws? What was it like—what will it be like—to feel your intelligence slip away, piece by piece, chunk by chunk, knowing you *are losing sentience, losing everything, and knowing that nothing, nothing can stop it?*

I wonder if the wild dogs, the wolves, will hunt us down, or capture us, put collars around our necks.

With minor modification in the forcefield's air filter, the CO levels inside the domes can be increased slowly, so slowly, that it will be like falling to sleep. In a month or two, it will all be over.

An ironic act, of course, as the domes were first built to keep out the polluted air on this planet, and now the air is clean. I will have the biosensors linked to the domes: when no vertebrate life registers, the domes will go down. Can't have all the trees dying a slow death.

O Lord Madaan, Lady Aurelian, it is time for us to come home to the Great Forest, past time.

Chapter X

Caleb, Phlarx, and Nox, June-December 2156

"**L**AND THERE, PHLARX, RIGHT THERE," CALEB SAID, "Land where, Caleb? There's been nothing except water for—oh, I see, the sand, those stone walls, land there?" Phlarx asked, as he banked the flyer into a wide circle over the night-black-and-silver waters rippling beneath them. It was just after midnight and they had been in flight for four hours since leaving Umium. Caleb had insisted they follow the route in the stories: down the Dividing River, to the Gulf (also insisting they use the human word), and southeast, past islands and the Warm Sea, to Continent Two.

"Caleb, we can be there, at top speed in less than two hours, if we go direct," Phlarx had protested. "Look at this map in the nav, see the yellow route line—"

"The stories say to follow the river, then southeast over the Gulf," Caleb said stubbornly. "Past islands and across the Warm Sea."

"Caleb—"

"The stories say to follow the river, then southeast. . . ." Caleb repeated, refusing to look at the small inset map. Caleb couldn't explain to Phlarx why the directions had to be followed, the prescribed route taken, the right words used, but he knew they had to be. The story had to become real.

"I heard you. Down the river," Phlarx said, sighing.

"Those walls are human-made. See, grey stones. Papa said the Summer Country would be just like this: on the edge of the sea, with white sand and green trees." Caleb glanced over at Papa, who was asleep, curled up on the seat. He reached back to touch the ring on Papa's neck, more a pink now, but still visible. The neck ring, he knew, would fade. But the three silver bars and a dark red half-moon, the Vaarchael family mark, wouldn't. Nor would the three yellow bars and sun on his own collarbone, the imperial family mark. Caleb turned around to Phlarx. "This is the Summer Country. We followed the directions, we have to be there."

Phlarx looked at Caleb but said nothing. He took the flyer down until it was just above the water. Caleb could see the white foam as the waves rose and fell, the water luminous in the moonlight. The flyer's black shadow trembled on the water.

"Yes, there was a dog—hew-mun city here. But, look, these buildings are broken, empty. See the vines coming out of the windows. Look," Phlarx said. They were flying parallel to the beach now and Caleb could see what Phlarx saw: the crumbling buildings, the vines, fractured pavement, the rubble. And jungle, the jungle had come back to this city.

"Look over there, the grey walls we saw—see them?" Caleb said. He had a feeling, sharp and clear, that humans lived behind there, even though vines had crawled up and over the stones, and trees grew close to the walls. "Go there."

Phlarx landed the flyer just inside the stone walls in an open plaza in front of a white clock tower. Only three of the numbers were left on the smashed-in clock face: 3, 7, and 10.

"Here we go," Phlarx said, and opened the flyer's roof. They both gasped when the night air hit them, warm, heavy, and moist. A bird screamed, and another, and another. "Nobody's here, Caleb."

"They're here. The night-watchmen will find us in a little while," Caleb said. He could see the signs around them in the plaza. There were new rocks in the cobblestones, and the asphalt had been patched. Lashed ropes held together some of the railed balconies. Some of the buildings were empty, yes, but not all. Then he reached back over the seat and shook his father awake. "We're there, Papa, we're in the Summer Country. Just like in your stories."

"Here they are, Caleb, your other hew-muns, your purple zone wolves," Phlarx whispered about half-an-hour later. His ears went flat against his skull, his crest drooped.

Caleb turned from Papa and looked where Phlarx was looking. Four men, armed with spears and bows and arrows, stood beneath one of the arches under a whitewashed building. One bearded man stood a step ahead of the others. Barking beside the bearded man was a big black dog. A dog, a real dog, like Max. Caleb wanted to run and touch the animal, feel its soft skin and fur, let it lick his hands.

"It is so hot here, even at night, and the air, so thick, wet, close," Phlarx said, and stood up. "Let them see me first, then you, Caleb."

"*Mira, un Leendauzee. Míralo, mira, matálo. ¡Matálo! Pero, mira, un muchacho, y un hombre.*" Look, a Lindauzi, look at it, look, kill it. Kill it. But, look, a boy, and a man. Phlarx ducked as an arrow flew past his hand, banging on the flyer's shield. "*No, espera, mira, el muchacho, el hombre. Espera.*" No, wait, look, the boy, the man. The man in front yelled back at the one who had let fly his arrow.

"Papa, be still. Come on, Phlarx, let's show them you're harmless." Slowly Caleb, then Phlarx, climbed out of the flyer. Caleb stood beside Phlarx and waited for the men to get closer.

"I feel just the edge of their emotions, sort of the backwash of what I feel from Ilox, but it's enough. They hate Lindauzi. They want to kill me with those spears and arrows they are carrying," Phlarx said and took a step behind Caleb. Caleb looked at Phlarx and then at the four men. Then he grabbed Phlarx's warm, hairy hand, and held it tight.

"*¿Niño, qué pasó? El es un Leendauzee. Eres un humano y éste es un lugar para los humanos. No es para monstruos,*" the head watchman said. Child, what is going on? It is a Lindauzi. You are a human and this is a place for humans. Not for monsters. Behind the head watchman, Caleb saw that all three of the others had arrows on string. And behind the watchmen, through the flickering red flames of the men's coronas, Caleb saw seven or eight others coming, yawning, in nightclothes, half-dressed, one or two almost naked, women with hair loose about their faces. A little girl came with one man, riding on his shoulders. Two more barking dogs. Well, he thought, nobody had been very quiet.

"No, no, listen to me. If you kill him, you kill my father. Don't hurt him." Caleb was sweating. He felt water dripping down his forehead and his back, pooling in his leather boots. The red tunic clung to his skin. Caleb gripped Phlarx's hand tighter, hoping he could stop the Lindauzu's trembling. *He's almost half again as tall as any of these people, his claws would tear them apart before they could get him with their arrows, and he's scared.*

Papa kept calling out Phlarx's and Caleb's names over and over.

"Chico," the head watchman said, *"este pueblo y este país es un santuario para los humanos. El monstruo no puede vivir aquí."* Boy, this town and this country are a sanctuary for humans. The monster can't live here.

"I'm sorry, I don't speak your language. I speak American, American. He speaks American, too. American. Papa, no, stay in the flyer—"

"I will look after Lox," Phlarx said, releasing Caleb's hand. He slowly stepped back and then reached into the flyer and picked Papa up and out. Phlarx held the man against his chest and smoothed his hair. Papa grew quiet and laid his head on Phlarx's shoulder. He clutched tufts of fur in his hands. The watchmen and the others shook their heads, muttering and scowling. The dogs finally stopped barking, but they kept growling and watching Phlarx.

One woman, however, looked sharply at Caleb. *"¿Americano?"* she asked. *"No habla español, habla americano, creo que sí, Pablo,"* she said and the head watchman turned to face her. *"El chico no entiende nada de lo que hablamos. Manda alguien por Maria Catalina Carvajal. Su abuela vino de América. . . ."* American? He doesn't speak Spanish, I think he speaks American. The boy understands nothing we are saying. Send someone for Maria Catalina Caravajal. Her grandmother came from America. . . .

Caleb watched and waited, sweating, as he looked first at the woman, then at Pablo, and then at all the others. What were they saying, other than American? At least the woman had gotten Pablo and the other watchmen to unnotch their arrows. Finally, after much rapid talk and hand waving, one of the watchmen ran off. Caleb thought the man would never come back, but he finally did, walking this time, with a very sleepy woman, yawning and running her fingers through long black hair. For a brief moment Caleb thought she was his mother: the same dark curly hair, olive skin. After another rapid conversation of hands and words, Caleb found himself facing the sleepy woman. Pablo stood by her, after waving the rest away.

"I speak some American. *Mi abuela,* my grandmother, she came from *el norte.* She told me stories. *¿Hablas americano?*" she asked gently.

It was slow clumsy talk, the broken American, the Spanish, between Caleb and Maria Catalina and Pablo. At times, Caleb had to ask Phlarx something and the rough Lindauzi sounds seemed to push the crowd even farther back. Several of the others drew crosses in the air or made circles with their fingers; one woman picked up a stone. Before she could throw it, Pablo turned and yelled at her. The dropped stone striking stone rang throughout the plaza.

Phlarx, sighing, finally set Papa down on his feet. After a terrified look at the strangers, Papa pressed himself back against Phlarx, hiding his face in Phlarx's fur.

"Well, they aren't going kill you, Phlarx," Caleb said when the talking seemed to be done and the crowd, tired and sleepy, started to leave. "We're supposed to go with this lady here. She's going to take us to her house. You have no idea how much the Lindauzi are hated." Caleb yawned. The sky was still dark, but Caleb could see a deep-blue grey at the bottom of the sky and it was getting warmer and warmer. He wanted to peel his tunic off and wring it out.

"I have some idea," Phlarx said heavily.

"*Me llamo María Catalina.* My name, Maria Catalina, *y tú?*" She repeated what she said, pointing to herself and to Caleb.

"Caleb. Ilox. Phlarx," Caleb said, pointing, and after she repeated their names, the woman led them through a confusion of narrow streets with the buildings so close Caleb felt sure they were about to fall over. The buildings were almost all white with arched windows, balconies, and carved red tiles on the roofs. Many were empty and every so often one was in complete ruins, scarred by fire, or collapsed into rubble. Trees grew through holes in the tiles, vines were window-lace. Caleb walked beside Maria and tried to answer her questions about Carolina and Jackson and Davy and Mama and Umium. Phlarx and Papa walked behind them, Papa clinging to Phlarx's hand. The head watchman took the rear, with his black dog at his side.

A few of the crowd followed them, keeping a safe distance behind them. Once when Caleb looked back he saw a woman making a cross, this time touching her head, chest, and shoulders. He decided right now was not a good time to ask Maria what the cross mean. The little girl broke free of her father and ran up and touched Papa's bare skin. Then Phlarx turned around and she found herself staring right at him. She screamed and Papa screamed. Both tried to run away.

"Very few humans live here in this place, Cartagena," Maria told Caleb as they walked. "How many here—I don't know— maybe two, three hundred? *Más se esconden en la selva—y nos escondemos*—how do you say—hide? Yes, we hide, *también. El humo de fuego,* out, down, not up. *En el pasado mucha gente aquí.* You are *los primeros extranjeros en muchos años,* the first strangers in many years."

"Where did they all go?" Caleb asked, as they turned down a street where two women, one old and one young, were unpacking two huge baskets, stuffed with funny-shaped things. He looked back: the little girl and her father had disappeared.

"*Frutas, para comer.* Fruit, to eat," Maria Catalina said. The fruit were unlike the apples, pears, grapes, and plums Caleb knew. The women spread a cloth on the ground and then started laying out the fruit. The older woman first put out long yellow fingerlike fruits, then thick-skinned longer yellow-green ones, and then, thorny green ones, with topknots. And sitting on its haunches, licking its paws, was an orange-and-white cat. Caleb wanted to touch the cat as well, to see if it would purr the way his mother said cats did, their little bodies vibrating.

"*Trabajamos antes el día*—we work before the day, *vivimos nuestras vidas en el oscuro*—we live our lives in the dark," Maria Catalina added and waved her hand at the doors and windows opening on the street around them. Lives hiding in the dark? Caleb wondered, glancing up at a sky slowly growing lighter. It was not until some time later he understood what Maria meant by a hidden life. Cartageneros rose an hour later every day, shifting daily the hours spent in the light and the dark. So the Lindauzi ships that pass over head, she later explained, can never be sure if they will find anyone. Although no Lindauzi before Phlarx tried to live in the purple zones, the ships and flyers passing overhead would use the zones for target practice. A sudden movement, a laser blast. Did Caleb understand why they had to keep changing the waking hours every day? Caleb finally did, when he remembered that although Jacksoners and Covenant-keepers and Footwashers didn't sleep in the day and work at night, they had lived in the shadows, they had lived lives spent running for cover.

"Many many dead from sickness, *la muerte grande después de la llegada del Leendauzee.* After they came," Maria Catalina said and jerked her head toward Phlarx. "They made us *enfermo*, bad, sick, you know," and she grimaced and made a face, rubbing her stomach.

Caleb nodded; he knew. He had heard the same stories from Papa and Mama and the storytellers around the Jackson night-fires. He had told Phlarx the same story on their four-hour flight from Umium.

At first Phlarx had talked. He worried that his father would send hounds out to bring him in, or to shoot down his flyer. Once labeled an atavism you were fair game. Out over the Gulf and the Warm Sea, Phlarx worried about how sick Papa was and if he would ever get well and what a mistake Phlarx had made when he had the vet cocoon Papa.

"Your people have made a big mistake here from beginning to end," Caleb had said and told him the story of the Lindauzi Arrival that Papa had told him: about how the Lindauzi had released the Virus so many years ago and the pogroms—everything, the whole story. Surely Phlarx knew at least some of the story. Caleb waited for Phlarx to say something, anything, he didn't know what, but the Lindauzu had said nothing at all.

At the end of the street, they came to another, smaller, three-sided plaza, bordered on one side by a street and the grey stone city wall, another by a three-story building, and the last, broken stones, bricks, weeds, vines, trees. The white face of the building faced the sea. Palm trees grew by the street. Caleb heard, behind him and faint in his ear, a woman shouting: *piña, papaya, melón*. But what a *piñapapayamelón* was, he had no idea.

"*Aquí*. Here, this place. *Mi familia* lives here, on the first *piso*. There are rooms for you above, *en el segundo*," Maria Catalina said, and they followed her up narrow stairs to the second floor, and then into a dark, faintly musty room. Caleb could make out, in the grey light, chairs, a table, and through an arch, a hallway. Phlarx sat down in a chair that sagged with his weight. He had to duck his head coming in. Phlarx closed his eyes, breathing heavily. His fur was damp and stuck up in odd places.

"*¿El Leendauzee está enfermo?* Sick?" she asked.

"The heat, it's bad for him," Caleb said and fanned his own flushed face. He had never been in a place so hot—even the summers in Jackson had not been this hot. Papa sat down on the floor, leaning into Phlarx's leg.

Please talk, Papa. Say something. We're here. We made it; why aren't you getting well?

"*¿Y el hombre, tu padre, no? ¿Tú papa está enfermo, también, si?*"

"My papa. Yes, he is sick, *enfermo*. In his head," Caleb said, feeling very tired and very young. "He has lost himself and—"

"*¿Maria, qué pasó?*" A dark-haired man stood in the door behind Maria, staring at Phlarx, slowly drawing a cross on his bare chest.

"*Ernesto, espera, permiteme explicar . . .*" Maria Catalina said and starting talking rapidly in Spanish, her words sharp and quick. The only words Caleb recognized were Lindauzi, American, and all their names. He was so tired and so hungry. *This isn't how it is supposed to be here. This is the Summer Country. People are supposed to be happy here and not afraid. But their clothes, rags, and they're skinny and they hide in the dark—*

"*O Caleb, chico, tú estás fatigado, casi muerto. Ve con Ernesto. Go con* Ernesto," Maria said and nodded toward the man who stepped forward and scooped Caleb up. "*Cuido de tu popy y el monstruo.* It's all right, *chico. Está bien.*"

Caleb slumped against the man, thinking how funny he smelled, of salt, the sea, fish. He closed his eyes and opened them briefly when the man laid him down on a bed and helped pull his tunic over his head, his boots off his feet. Then Caleb rolled over onto his stomach and fell asleep to the sounds of Phlarx's and Papa's voices, and the softer sounds of Maria Catalina's.

Over the next few weeks, Caleb, with Maria Catalina's help, told and retold his and Papa's and Phlarx's story. With each retelling the Cartageneros gradually and grudgingly accepted Phlarx— enough, Phlarx said, that the edge of their hatred was dulled, it gnawed at him a little less. Some, in spite of themselves, admired him. Love, Maria Catalina said, is love, after all.

The three of them stayed in the house by the sea. Phlarx and Papa rarely, if ever, left the house, even when the Cartagenero day was mostly in the night and the air was a little cooler. Then Papa would go out on the balcony and sit in an old rocking chair, watching the sea move and change shapes and colors, as the moon painted and repainted the waves. Or, when the Cartageneros were up in the daylight, he liked to watch the fishermen in their long black boats trailing their nets in the water. Phlarx sometimes sat with him, with one hand touching Papa, and watch the sea as well. He told Caleb of when they were younglings at the beach and how Ilox had loved the sea and how they would both run on the sand. And he talked with Caleb of the Spanish he was learning to read, a language Phlarx found even harder to speak than American. He would read aloud to both Caleb and Papa. The Cartageneros didn't want Phlarx to even touch a human book at first, but Caleb told them how his people had cared for books and promised he would take care of the old, old, rebound books. They are sacred, he told them.

"There are things in these books about this place I never dreamed of, things I don't think any Lindauzi knows about hewmuns. This God, this *Jesús Cristo.* I think he may be Lord Madaan in a different skin. This *Espíritu Santo,* Lady Aurelian. Or maybe she is *El Cristo,* he the spirit. I wish we could come here again," Phlarx said.

Caleb also heard about God and *Jesús Cristo en La Iglesia,* from Padre Hernando, the priest. He didn't have white fur, but he did wear, in *La Iglesia,* a dark sash across his chest. Maria Catalina insisted he go every Sunday with her and Ernesto Luis and their children.

"*Tú puedes bañarte tu cara.* Your face, Caleb, wash. *Vamos a La Iglesia esta mañana, es domingo.* Sunday," Maria Catalina said to him one morning a week after he, Papa, and Phlarx had arrived in Cartagena.

Caleb looked at her, puzzled. Wash his face, sure, if she wanted him to, but *La Iglesia?*

"*Nunca,* never to *La Iglesia? Tu tribu*—oh, I don't have *bastante americano.* OK, your people, you prayed *a Dios,* to God?" Maria Catalina asked, sitting down beside Caleb on his bed. It was late in the morning, the "day" having begun four hours after sunrise. The light coming through the window was a white shaft cutting through the room's shadows, dividing the space into three: dark, grey, and white. Caleb and Maria sat in the darkness. Through the open door, Caleb could hear from the floor below Ernesto Luis and the others cooking. The smell of frying fish was everywhere.

"Oh, *God,* Father Art. Father Art in Heaven, hallowed be His name. But He was always angry, and He and His Son went away and left us with the Lindauzi. That's what Aunt Sara and all the Jacksoner storytellers said. There were churches, places where He used to live, but He never came to them or anywhere, anymore," Caleb said, turning his head to one side. Maria Catalina didn't look quite as much like his mother as she had on the first day, she was bigger and thicker and older, there was grey in her hair and in Ernesto's. Still, she felt like Mama.

"Church, tall crosses, yes? Well," Maria Catalina said after a long pause, interrupted by Juan Dario, her oldest son, to tell them breakfast was ready. "I think He and His Son did not go far away. They are here in church, *en La Iglesia*. Now wash your face."

Caleb sat near the front of the church with all the Carvajals on a long wooden bench. He understood very little of what Padre Hernando said, other than *Dios* and *Jesús Cristo*, but the man's voice was kind and gentle. He wondered as he sat there and looking around the room, a wide space, with rows of benches, and tall, tall windows, most of which were broken, a few with pictures in colored glass, if Phlarx was right. Would this priest know if Lord Madaan was the same as *Jesús Cristo?* Had Madaan changed skins when he came to Earth? If they were the same, then wouldn't their words be the same? Did that make humans and Lindauzi in some way alike? Then why had the Lindauzi done what they had done and why had Lord Madaan-*Jesús Cristo* let them?

Phlarx had asked if *Jesús Cristo* and this God could forgive the Lindauzi, did Caleb think so?

"I knew some of the story you told me when we flew here, but not all of it. But, I believed in the Project—we all did—even though Father bored me with it. But after I realized how I hurt Ilox because of the Project and now that I know all that we did—I can't forgive myself. Can God?" Phlarx had said.

Caleb shook his head and stood up with the Carvajals and everybody else in church. Forgiveness for the Lindauzi was just too big to think about.

Caleb knew Maria Catalina and Ernesto Luis and their two sons, Juan Dario and Luis Xavier, and their daughter, Maria Elena, all thought the padre was a good man. He wanted to think so, the man's voice was so kind, but he had to be sure. And Caleb was a little afraid of the man, so he kept his questions to himself and listened carefully each Sunday, understanding more Spanish each time. Perhaps, he thought, when he had learned enough Spanish, he would hear the priest answer the questions when he talked up there in front of the church. Caleb learned when to stand and to kneel and how to make the Sign of the Cross, and he waited.

In July, a month after Caleb's first visit to the church, Ernesto Luis told Caleb it was time for him to learn a trade, a way to make a living, a way to live and feed himself and others. Ernesto Luis listened, as Maria Catalina translated, when Caleb told him in Jackson he would have become a Reader. His mother had been a

Reader and her father and her mother—the Hulberts had always been the Readers for Jacksoners.

"At night around the fire, I would have read from the old story books and I would have written names on the life-necklaces. In Umium, the Lindauzi taught me to be a show-dog."

"Here, you read, yes," Ernesto Luis said, beginning in the American his wife had taught him, and ending in Spanish, *"pero, como un miembro de mi familia, tú te pondrás un pescador."* Fisherman, Caleb understood.

Beginning the next "day," under a full moon, and for every day thereafter, except Sunday, in the long black boats Papa loved to watch, Caleb and Ernesto Luis and Ernesto Luis's two sons, went out to sea to fish. They would spent half the day, whether beneath the stars and moon, in the grey dawn or twilight, or beneath the sun, on the sea. Sometimes they came back with boats heavy with fish, sometimes with only a few.

Caleb grew lean and tough and dark.

Maria Catalina was Caleb's teacher as well. She taught him how to cut and eat and cook coconuts from the palm trees that grew in front of their house. She taught him the names of all the fruits the women sold on the street corners from their baskets: *maracuya, banana, papaya, guanábana, níspero, zapote, aguacate.* She taught him to cook and eat all of them. And as the months passed, Caleb began to learn the tempo of life in Cartagena. June, *junio,* like May, was a dry month, then July—*julio,* and the rains began again in *agosto,* hard, heavy thunder showers almost every true afternoon, lightening scrawling down the sky into the ocean. The showers came and went, leaving the air hot and wet and close. There was a time to hoard water and a time to play naked in the sudden afternoon showers. There was a time, *septiembre y octubre,* when the rain fell for long grey hours, filling up the streets with suddenly cold rivers. The world would be swallowed up in the grey rain. Once, dim in the storm, Caleb saw what Dario said was *un tornado, una tromba,* a dark spiral falling out of the sky into the ocean. There was a time, beginning in late *noviembre,* when the dry returned and the wind blew so hard it was hard to walk in the streets and the window shutters and doors had to be kept closed or even the plates would be blown to the floor. And plates, Maria Catalina said, did not grow on trees, *la alfarera* made only so many at a time and she took Caleb to watch *la alfarera* and her wheel and the clay pots and plates growing out of the woman's hands.

Caleb learned the sounds of Cartagena as well, *los loros*, the screaming brightly-colored birds in the trees, the waves pounding the sea wall, the wind and the sudden rain on the roof. And he learned the names of things: wind, *el viento*, rain, *la lluvia*, women, *las mujeres*, men, *los hombres*. Everyone was his Spanish teacher, all the Carvajals, the priest, the women with their fruit, the wild-eyed farmers coming in out of the jungle, *la alfarera*. By the end of *septiembre*, their fourth month, Caleb dreamed in Spanish.

The only place he spoke American and Lindauzi was with Papa and Phlarx. After fishing, after learning how to mend and make nets, after swimming with Juan Dario and Luis Xavier, Caleb would always go and sit on the second floor balcony of the house with Papa and Phlarx. At first Juan Dario and Luis Xavier asked Caleb to come with them after swimming or fishing or net mending, but he always said no. Caleb wanted very much to play with the Carvajal boys, and their friends—but if he did, he was afraid he would miss Papa coming back—even for a minute. He wanted to play with Maria Elena, who was just a few weeks younger than Caleb, but it was the same. Maria Catalina told Caleb to let his father and the monster be by themselves, if just for an afternoon, but Caleb couldn't.

Besides, Caleb thought, Papa and Phlarx were always waiting for him to come. Papa knew Caleb now, and called him Caleb-boy, and by *octubre*, could remember Caleb was his son, most of the time, and that he had had a wife and another son and they had lived, all of them, far, far away. And he even begin to use the word *I* again for himself. Sometimes Caleb thought, sitting with them as they watched the sea, his father remembered everything and was trying to find his lost language. Papa's eyes would grow suddenly brighter, and he would reach out and rest his hand on Caleb's head. And then the fire was gone. The fire, though, Caleb saw, never went out for Phlarx. Papa and Phlarx were never far enough apart that one could not reach out and touch the other.

Phlarx talked and talked and asked Caleb questions, about what Padre Hernando said in church about *Dios*, and *Jesús Cristo*. He asked Caleb about fishing and was Caleb able to sense these animals here as he had in Umium (Caleb had told the Lindauzu how they had escaped) and did the animals have the same thoughts? The answers were yes and yes, although Caleb told no Cartagenero he knew what the goats thought about when they were milked. He remembered how it had felt to be a halver. Phlarx wondered and talked about what might have happened in Umium and he was the one who told Ernesto Luis in late *octubre* that it had been a long time since any Lindauzi airship had passed overhead. And no more were probably coming.

Caleb had to bring Ernesto Luis up the stairs to the balcony for Phlarx to tell him. Phlarx had become very weak and tired. After Ernesto Luis left, Phlarx said nothing for a long time, and then, he turned to Caleb and spoke in a low, tired voice. "He still hates me, they all do. I feel it. Oh, I know, Caleb, what you told me, they respect my love for Ilox and his love for me, but they still hate me. I don't blame them; we did terrible things here. I did a terrible thing to Ilox. Even you hate me, a little, don't you?"

"Phlarx, I used to, but not anymore. I really don't," Caleb and realized for the first time it was true. Did he love the Lindauzu? He didn't know, but he didn't hate him.

"That's something. I'm tired; I'll talk to you later. Oh, yes, Ilox, tell him your dream. And then, Caleb, tell Ernesto Luis and the others they don't have to shift their waking hours anymore," Phlarx said and went back into their room. Caleb noticed for the first time the bare patches in Phlarx's fur, the light brown tufts he left behind in his chair.

"Phlarx not well, Caleb-boy," Papa said and stood up. "I not well either."

"Papa, your dream? Phlarx said you had a dream to tell me?"

Papa nodded and sat back in his rocker. "I dreamed. I dream. In a place where I have, where I was, in the center of an enormous golden room, surrounded by Lindauzi, red, black, white, grey, yellow-furred Lindauzi, all trying to touch me, stroke my hair, all of them, so many, and I run, I hide, cover my face, their claws on my skin, the air is gold, shining, like light on water, and I can see the Lindauzi behind the light, the gold, they are tired, sleepy, so sleepy, they lie down, one, two, three, one, five, I am in the golden room and all around me sleeping. I dreamed, Caleb-boy; I dream."

"But what does it mean? All those Lindauzi asleep?" Caleb asked as Papa stood back up.

"Not wake up," he said, and holding onto to the railing and then the chair and the wall, followed Phlarx.

Caleb sat down in Papa's empty rocker and stayed a long time, watching the sea, rocking back and forth, thinking about Umium and its golden dome and its gardens and fountains and the big triangular palace and how hollow his voice would sound if he were there.

*   *   *

Everyone said Papa's dream was just a dream and how could he know what had happened in a Lindauzi city thousands and thousand of kilometers away? He was crazy, wasn't he, hadn't the boy said the Lindauzi had made him crazy? Oh, he was crazy all right, but the boy said he had the same dream over and over. And didn't God talk to people in dreams, yes? Didn't God send people dreams of the future? He told *José* to flee to *Egipto con María y El Niño*? And didn't *José en El Testamento Viejo* dream of when his brothers would bow down to him? There have been no more Lindauzi airships and flyers in the sky. Does that prove they are all dead?

So, by ones and twos and threes, the Cartageneros came to ask Papa to tell them his dream. And they asked and asked and asked, until when the twentieth and twenty-first person came and asked and asked, and tried to get Papa to explain for yet another time, he started crying and hiding his face.

"Stop, leave him alone," Caleb yelled. "He told you his dream. Leave him alone."

But, *hijo*, the dream, how can we be sure? *Tu popy está loco. . . .*

Padre Hernando had the answer: go and look. And after another week of talk, five men and five women headed south, riding on burros, to find out.

In the last week of *noviembre*, the sixth month after their coming to Cartagena, Phlarx took to bed never to get up again. The winds brought no relief, nor did cutting Phlarx's fur short and close to his skin. And after Phlarx became ill, Papa become ill. All that month and into *diciembre*, Caleb would come home to sit with the two of them in their dark room, the window shutters closed during the "day" to keep out any light and the trade winds. He sat by their bed in a rocking chair he had brought in from the balcony. Caleb fed both Phlarx and Papa after they became too weak to sit up.

At first Caleb tried to argue Phlarx into health.

"You've got to get up. You can't give up, Phlarx. Papa, don't let him."

"I'm dying, Caleb. The heat, the wet—"

"You should have never left Umium, but you did, you're here—"

"No, listen," Phlarx finally said after he and Caleb repeated the same argument for the umpteenth time. "Listen," and he laid a hand on Caleb's shoulder. Caleb flinched at the touch of Phlarx's claws but remained still. He could see on the Lindauzu's other hand that his claws were cracked and split.

"Phlarx? Caleb-boy?" Papa sat up and reached for Caleb. Moving carefully, Caleb got out of his chair and sat on their bed so that Phlarx could hold one hand and Papa the other. Sometimes, Caleb thought, they were two halves of the same creature.

"Listen. Remember, I told you we were all dying. I would have died there or in Kinsella without Ilox. Maybe a few more years, but I would have died. Or I would have been killed; I told you what happens when you show any signs, even the smallest, of being an atavism. I doubt Morix would have stopped them. I'm probably the last—everyone died in Ilox's dream. And I am dying now. I'm sorry, Caleb, but when I die, Ilox dies. I'm sorry, Caleb," Phlarx said, speaking slowly, his breathing labored. He let go of Caleb's hand and closed his eyes. A moment later Papa let go of Caleb's other hand and then rolled over to put an arm across Phlarx's chest.

Caleb sat very still listening to the sound of their breathing. Through the shuttered window he could hear the waves breaking on the sea wall. The winds moaned against the house. A woman yelled at her son to come inside; somebody nearby played *una guitarra*.

Then Papa spoke in a grey voice out of the room's shadows. "Caleb-boy. Remember, I, Caleb small against chest, looked for Caleb black river looked looked. Here Caleb-boy Phlarx here" and Papa touched Caleb's hand again and stroked the now-sleeping Lindauzu's forehead. "And here," and Papa touched his own head.

"I want you to stay here," Caleb said, turning to Papa. He got up and walked over to sit on his father's side of the bed. Slowly and carefully, he stroked his father's hair, now long again, curly, the yellow streaked with grey.

"Caleb? Caleb-boy?"

Caleb sat up quickly in bed. Papa? He glanced around the room, blinking his eyes at the sudden light. The "day" had ended at dawn; was it noon now? It was hard to think, his head was so heavy with sleep.

"Caleb-boy."

Where were his clothes? There, by the door, his shorts, where was his shirt?

"Caleb-boy! Phlarx can't wake."

"I'm coming, I'm coming." Caleb gave up finding his shirt and ran out of the room and down the short hall, stumbling as he pulled on his shorts, his feet missing the legs. He slammed open the door to Papa and Phlarx's room. Papa was on his knees in bed, stroking Phlarx's fur, pulling at Phlarx's arm, pushing Phlarx's head. Papa was crying.

"Caleb, help Phlarx going bring him back he's going I want him back bring him . . ." Papa kept pulling and pushing until Phlarx groaned, low, soft, more of a whisper than a groan.

"I don't know what to do, Papa. I'm not a healer. I'll get help," and Caleb ran out of the room and down the stairs, calling Maria Catalina and Ernesto Luis. *Don't die, Phlarx. Please don't die. Papa will die and I will never get him back. But, maybe, if Phlarx goes, Papa will come back — no, what am I thinking — it's wrong to think this —*

"Help, Maria Catalina, Ernesto, help me," Caleb yelled into their bedroom and ran back upstairs. Papa screamed when Caleb was back at the top of the stairs, his scream becoming a howl swallowed by the wind outside. When he got back to their door, Phlarx was howling, throwing back his head and arching his back, his claws tearing and shredding the sheets.

"*¿Santa María, qué pasa?*" Maria Catalina pounded up the stairs, followed by Ernesto Luis and Juan Dario, Luis Xavier, and Maria Elena. "*¿Caleb, qué pasa?*"

Caleb stepped back to let her in the room. "Papa says Phlarx is dying and Papa is dying, too. Can you help, please help me, help them," Caleb said and started crying.

"*O hijo, ellos no tienen remedio.*" They are beyond help.

Phlarx howled again, a long, low cry reminding Caleb of the dogs in Jackson on the hunt or at a full moon. Papa wrapped himself around Phlarx, burying his face in the Lindauzu's chest fur. Phlarx jerked and shuddered, and then his head jerked back and forth. Papa jerked and shuddered with Phlarx, his head jerked back and forth. Then Phlarx gave a sudden gasp and his head fell back, his hands relaxed, his claws retracted. Papa gasped, his head dropped against Phlarx's chest, and they were both very still. No one spoke.

There was only the sound of the wind.

"They were part of each other. I want them buried together," Caleb said, refusing to look at either Maria Catalina or Ernesto Luis. "I don't care where, just together."

"*Pero, Caleb. Phlarx no fue un hombre y Cartagena es un lugar de hombres. Tu popy fue un hombre. Su tumba pertenece en la ciudad, en el cementerio de La Iglesia, en tierra santa. Al Leen-*

dauzee le debe enterra afuera de la ciudad. ¿Entiendes?" Ernesto Luis said. But, Caleb. Phlarx wasn't a man and Cartagena is a place for men. Your papa was a man. His grave belongs in the city, in the church's cemetery, in holy ground. The Lindauzi must be buried outside the city. Understand?

They were in the living room downstairs. Above Papa and Phlarx lay, covered with palm fronds, because this is how we treat the dead, Maria Catalina had explained. It was early in the "morning" and outside it was twilight and the first stars were coming out. Caleb had not gone back to sleep after Papa and Phlarx had died. He had sat in the *hamaca*, sipping the strong sweet *café con leche* Maria Catalina had insisted he drink, and swinging, pushing against the tile floor with his feet. Ernesto Luis told him the funeral had to be tomorrow. Any longer and the bodies would start smelling.

"I understand. Phlarx wasn't a man and Papa was. I don't care; I still want them to be buried together. Don't tell me I am just a boy, either."

The Carvajals looked at each other then, clearly exasperated with their foundling child. Ernesto Luis ran his fingers through his grey-and-black thick hair and looked up at his wife. She sighed, steepling her hands together. "I will go for Padre Hernando."

"Go get the priest. I still want my father and Phlarx to be buried together, side by side, if they can't be buried in the same grave," Caleb said in Spanish and then repeated himself in American and Lindauzi, so what if hearing the growls and snarls made the two adults cringe. "If you bury them apart, I will go at night and dig up the graves and bury them together."

"You are a foolish boy, this isn't right—wait, I will go with you, Maria," Ernesto Luis said, clearly angry.

Caleb sat stonily in the *hamaca*, holding the empty *café con leche* bowl in his lap, until the Carvajals returned with Padre Hernando. Caleb wondered briefly where the Carvajal children were —sent out to be away from the monster-lover American? He didn't care.

"*Caleb, favor de caminar con Padre Hernando.* He wants to walk and talk with you," Maria said, the black-sashed priest behind her, his hands together, his grey hair windblown, and his corona, a pale, pale white light all around him. Caleb wanted to ask if all priests had to have grey hair, but decided it wasn't really the right time.

For a long while, the padre said nothing as he and Caleb walked. They walked down by the sea wall and then down on the beach, their feet leaving imprints in the sand, the wind tossing spray in their faces as it tried to push them up the beach. Night fell as they walked, the blue becoming black, the stars, and then a crescent moon, a white half-circle in the sky. And out at sea, were those dolphins? Caleb wanted to take a boat out to where the dolphins swam, lay his hand in the water and call out, and wait to touch the dolphins themselves. What did they think about out in the sea?

"*Hijo*, let's sit here, on this old drift log, with our backs to the wind, so we can talk," the padre said and gestured with his hand beside him. "I will speak slowly, *mi hijo*. I know you speak Spanish well, but I am a slow talker and I want us to understand each other. Tell me why you want your father buried with the monster?"

Caleb waited until three more waves broke behind them, sending a wash of foam around the driftwood to almost touch their feet. Tide coming in, he thought.

"Papa and Phlarx were two halves of one person, one creature," Caleb said, speaking as slowly, and using American words when he couldn't remember the Spanish. After today, he thought, I may never speak American or Lindauzi again. "Each was the soul of the other. They were bond-mates—what did the Lindauzi always say? Heart to heart, mind to mind, soul to soul."

"You believe Phlarx and all the Lindauzi have souls?"

"Yes. Papa told me even though the Lindauzi did horrible things here, that we all come from the same universe. The same universe that Father Art—*El Señor*—made. So He made humans and He made the Lindauzi," Caleb said, kicking at the sand with his feet. He had one hand up beside his face to block off the wind.

"Yes," the priest said after a long pause, "I believe that is true, and I believe they have souls, but Caleb—"

"Papa and Phlarx were more than brothers," Caleb said quickly, "more than husband and wife. They were part of each other. They loved each other so much, so much it hurt sometimes to be with them. Papa loved me, he loved me and Mama and Davy a lot. But he never stopped loving Phlarx, even when he didn't see him for years. I think in his heart that love was always first. They should be buried together. That's all," Caleb said, knowing he sounded angry and knowing he was angry with both Papa and Phlarx. With Phlarx for finally and forever winning by taking Papa with him to the Great Forest and with Papa for never finishing his return from the black river. And with both of them for leaving him alone.

"*Hijo*, you know, I know, every human in Cartagena, every

human hiding in the jungle, every human anywhere outside the Lindauzi cities and houses knows what they did. Some might say that they only did to us what we have done to ourselves — one day I must teach you human history before the Arrival. Someday I hope there can be forgiveness; I am ashamed that I never met this Phlarx. But people can't forgive now, Caleb, not yet. Even that your father loved the Lindauzi isn't enough. It should be, I know," the priest said, holding up his hand before Caleb could speak. "Let me finish. That no one has rushed into the Carvajal house and taken the Lindauzi's body and flung it into a pit is because of their love for you and their pity for your father. What do you think will happen when the mission south comes back in six or seven months and your father's dream is true: The Lindauzi are dead, their cities are empty? There will be no mourning for the Lindauzi. Do you understand why men don't want your father buried with an alien?" the priest said gently. "Let's walk to the church, Caleb. There is too much wind. Let me think; there we will talk some more."

Caleb had grown to love the church. He liked the way it smelled of old, cool stones, and yet fresh and green from the garden that grew to one side, walled off from the streets. He liked the dark wooden beams in the roof of the sanctuary, some darker than others, the newer ones golden and virgin from the jungle. When he came there alone, Caleb walked in the garden and in the sanctuary, running his hands along the smooth wood of the pews. The Jacksoners' garden had been all vegetables, and fruits, and the garden in the imperial palace only flowers and fountains and grass and alien trees. The church garden was smaller than both the other gardens, and was green and there were *orquídeas* — deep blue, purple, white, pink — and white pebbled paths and statues of saints, the padre said, salvaged from other churches. There aren't enough of us for more than one, he had told Caleb. But mostly the church garden was quiet, like the church.

Padre Hernando and Caleb sat down in a pew close to the altar and where, once, before the Virus, there had been a glass, wood, and stone tomb of San Pedro Claver.

"He lay there for almost five hundred years, and people used to say he kept Cartagena safe and healed the sick," Maria Catalina had explained. She had taken Caleb to the church on *el ocho de septiembre, la fiesta del santo viejo.* "Even with his body gone, and his tomb smashed, I still come," she said, "*cada septiembre,* to lay flowers and palm fronds and light candles. Hundreds came here in the days of the Virus," she had told Caleb, "but no one was healed. Boca Grande, the new part of the city, burned, the churches burned, and the *santo* was given to the sharks."

For a while Caleb and the padre sat in the quiet. Outside Caleb could hear night-sounds: wind, birds, a bat. But it was quiet.

"That's better. The wind was just too much. Now, Caleb, I was thinking as we walked here. I can do this. Your father and the Lindauzi can be buried side by side. Your father will be buried in one corner of the church graveyard, where the wall has fallen, and on the other side, in unconsecrated land, your Phlarx will be buried. Yes?"

"Yes," Caleb said, and that is how it was. They walked back to the Carvajals and the priest called men from up and down the street to dig the graves. Then Ernesto Luis and his sons and the priest and Caleb carried the bodies to the graveyard, and by true morning, Phlarx and Papa were laid in their graves. The priest then sent everyone home to sleep. The next "morning," Padre Hernando said *la misa* and blessed each grave, ignoring the sharp intake of breath when he blessed Phlarx's.

Padre Hernando laid the first palm frond on the raw earth of Papa's grave, weighing it down against the wind, with a dark stone. Next, he laid his hand, briefly, on Caleb's head, and then he was the first to leave. Maria Catalina and Ernesto repeated the priest's actions, then their sons, and they left. Then, in twos, threes, in family groups, in couples, the other Cartageneros laid palm fronds on Papa's grave, weighted them with stones or small chunks of rubble, and left. Caleb looked up only for the priest and the Carvajals. As the others came and went, Caleb, his head bent, stared hard at the fresh earth of the two graves, only one covered with palm fronds. Some of the others said Caleb's name, touched his shoulder, his hair, but Caleb only shook his head and stepped back and out of reach.

When Caleb was sure everyone had left, he knelt to set aside the stones and then, frond by frond, moved them to cover all the fresh earth, over both Papa and Phlarx.

"Wait, let me help. And I brought flowers—there are always flowers for funerals—until today."

Caleb looked up. Maria Elena had come back, her arms filled with *orquídeas* and other flowers whose names Caleb had either not yet learned or could not remember. She stood a meter or so away, waiting. Caleb stared at her for a long moment, trying to see past her dark eyes, her long, even darker hair woven into a thick braid, into her head, her heart, wanting to see why she had come back. Why was she doing this? Then he shrugged—it didn't matter why—nodded, and the two of them soon had the graves more or less completely covered. There were only enough stones to hold down the fronds; already, as they stood and examined their work, the wind was pushing and picking up the flowers.

"I am going to make a cross," Caleb said, one last red flower in his hand, "and put both their names on it. I dreamed about them last night. Papa and Phlarx were running and running down an empty beach, kicking up sand and water. Just the two of them, running beneath a clear sky and birds—like gulls—barely moving, riding thermals as if they were leaves. Papa caught Phlarx or maybe Phlarx caught Papa, and they fell—no, one pulled the other down to roll, laughing, in the sand, one on top of the other. Their beach was in another country, a country of tall silver trees, the silver trees from the palace roof. What do you think it means?"

Maria Elena shook her head. "That they are happy?"

Caleb nodded. Maria Elena stood beside him, by the double grave, watching as the flowers were blown away, some flat against the stone wall directly behind Papa's half, some through the hole in the wall, now filled by Phlarx's half. Some into the air, the petals like huge flakes of multicolored snow. Finally she touched Caleb, lightly, on his forehead, his cheek, and left. Caleb crossed himself as Padre Hernando had taught him, and then took the last flower, the nameless red blossom, and, petal by petal, scattered it onto and over the grave, and into the wind.

"Ashes to ashes, dust to dust. I give back what was given. Please hold Papa and Phlarx close, in the palm of Your hand. Take them to the promised land of milk and honey, the summer country on the other side of the golden river. Ashes to ashes, dust to dust."

Three thousand copies of this book have been printed by the Maple-Vail Book Manufacturing Group, Binghamton, NY, for Golden Gryphon Press, Urbana, IL. The typeset is Elante, printed on 55# Sebago. The binding cloth is Roxite A. Typesetting by The Composing Room, Inc., Kimberly, WI.